THE
STUFF THAT
DREAMS
ARE MADE OF

ALSO BY RILEY MASTERS

Fortune Hunters
(Boston McBain Book #1)

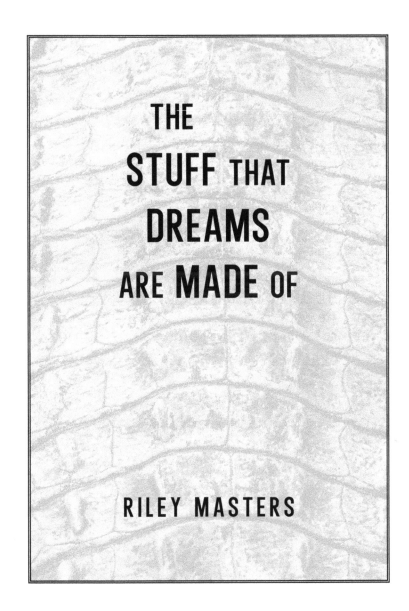

THE
STUFF THAT
DREAMS
ARE MADE OF

RILEY MASTERS

Lost Haven Press

LOST HAVEN PRESS

Book cover and interior design by The Book Cover Whisperer: ProfessionalBookCoverDesign.com

Library of Congress Control Number: 2020914129

ISBN: 978-1-64999-595-7 Hardcover
ISBN: 978-1-64999-596-4 Paperback
ISBN: 978-1-64999-597-1 eBook

FIRST EDITION

THE
STUFF THAT
DREAMS
ARE MADE OF

PRELUDE

*{ Eastern Angola, near the border with the Democratic
Republic of the Congo, August 2018 }*

Outside the reach of the headlamp, the tunnel was pitch black, climbing ahead at a steep angle from eight hundred feet below the earth's surface. Daniel Neto's beige coveralls and orange safety vest were caked with dust. His footsteps shattered the silence of the empty mine and threw echoes out ahead of him, the boots crunching loose dirt and stones as his legs and heart pumped faster.

At last, he saw a distant glow that signaled the elevator to the upper levels and the exit from the mines. He quickened his pace. After another minute, he stopped and turned his head to listen again. The only sounds were his heartbeat and the fading traces of his own footsteps. The rest were his imagination. His hand fell to the brown leather satchel on his hip, and he secured the strap across his chest. Neto reached the elevator cage, and the closing of the door rang out in the dim light like the slam of a prison cell in the dead of night. The lift rose toward clean air, and his breathing eased.

At the surface, the geologist pushed open the iron gate and emerged into the cool of the Angolan night. His shirt and coveralls were soaked in sweat. The dark around him hummed with life from massive generators high above that powered floodlights and conveyors scattered on the heights. His eyes rose up to take in the climbing walls of road levels that circled the main pit of the mine, rank after rank, as a football stadium looms the night before a great match. At the top of the pit, monstrous earthmoving equipment stood idle, modern dinosaurs with massive treads and steel arms vanishing beyond the light. Voices carried across the night air along with the electric hum.

Neto walked slowly to his vehicle, scanning for miners or engineers on the rim above him. His Mercedes four-wheeler was parked near the mine entrance, and he held his breath as he turned the key. The engine struggled for seconds, then turned over. The vehicle climbed in a long corkscrew out of the pit to the buildings in the compound above the mine.

The geologist parked in front of the mineralogy research office, went in, and locked the door. He checked outside the window before pulling down the shade. He sat at his desk for a moment and turned on a desk lamp to catch his breath, think, and write. Who could he trust? Only one person came to mind.

Neto pulled out a blank sheet of paper and pen. He turned on the fax machine and thought of several lines while it came alive. He wrote quickly, then signed it, punched in the number, and sent it off.

Unlocking his desk drawer, he pulled out his mineralogy survey report with the results of his latest analysis from the deepest tunnels of the mine. In the last two weeks, he had covered each of the new sections that had been opened over the past six months. Then tonight, he had passed through the gates at the bottom of the shaft to investigate the farthest reaches of the tunnels that branched off into areas marked as off limits to the research teams. Tonight, he finally understood. From his pack, he withdrew several plastic bags and glass vials of samples, scribbling in the margins of his report as he examined the labels he had placed on them.

The phone on his desk rang, sending his heart to the ceiling. He stared at the caller's number, and his pulse rate crept higher. No one should have known he was here at this time of night. He didn't answer, but his mind began to race. Someone did know or had been alerted by one of the field managers on site. The phone stopped ringing. Neto looked at his watch and thought hard.

He turned on the copy machine and made two copies of his document with the notes in the margin. He put the original in his satchel with the samples and placed the other two in envelopes. Neto wrote the same address on each and put one on the top of his own outbox. The other he placed in the office manager's outbox under several other fat envelopes and letters waiting for tomorrow's mail pickup.

There was a fresh set of khaki clothing in his locker. He changed quickly, picked up the satchel, and switched off his light. He opened the door and scanned the grounds, but no one was in sight. Light from adjacent buildings and faint laughter filtered through the night air. He got in his Mercedes and turned the key. The engine turned over . . . and over . . . and over. He tried for two minutes, his breathing and heart rate matching the groan of the starter, his hand nearly snapping the key.

The truck wouldn't start. The night was cool, but Neto was sweating again. His eyes darted to the mirrors and the windows, but there was no movement. Only his own dark face and fear-filled eyes. What to do?

Leave, and quickly.

The nearest people were twenty miles away, where the bridge crossed the river downstream. They knew him there and would help. He was young and a good runner and could make it easily before daybreak. There were animals in this part of the country, but most were unlikely to trouble him if he stayed to the road, moved with noise, and used his light. It was rare for an animal to attack a man if it was not very hungry.

Neto put the satchel over his shoulder and walked to the gate with his eyes and ears open. The two men standing in the small shack were dressed in camouflage fatigues, with pistols on their hips and FN automatic weapons slung over their shoulders. He nodded at them as he continued out of the gate, saying something about a brief stroll for some night air. They said nothing and did not stop him, but they eyed him with suspicion as he walked around the barrier pole that crossed the gravel road between the fence. The sign reminded visitors in English and Portuguese: Mining Entrance—Extremely Hazardous. Private Property. No Unauthorized Entry. Trespassers Will Be Dealt With. The thought came to Neto late: *Who goes out for a walk in this area late in the evening?* He was only a hundred feet down the dirt road when the shrill sound of the ringing phone broke the silence.

A voice echoed behind him as he kept walking. The geologist could not make out any words but heard the tone rising. Then the second sentry joined in. Neto picked up his pace, angling to the side of the road. As the pitch of the two voices grew louder, he left the road and ducked down into the tall grass not a moment too soon. A floodlight from the guard post sliced the dark, reaching out down the road, searching for him.

The beam moved up and down, then swept toward the grass a hundred yards out from the fence. Neto fell flat onto his stomach. After a few seconds, the light went out. The geologist thought he heard the roar of an engine in the direction of the compound. Without thinking twice, he rose to a crouch, turned, and crept for the tree line. When he reached the trees, he stopped for a moment to think. Neto wiped the sweat from his eyes and considered his options. Wait for a minute and go back to the road, or make his way through the jungle near the dry grass and stay out of sight? What if he went back? He closed his eyes and fought for the courage to do what was right. If he returned to the mine, nothing would change. They had already warned him. And now they would know he had gone to the deepest recesses of the dig.

The bark of the Dobermans reached out across the night. Daniel Neto no longer needed his imagination to feed his fears. They were coming for him.

The river. With luck he could make the Zambezi River a kilometer away, two at the most. He reached into his satchel and pulled out a compass and flashlight. In the pitch black of the forest, he had no choice. He held them both low to the ground to hide the light. In seconds, he had his bearings and set off as fast as he dared, trying to minimize noise and glow.

The whir of insects and the cries of night birds increased as he penetrated farther, past the first trees and thick brush. He wiped the sweat and bugs off his face, and the odor of jungle rot mixed with the smell of fear. The sound of the dogs and engine faded. Daniel kept moving, dividing his attention between the sights and sounds around him and the road behind him. After five minutes, he stopped, turned off his light, and listened. There were voices, but far away. He kept moving, alert to the treacherous footing and wary of branches that were dry at this season of the year. After ten more minutes, he stopped again. Nothing but the birds. The brush was sharp and thick now, and the trees began to close in as well. After fifteen minutes more, his fight against the forest had become much harder, and he was less sure of the direction. Neto pulled out his flashlight, but as he fumbled for the compass, it flew from his sweaty hand into the bush. Cursing, he swung the light around, crouching down to search for the compass.

He couldn't find it. But the leaves under his hands were wet and slippery. He must be getting nearer. He was going to make it.

The noise from the birds and wind in the leaves had grown louder, but suddenly human voices pierced that sound and with them, the bark of the dogs, closer now. The geologist switched off his light and began to move forward in the direction he hoped to find the river, his hands extended out in front of his body, reaching for tree limbs and brush.

Faint but clear, he heard the rush of water. As he forced the branches aside, his rising fear began to push him faster, disregarding the noise. He slipped once, then again, but his mind fought for the river and safety and blocked out any thought but reaching the water. The shouts were getting closer now, and when Daniel turned his head he saw the twinkling of lights cutting through the forest, following the path he had made.

He did not hear them coming until the last rustle of brush. The Dobermans took him down from behind as the night reverberated with the shrieks of dozens of colobus monkeys scrambling higher into the trees. The snarls and barks were even more terrifying than the jaws locked on his leg and arm. But they were not creatures of the wild. They were there to hold and terrify him. In another minute, a harsh voice called to them, and the dogs were pulled away. In their place, he saw he was surrounded by his pursuers, and as the quiet returned, his fear of the lights that now blinded and illuminated him and the bodies on the other side of them brought despair.

"You picked a nice time to go for a walk in the woods, Neto."

The silky voice spoke in Portuguese as a man stepped forward into the light so Daniel could see him. His bulk blocked out some of the lanterns while others pointed out into the darkness to hold off the night for a few more minutes. The light around him was bright enough to illuminate his white smile. His slow voice was tinged with humor and curiosity.

"Where were you going at this time of the night? To see some friends in the village? That's a long way to go. Maybe a date with one of the girls? What could be so important? I guess when you need a whore, the time of night doesn't matter, eh?"

Daniel stood and put his back up against a tree, his breathing labored and his face covered in sweat and dirt. Few words came to him. He had never been a good liar. He had always valued the truth too much. "I . . . I needed to think . . ."

The leader lost his smile and nodded. "Yes, you did need to think. But I guess you did not decide the right way." He shone his light on Daniel's satchel. "You needed to bring work with you to think in the dark, Neto? What's in the bag, Neto?"

Daniel held the satchel closer to his body. "It's not work; it's—"

The large man swung his lantern into Daniel's face, stunning him and sending him to the damp forest floor. He struggled onto all fours, his head spinning. The man ripped the satchel from his body and kicked him in the stomach, sending him sprawling against the tree. Daniel was retching on an empty stomach, gasping for breath. The big man searched inside the satchel with his light. Then he glanced at Daniel struggling to his knees and pulling himself using the tree. He smiled again.

"I do not think these belong to you. They look like they belong to the company. We warned you what would happen, Neto. But you would not listen." The big man shoved him to the ground. "And I am glad. Because the big boss gave me the green light to handle things my own way. Now I get to have a little fun in this nowhere shithole I have been sent to for a change."

He stepped aside, then nodded to the group of men who had been hanging back, laughing at his every word. They beat the geologist savagely, with clubs and lanterns, fists and feet. They hit and kicked him until his ribs were broken, and he stopped begging them for mercy from a swollen, blood-soaked mouth. Somewhere inside, a part of him started to pray. And finally, his prayer was answered. They stopped. Daniel groaned and rolled over onto his back, the cool, wet ground providing solace as the quiet returned and the men stepped back.

The big man had been watching in amusement while his men enjoyed their fun. Now, in a smooth motion, he stepped forward and drew his machete, swinging his arm in a wide arc to bring it down on Daniel's ankle, cutting off his right foot. As the dark silence was shattered by Daniel's scream, the foreman raised his arm and hacked off the left foot. In the light of the lanterns, the geologist's life pumped out, soaking the leaves around him.

After a few minutes, Daniel's screams turned to moans and cries for help. The men all stepped back and watched, shining their lights at random into the jungle, awaiting orders to finish their work.

The leader inhaled the night air and exhaled loudly. "You were right after all, Neto. It was a nice night for a walk. OK, boys, let's go, back the way we came."

A short, thin man made a chopping gesture with one of his hands and drew two fingers across his own mouth. "If we leave him, we should take his hands, too, and cut out his tongue so he does not talk to anyone."

The big man grinned and shone his light into the trees, examining the darkness. "He will not be talking to anyone except for our friends and neighbors. Besides, I want his tongue in place so we can hear him sing. Listen."

He picked up the leather satchel again and examined the contents with his flashlight. Then he smiled down at the bleeding man on the ground clawing at his boot, begging him for life.

"Plea- please . . . don't leave me here. Don't leave me . . . I . . . I won't . . ."

"Adeus, Neto." He led them away, lights flashing and machetes hacking away at the brush to announce their departure.

Daniel Neto listened to the sounds of their retreat and struggled to stifle his moans. He bit his tongue and fought the pain tearing through his legs from the bloody stumps. His mind tried to grasp and accept that his feet were gone, even as it grappled subconsciously with the approach of a more primordial danger. His eyes were full of tears, but he did not need to see to know that the brush was moving. As the sound of a large human presence faded, the dark was coming alive.

Dragging his body forward on his forearms, he tried to concentrate and listen for the river, praying out loud as he crawled. He heard the water and pulled himself faster. Gritting his teeth, he fought back the tears and agony and prayed to God for strength to keep moving. He knew he was almost there when he pulled aside the branches of a bush, and the sound of the rushing river met him. In the moonlight he could see water and the far bank.

What Daniel did not see was the low reptilian shape in the waving grasses next to the near bank. The sound of the river and growing cacophony of the monkeys above drowned out the approaching swish of the brush and leaves as a shadow moved through the shallows and mud.

As he felt the first moist earth in his hands, there was movement in his peripheral vision. He rolled over and saw a dark, fast-moving blur at the level of his eyes, then the narrow red slits reflecting the light from the river. He had only a second to react before the crocodile's long jaws were on the bleeding stump of his ankle. The teeth were a vise made of razors, ripping into his leg. Daniel's hideous screams filled the dark again and again as the creature tore into muscle and bone and worked its way up his leg. Then the reptile began to use it powerful legs to drag him toward the riverbank as he fought to grab hold of branches and tree roots. Hundreds of birds and monkeys added their terrible cries to the scene of horror as they fled the trees.

As the group of men returned to the road, the jungle night echoed with distant screams, one after another, until they faded away.

Their leader smiled and slung the satchel over his shoulder. He inhaled deeply again. "A beautiful night, isn't it, boys? Who's hungry? Let's get something to eat."

ONE

The path was getting tougher to navigate quickly, carpeted with wet leaves and slippery rocks. Logs blocked the trail at knee or waist level, forcing him to either vault them or slow down and climb. McBain glanced at his watch, breathing hard. He couldn't afford to slow down; he was in a race against the clock, and time was running out.

The investigator calculated he had traveled almost five miles. His legs were tired, scratched, and sore, and his cargo shorts and khaki shirt were soaked with sweat, his light brown hair matted with traces of leaves and mosquitos. September in New Hampshire was supposed to at least start to cool, but the summer heat and humidity were suffocating, even along the coastline.

He pushed on, splashing across a small stream just to feel the water. The air was thick with moisture and the dank smell of mud and leaves. A passel of ducks exploded into the air to his right as he plunged into the underbrush toward the beach. The path barely a thread at this point, he focused on the ground ahead of him, trying to move forward against the thickets that tore at him. Angry that he had agreed to come here, he tore back just as hard.

After another minute, the trees and undergrowth thinned out, and the path broadened. McBain heard the distant sound of ocean waves and felt the surge of energy that came with the growing appearance of sunlight. Then he was dancing over fallen tree limbs and granite slabs and on the strip of beach at last. He turned left and headed north.

McBain glanced behind at the trail he had left, then kept moving at a jog.

At last he thought he couldn't possibly move any faster in the deep sand and stopped to take thirty seconds, breathing hard.

He didn't get thirty seconds. The crack of a gunshot to his left ripped the air as the branch on the log of driftwood beside him shattered. He fell to the ground. His head whipped around, but he couldn't see anyone along the undulating line of seagrass and dunes. This wasn't part of the plan. He stopped wondering why he was here and took off, moving at a pace that would have left his old self standing still.

McBain guessed that the trailhead and his car were a quarter mile away at the most. At first, he scuttled along in a crab walk, scanning the dunes and tree line to his left. His quads were burning, and he stopped twice to listen but heard only the cries of seagulls and the sound of the surf behind him. Seeing the wooden post that marked the spot, he broke into a run. His feet drove against the sand, and the beach rose up to a break in the dunes.

The investigator reached the gap at the top of the rise between the high dunes. With sweat smearing his eyesight, he glimpsed the shape of his green Range Rover at the trailhead a hundred feet away as he collapsed onto the sand. His chest was heaving as he struggled for breath through gritted teeth, getting ready to sprint for the vehicle. He tilted his head to look up and squinted at the glare with bleary eyes.

Suddenly the sun was blocked. A silhouette stood three feet away from him, throwing a shadow across his prostrate figure. McBain rubbed dirt and sweat from his eyes. She was a vision of youth and fitness, dressed in olive drab and white athletic shorts and halter top, with a body that curved up five feet eight inches from the white trainers on her feet to the faded blue baseball cap with a red italic letter *B* on it. A braided ponytail held her auburn hair back from high cheekbones and suntanned, freckled face. An army pack was slung over one shoulder, and her upper chest and stomach glistened from the heat.

"That was pathetic," Boston O'Daniel said. She adjusted her Ray-Ban aviators and applied sunscreen to her lips. "Two minutes behind your last time. And you're breathing like an asthmatic."

"Wha . . . somebody . . . shot . . ."

"That was me," she said, dropping the backpack to the sand.

He wiped his eyes open and straightened, heart still pumping in overdrive. "Wha . . . ?"

"You shouldn't have been standing around there on the beach, so I gave you a little encouragement to get you to the finish line."

He bent over, hands on knees again as he wagged his head back and forth. "You could have . . . hit me . . ."

Boston rolled her eyes and curled her lip. "Oh please."

He was still inhaling deeply. "Christ . . . I'm not . . . as young . . . as you . . ."

She pushed her sunglasses down on her nose and scanned him. "You just turned forty a couple weeks ago, Boozy. When Gordy Howe was forty, he scored forty-four goals and a hundred points."

Doubled over, McBain sucked in air as his eyes rolled up at her. "Who?"

Boston put her hands on her hips. "Gor . . . Forty isn't that old. Or it shouldn't be."

"We'll see . . . how it feels . . . when you turn . . . thirty . . ."

She ignored him and fished around in her backpack. "I don't know what you're talking about."

"Next . . . year . . ."

Boston pulled out a quart of Poland Spring and handed it to him. "Save it. Here, drink. I told you before: you should always have water with you.

You never listen."

He almost choked himself on water. After another minute, he felt better. "Hey, I expected to be retired on a beach somewhere in the Pacific by now."

"You are on a beach."

"Hilarious. Besides, you're the one who's always cracking the 'older man' jokes. No wonder I've started looking for gray hairs."

"Fine. You know, you've made a lot of progress in the past three months. You're down from two hundred to one ninety and dropped an inch off your waist. According to the scale I looked up, a healthy six foot, forty-year old male should weigh in at around one seventy-five or one eighty. You don't look half-bad for a walking cocktail. Not as fit as when we first met, but not bad. If you would give up the cigarettes and shave back the drinking just a little, you'd be surprised at how fast you'd progress. You might even hit your goal by Christmas. Then you could reward yourself with some new clothes."

"The key word you used was *healthy*. And you mean your goals. As far as the smoking, dream on. Sometimes it helps me think. Besides, I barely smoke a pack a week. And I don't smoke in the office."

"Stop whining like a little girl," she said. "And it's closer to two. I'm sooo sorry you feel sooo pressured to get in shape. Pardon me for caring enough about your health and our business to encourage you to eat right, exercise, and do the right thing for your body."

McBain twisted his torso back and forth to stretch his back. "Sarcasm doesn't suit you, Boston."

"Fine. Then just do it for my sake. Do I really ask that much of you? The Baker case might easily have involved a gang of very tough people—"

"But it didn't."

"—and I'd like to think you'd have my back if ever there comes a time I need you in a bad spot. Remember, I know you've got it in you."

McBain stopped stretching and looked at his partner. "Guilt, on the other hand, you do very well."

"I'm Catholic; what do you want? Look, I'm sorry, we said we wouldn't talk about that. But this is important for me, for us."

McBain finished the bottle of water and nodded. "OK," he said. "I'll do better next time, and I'll cut back on the smoking, maybe even my drinking. For us." He took a step toward her. "Come here. Give me a hug."

She straight-armed him in the chest and recoiled. "Ugh. Shower, please. Let's get to the office. I'll drive."

He threw up his hands. "It's Saturday. I just finished a five-mile obstacle course. And I've been shot at."

Boston shook her red ponytail. "We agreed on this weekend. We've been too busy to catch up until now. Those files won't review themselves . . . little girl."

TWO

C ool air and music wafted in through the open windows above the square on Tremont Street. Boston got up from the conference table and closed both of them. She turned on the air conditioning for the office. A fall afternoon breeze was driving out the humidity, but the three-room office in the South End was on the third floor of an older building with no cross circulation.

"I was enjoying that," McBain said.

"I can't concentrate with that racket from the square."

"That racket was some not-bad Miles Davis."

"Yeah, well, Miles isn't helping us get through this stack of requests any faster. Besides, I know you. You're all dressed in black. Four o'clock and jazz on a Saturday equals cocktail hour. We need to buckle down and get through these this afternoon before we head over to Holiday."

McBain exhaled wistfully, rolled up the sleeves of his black cotton shirt, and took a sip of iced tea while he ran his fingers through his mane to ensure he'd gotten everything out. He picked up another file and scanned the pertinent facts. A minute later he tossed it back onto the table on top of a pile of other manila file folders in the stack labeled no. The no pile held most of the folders the partners had already reviewed. The yes pile held two files and the maybe bin seven.

"What's wrong with the Carlton file?" Boston asked.

McBain shook his head. "They're looking to get back just under a million bucks. Not worth our time."

"OK, fine," she said. "We still haven't decided on a cutoff."

"That's because you're getting greedy," he said with a wink. "Personally, I think five million is too high. I still don't get it. You've nixed some interesting possibilities already. Once upon a time, we would have jumped at some of these noes."

She brushed back her hair and smiled sweetly. "We agreed to raise our limit so we wouldn't have to raise our rates. And with this many leads, we can afford to be choosy. Now that we've collected some big paydays, we have a chance to clear the decks and line up our next few jobs. We have the opportunity to be more selective, which means we can accelerate our business plan and move up our time frame if we pick bigger cases. After four and a half years and some of our recent wins, I think we can market ourselves as a premium service, don't you?"

"Oh, I agree," McBain said. "Besides, I can see that you've been shopping again. Is that a new Chanel bag? And what is Jimmy Choo running these days?"

The redhead glanced over at the quilted designer flap handbag, sitting on the end of the table like a trusted friend.

"Good eye, McBain," she said. "Why, yes, Coco is new, a little bonus to myself. You know, I'm always impressed by how much you know about women's fashion. Are you sure you haven't switched teams?" She raised her finger. "No, wait, I forgot: Melissa trained you."

"Ha ha. That's not very nice." He lost his smirk. "True, but not nice."

Boston pulled her hair away from her cheeks. Small emerald earrings sparkled in the afternoon sun along with her sea-green eyes.

"If you're going to charge premium prices, you have to dress the part, McBain." She spread her arms apart. "We have to look like we're worth it when people walk in through the front door."

He folded his hands on his lap and eyeballed her. The top buttons of her royal-blue silk shirt were open. A slim gold pendant hung around her neck and fell between her breasts. The rest of her curves were hidden under the table, wrapped in a snug black skirt. She tapped her Jimmy Choos against her chair.

"You certainly look premium to me," McBain said. "But seriously, for this first cut, can we at least consider some of the under-five files? We can always eliminate them in another round."

Boston sighed. "OK, like who?"

"What about this one? Potential three-million-dollar settlement for the client if we prove they were ripped off."

She paged through the folder, then groaned and wagged her shoulders. "Artwork? Really? I know you're a fan of museums, but we don't really know anything about the art market. It could take us a long time to get up to speed and even figure out if we had a case."

"You're right. I'd rather wait for a chance to crack the Isabella Gardner heist anyway. Next?"

She shook her head, opened another one, ran her finger down the page, and handed it to McBain. "What about this one?"

He read it over, jiggling the ice in his glass. "Hmm. It meets the five-million threshold, but that's only because there are so many people involved. Another small-town Ponzi scheme with over twenty victims. The guy is probably either ready to bolt or has spent the money already on cars, whores, and boats. I sympathize, but it probably isn't worth our time. Send it to Dave."

"He sent it to us."

"Oh," McBain said. "Tough luck for them, but their money's gone. That's the problem with Ponzis. By their nature, there's almost never a stack of gold sitting somewhere. The new suckers put money in to pay off the older suckers and keep it going, or else the runner spends it until the whole thing blows up. Anyway, if the pattern holds, we would never be able to put any pressure on him to cough anything up. He'll just pull up stakes overnight, move two thousand miles away, and start over again. He's probably done it before successfully; that's how he landed here. He knows the chances he'll ever spend a day in jail—slim and none."

She nodded and placed the folder back on the no stack. "Sorry, I forgot: stay away from Ponzis. Although I did read in the news that the Chinese executed some woman for running a seventy-million-dollar Ponzi scheme in Shanghai. Too bad they don't do that here. Wouldn't that be great to have as leverage in our bag of tricks? What else do you have?"

A corner of his mouth went up. "There's always this one." He tossed it over.

It took Boston three minutes to read through the folder, and her expression veered between skepticism and curiosity as her eyes scanned the pages. "Where did this come from?"

"A referral from one of our satisfied customers—Kelly Parker."

"Of course. Still keeping in touch with you, is she?"

McBain examined his fingernails. "We must have made a good impression getting their money back from the investment firm. Anyway, you can't say that one is run of the mill."

Boston whistled. "No, I certainly wouldn't say that. Let's make sure I understand. This woman wants to hire us to make sure she isn't edged out of her 'rightful share' of the estate when her father dies in the not-too-distant future, correct? She's afraid her siblings or some new trophy wife will conspire to cheat her out of what's hers?"

"You certainly have to give it points for originality," McBain said. "I've heard about these rich family fist fights over money before, but they usually happen after the old guy's dead. This must be quite a prize bunch of brats. The potential inheritance and fee do look pretty sizeable, so we should consider it."

She rolled her eyes and tossed the folder on the yes pile. "Well, we certainly are moving up the food chain. Now people are hiring us before they've even been ripped off. Let's give it two stars for being a first and put it at the bottom of the yes pile. The man isn't dead yet, so I suppose we have some time. Jesus, and I thought my family was complicated. Keep going."

By six o'clock, they were finished. Boston ran her manicured fingers through the files that had made the cut. "Six, seven, eight . . . nine potential new cases. Add that to the three we've got in the pipe already, and it should make for a pretty full autumn and winter."

McBain frowned and tapped his cigarette pack on the table while he did a calculation in his head. "Hmm, so if even half of them work out, we're looking at nonstop work, including some weekends, through April or May, right?"

"Don't start."

"We haven't had a break all year," he said. "Remember, I cancelled my August trip after things picked up in the summer. That was supposed to be our slow time."

"So what? You're complaining about being busy and having a backlog of potential cases for a change? For our first couple years, we were starving. Up until late last year, we were still searching for new clients. Since the Baker case finished, Dave and Dee Dee have sent us a ton of new possibilities. That plus the walk-ins from referrals got us this stack of backed-up files as it is. We finally have our pick of profitable new prospects that can make us some serious new bank and bring us closer to retirement. Now all you want to do is go on vacation."

McBain got up and opened the window again. The sun was slanting west, and Tremont Street was crowded and noisy, though the jazz band was taking a break. He watched the foot traffic along the sidewalks and eyed the steakhouse and sushi restaurant across the street while he thought out loud.

"That's not entirely fair," he said. "I want to score as much as you do, and I like the idea of bigger jobs. But I've worked longer than you, and given the pace we operate, juggling multiple clients at once, and the hours, I'm worried about burnout."

Boston laughed and rolled her eyes. "I thought you wanted me to lay off the old guy jokes. Now you're talking about burnout? We're finally getting some momentum. Where's your sense of adventure?"

"Don't look at me with those big skeptical eyes. It's got nothing to do with age. Based on experience, I can tell you it's true. You've got a full head of steam now. But any therapist will tell you there's a risk of burnout in any profession, no matter how young and invincible you think you are. Sure, we could push the pedal to the floor on this stack. We could just as easily make mistakes in three months time too."

She didn't look convinced. "And what about our plan to score serious money, then retire as soon as possible? Who was the one talking about the beach a few hours ago?"

He came back to the table and sat next to her. Boston was instantly wary.

"That's still the plan. But you know how else we can accelerate our business plan? By adding a partner. That's the only way we're going to get any breathing room here."

She frowned at him. "McBain, we've talked about this theoretically, but interviewing and picking someone who is able and willing to work with our rules, or lack thereof, is a long-term proposition. I don't see how that gets us a break anytime soon, or you on vacation."

He nodded at the table.

"We need somebody who can jump in right away, who we don't have to train. Someone we are already comfortable with and can trust."

Boston grabbed a rubber football with the New England Patriots logo off the conference table and started tossing it at the ceiling. "Maybe we can check out the directory of the Fraud Association and see who looks promising."

"Possibly," McBain said. "But that could take time. Ask around, identify some candidates, and research their skills and work. I'm not exactly flavor of the month with the folks over there. They tend to frown on people who bend the rules with an 'end justifies the means' attitude. That might take months, or longer. Then they would have to accept our approach to getting results and be willing to work with our style. It would be nice if we had a candidate who had at least some firsthand experience with a wide range of investor fraud cases, knew the law and the ins and outs of putting pressure on the swine to do the right thing without getting caught."

Boston stopped throwing the ball, folded her arms across her chest, and sat back. "Seems you've been thinking about this for a while. You already have someone in mind?"

"The only one who's as good as you is Dave."

"We've been through it before with him, Boozy. You know what he'll say."

"We only brought it up once, and that was three years ago," he said. "A lot has changed since then. We're more secure, we have a good pipeline of leads, and are making great money, and he's still stuck at the same level in a government bureaucracy that's been taking a well-deserved pasting in the media for ineptitude."

Boston shrugged. "All true. All good points. And none of them will probably mean squat. You know Dave better than I do. But hey, I'm game to try. Don't ask, don't get, Dad always says."

"I'll call Dave and set it up. You can't get him into the city on weekends, so let's try to get him to dinner after work somewhere near South Station this week. We haven't been anyplace nice for a month anyway. Dave loves a good steak. What do you think—the Palm?"

Boston's face lit up. "The Palm."

THREE

The Palm was in the Financial District by the water and not far from South Station, but otherwise as far away from the noise and angst of the migrating commuter crowd as was possible. The modern-American menu and décor were figuratively on the other side of the railroad tracks.

The sidewalks were pressed with commuters heading for the rail lines out of Boston to start their weekend. Dave Thomas had insisted on Friday as a condition for having a drink. McBain leaned against the bar that looked out wide windows across the highway to Boston Harbor, wearing his favorite Hugo Boss blue suit with subtle pinstripes and a red Hermes tie against a crisp white custom-tailored shirt with his initials set in small letters on the pocket. The suit was fitting him well again after years in the closet. His partner sat next to him, a ruby pendant draped over her scoop-neck blouse and light-gold suit jacket, legs folded under a matching skirt that hugged her body and fueled the imagination of the two dozen men and women surrounding them.

They had finished a round of perfect manhattans when a rumpled middle-aged fellow in a gray suit meandered in and hovered by the reception stand, looking lost and out of place. The collar of his shirt was unbuttoned, and he played with the knot of his tie for a moment, as if thinking about pulling it up. He seemed half-inclined to walk out when he spotted Boston to his left, waving to him from the bar.

"Hi, Dave. Good to see you again." She hugged him and pulled him in to sit next to her.

"Wow," he replied.

"Thank you," she said.

"Thanks for inviting me to dinner, guys," Dave said. His head swiveled around to take in the restaurant and crowd. "I'd never come here on my own. Nice place."

"Dave," Boston said, "we wanted to thank you for all the business you've sent us over the last few months, not to mention earlier. Order anything you like. We'll finish our cocktails and then grab some dinner. On us."

"Do they have beer here?" he asked.

"Yes, but I'm not buying it unless it's the most expensive," McBain replied. "You can try something more foreign than Heineken for once."

McBain ordered his friend the best Belgian beer on the menu. Thomas drank half of it quickly, as good a sign of approval as any. When their table was ready, they moved into the restaurant. The high ceilings reverberated with the symphony of the weekend.

The waiter arrived, and McBain exchanged a few words with him in French. He ordered another round and asked for the sommelier to stop by after they had chosen their meals. They looked over the menus.

"I don't think I realized your French was that good," Dave said. "I thought you only spoke a few words of tourist French."

McBain shrugged. "Needs some work. Another good reason to come here more often and chew the fat with Julien. He comes and goes between here and his village near Avignon in southern France quite a bit. It's good practice for me to converse with someone who doesn't speak Parisian French."

Boston glanced over at him and smiled. "McBain is being modest. He was fluent before he came to us, Dave. He's promised to take me to Paris someday. Maybe we can think about expanding our business internationally. I'm sure they have financial crooks in Europe too."

McBain raised his drink to his partner and touched her glass. "Someday." His eyes lingered on her face for just a moment, then he turned to the table and raised his glass again. "Here's to a vacation on the beaches of Saint-Tropez and a stroll through the vineyards of Burgundy. Let's take a look at the menus, then we can talk about vacations and other things."

Their table was close to the front windows, and the shades were drawn to deflect the beams of sunset flooding the setting with natural light. The rest of the room curved away, past white columns that enhanced the modern décor and reached to the recessed lighting.

Choosing courses took time, but they were ready when Julien returned. Boston ordered bacon-wrapped sea scallops and a prime bone-in rib-eye steak cooked rare with mushrooms and asparagus. McBain chose filet mignon au poivre on a bed of spinach with mashed potatoes. After much cajoling, they convinced Dave to have several selections and ordered him the gulf shrimp; risotto with Maine crab and jalapeno; and the best rib-eye steak with potatoes, haricot verts, and red wine sauce. As a token, the men ordered the cherry sorbet with Brazil nuts for dessert while Boston requested the crème brulee.

McBain closed the menu and handed it to the waiter. "I know you can eat it all, Dave. So don't play shy. We don't buy someone dinner here every day."

The sommelier arrived, and Boston and Dave heard more of McBain's restaurant French while the two men exchanged thoughts on the wine list and chose several bottles of white and red for their courses.

"So," Dave said, "tell me about the vacation plans."

McBain put on a sad face. "Much as I would love a trip to France, Dave, the fact is that we just have so many leads that we have to start working Saturdays. My partner is a slave driver."

Boston reviewed some of the cases they had looked at, raising her eyebrows at the most unfortunate of the ripped-off potential clients. Dave Thomas listened to them, shaking his head in genuine sorrow and amazement between bites and sips of wine.

Finally McBain leaned forward in his seat. "I'll be straight with you, Dave. Counting the other stuff that comes in to us, we've got so much business lined up we can't handle it all. We need help. We need another partner. We need you."

Dave sat back, chewing his steak, his eyes wide with shock. "Are you serious?"

Boston nodded. "Absolutely, Dave. I wouldn't be here if we didn't both agree that this would be a great idea. What do you think?"

The government man looked at both their faces.

"You know how highly I think of you two and the things you do to help people who have been cheated. But you're—how can I put this? You're a premium service for those folks who can afford you or who have lost big money. What about the investors and shareholders who get taken to the cleaners? What about the ones who can't afford you?"

McBain sipped his wine and glanced over at his partner, who was busy biting back a smile along with her steak.

"Yeah, well, premium or not, the important thing is to get people their money back and send a message to the scam artists and scumbags in the business that they're not untouchable. I think you'd agree that our process is much faster and more effective than the SEC's."

Dave leaned forward. "Yes, but then you two don't always follow the rules yourselves, do you?"

Boston swirled her wine in the glass. "Now, Dave, you have to admit that federal regulators like to operate in the fuzzy gray area of the law as much as we do. That ambiguity comes in handy sometimes. Can we help it if that zone is so wide? With the kind of people we all deal with, you often have to fight fire with fire."

McBain leaned back in his chair, waving his wineglass.

"Dave, I don't have to ask you; I know what you get paid. We're talking about five to ten times that much money. Plus, we work cases through from beginning to end and see the investor get their money back. See them happy. We don't watch the cases plea bargained away to some slap on the wrist that lets them deny responsibility and hand shareholders the bill, watching these big firms hire some million-dollar lawyers who have been through the revolving door in government. I know you've got to be frustrated. You read the same stories we do: 'They're all in bed together, the politicians and regulators and Wall Street.' The little guy gets shafted while the politically connected get away with financial murder."

Boston placed her hand on her partner's expressive elbow to keep his wine from spilling and kept her voice level to avoid attention. "I've heard you complaining to us in the past too. The infighting between agencies, the bad press for the SEC whenever a Madoff or an Alan Stanford hits the headlines, the sneering from the big SEC lawyers in DC or New York, and the lack of people and resources in the Boston office. You've told us about all of these problems, Dave. You know us pretty well, plus it wouldn't hurt for us to have your guidance every day as we look at and work these cases. Like McBain said, with your help we can take on more clients, solve more of these cases, and get people their money back. Everybody benefits."

McBain leaned forward and lowered his voice. "Come on, Dave. We all read the inspector general's report on the Stanford case. Black eye doesn't begin to describe it. Guys like you, and even more junior, had Alan Stanford pegged for eight years. The lawyers at the top couldn't be bothered, or even worse. The guy that was head of enforcement quashed the investigation and left the agency to work for Stanford, then even tried to represent him in the case. Are you kidding me? That was worse than criminal. Didn't they disbar him? Eight billion dollars, Dave. Investor money down the toilet."

"A lot of changes have taken place since those things came to light," Dave said. "New procedures, new people, technology. We have a new head of enforcement here in Boston too. Things are much better now than before the whole Madoff and Stanford wave."

Boston and McBain spent the rest of the meal plying their potential partner with persuasive logic and expensive red wine. At last, dinner was over, and Dave Thomas looked at his watch and mentioned the last train from South Station. They finished their port wine with a fine sherbet and crème brulee. Thomas dabbed his lips as McBain paid the check. Boston reached across and took Dave's hand.

"Will you at least think about it, Dave?" That face and smile were hard for any man to say no to.

He nodded. "OK, Boston. You guys make some good points. Let me think about it over the weekend and talk to the wife. Maybe you can drop by my office on Monday. I'll give you an answer then."

FOUR

By Monday, Boston was eager to start thinning out the new client requests and set up meetings with several prospects. McBain convinced her to hold off until they had made one last pitch to Dave Thomas. The pair paid visits to several contacts at mutual funds and bought lunch for two of the hedge fund managers they were on good terms with.

They arrived at the offices of the US Securities and Exchange Commission on Arch Street in late afternoon and took the elevator up to the enforcement division and Dave Thomas's office on the twenty-third floor of the glass-and-steel tower. His staff of researchers and accountants beavered away in their cubicles, up to their eyeballs in complaints and investigations.

Thomas waved them in with a phone in one hand and a Coke in the other. His jacket hung on a chair, and his shirt sleeves were rolled up.

"Sorry, guys" he said as he hung up and straightened his glasses. "Busy day and week already."

"There's a surprise," Boston said. She brushed off her camel-colored business suit and sat across from Thomas. Her partner peered out the window of the office onto the Financial District and the clear autumn sky.

"Well, Dave," McBain said. "Any other thoughts over the weekend? Or today, for that matter? You could be looking at a busy week here or a busy and more lucrative week with us. What do you say?"

Boston smiled. "More important, what does the wife say?"

The regulator opened his hands and his face told the story.

"She was really tempted," Dave said. "The thought of me spending my days with a beautiful redhead didn't even seem to put her off. When I told her about the money and flexible hours, she wanted to hear more. I described some of the cases you two have investigated for your clients and how quickly you were able to get their money back."

"But . . .?" Boston said.

"In the end, she's just too conservative. The potential upside didn't offset the notion of that government security and pension. She's just a simple, suburban Massachusetts girl who doesn't need that much. She'd rather have the security and me home at seven and not have to worry about . . . um . . ."

Boston shrugged her shoulders and opened her mouth. "What?"

McBain's face fell. "About me."

Dave leaned forward on his desk and folded his hands. "I guess she's just concerned. I've told her about some of your cases over the years and about how proud we all were here of what you did with Roche. But she's thinking of those things in a different way."

McBain nodded his head, his eyes on the credenza to his left.

"She's not being judgmental, McBain. She just doesn't think it's a good choice for me. She knows how much I love the work here. I'll keep working on her. Maybe she'll change her mind. After hearing your pitch the other night, I really am more torn than ever. Give me a little time."

Boston looked at her partner. He came over and sat down next to her. "She's got a fair point, Dave. I can be a loose cannon at times. I'll work on that. Maybe if I prove myself, she'll come around in the future. The offer is open anytime."

The regulator smiled. "Thanks. And thanks for understanding. Anyway, now that I have you here, I'd like your thoughts on something." He sat back and put his hands on a file. "A friend of mine called me over the weekend about a problem he has. His name is Harold Rogers. He has a pretty hot company called Harold Rogers Technologies, more commonly referred to as HR Tech. Harold started the company thirty years ago. He's an engineer and geologist who sells services to big energy companies. Harold and his people recently developed some unique technology that's extremely useful in the extraction and processing of natural resources, minerals in particular."

McBain said, "I don't know the company, but I've seen the stock. I think it doubled in the past few weeks. He's in play."

"Correct, but the play seems to be pretty much over."

Boston perked up. "What do you mean?"

"The contest is close to being settled. One particular bidder is going to get the company. That's the reason the stock has been a meteor."

She shrugged. "Sounds great. Your friend sells his company for a fortune and retires. Why would he call you?"

"He has some concerns about the bidder. The would-be acquiring company is listed in Europe, headquartered in Africa, and registered in Mauritius, an offshore tax haven. The company and the guy who owns it have a bit of history in the mining industry. And he has quite a reputation in the investment community as a hardball player. Some of his fellow investors in hedge funds and companies haven't always done as well as he has out of his deals. There were some suggestions in the past about shifting legal domiciles and new shell companies appearing. I found some examples of accounting firms changing at opportune moments, a fund that was dissolved with the minority investors and limited partners being diluted or cleaned out."

McBain brushed some lint off his suit. "C'mon, Dave. Your friend must be a big boy. When you get to this level, there's no point talking about fair or unfair. Investing is bare-knuckle boxing; you know that. You hire good lawyers and bankers and take your chances."

Dave nodded and opened the file on his desk.

"The problem is the acquiring company is located offshore. I told Harold there's not much we could do for him, even if he did have grounds for suspicion. We don't operate overseas and don't have the authority to investigate the company or investor. I thought maybe there might be some offshore tax issues that could give us a reason to poke around, so I brought it to our new enforcement director, but she said it was a waste of our time to look at something like this."

"She's probably right," McBain said.

"I thought you two might be interested in doing some due diligence for Harold."

Both investigators chuckled. "Why on earth would you think that, Dave?" Boston said.

"You're perfect for the job," Dave said.

"Thanks, I think," she said.

"Dave," McBain said, "there are tons of firms dying to get work like this. Why don't you just send Rogers to one of them?"

"The board of HR Tech has hired some bankers to perform the due diligence. They are already well along and, in fact, very excited about the prospect of doing the deal."

"So what's the problem?" Boston asked.

"Harold doesn't trust the bankers. He thinks they have a conflict of interest in getting the deal done. They keep using the word *synergies*. Harold's a bit old fashioned."

"There usually are synergies on a deal like this," McBain said. "For the banks. Merger fees, future stock and bond underwriting deals, other quote unquote 'advisory work,' loans, you name it. With the stock already soaring

I'm sure that, to these guys, the deal is as good as signed. The only fighting that's going to take place is when it comes to who gets lead manager role and has the edge on future business."

Dave said, "At any rate, it was the board that hired the bankers. And Harold doesn't trust investment bankers. He thinks they're all either incompetent morons or self-serving parasites."

McBain smirked. "Well, not all of them. In fact, some are extremely competent parasites."

"Harold wants another party to look at the deal and the bidder, one he picks himself and he can trust to work for him and his company's best interests. Remember, he built this from the ground up. It's his baby."

"I know how he feels," Boston said. "But I don't really see what this has to do with us. It's more corporate accounting or legal work than investment oriented. We help individual clients get their money back. Your friend hasn't been robbed or cheated. From what I can see, he is about to become very rich. We don't do this kind of work."

"Not normally," Thomas said. "But that's only because you don't have to. Due diligence is about more than looking at the books. It's about knowing what questions to ask and digging until you're satisfied you have the real answers. And nobody is better at that than you two. You have an instinct for when something is not right with the numbers or people and no tolerance for bullshit. Not to mention the fact that you're both naturally suspicious and always assume your client is getting ripped off."

McBain was shaking his head. "Yeah, well, you know how I feel about corporate work and Wall Street in general. I did my time in the big house as a trader, and traders and bankers get along about as well as the Montagues and Capulets. Besides, like we said at dinner, we've got lots of good leads lined up to start on. Why would we need the headache of a boring merger due diligence?"

"Well, for one thing, it should be a piece of cake compared to your normal jobs. And there's no gray area—just a simple, legal, and legit review of the acquiring company and its owners; the deal terms; and the books and maybe an independent valuation. Plus, it shouldn't take much time at all. The board wants the deal wrapped up and signed in a few months at the outside. Not to mention there are a bunch of other teams pulling out information and facts for you to piggyback off. And because Harold is willing to pay investment-banker rates to have his own people on this job."

"In other words," Boston said, "it's easy money."

"Yep," Dave said. "Probably some of the easiest you've ever made. Not to mention legitimate."

Boston and McBain both feigned shock and threw up their hands.

The door to the office opened. The investigators turned around to see a stocky woman in a gray suit and white buttoned-up blouse, with shoulder-length, graying dishwater-blonde hair and wire-rim glasses that magnified steady schoolmarm eyes.

She nodded. "Thomas. I didn't realize you were occupied."

Dave stood up and waved his hand. "Good afternoon, Ms. Strasser. I'm glad you stopped by. I'd like to introduce you to Mr. McBain and Ms. O'Daniel."

The woman evaluated them. "I see."

Boston and McBain glanced at each other and rose slowly.

"So, I finally get to meet the famous team who took down Richard Roche."

Boston was the first to stiffen at the tone. She smiled. "You're welcome."

"I'm not sure the SEC should be thanking you, Ms. O'Daniel. From what I have learned over the course of the last few months, the case was almost thrown out on technicalities. Not least because of some questionable actions on the part of Mr. McBain. Mr. Roche might easily be sitting on a beach in South America instead of in a prison cell."

McBain sat back down and crossed his legs, scanning her severe face. "But he's not. And it certainly didn't hurt your reputation or the agency's, did it, Ms. Strasser? You seemed to enjoy those news conferences I saw on TV. We did the work; you got the credit and some badly needed good press. Is there a problem?"

Strasser folded her arms. "The problem, Mr. McBain, is that your cavalier approach and tactics almost resulted in a murderer and swindler going free. Perhaps if you had come to us with your information at the beginning, we might have been able to bring him to justice without the risk you injected into the situation. I don't suppose it occurred to you that you were just lucky."

He looked at his partner. "Every day, Ms. Strasser."

"Frankly, I think it's a wonder that you're not in prison already yourself, Mr. McBain. From what I've learned, you take many chances, some of them of questionable propriety. You and others like you should leave investment fraud to the professionals. It is, after all, our area of expertise."

Boston leaned back on her hip and folded her arms right back at her. "Yes, there are others like us, Ms. Strasser. The Association of Fraud Examiners, for example, is a fairly large organization, full of people who feel the way you do about investors being cheated. People in the accounting, legal, and investment professions, or in companies, who have a high sense of ethics and responsibility for unearthing financial crimes or blowing the whistle on fraud."

The SEC director grunted and offered a thin smile. "Yes, I know about this organization. I understand a number of my people are members, and I don't approve. There is a system of justice in this country. When laws are violated and people are cheated, they bring their legitimate complaints to the proper authorities. This association seems to me to be composed of individuals who work outside the government sector, many of them with a potential conflict of interest in investigating and reporting financial fraud. Others are no better than bounty hunters, looking to make a quick buck, only pursuing an opportunity where they can make a high percentage of fees when the government prosecutes a case, such as a whistleblower in a corporation. We expend the time and resources, and they take home a large check for doing what should be their civic duty. Hardly an equitable arrangement for either the investor or the taxpayer. In my opinion, they're part of the self-regulatory problem with the industry. I intend to suggest the SEC review our cooperation with your association."

Boston took a step forward, but McBain put his hand on her arm. "Well, it's not exactly our association, Ms. Strasser."

Strasser looked at Boston's suit and jewelry and pulled her own jacket straight. "Good day," she said. "Thomas, come to my office when you're finished here. I have a few things I'd like to go over with you."

After she left, McBain and Boston turned back around and stared at Dave. He held up his hands. "I know. I know what you think."

Boston's eyes narrowed. "No, Dave, you really don't."

"She seems a bit hard, but that's only because she is so committed to doing right by the investor. She has a good track record in Washington with making reforms to some of our procedures and prosecuting insider cases. Elizabeth Strasser is a lawyer who works by the numbers, but only because she wants to convict people who cross the line and rip off investors and shareholders."

McBain said, "You used *Washington* and *lawyer* in the same breath, Dave. That's two strikes already."

"Ms. Strasser was the one who determined we didn't have the time or resources to devote to the Rogers case. She's very cost conscious and focused. She looked at the deal thoroughly on the merits and decided it wasn't a good use of our time. Even you agreed we can't fault her for that. This is the SEC, and there's no suggestion a crime is being committed."

Boston looked at her partner, who was sticking out his lower lip in thought. "And she vetoed even looking at the merger, eh?" she said as she sat down.

McBain rubbed his chin and glanced over at her. "You say the board wants it wrapped up in a few months. Let's call it six to eight weeks tops, to allow for some slippage and back and forth. Starting from scratch, we'd have to get up to speed and understand the industry and the deal, do the accounting and investigative work, look under any rocks, find people and do some interviews; say one hundred hours a week. That's eight hundred hours we'd bill him, plus expenses. What do you think, partner?"

She was playing with her enameled Hermes bracelet, but she had done the calculation already herself. "Are you sure this won't turn into one of those long, drawn-out takeover circuses I've read about? We have a stack of requests from people who are waiting to hear back from us."

Dave shrugged. "Well, there are no guarantees, but with everyone so keen on the acquisition, I've rarely seen a deal that looked so promising. It's not a hostile offer. And as I said, Strasser already looked at it and didn't really think there was anything objectionable. Barring you two discovering something troubling, I don't even see it lasting six weeks. McBain is just being conservative in his estimate."

Boston finally nodded at her partner. She and McBain stood up.

"OK," he said. "We'll talk to your friend."

"Thanks, guys."

McBain pointed at Dave across the desk and grabbed his fedora. "If we're going to take this job, just make sure this guy understands two things: We have our own way of working, and we're not cheap."

Dave Thomas folded his hands on his stomach and smiled. "Oh, don't worry, he already knows. How else am I going to get my next five-star dinner?"

They were leaving his office when Boston stopped in the doorway and looked down the hall at Elizabeth Strasser, standing in front of a group of SEC examiners. They had all the appearance of terrified galley slaves, and the sound of the SEC director lecturing them about the quality of their work and appearance echoed down the corridor. Suddenly, Boston turned and stared at Dave Thomas, who was leaning back in his chair with a twinkle of satisfaction in his eyes. A little smile crept across her lips.

"You knew she was going to stop by your office while we were here, didn't you?"

Thomas shrugged. "Her office is just down the hall. She stops by occasionally during the day."

McBain turned from his partner and narrowed his eyes at Dave. "Why you dirty, manipulative sonuvabitch."

Boston sauntered over to the federal examiner's desk and leaned across it. "I don't care what you say, David Thomas, I promise you this: You are coming to work with us someday."

As she walked by him out the door, McBain shoved his hat on his head and jerked his thumb toward the pudgy fed.

"Good luck getting him to work out, Boston."

FIVE

At five-thirty, Boston and McBain locked their office and strolled along the tree-lined streets and past the brownstones of the South End to the Holiday Lounge. Cocktail hour at Holiday was in full swing, and the favorable autumn breeze brought out a good-looking crowd searching for quality jazz, beverages, and short-term relationships. After waving to Michael behind the long L-shaped bar on their right, they occupied an empty booth farther to the back of the restaurant side of the lounge. A trumpet, bass, and sax were setting up near the window overlooking the street. The piano player had not arrived yet, but Sarah Vaughan was setting the mood just fine over the speakers.

The investigators ordered a round of gin martinis and were easing into the music when Dave Thomas entered the restaurant accompanied by a white-haired gentleman in a blue suit. In contrast to his wrinkled face, the older man's attire was dignified and classic, a crisp white pocket square matching his pressed shirt and rep tie. McBain joined Boston on one side while the two men slipped in across from them. Dave did the introductions.

"Harold Rogers, I'd like to introduce Boston O'Daniel and Mr. McBain."

The older gentleman shook Boston's hand and reached for McBain's. "Please, call me Harold. That's a charming name you have, young lady. Do you have a first name, Mr. McBain?"

Dave said, "No, he doesn't."

"My friends sometimes call me Boozy."

Rogers looked at Dave Thomas, his face wrinkling even further into a question mark.

Dave raised his hand as he saw a waitress. "Let's order you a drink, shall we?"

She brought Thomas a Budweiser and Rogers a glass of cabernet, along with two baskets of fresh calamari and a large plate of iced oysters on the half shell.

After scrutinizing the seafood, Harold Rogers didn't look hungry. McBain took note of his face and handed him a menu. "Harold, Dave tells us that you have a situation we might be able to help you with."

Rogers said, "I certainly hope you can, Mr. McBain. I'm trying to do what's best for my company and shareholders. But, if you'll forgive me, although David recommended you highly when he suggested we meet, I must say I'm still a little uncertain about what it is you both do and whether you are the right people for me to be talking to."

McBain sat back, and Boston took over, her red hair and ruby necklace dangling over a light gray suit jacket. "Let me give you a little background. Then you can decide whether you're wasting your time or not. At the very least, you can enjoy a glass of wine and some jazz while we talk.

"McBain and I are what you might call financial detectives. People come to us when they feel they have been cheated out of their money. Dave said that you have built a very successful company that is the subject of a takeover offer. We also have built a small business over the past four and a half years, helping people recover or protect what's theirs, usually from unscrupulous characters or scam artists in the money business, people who have no qualms about ethics or professionalism. You could say we try and get the financial results that Dave and the regulators are after officially, but we work privately and outside the standard legal channels. On the other hand, we don't look to send anyone to jail, and our methods for getting people their money back can be somewhat unorthodox if the situation demands it. In short, we do whatever it takes to find out the truth about a given financial problem and get the best results for our clients.

"As to our ability and credentials, we are licensed private investigators and members of the Association of Certified Fraud Examiners."

Rogers said, "I've never heard of such an organization. I didn't know such a thing existed. I thought fraud only occurred on Wall Street—insider trading and that sort of thing. Naturally, I've heard of Ivan Boesky and Bernard Madoff."

Boston watched Dave Thomas wince at the name. "It's a sad comment on human nature, Harold," she continued, "that my partner and I have never been without new business, especially since the stock market began to melt down a few years ago. Investment and corporate fraud are much more widespread than people realize. That may be one of the reasons so many innocent people get taken by scams of every kind. It happens to small-town merchants, professional athletes, and movie stars, as well as sophisticated investors.

"As far as results go, we can give you a dozen recommendations from satisfied clients, confidentially, of course. My own specialties run from portfolio and securities analysis to investigating the backgrounds of the targets of our clients' claims."

Rogers took a sip of his wine and nodded, scanned the menu, and ordered a cheeseburger from the waitress. The older man grew more at ease as he absorbed Boston's words.

"Well," he said. "I am intrigued. I'd be interested in hearing more about your experiences in time. Right now, my concerns run more to the level of corporate shenanigans than Madoff-type scams."

McBain pulled over his martini. "I spent years working on Wall Street, trading equities, options, and futures. During that time and since then I've been known as a pretty successful short seller. I became a successful short seller because I often either smelled a rat or assumed someone was lying to me, either in the financial statements or in the investment research. There are lots of reasons for suspicion when it comes to the quality of the work and opinions in the investment business. Some of it is due to incompetence or ego, some of it poor training of young analysts coming up, most of it the structure of incentives. The unspoken rule is you go along with everyone else and you're OK. Better to be wrong with the crowd than stick your neck out, be right, and offend any executive of a big company, or worse, make them look foolish. Most of the time you can get away with that; other times, somebody suffers. Rarely is it 'the talent' on the Street.

"When Boston and I look at a situation, we don't trust other opinions just because they come from highly paid supposed experts. Between her eye for numbers and feel for people and my experience looking at corporate PR smokescreens, patterns, and bogus transactions, we evaluate a given scenario with skeptical eyes and assume the worst until proven otherwise through our own exhaustive research, investigation, and confirmation of the facts behind the numbers."

Boston said, "So one thing we can assure you is that if my partner and I start an investigation, our premise is that our client has been or is going to be ripped off somewhere, somehow. And we approach the case accordingly. Now, I'm not sure how all this applies to your problem. From what little Dave has told us, it sounds like a pretty straightforward takeover deal and merger due diligence. But if you think for some reason you might need the services of someone to protect your financial interests, I doubt you'll find anyone more qualified or determined than us."

Rogers looked over at Dave Thomas and nodded slightly before addressing the investigators. His eyes flickered with a keen light.

"Very interesting, Mr. McBain, Ms. O'Daniel. There could come a time when we may want to talk about your unorthodox methods. For now, I'll simply describe my needs. I am, by profession, an engineer and a businessman. I've built Harold Rogers Technologies over the past thirty years, first starting out with my own capital, then taking my company public eight years ago as we expanded. Our technologies have focused largely on hardware and software that helps energy companies identify and obtain natural resources around the world. About ten years ago, we began to develop tools that would work in the mining sector as well. As good fortune would have it, my research team and I developed some unique technologies that have proven to be invaluable in locating, identifying, and processing rare earth and strategic minerals."

"Rare earth minerals," McBain said. "You mean like platinum and gold?"

"Sapphires, rubies, emeralds, that kind of thing?" Boston said with enthusiasm.

The gentleman stared at them, then at Dave, then back at the detectives. He sighed.

"No, that's not what I mean. Rare earth minerals aren't precious stones. They are valuable commercial minerals of the lanthanide and other groups of chemical elements that are not commonly found in large quantities and are often difficult to find and process. What makes these items even more valuable is that they are often in great demand because of their use in either critical national defense technologies or popular consumer or industrial products. Most people have never heard of these in the way they may be aware of gold or copper. Yet they are increasingly used in everyday products. Some people call them the vitamins of the chemical chain."

"Count me as impressed," McBain said. "Like what, for example?"

"Do you own a smartphone?"

McBain pulled his from his suit pocket. "Of course."

Rogers leaned across and looked at the model. "Your phone uses a number of critical minerals, including a rare earth metal called tantalum, probably mined in China or the Democratic Republic of the Congo in Africa. A smartphone contains about forty milligrams." The engineer warmed to his subject. "That's just one of the most widely used metals. The most in demand include neodymium, niobium, dysprosium, europium, terbium, and yttrium. Their critical everyday uses range from batteries in electric cars to magnets to lasers to large wind turbines used in wind farms. These metals, along with other strategic minerals such as rhodium, are used not just in green technology but everyday medical technology and important defense industries."

Boston screwed up her face. "Dyspepsium?"

"Jeez," said McBain. "And I thought derivatives jargon was obscure. You sound like some kind of Star Trek geek, Harold."

Rogers took a drink of wine and inhaled for a moment. "You understand options, correct?"

"Sure."

"Just think of them as Greek symbols, Mr. McBain. Perhaps that will help."

"That works."

Dave fished around in the dish of calamari and interjected, "You two can get up to speed on the details of the industry later. For now you just have to understand that global demand for these scarce metals has made Harold's company a hot property. As the rare earth sector has heated up, HR has attracted a number of offers. He's rejected several, but now the board is insisting they accept this most recent one from the new bidder. Given the size of the premium to market, they really have no choice from a fiduciary perspective. So the deal is on the table, and barring any problems in the discovery phase, the merger will go through."

Boston said, "I don't get it. You built the company over thirty years. So why are you selling at all if you don't want to cash out?"

"If it was up to me, I wouldn't be selling the company, Ms. O'Daniel. When the company went public, I was diluted. I am the largest shareholder, but I only own a third of my company, so I can't really block the sale. David is right. This offer is very attractive from a shareholder perspective. The board loves it. So does my senior management team. The acquiring company is, in theory, a perfect match with HR. The analysts and investment community are referring to it as two plus two equals ten."

McBain finished his martini as he listened. "I have to admit, though I've seen your stock soar, I haven't paid much attention to the deal. Who is the offer from?"

Rogers shifted in his seat and swirled the wine around in his glass. The older man's eyes changed, became more than a little edgy as he replied. "A company called Africa's Future Resources. The shares are listed in Europe, but the company is, in practical terms, based in South Africa. AFR owns a large asset base of mining sites and leases throughout Africa and a few in Central Asia and South America. More important, in the past few years they have amassed mineral rights in a number of critical strategic locations that, if fully developed, could prove to be significant new sources of rare earth minerals. That's why investors are valuing the combined company so highly. With our technology, new separation processes, and artificial intelligence data research, they could locate, identify, extract, and process those minerals at an exponentially faster pace and lower cost."

Boston made a few notes. McBain said, "I don't know the name. What do you know about the owners? European, South African?"

"AFR is majority owned by a man with the last name of Henry, very successful in the commodities business."

Boston and McBain looked at each other with wide eyes. She leaned toward Rogers. "You don't mean the guy who owns the Red Sox? Whoa!"

Once again, Rogers implored Dave Thomas with a desperate look. Thomas took a swallow of beer, and Rogers finally said, "No, young lady, he's not the man who owns the Boston Red Sox."

"Whew, thank God for that."

Dave finished his beer and jumped in. "Rodney Henry is a big name in the international mining business. He's been a serious player for years, but he maintains a low profile, so I'm not surprised you haven't heard of him. He made a reputation as an i-banker first, then with some pretty shrewd investment calls on his own. A couple years ago, he moved into owning hard mining assets as a pure play and has been quietly buying up mineral rights around the world under the radar, going head to head with the Chinese and the global mining conglomerates. With these big strikes in rare earth and strategic minerals, he could vault into the big leagues. We're talking billionaire territory with a stranglehold on a good portion of critical resources that aren't already owned by China, not to mention some leading-edge processing tech. That makes him important not just in the industry but in Washington."

Boston said, "What exactly are you looking for, Harold? I'm still not sure why you need to hire anyone, especially an investigator. What are you worried about?"

"Ms. O'Daniel, you asked me why I was cashing out. In practical terms, I'm not. The company will be purchased through an exchange of shares. So I will, in effect, become a large shareholder of Africa's Future Resources stock."

McBain pushed away the empty plate of oysters and leaned back. "Now I'm beginning to see why you're nervous. Either way you play it, you're going to be a minority shareholder in Henry's company. A much smaller fish in a bigger pond."

Rogers said, "The international mining fraternity is a very insular community, Mr. McBain. I've asked around discreetly. Mr. Henry has a very tough reputation. Various stories have circulated over time. Henry has been very successful, and so have many of his investors. But I've heard that some of his former hedge fund partners and minority shareholders haven't always been quite so fortunate. Nothing that anyone would go on record about or could be proven in legal proceedings. I'm a good businessman and technologist, but I will admit that when it comes to corporate politics and machinations, I'm out of my depth against a man like that. I just want to know what I'm getting into and that the future of my company and investment are being protected. I've known entrepreneurs who were maneuvered out of both their own companies and their investment capital over time. I don't intend to become one of them."

The investigators looked at each other, then at Dave. "And you've got nothing on record, Dave?" McBain asked. "This is the guy you said Strasser looked at and gave a pass to?"

Dave nodded and picked at the cold calamari. "Nothing but rumors, unsubstantiated accusations, and complaints that never went all the way to trial. One or two lawsuits by former investors that are tied up in the courts with countersuits. No regulatory filings or charges. You could say the same for hundreds of cases. And like I said, he mostly operates overseas now."

Boston smiled at Rogers and said, "And you don't think the bankers and lawyers the board hired will watch out for you?"

"To be frank, no. They may do their jobs well, but at this point, everyone is entirely too enthusiastic about this deal for my comfort."

"You're right to be cautious," McBain said. "I don't know anything about this Henry's reputation yet, but if he is as sharp a corporate knife fighter as you say, with Wall Street training, I'd be nervous too. On the other hand, no disrespect, sir, but Bill Gates and Steve Jobs didn't become who they were by being fair-minded doormats. The billion-dollar club is filled with smart, tough men and women with blood on their hands. Either way, you can be sure he'll be looking out for his long-term interests. And I'd bet that they don't dovetail with yours. I remember hearing in school about a huge merger that created a financial conglomerate back in the nineties. One minute, the two mega-executives were shaking hands on the stage looking like the best of friends. A year later, one of the guys was a footnote to corporate history."

Boston plucked at an olive in her drink and smiled. "Not to mention, the whole thing is starting to have the feel of too good to be true, isn't it? With everybody this happy, I'm already suspicious myself, and we haven't even looked at the deal."

More food arrived, and the investigators took notes and asked a few more questions about the transaction and how far along it was. Rogers and Dave Thomas finished their drinks.

"Goodnight," McBain said. "Boston and I will make some notes here while we have a few drinks and listen to some music."

"Take care, Dave," Boston said. "We'll think about some ways to approach this that might work for you and send you a proposal tomorrow, Harold."

Rogers buttoned his jacket as he and the regulator looked for a taxi outside Holiday. "So, David, to safeguard my life's work, you've sent me to a swimsuit model and an alcoholic. I hope you know how much trust I'm placing in your recommendation."

Thomas smiled and pulled at the older man's arm. "Let's take a walk for a few minutes before we find a cab, Harold. I'd like to tell you about a story you may have seen in the papers not long ago. And about how much I think of those two people."

SIX

The Mandarin Oriental Hotel is a sleek architectural gem set in the belt of high-end stores and posh restaurants of Back Bay on Boylston Street. On a perfect fall evening, the black SUVs and parade of high-priced sports cars swooped down on the glass-and-steel entrance, suits and dresses alighted from each car, one after another as they arrived for a special event. Now and then, a Maserati or Lamborghini swept into the lane, and uniformed valets would swarm over it like a smiling pit crew.

Boston and McBain waited on the marble floor of the lobby for Harold Rogers, admiring the art deco design and furnishings and observing the expensive clientele circulating for pre-dinner cocktails at Bar Boulud. The investigators did not look out of place. McBain's custom gray pinstripe was his most expensive suit, and his dark-blue tie matched his cufflinks. Boston was dressed in a form-fitting, dark-green Gucci blazer over her cocktail dress, a small diamond pendant with matching earrings, and a gold Hermes scarf. The redhead also wore designer eye frames with razor-thin lenses.

Rogers arrived punctually at six-thirty, and the three rode up the elevator to a penthouse-level hospitality suite. Boston touched their client lightly on the arm. "Are you ready?"

The white-haired gentleman exhaled loudly. "As ready as I'll ever be. I'm sure I'm not terribly comfortable at role playing and intrigue."

McBain straightened his fedora in the reflection. "Not to worry, Harold, we are. You just stick with the plan and introduce us as your independent consultants and smooth out the happy news with your board. We'll take care of everyone else."

Boston pulled at his sleeve and whispered. "Try not to insult too many people tonight, McBain. The idea is to get everyone comfortable with our role in this so they'll feel free to share information. Just another pair of green-eyeshade types to—"

The doors slid open. "Showtime," McBain said.

They entered an expansive hospitality suite with a wall of glass looking north over the brownstones and shopping districts of the Back Bay toward the Charles River, with Cambridge and the halls of MIT in the distance. The room was filled with over three dozen suits, mostly men, with a few cocktail dresses scattered among the crowd of investment bankers, senior executives from the two companies, and members of the board of directors of HR Technologies. McBain observed with pleasure that he was the only man with a hat. As he checked it with the event receptionist, he also noted that no one who was paying attention was looking at him as long as he stood next to his partner.

"Boston, I don't think it's your pair of green eyes that those gents are staring at."

"Shut up."

Four of the men observing them had staked out the small bar. Rogers led the investigators over and introduced them to some of the HR board members. The executives were confused, and their reactions showed it; they were no doubt startled by the glamorous appearance of their company chairman's guests.

One thin-haired man in a weathered blue suit seemed eager to pepper Boston with questions about her background and even more interested in getting her a cocktail. No one professed interest in McBain's background.

She smiled at the group and answered their questions politely. "I can assure you, Mr. Harrison, Mr. McBain and I have performed many due diligence analyses at this level of complexity. I did honors work in merger accounting at Boston College years ago and have worked as a private consultant on both equity and quasi-equity transactions. Mainly, we work with closely held firms, assisting private investors with valuations. We've worked with a number of venture capitalists and private equity firms on buyouts, pre-IPO valuations for different rounds of high-tech fund raising, and off-market valuations for acquisitions and exits. If they approve, I could provide references for several technology company purchases in the New England region that we've been involved in. We also have relationships with the incubators and research labs at MIT and Harvard Business School and work with any number of professors there to advise them on how to monetize ideas."

Fifteen minutes of red-haired charm later, the board was welcoming the addition of the consultants with hearty laughter and open arms, fortified by Rogers's confirmation that he would be paying the new advisers out of his own pocket. If anything, their confidence in the certainty of the impending deal was even more assured.

At this point McBain determined that, with that part of the plan anchored, it was time to meet and greet the other parties to the transaction, starting with the bankers of the acquiring firm. As the three of them drifted away from the bar and the board members, he spotted several candidates mingled together with what were in all likelihood some of the executives of Africa's Future Resources.

"Is Henry over there, Harold?" he asked.

"No, I don't see him yet."

McBain jiggled the ice in his glass of vodka. "Tell you what. Why don't you two keep an eye out for him while I go over and introduce myself to our hosts and some of their talent."

Boston knew the look in his eyes and covertly elbowed him as she turned aside. "Just remember what I said . . . underplay."

"You worry too much, partner," he said, dabbing his lips with a vod-ka-soaked pinkie.

She closed her eyes, her lips slightly parted.

Boston and Rogers picked up small plates of smoked salmon and caviar and grabbed a corner table with comfortable chairs. Rogers sipped his white wine while Boston drank spring water.

"While we're waiting for his big entrance," she said, "why don't you fill me in on what you know about Henry's background? Since we didn't have time to do much research before this meet and greet was scheduled, I'd like to hear your impressions. Let's see if I can spot him before you point him out to me."

Rogers raised an eyebrow. "Oh, I'm fairly certain you'll know when he walks into the room. My two brief meetings with the man have focused on the general offer terms of the deal, but I'll tell you what I've learned about him from others.

"His story is quite the rags-to-riches saga. I think he tries to stay out of the public eye, but his is a classic American success story. Word has it he comes from a background of poverty, somewhere in the mining country of Appalachia. I don't think he talks about it, so that information is a bit vague. The details probably don't mesh well with his business profile and aspirations. No one says much about his early life or family. He went to college for mining and mineral engineering. He served five years in the army, then came out and went to work on Wall Street for one of the big firms. Henry became a star in their corporate finance department and then specialized in mergers and acquisitions for the mining sector. After making the firm a lot of money, he decided to go out on his own and set up an investment fund. Or should I say several. Ugh. I wonder if they have anything else to eat, I . . ."

Boston smiled and signaled a white-coated waiter. "I found caviar is an acquired taste, even when it's good. I'm still not sure I've acquired it. This fellow seems to have some things more up our alley."

The waiter placed small plates of shrimp, mini-pizza slices, puff pastry cups, and bruschetta on their table. Rogers sampled a few and continued between bites.

"As I indicated the other night, he had some spectacular successes, but his partners and investors didn't always seem to come out quite as well. He had some home runs, but one or two funds were dissolved after suffering poor returns or outright losses on big bets. One of his more notable triumphs was against some short sellers who had bet big against him on a particular stock. Henry went after them legally and publicly and reportedly put pressure on several analysts who were hedging their opinions. Eventually, he outlasted them and was proven right, and the shorts were wiped out. I was told he made quite a killing on that deal when they had to cover their positions. Years ago, he spotted the evolving demand for rare earth metals and other strategic minerals earlier than most. It seems he decided the most profitable play was to own the mineral rights to the assets directly. Since then, he has cultivated relationships with important government officials in several countries in order to outmaneuver both major private mining companies and big foreign investors like the Russians and Chinese."

Boston continued to scan the room. "And what do you think of that strategy?"

"It's a gamble, but I have to admire it. I've been involved with energy and resource development for decades. He has taken on a lot of risk in some very dicey corners of the world, places I wouldn't venture myself. Contrary to what you may think, I hope Henry is correct. I don't have that kind of tolerance for risk, but if it pays off, I stand to profit handsomely as a major shareholder of AFR."

She smiled at his dignity and modesty. He had worked hard to create something lasting, and though the sale might not have been his first choice, he was on the verge of a personal and public triumph. "Well, Harold, let's just hope we're all being overly cautious. We'll do our job and make sure you are protected financially, and your legacy is secured. The rest will be up to Rodney Henry."

And when she looked up, he was by the door to the hospitality suite, shaking hands with two men who had the look of very expensive lawyers. Three of the HR board members were gravitating toward him eagerly from the bar.

The first thing Boston noticed was his suit. Savile Row custom-tailored, window-pane blue-gray, it fit his solid figure like a ten-thousand-dollar glove.

The second thing she saw was the hands.

In an instant, she processed everything Rogers had just told her in the context of Henry's bearing and appearance, but especially his big hands. As she watched him interact with the others, she observed a deference in their demeanor that was not just a reflection of his financial position or role in this deal. Henry did not look or act like a smooth-talking corporate operator or Wall Street dealmaker. There was no plastered-on smile or polite laughter. Standing among these Ivy League degrees, he exuded a quiet confidence as he listened to them talk: a silent confidence free of arrogance. He stood six feet tall, with a full head of brown hair streaked with battleship-gray that placed him somewhere in his forties. The blue eyes were steady and intense, his expression neither welcoming nor hostile. She could tell he was actively absorbing information when someone spoke to him, and if someone was foolish enough to waste his valuable time, that fool would regret it.

As he gripped the hands of these high-priced lawyers and executives one by one, there was an exchange of unspoken communication. With men like Henry this wasn't just a handshake; it was a personal challenge, like wrestling or boxing. If you were a man, it was intended to take your measure, intimidate, or master. If you were a woman, possess. Far from presenting himself as a high-priced executive, he had the bearing of the kind of man who ran a trucking company or construction empire that he had assembled the hard way, with twenty-hour-a-day shifts. She judged him to be a throwback to an earlier time, when men were measured by something more than certificates on the wall and financial cleverness. He had the look of a man who built things from the ground up with his hands. His business. His fortune. His life.

Henry's attention turned to the pair at the corner table. As Boston watched him approach, she was barely aware that they were already standing. She knew one thing already: She would have to be very careful. They were about to burrow deeply into the life and affairs of a very serious predator. For some reason, she found that idea thrilling. She wasn't aware that her green eyes were blazing behind the glasses, but inside, she was smiling. For the briefest of moments, her tongue flicked out between her lips.

"Harold," Henry said as they exchanged a handshake. "Good to see you again so soon. I'm glad you could make it on short notice."

"I don't think I had much choice, Mr. Henry," Rogers said. "At the pace these discussions have been going, missing out on any meeting could be dangerous—or expensive."

Rodney Henry's eyes shifted over to close with Boston's.

"May I present Ms. O'Daniel, one of my independent merger consultants. I've retained her along with her partner to assist the board in finalizing the valuation and agreement details."

"Another firm, Harold?" Henry said. "You're not happy with the ones the board chose?"

"They're fine," Rogers replied. "Just a belt-and-suspenders approach. I'm sure you can appreciate that as a self-made man."

They were already clasping hands. Henry glanced down at her fingers as they shook. "That's quite a grip you have, Ms. O'Daniel."

Suddenly Boston remembered that her hands were rough. It was one thing that not even an expensive manicure and designer accessorizing could disguise. She released his hand.

"Sorry, Mr. Henry. They're not very ladylike, I know. I worked in a body shop to pay for college."

"I see," Henry said. "That must have been an impressive body shop."

"It still is."

His eyes swept over her, then the corners of his mouth rose. "Yes, I'll bet it is. You still work with your hands when you're not consulting on corporate mergers?"

"When I get the chance."

He nodded and crossed his arms. "Don't try to hide it. I work with people all day long who've never done a day's hard work with their backs or hands. Be proud of who you are and where you come from."

"I am, Mr. Henry."

"Did you break your nose working in the shop as well, Ms. O'Daniel?"

She reached up and pushed at her glasses. "Something like that."

"I'm sure it didn't affect your work at all. It's good to have another pair of sharp eyes on deck. The more smart people we have working on this, the sooner we can all put our signatures to the dotted line and build something else to be proud of. If Harold hired you, I'm sure you're well qualified to help make this happen."

Boston tilted her head and turned to Rogers. "Perhaps we can introduce Mr. Henry to my partner, Mr. McBain. He's over there with that group by the window."

Henry nodded. "That's part of my management team. And some of the investment bankers from Whitney, Mitchell."

• • •

WHEN HE LEFT Boston and Harold Rogers, McBain wasted no time in wading into the gaggle of bankers, lawyers, and AFR executives on the other side of the suite. Some of the bankers were busy discussing their renewed fortunes and future purchases associated with the rising market, a subject dear to McBain's heart.

"Good evening, gentlemen, ladies" he said. "My name is McBain. I'm a new member of the HR Tech team. I just wanted to introduce myself since we'll be working together. Nice watch, by the way. Rollie? Cheers. Here's to the happy couple."

The party fell silent for a moment while the evaluation took place. Between the irreverent intrusion and the expensive suit, the group was nonplussed. The AFR executives glanced at one another, then at their investment bankers. One of the more experienced bankers eyed McBain with suspicion from beneath a shining bald head. With all the egos involved, there is a pecking order in investment banking. The others waited for their most senior man to set the tone.

"We haven't met before," he said, without offering his hand. "I'm Todd

Mortimer of Whitney, Mitchell, and Company, the lead adviser on this deal. Who are you with?"

"I'm with Harold Rogers. And with that redhead over there sitting next to him."

"No, I meant what firm."

"So did I." McBain smiled, his eyes laughing at the banker over the rim as he enjoyed his vodka.

The group shuffled their feet, even more perplexed.

The investigator straightened his blue tie with his free hand. "I used to work for Morgan years ago. In New York, if that helps you."

"Which Morgan?" a young blonde woman asked.

"Exactly."

Another banker in double-breasted Armani chimed in, "In mining mergers and acquisitions?"

McBain shook his head. "Nope. I traded equities and derivatives on the prop desk and for some of the big customer accounts."

The confused faces looked at one another, then searched his face for hints of humor. "Wait, you were a trader? How did you—?"

"The firm and I decided my penchant for short selling stocks didn't fit with their overall rosy outlook on certain companies. So now I do valuations and due diligence for private equity players and VCs. The only difference now is that I set my own hours. And that I always look out for the interests of my clients first without worrying about being fired."

The investment bankers shifted and looked at their Omegas and Rolexes. Two of the AFR executives coughed into their smiles.

Todd Mortimer smirked.

"Come on. Equity trading and short selling? Whatever your talents as a trader and stock picker, Mr. McBain, M and A at this level is an entirely different game. No offense, but most of us have a background not just in corporate finance but specifically in mining company valuations, acquisitions, and spin-offs. We've been working this deal for six months."

McBain flashed a grin. "Not that the phrase 'interests of my client' means anything to you, but I'm here at the request of one of the major shareholders of HR Technologies. I'm sure you don't object to another set of eyes hovering around to double-check your math and the stack of term sheets or merger agreements and make sure all parties are satisfied the deal is fair. After all, it's not coming out of your pocket."

He crunched an ice cube.

The short, dark-haired Rolex banker grunted behind his polished smile and shrugged.

"If Rogers wants to pay someone out of his pocket to sleep better, we've got no problem with that. But I hardly think you'll have much to add other than a bill, McBain. We have five governments that have already approved this transaction on a preliminary basis, including Treasury, Defense, and Justice here in the US. Ten of the finest international law firms have reviewed it. Six investment banks. Ten major commercial lenders. Mining experts, international political risk experts, government legal consultants, lobbyists . . ."

McBain laughed. "In which case, I'm getting five hundred an hour for surfing off your work. Sweet. Keep it quiet, will ya, guys?"

Double-breasted Armani stood tall and chimed in. "And you think you'll have more value to add than Citi, UBS, Barclays, JPMorgan, and the other firms? We have the best banks on the Street behind this deal."

McBain glanced at the ceiling for a moment, then looked at the AFR executives. "Good point. All fine firms," he said, "and you guys at AFR should have confidence you're getting your money's worth. And after all, it's not like the mining M and A guys at UBS lost the sixty billion Swiss francs or got indicted by the Justice Department for tax evasion. And the Citi boys had nothing to do with the subprime meltdown. They're good, for ex-government employees. And you can't fault the Barclays team for that interest rate–fixing scandal. I know from personal experience how hard it is to trade derivatives, so I can sympathize with the JPMorgan department that lost six billion on that Whale thing a few years back. Anybody can make a mistake, as we just saw when a certain elite firm with lots of government clout got dragged into that bribery scandal in Malaysia and got blown out to the tune of five hundred million Euros on their portfolio of German bunds in the same week. Maybe they were refugees from Lehman, Bear, or Merrill after they tanked. And poor Goldman, what with that big bulls-eye on their forehead, I'm surprised they don't use the same logo as Target. If anything, all this should underline the commitment to do better for their customers elsewhere. Just because these big boys can't manage their own businesses is no reflection of the work they'll do for you."

McBain inhaled to prepare for his next round of mockery and saw the crowd stiffen. They all straightened their spines, and corporate smiles replaced the grimaces on their faces and not because of his wit. The scene was reminiscent of a crowd of courtiers bowing away as the king approached.

"Mr. McBain," Harold Rogers said from behind him, "I'd like to introduce you to Rodney Henry."

McBain spun around to evaluate the man he had been waiting to meet. In an instant, he saw the hands, too, and he didn't like what he saw. He rapidly came to the same conclusion as his partner, but there was something else that made him uneasy.

In the ten years that he had worked on Wall Street, McBain had developed a comfortable contempt for most of the big shots he met. Over time, he had felt assured of several things, the most important of which was that net worth rarely bore any real relationship to actual worth as an accomplished human being. In the seconds that he wrestled with Henry's grip and gaze, he suspected something very different was behind that confident visage. Something that was a more formidable source of personal power and ego than mere wealth. Taunting mere investment bankers and corporate executives was child's play compared to dealing with this. The easy part of the job was over.

"Mr. McBain," Henry said as they shook, "glad to have you and your partner on the team."

The investigator fought the urge to massage his right hand when Henry released it. "Technically," he said, "we're on Team Rogers for now, Mr. Henry. From what I've been hearing, you've got a pretty crowded bench of big-name players as it is. But as I was just saying to your managers and bankers here, I'm sure we'll all be opening the champagne to celebrate in short order."

"Of course," Henry said. "I'm confident you and Ms. O'Daniel will still prove invaluable to your client."

"We always do."

"Do you have experience in mining, Mr. McBain?"

"I've done pretty good with commodity futures and options. I also have experience with Wall Street, with takeovers, and with making sure my client's interests are protected."

No reaction. "And are you familiar with Africa?"

McBain thought for a moment. "I've been to the Seychelles for diving and climbed Mount Kilimanjaro once. I spent some time in Cape Town, South Africa. I saw plenty of mines from the air; does that count?"

The group of investment bankers had been shouldering their way forward to become part of the conversation. The alpha-male primate instinct was strong in the financial world. Todd Mortimer smirked his way to the front.

"Those mines are the past, McBain, gold, copper, or iron ore. Most of them fully developed, some played out. What Rod and AFR are doing is literally cutting new ground. Like we told you, there are a half-dozen governments involved with approving this deal. This merger will produce one of the biggest and most advanced cross-border mining companies in the world. AFR has rights to places you've never even heard of, let alone been to."

Rogers said, "I have to admit, Mr. Henry, aside from making the discoveries themselves, getting those government approvals struck me as a very impressive feat. You must have pulled quite a few strings to edge out Anglo, BHP, Lohnro, and the others for the mining rights to those lands."

Henry shook his head. "Africa isn't for the soft hearted, Harold. Or the soft headed. Doing business in Africa requires not just skill but patience, persistence, and most of all toughness, particularly if you are on the leading edge, like we are. It's all based on understanding the people we're dealing with and convincing them of the long-term benefits we can bring, how our interests can advance theirs. We've cultivated those relationships over years, much the same way you developed your software. We made mistakes and learned. And this is where it pays off."

McBain gestured to Henry with his glass. "I can't place your accent. It almost sounds southern. You're certainly not from Africa yourself. Where are you from originally?"

He turned to the investigator. "You don't have to be from Africa to do well there, but you do have to adapt, and quickly. People tend to romanticize the place or fear it from the comfort of their living room. In reality, it can be an unforgiving continent. So outsiders either figure out how to operate in that environment or go home licking their wounds. I found that if you do adapt and immerse yourself, almost any part of Africa can feel like home. Of course, as your client has pointed out, for both animals and humans the competition for life is fierce in a way most of us can't imagine. Have you ever killed a man, Mr. McBain?"

The group fell silent. McBain narrowed his eyes, his drink halfway to his mouth. "What does killing have to do with anything?"

"I've seen the kind of grinding poverty that brings people to the point where they'll kill to feed their family. The kind of hunger that gnaws at a mother's belly for days. Yet all she can think about is how fortunate she is to have any job as she walks ten miles to go to work each day because she can't afford to pay for the overcrowded, rickety bus. In Africa, it's more often than not the norm. But things are changing. We're a part of that change, helping make it happen. And it's all because of the careful development of the natural resources of the continent.

"Most people aren't even aware of what's happening. Think about it. Ten years ago, if anybody told you Uganda had oil reserves, you would have laughed at them. Today, Angola is a rising power. They're still hitting new finds in oil and gas. And that's just energy. Angola is twice the size of Texas and only has twenty million people. Conservative estimates of her natural resources are being expanded every year and include mining, timber, you name it. And look at the demographics. Nobody talks about Asian tigers anymore. It's African lions now. Investors are still fighting to get into Zimbabwe and Congo despite decades of war and tribal politics. Ghana, the Ivory Coast, Cameroon, even Rwanda are all being evaluated.

"China is all over Africa. So is India. And all over our deposits in the region. I've had to fight their companies tooth and nail, from corporate boardrooms to small government offices in crowded third-world capitals where one doesn't go without bodyguards and bottled water. I wonder what the Chinese know that Western investors don't. So while the risk averse and skeptics here prevent us from investing, those countries are pouring in billions and buying up the rights to everything the twenty-first-century economy needs to grow."

Rogers raised his glass of wine. "Yes, but you've pointed out two parts of the problem with so much competition and money going into a continent that may not be quite ready for it. So much ready money paired with so much poverty has led in the past to corruption and greater disparity in the distribution of sudden wealth. We've seen this with diamonds, gold, and oil in Nigeria and the Congo. We're all familiar with the concept of blood diamonds. How are we any different from the Chinese or the old imperial powers?"

Boston and McBain watched for an emotional reaction, but Henry's face remained impassive.

"You're right," he said. "But you put your finger on the way you and I can make a difference. I've already established relationships with government agencies in many of these countries that are responsible for public welfare, like housing, power, and education. When this deal goes through, it won't be just the shareholders who benefit, and not just the well off in Angola or Zambia. AFR will be involved in creating jobs and businesses in these far-flung provinces that have barely seen any development. Everyone keeps talking about making a difference in Africa. Well, you can't have a bigger impact than starting projects that will bring real work right away. And not just mining jobs. Demand for ancillary services will mean more employees in trucking, construction, services, food, you name it. Eventually, even high-value light manufacturing jobs that will require education, training, and skills transfers and demand for housing and clean water and electricity."

Boston crossed her arms and stood by her client. "You certainly get points for your sense of social justice, Mr. Henry."

For once, Henry shook his head with dismissal. "I have no use for such a simplistic and meaningless term, Ms. O'Daniel. I'm not a philanthropist or someone who pretends he's making a difference. We're not handing out make-work jobs to people to make our company appear morally superior. I look at global economics. When we go in to develop projects, we expect to make money. We hire and train local people because it benefits us as well as the host country in the long run. In my view, they are an untapped resource that we've identified, and others haven't. I see opportunity, and I see the future of business in these countries, in Africa."

McBain said, "That must be why Whitney, Mitchell is involved. They're known for their philanthropic devotion to poor people in emerging markets. Their presence must be a great comfort. Is that why they're lead manager on the deal?"

Baldy Mortimer jumped in. "Whitney, Mitchell is one of the top M and A boutique firms in the world. I guarantee you we have the connections and weight to manage all the moving pieces and push this across the line with any government or regulator in the world."

McBain finished his drink. "Boutique. I've always loved that term," he said. "It sounds so charming and harmless when you put it that way, like a small shop on Newbury Street or Madison Avenue. I remember watching the migration of the dealmakers from the collapsing houses into their own shops—boutique firms. Calling Whitney, Mitchell a boutique is like calling a pit full of spitting cobras and black widows a terrarium."

The cloud of bankers and lawyers recoiled. Rodney Henry chuckled and shook McBain's hand again. "On that note, I'll say good evening. I think

I'm going to like dealing with you, Mr. McBain. My people will be pleased to provide you and your partner any information we've given to Charlie Mitchell or anything else you need. Take care."

He turned, then nodded to Boston. "A pleasure, Ms. O'Daniel."

Henry walked away and was joined by one of his executives and several members of the board of directors of HR Tech. The crowd dispersed.

McBain followed him with his eyes. So did Boston. He tapped her on the elbow. "I'll bet there are only two people in the world who call Charles Mitchell Charlie," he whispered. "And Mitchell's wife is the other one."

SEVEN

Boston leaned forward in her seat, straining to hear the play calls over the noise of the crowd. The screams faded as the quarterback started the snap count. Moments later, the tailback hit the line and was stopped, but Brady was already four paces back and releasing the ball. He led his man perfectly, and the receiver had the corner beat by three steps as he caught the tight spiral. Boston leaped to her feet and joined in the thunderous roar. It reverberated throughout the stadium and reached manic proportions as the receiver raced sixty yards into the end zone. The Patriots had scored their third touchdown of the quarter and now held a commanding lead over the Jets heading into the final fifteen minutes.

"Damn, he's good!" She high fived her neighbor and sat down.

McBain had remained in his seat, finishing a hot dog. "He's married, you know."

"Who?"

"Tom Brady."

"Of course I know. I'm just pointing out how great he is."

"I hear his wife isn't bad looking either."

"McBain, given that you are the only man in this city who knows nothing about the Patriots or football, I don't expect you to appreciate his wicked awesomeness."

"I can't help it if I like baseball instead of football," he said.

"You live in Boston now, man up. Besides, I'm just admiring one of the greatest quarterbacks ever to play who's operating at the top of his game."

"Speaking of which, we should talk about how we want to approach the Rogers case."

Boston glanced at her watch, calculating how much time until the commercial break ended. "I guess the usual sweep and dig to start."

McBain eyeballed the stands for another vendor. "Should be easy to start with," he said. "Most of the collection work has already been done by the drones in the banks and law firms. We can start by accessing the data room they set up for the deal and see what they've got there in terms of corporate documentation, then decide what we want to examine in detail."

"What do you mean, data room?"

"Oh, sorry, you haven't dealt with that before. When they're doing a deal, the bankers and lawyers set up a virtual data room where they put electronic versions of all the relevant documents for the deal: private financial information, important legal contracts, audit reports, regulatory files, stuff like that. It's like an online digital vault. It's very secure, and you can set up all kinds of access levels to allow people anywhere to download files and numbers based on their seniority or need to know. Great for international deals like this one with lots of parties involved."

She raised her eyebrows. "That will be handy. I usually have to spend a lot of time tracking down information. OK, what do we know? We know Henry wants HR Tech in the worst way, otherwise he wouldn't have offered such a large premium to market. We know he's got mining assets, and Rogers has the technology to get to and process them. Assuming he's up to anything, you'd have to figure he'd try to get the technology without paying for it somehow, right?"

McBain glanced at her sideways. The dark-blue Patriots jersey with the number twelve fit her better than Brady. "Very good. Which means either

AFR might be trying to get access to their intellectual property by peeking at the company, then backing away at the last minute, or they do intend to buy HR and the tech, then try to manipulate the situation to invalidate or dilute Rogers and the other shareholders."

"So you think maybe Henry has guys trying to steal the software design? I've heard of that before. Can he use this data room thingy for that?"

"I'm not sure. Could be the old 'open your kimono' gimmick. Let's make a note to ask Rogers if that's even possible. Otherwise, I would think it would have to be what he fears, that somehow after the deal goes through, he gets the shaft."

Boston said, "So that means: What do we do with the information they give us? Sort through it and decide if there's a clause or a financial out they can use to cheat Rogers? Maybe some kind of performance clause for HR's products?"

"Probably, though I'm guessing it won't be in there. Rogers may not trust the board's lawyers and bankers, but they're not stupid, and they don't want to get sued. They get paid to comb through documents and evaluate what they see. In some ways, it pays for them to find mistakes and challenge issues or language the other side tried to insert—more billable hours and higher fees the longer it takes to close. No, I think we'll just have to figure out what we don't know but can guess or deduce from the facts and suspicions."

Boston watched as the Patriots lined up for the kick.

"From there, we decide what information we need to feel secure," she said. "I think we should take a look at the history of the two companies, especially AFR and Henry. We should be able to find out much more about his business history than what little Rogers did. If a trick worked before, Henry will probably try something like it again."

McBain said, "Right. Which means we go over how the other investors Rogers and Dave were talking about got burned. Let's put that at the top of the list."

"I'll start there for now," Boston said. "We have to figure out where we get that information and who we need to talk to. If they'll talk, that is."

She rose and chanted with the rest of the crowd. McBain spotted a vendor and tried waving for another hot dog, but the man couldn't see him through the sea of red, blue, and white jerseys. It took him a few minutes to get two more dogs to keep himself occupied. After the Jets called a time-out, he elbowed Boston.

"Let's not forget the most important part of the job. We've heard all the hosannas about Henry. You don't get where he is without making enemies. I want to know about the negative stuff and the rumors. I want to know more about him personally. You noticed how he dodged my question at the reception the other night."

"He didn't dodge it, McBain. He ignored it. I got the feeling he doesn't share his personal life much. Certainly not at cocktail events for business deals. Hey, you got a laugh out of him with your Wall Street cracks—consider yourself successful."

He finished chewing and looked at her face and eyes, focused on the field. "According to Rogers, you were a big hit with Henry yourself. I think you probably got more of his attention at the party than the lawyers or board members. Rogers told me Henry seemed quite impressed."

Boston sat down and shrugged. "If Rogers's information is correct, Henry probably felt some kind of empathy with my working-class background. He certainly is perceptive—even noticed my broken nose. Nobody else picks up on that, especially when I'm dressed in Gucci."

"Did you tell him how it was broken? The last time, I mean."

She leaned back and stared at him. "Of course not. What are you thinking?"

He held up his hot dog–filled hands. "I was thinking you might play on your common background to put him at ease. I was thinking the man would be intrigued to learn more about you when he discovered you were more than just a pretty face. Maybe you could draw him out on his own history."

"Not yet," she said, and her eyes narrowed even as they observed the game. "Never give them too much too soon, McBain. Make them work for it. Men like him want a challenge—you don't give him your life story in the first five minutes. If he's at all curious, he'll come back for more. You find out what he wants and keep it just out of reach."

"Well, well," McBain said. "Did you learn that from your mother?"

"No, I learned it fishing with Dad. You should come with us sometime. It's very relaxing."

"I fish the olives out of my martini; does that count?"

She rolled her eyes, shook her head, and zipped up her fleece vest. "I think our next stop should be Dee Dee. If anybody can bring us up to speed on all things Henry, she can. I'll call her when I get home and see if she has time to help."

"Works for me."

They watched the Patriots drive down the field for another few minutes. Then Boston turned to him and said, "By the way, you never told me you had been to Africa."

He was quiet and distant while he finished his last frankfurter. He reached down and nursed an untouched beer. "That was before your time," he said. "With Mel."

"Want to talk about it?"

"Not much."

"I thought we agreed no secrets."

His eyes sparkled a little. "We did. But I wouldn't want to give you my whole life story in five minutes, would I?"

"We've been together four and a half years." She waited another ten seconds while he pretended to watch the game. "Jerk."

McBain smiled and blew a kiss at his partner. He was beginning to like football.

EIGHT

October brought two things in abundance to New England: the multifaceted pageantries of local sports and autumn colors. Boston met McBain early at his apartment in the South End, and they admired the red and gold leaves while enjoying a walk past the multicolored banks of flowers in the Public Garden and across Boston Common. The investigators stopped for scrambled egg sandwiches and coffee and watched the tourists and children playing in the park. McBain took pictures with his phone of Boston kneeling next to a group of kindergartners as they sat on the bronze duckling statuettes in the Garden.

They wound their way through the maze of the Financial District to Post Office Square, had another coffee sitting outside on a bench next to the kiosk, then took the elevator to Dee Dee Franklin's office at the *Boston Business Journal*. The managing editor was seated in the conference room with a half-dozen people. Her dark eyes were set in stone, black hair pulled back to reveal the prominent profile of a Nubian queen displeased with her subjects. After five minutes, the staff of chastened researchers and writers scampered out of the conference room. Franklin grabbed a coffee from the steel container on a credenza, saw the investigators, and waved them in.

"Good morning, Dee," McBain said. "Are we interrupting?"

Franklin straightened her crimson blazer and gold necklace and sat back down. "No, you are right on time. I was just providing some encouragement to the staff. Hi, Boston."

"Not on our account, I hope," Boston said.

"Not exactly. But in the course of researching your new case, it became clear that some of my people have become entirely too complacent about their reporting lately."

McBain grunted. "Let me guess, stock market going up again, everything coming up roses. Rainbows and unicorns from now on thanks to the Federal Reserve's printing press."

"Pretty much," Dee said. "I know bankers and investors have short memories, but I didn't think I'd have to remind newspeople. Jesus Lord, it's not like the last meltdown was that long ago. I gave them some extra homework to do: go back and research some of the rose-colored financial reporting crap that was written about some little companies called Enron, WorldCom, and Lehman. Not to mention Madoff. You don't take anyone's word for anything. You dig, dig, dig and ask probing questions."

"Speaking of which, any luck on Rodney Henry?" Boston asked as she pulled up a seat at the table.

The editor arched her eyebrows and tilted her head, tapping a file folder with her pencil. A yellow legal pad next to it was covered with bullet points in elegant script.

"You two sure picked a prize bull to tangle with this time," Dee Dee said. "Where did you get this one?"

McBain picked up a bottle of water from the side table and leaned against the wall. "Dave Thomas tricked us into taking it on as a favor to a friend."

Franklin sat quietly while Boston filled her in on Harold Rogers's concerns.

Dee Dee was not amused. "Rogers is right to be cautious."

"You've got something?" McBain asked.

"I'll let you judge," she said. "I'm always more concerned by the things I can't find out, but in this case, I'm getting some uneasy vibes on a couple fronts."

"Like what, for instance?" Boston said.

The editor ticked off the first bullet point on the legal pad with her pencil. "The first thing we did was check out the available press on Henry, going back as far as we could. Then I started making some calls to the editors and writers who had done the few pieces on him and the ones who had tried to. Investors aren't the only ones your man plays hardball with. Henry knows how to work the media like a pro."

McBain frowned. "Strange. When we met him, he didn't strike me as the media-friendly type."

"There's a big difference between friendly and savvy," Dee said. "My guess is he knows how to tell whether a reporter is hungry or not. There's a real art to reading what a reporter is after from her own perspective. I've already taught you both that newspeople are just like anyone else, with their own goals and ambitions. Let's just say Henry has played the game as well as any, and he has a knack for cultivating good press. Or crushing bad press.

"If it's a two-way street, both sides can benefit. Access to a story can help a reporter's career, just as access to a customer can help a salesman. Henry appears to have a feel for that. You smooth talk the right news channel, make her believe she has exclusive information, throw some parties with lots of rich friends, maybe dispense a couple of gifts or trips here and there—discreetly, of course. The reporter gets a great story and reputation for access; the subject manages the version of the truth that gets to the public."

McBain nodded. "Same with Wall Street research. Access to senior management can make or break an analyst, especially one coming up the ladder."

"Exactly," Franklin said. "And that's happened here as well. Nobody was able to confirm anything, but I got the impression Henry wasn't shy about threatening an analyst or a firm if they started to put out bad news or imply something he didn't like. From what I've seen, two or three analysts made their careers by boosting Henry's reputation and stock picks over the years. You know the story, McBain. One hand washes the other. Once a reputation gets rolling, it builds on itself. Then you've impressed the bankers and investment community with your record and BS, especially the younger ones who don't have the chops to challenge the conventional wisdom."

"And if somebody doesn't play along?" Boston asked.

The editor kept moving down the page. "Henry isn't shy about going after people, legally and otherwise," she said. "He has worked to discredit news stories and negative research about his company or stocks he has an interest in. He sued one accounting firm and had a high-profile analyst fired for putting out a negative rating and story. You know about the short sellers who went up against him. What you don't know is the effort he put into pressuring the analysts and slandering the shorts until they had to break. When they covered, the stock soared, and your boy made a bundle. Nobody could confirm it, but there may have been some question of money changing hands after he finally sold off his position at a profit."

The investigators absorbed this information, scribbling furiously.

Boston smiled. "Rogers was right to go looking for help. Seems like Mr. Henry is shaping up to be one of our typical targets after all. No wonder he gets along so well with Whitney, Mitchell and the other bankers. Got any names we can try?"

Franklin slid her a page from the memo pad.

McBain grabbed a coffee and shook his head as he sat down across from his partner. "I'm guessing there's something else too. The Street loves guys like this. Like the geeks or hangers-on who want to be in with the tough guys at school. He's a man in a way that they know in their gut they're not. He's savvy in a financial way, plus he has the balls of a fighter who's earned his way with his fists and guts, not just brains and guile. It's all the difference between a man who has been in combat and one who dresses up in camo and plays paintball on the weekends. And they know it in their bones every time they meet him."

Dee Dee opened the file folder on the table. "And he is extremely guarded about his personal life."

"OK, let's talk about that," McBain said. "What were you able to find out about the man personally—his background, history, social life? He just blew me off when I asked him where he was from."

"Not surprising," Dee said. "Henry is forty-six years old and comes from a Kentucky coal-mining family. Not sure if he ever worked the mines, but he grew up dirt poor and certainly worked hard as a kid. I'm still trying to find contacts down there who can tell us more about that. Not exactly the kind of stuff you want to find on Page Six. He has a big-gun public relations firm to make sure the world gets to see the profile he wants and works to bury or erase the stuff he doesn't want known."

Boston started to doodle on her notepad. "So how does a coal miner's kid get to become an international mining titan?"

"He got into Virginia Polytech, one of the top mining programs in the world, on an ROTC scholarship and graduated with honors in mining and engineering. Did five years in the army, then left for Wall Street. The army was where he first spent time in Africa. On the Street he made his reputation in corporate finance and mergers in the mining sector, building a pretty impressive international rolodex while getting his boss fired for incompetence. That's when he started making connections across Africa, Australia, Central Asia, and South America. The rest you seem to know. Went out on his own as an investor, set up some hedge funds, then created Africa's Future Resources and started acquiring hard assets and mining rights directly.

"Worth around five hundred million dollars, but most of it is tied up in AFR stock and assets. Has homes in Cape Town, London, Saint Bart's, and a couple other places, but they are owned by the company through corporate shells. Also owns a pretty nice ocean-going yacht that's docked in Nantucket right now.

"Interesting bit here. He entertains at the society level and mingles with the party crowd, but I think it's mostly a public relations front to manage his network of contacts, introducing people to wealthy or influential contacts as a way to recruit favors. Funny, but if you look closer, it's almost as if he doesn't enjoy it—just part of the image."

"Women?" McBain said.

Dee Dee turned the page. "Ah, now things get a little more fascinating."

Boston put her pen down. "Tell me."

"In addition to good money in his investment banking job, young Henry also made a killing the old-fashioned way—he married rich."

McBain leaned back in his chair. "He's married?"

"She died years ago," Franklin said. "She was much older than him, anyway—a widowed German countess on the international social circuit at the time they met. She lasted about five years, then left him a tidy little fortune to build on."

"Wow," Boston said. "Any hint of foul play?"

"Not that anyone could tell, but it gets better." Dee Dee smiled.

Boston arched her eyebrows and her fingers. "Go on."

"He was married once before."

McBain watched his partner while Dee Dee flipped another page.

"Details are hard to come by," she said, "but it seems he was married to a college sweetheart. She was with him during his army years, but not too long into his Wall Street career, he left her for the widow Von Moneybags.

According to my information, she died not long after that. If he's ever talked about her, nobody can find it."

Boston toyed with her pendant and looked at the ceiling. "Interesting. Two dead ex-wives at opposite ends of the social scale. It would be helpful to know how he really felt about each of them. That might be useful if the time comes."

McBain grunted. "Quite a coincidence. But frankly, I don't lose a lot of sleep over dead ex-wives."

Boston frowned at him. "I'm serious, McBain."

"So am I."

"Ignore him, Dee. What about now?"

"Henry's a loner. He never lets anybody get too close, especially women. Whenever he shows up at these society events, he always has some arm candy with him. If he's associated with anyone, it's just some socialite or Euro party girl for a short period of time as a way of making connections. The next time he appears, it's with someone new, another cookie-cutter beauty."

"What's his type?"

Dee Dee smiled. "Well, in a couple ways you're his type."

"Red hair?"

"Young, attractive, fashion conscious, lots of curves."

McBain chuckled as he poured himself a cup of coffee. "Well, if he likes 'em dumb, he's in for trouble. He doesn't know you're an accounting prodigy."

"Are you calling me a child?" Boston said.

"Not at all. You're more like a thirty-four C Einstein. Heh heh."

"Huh. You're so funny . . . and it's thirty-six."

McBain choked on his coffee.

Boston smiled sweetly at him. "You must have me confused with some-one smaller, like your ex-wife."

Dee Dee laughed and closed her folder. "Stop, stop. Let's focus on the details here. You two can bicker on your own time. What did you make of him when you met? Think he's out to shaft your client?"

"After hearing from you," McBain said, "more than ever."

"Maybe."

McBain and Franklin both looked at Boston.

"I'm more suspicious now, of course," Boston continued. "And I think we should subtly communicate to Henry that we're aware of his background and not intimidated by his tactics or history. But so far, we've still got the same picture—the guy plays hardball with investors, competitors, the media, and everyone else. Our job hasn't changed—protect the client. It sounds like plenty of people have made money with Henry too. So if we do our job right, Harold Rogers comes out of this a rich man. Another happy customer. What do we care about Henry's other goals?"

"I don't like him," McBain said. "And I don't trust him."

Boston spread her hands and scowled. "You don't like him? McBain, what does that have to do with anything? We don't like or trust anyone in this business, especially someone a client has hired us to investigate."

McBain shifted in his seat and stared at the table, looking at something the others couldn't see and trying to convince himself he was focusing on facts.

"You heard Dee," he said. "This guy is hiding a lot. He manipulates people. He's evasive and crafty. There are too many blanks about him. I'd feel more comfortable if he was just another rich dealmaker with too much money and ambition. He's up to something with this whole deal. Sounds like he isn't even about the money. He's out to prove something—poor kid from the hills taking what he wants and crushing everyone in his path."

His partner drummed her fingers on the table and waited for him to finish. Then she shook her head in exasperation.

"Now that you've met him and he's not your average Wall Street glad-hander, you think he's dirty? Come on, McBain. Compared with the pampered crooks we usually deal with? What, he has a little dirt under his fingernails, so he must have cheated his way to the top? You of all people should be cutting him a little slack; you weren't born with a silver spoon either. For once, a guy worked his way up the ladder without relying on Daddy's connections or his trust fund. We don't have to trust Henry to recognize what he's done. If he's out to screw Rogers, we find out how and stop it. If he's not, we do our job and take home a nice paycheck. You 'don't like him'? Don't make it personal."

Dee Dee eyed them both with a frown, then held her palm up and shoved the folder over to Boston. "Here's the file," she said. "I'll keep digging on this end and send you more as I get it. How are you going to approach it?"

Boston walked around to the credenza and leaned against it while she picked up a bottle of water. She eyed the back of her partner's head. "Well, if McBain has no objections, I'll take the lead with the data and accounting side. We can sit in on some of the negotiations over the next couple weeks and start posing questions to the bankers and lawyers as we weed through the financials and term sheets. Meanwhile, he can satisfy his craving for dirt by contacting the people who've been burned by Henry over the years to see what tricks he has in his bag. Maybe he'll actually come up with something that resembles a fact to support his gut feeling."

McBain opened the folder on the table. "Yeah, I think I'll start by finding out more about his two ex-wives. Be interesting to see how they died. Maybe I can learn some of his tricks too."

NINE

Two weeks later, a cool October was well along when Harold Rogers arrived at their conference room midafternoon for a progress report. With the able assistance of Dee Dee Franklin's whip hand and the covert support of Dave Thomas, the investigators had burned up the phone batteries and hunted down sources who might help them build a profile they could analyze even as they absorbed a small library of deal documents.

McBain had indeed learned about Henry's two dead ex-wives, or at least as much as he could through public information and his old Manhattan society gossip connections. The German heiress had died peacefully of natural causes at the age of seventy-six, forty years his senior but, by all accounts happy, in every way. Even the most fervent Henry-haters among his former peers or competitors seemed certain of that.

Wife number one had simply disappeared not long after Henry began his successful rise on Wall Street. A classic country girl in the Big Apple, she had always seemed a fish out of water in the fast company of Manhattan's big-finance culture and appearance-driven society. The consensus was even more common than with the heiress. Where big money and the rise to fame and success were concerned, the scenario was as familiar as putting old comfortable furniture from your college days out by the curb once the first big bonus comes in, a ritual older than the trophy wife. The first ex–Mrs. Henry had returned to wherever she had come from before Virginia Tech, leaving behind few memories and no friends among the people McBain had interviewed.

The same might have been said about Henry's disgruntled investors and limited partners, though in McBain's view they had less excuse. All had lost money with Henry when investment funds or stocks he had managed collapsed. When pressed for details, it seemed most had not paid attention to the finer points of their limited partnership agreements or their investments. Nor had they seemed to grasp the basic mathematics and gravity of commodity investing, insisting that they had been cheated by an 'unexpected' decline in a commodity or stock's price. Despite asking each of them as many leading questions as possible, nothing of a fraudulent or nefarious nature emerged that implicated Henry in anything illegal. Ethics, as always, were another issue. In the end, McBain was forced to bite his tongue and resist the temptation to explain hedge fund investing to at least one supposedly sophisticated investor who had once worked at a leading money-management firm.

Others were unwilling to speak due to pending lawsuits or settlement agreements. The only encouraging result of his dirt-digging investigation of Rodney Henry was the discovery that the man was widely loathed by former banking colleagues, ex-employees, and investing competitors alike, as well as many in the mining industry.

Rogers absorbed it all with keen interest as he listened to McBain read from the list of expletives and condemnations of Henry's hardball deal tactics.

"My favorite call was with the analyst who claims Henry had him fired," McBain said. "The guy was pretty widely respected at the time too. Didn't stop the brokerage from looking at the commission revenue they earned from Henry and making a quick decision."

Boston brought Rogers a cup of tea, which he sipped thoughtfully. "Was the analyst accusing Henry of wrongdoing?"

"Not specifically," Boston said. "But he had downgraded and was bad-mouthing a gold-mining stock that Henry had a big wad of cash in. Seems he doesn't take kindly to dissenting opinions. And he's got a long reach."

McBain tossed a copy of the original report over the table to Rogers. "The analyst also suggested not too subtly that there might have been some manipulation of the company's stock price at year end involving Henry in order to beef up management compensation at just the right time. Maybe a little quid pro quo that other investors weren't getting. He couldn't prove it before he got canned, and the SEC declined to investigate, as usual. At any rate, about a year later, the guy's forecast proved to be right on the money. The stock tumbled and became a dog. After Henry had exited his position, of course."

Their client browsed the pages, then looked up. "I'd like to talk to him if I could."

McBain inhaled through his teeth. "Unfortunately, he's not eager to talk much about Henry. We got as much as we could from him before he began to realize where it was going. Then he got real nervous and hung up. Like Boston said, Henry's got a long reach, and it seems to have gotten longer as his reputation has grown. After he was fired, the guy was blackballed from the industry. He finally got a job with the Interior Department in Montana. We got the impression he lives in fear of Henry finding out where he is and finishing him off like Custer at Little Big Horn. Wasn't that in Montana, Boston?"

Rogers sat back and sighed. Boston tapped her pencil on the table and shot McBain a dirty look.

"Moving on," she said, and walked over to a whiteboard covered with a checklist. "I've finished looking at the most important documents in the data room and started a financial analysis of the transaction myself. I'll match it up with the work your board's bankers are doing on the fairness opinion and the valuation presented by Whitney, Mitchell. Nothing major stands out yet, but we'll need your help walking through some of the underlying accounting stuff that might be specific to the industry or your company."

"Of course," Rogers said. "Let's schedule some time for you to sit with me and some of my businesspeople to go over the industry dynamics. And I'll make our accounting and finance people available as well. This is something of a unique combination."

Boston pointed to another line on the board. "Speaking of that, I've also identified potential clauses in these documents and in the initial term sheet that look suspicious. They have to do with the performance of the company's technology and business units after the merger."

Rogers sipped his tea and nodded. "Yes, I'm aware of those. In theory, they penalize us and dilute our ownership if our technology fails to perform as expected over an initial two-year term. But, as I assured our attorneys, I have every confidence in our new products. We spent years in research and development, and everything has been thoroughly tested in the field."

The redhead puzzled over that for a moment. "Any chance somebody from Henry's side could sabotage the technology during that period, maybe make sure it doesn't perform to specifications?"

Rogers sat up like a proud grandfather. "Since you're new to this industry, I should be clear. HR's processing technology isn't sitting on one big computer somewhere, waiting to be penetrated with a virus. Aside from the results in the R and D stage, variations of our new software and systems have already been deployed to several companies and are being used with great success around the world in the energy industry. My confidence is built on our track record. No, I don't really see that as a threat. I suppose, in theory, someone could deliberately misuse it at a mine or processing plant. But why would they? As I've said, the great value of the deal is the technology paired with the vast potential reserves AFR owns and plans to develop. Our technology will lower the cost of discovering, extracting, and processing rare earth minerals from these regions by a significant margin, increasing the profitability of the projects far beyond what otherwise might be possible. There really is no benefit to trying to sabotage the development of the minerals. The entire company's market price would suffer."

Boston shrugged and put a check mark next to the item on the whiteboard.

"I do have a simple question for you, Harold," McBain said. "Why the all-stock deal? Wouldn't it be better to take out some cash, either do an all-cash buyout or half cash, half shares? I can't help but think there would be much less risk on your part if you take some money off the table up front."

Rogers nodded. "In theory you're quite right, Mr. McBain. But I don't think AFR is in a position to make a cash offer. And there are tax accounting issues. Also, my board and senior managers seem to be pleased with the notion of owning AFR stock. The shares have tripled in the past two years, and the market consensus seems to be that owning them promises tremendous upside when the two companies begin to realize the benefits of our combination. Plus the market forecast is promising."

McBain smirked. "Yes, isn't it always?"

Boston picked up a blue marker and moved to an empty whiteboard on the wall. "So AFR has taken off in the past two years," she said, drawing a line that climbed to the right. "I'd like to know why. That's the only way they can afford the rich price. I've looked at the numbers. Before then, the stock was just an average performer, and not even a major player in the industry. Why don't you tell us what you know about their mining assets and value?"

"Well," Rogers said, "it's the new African mining rights, really. The game now is all about finding new alternatives to depending on China for rare earths, since they control over ninety percent of the world's production of metals and so much of the supply chain for final products. Companies are looking at potential new developments everywhere from Canada and the US to the sea floors off Japan. Once new discoveries were made in South Africa, the more intrepid pioneers started looking at previously unexplored territory that was not far from major mining belts. That was when the first reports came out about their discovery of these new potential deposits of critical rare earth minerals in an obscure region that overlaps three countries. They outbid the Chinese and Russians for the mining rights, putting together a cross-border team that convinced the governments of Angola, Zambia, and the Democratic Republic of the Congo to cede rights to them for a percentage of the revenue and a commitment to help develop the area. AFR became immensely valuable after that."

She looked at the ceiling while she fiddled with her ruby pendant. "OK, so it's the reserves that made their stock take off."

McBain smiled at his partner, then said, "And who decides how much the reserves are worth?"

The executive brightened as he warmed to his subject. He stepped up to the whiteboard with a marker and began to list steps. "It's a long, complex process. Here's the potential discovery, then the initial tests are performed on the area in question, then assay samples are extracted to examine the type and quality of the ore, along with the possible range of minerals in the designated geographic area. In a relatively unexplored region like this one, you could see everything from these rare earth minerals to copper or iron. If those samples look promising enough, a larger feasibility study called a preliminary economic assessment, or PEA, is performed to judge the overall quality and scope of the deposits and estimate whether they are economically worth developing. Then an independent evaluation is conducted by a qualified third-party specialist as a check to confirm or dispute the findings. At all these stages one conducts tests in accordance with industry standards and at different depths to determine the size and potential value of the deposits. Once that is determined, market prices and demand forecasts would dictate the worth to the owner of the rights."

"So at what stage are these new African mines?" Boston asked.

Rogers underlined the feasibility stage. "We've finished the PEA, and we're almost through with independent evaluations. AFR submitted theirs to the local governments already and received the go-ahead."

McBain said, "Anybody else take a hard look?"

"Who hasn't?" Rogers said. "Something with the potential to have as much impact on the rare earth market as this drew a lot of scrutiny. We already knew that the Chinese were keenly interested in the early stages, and several of the big international mining companies as well. Several industry analysts have been to the area and seen the mining development as it has evolved. Since AFR is a public company, their audit people and the stock analysts who cover them have gone over the details and met with the engineers. Media attention has focused on the company and followed them from the very beginning, including any number of specialized newsletters that scrutinize the global mining industry. *The Rare Investor* is the premier publication that covers developments in the rare earth mining sector. They were on top of it from the start and have done in-depth pieces that have confirmed the potential of the Angolan and DNC mine sector."

"So AFR passed muster with all the right checks," Boston said.

"At every step of the way," Rogers said. His face crinkled up in a grin. "That was a concern of mine as well. Especially as I'm not an expert on African mining, and these are new, undeveloped areas of Angola and

Congo, stretching across the border to Zambia. I certainly wasn't going to take anyone's word for it. So together with AFR, we hired an independent engineering firm called Coutinho and Company to conduct an independent assessment and give me their own opinion on the quality and quantity of the main strikes in Eastern Angola. They're from Brazil and made a major contribution to the discovery and development of some Brazilian rare earth mining sites at the upper reaches of the Amazon, including the big one at Cabeca do Cachorro."

Boston put her palm to her face. "Not Brazilians again."

The older man nodded enthusiastically. "I assure you they are among the best mining consultants in the world. We've also gotten opinions on legal and political risk, given the overlap of the mining sites between the three countries. The Katanga copper belt is east of the AFR sites, with lots of deposits of everything from copper and cobalt to uranium. I've seen the analysis; it's very impressive. We are looking at major finds that could include a number of critical rare earths for use in commercial and military fields."

McBain stood and looked at the whiteboard. "They confirmed everything?"

"So far. As of three weeks ago, all their findings are in agreement with what we've been told by all the experts, not just AFR. I'm expecting a final sign-off before the deal closes, although the deal is more or less independent of what happens there. Everyone agrees it would be ideal if the results were announced very close to the merger's closing." Rogers finished his tea and dabbed at his mouth with a napkin. "Frankly, I was hoping that between their final sign-off and yours, the last pieces would be in place, and I could rest easy. Everyone else seems eager to get this deal done and get these two companies together: my board and senior management, many of the employees, the bankers, lawyers, even politicians."

"It all seems so perfect," Boston said. "That in itself usually makes us suspicious. So how much time do we have to finish our own digging and either find something or give you our all clear?"

"The board is putting pressure on me to stop holding out," Rogers said. "I haven't been able to offer them a good reason, and we do have a fiduciary responsibility here. If the report comes in from Coutinho in Africa that confirms the project potential, I won't have much choice."

McBain asked, "Where are they located?"

"Who?" Rogers said.

"Coutinho and Company. Your consultants."

"Pretoria, South Africa, and Luanda in Angola. Why?"

Boston looked at her partner.

"I want to talk to them," McBain said.

She walked around to face him.

"In person."

"What are you talking about?" she said.

"We can look at all the documents we want," he said. "This whole deal and the valuation are premised on the value of these mining rights. I want to do a face to face with the company Mr. Rogers hired and hear what they have to say about it. And I want to talk to some people involved in this thing, in Africa, not here. Mining types, government officials, and others who may have dealt with Henry over the years. He talks a lot about all the people he knows. If there's anything going on that our client should be aware of, we're only going to hear it from meeting with people that have seen him in action or been on the receiving end of his business dealings."

Boston spread her hands and inclined her head toward the board. "Can't we do that from here?"

McBain glanced at her sideways, checked himself, then spoke to the client as he looked over the whiteboard.

"I'd like to talk to a number of those involved with these steps, Harold. If you can give me the names of your contacts in Africa and anyone else, I can set up meetings with them. I know a couple of people down there who can probably introduce me around Cape Town and South Africa to government contacts or Henry's competitors. They're usually a good source of information. Maybe the board's bankers and lawyers can pass me some names too. When are you expecting final sign-off on the investigation?"

"I was hoping to have it a week ago. They said they're still waiting to hear from their chief mineralogist at the site. I'll contact them about it when I inform them you're coming. They'll make all the documentation available and give you the names you need. And thank you, Mr. McBain. I'll feel much better after you've had a first-hand look at the situation on the ground in Africa."

TEN

The balcony of Boston's apartment in the Charlestown Navy Yard looked east and south to the USS *Constitution*, the harbor islands, and the sea. White sails flapped on the horizon or bobbed at anchor in their berths as the stiff ocean breeze pushed whitecaps up the Charles River. Across the waves, the city's skyline glittered in the afternoon sun. McBain put on his sunglasses and Red Sox cap as he sat at a glass table in khakis and a black polo shirt, gazing out over the piers at the city, sailboats, and ferries.

He sipped a glass of chardonnay and tried to enjoy the beckoning calls of the gulls and tidal smells wafting up from the docks and sea, despite the slamming doors behind him. After five minutes, he took off his sunglasses, got up, and went inside, wandering around her bedroom as he listened to the shower run. He went to the dresser and, spotting her antique jewelry box, rummaged through until he found what he was looking for. He slid the chain and medallion into his pocket.

McBain returned to the living room and lingered over the O'Daniel family photographs staged on a table by the old stereo and record albums, straightening the picture of Boston and himself dancing at a formal dinner. After another ten minutes, she was still in the shower, so he pulled some mixed berries out of the refrigerator and sat at the granite island in the kitchen, looking at a copy of *Car and Driver* while he ate and drank his wine.

A door opened with a mild thud, and when he lifted his eyes from the picture of the new Audi, Boston was standing across the island with one pale-green towel wrapped around her body and another holding her hair.

Her bare arms were crossed, and her eyes were emerald daggers.

"So you're still mad?"

A damp foot was tapping the Mediterranean tiles.

"Will you at least talk to me?"

A long breath with the hum of a racing engine was all he got.

"Are you going to get dressed?"

She took out the bottle of Rombauer chardonnay and filled a glass.

"You know I don't like surprises," she said at last. "We should have talked about a trip to Africa before you sprang it on me and committed in front of Rogers."

"I'll keep apologizing all day and night," McBain said. "And repeating that it only came to me at the end of the meeting.

"Why the hell do you have to go to Africa?" she asked.

He plucked at his berries. "If you would cool off, I think you'd remember that meeting people in person, looking them in the eye, reading their body language, and being there to examine things on the ground is the right way to do this. This thing is different; it's overseas, where the mining people and assets are. That makes it extra challenging. You know that. How can we possibly do a proper due diligence if we can't talk to people face to face and get a feel for who's lying?"

"We have done a proper due diligence," she said. "We've been poring over documents and talking to people in Boston, New York, Washington, Colorado, and Montana. I've quizzed the board's bankers and lawyers and everyone Rogers has put us in touch with. You've talked to all the names Dave and Dee Dee gave us about Henry's business dealings, track record on Wall Street, and, of course, your favorite subject, his dead ex-wives. The guy is tough but legit."

"So far," McBain said. "Look, everything we've turned up suggests Henry is . . . well, not clean, but not obviously able to screw our client out of his company and shares. You heard Rogers; the board is pressuring him to join the parade and sell his shares. If we can't come up with something over the next two weeks, he's going to have to give up the fight and commit to the deal."

"And that's a bad thing?" she said. "Our client gets rich, we take home a nice check for a couple months work like we planned, and that's it—story over. Happy ending for all concerned. Except, for some reason, you've got a bug up your ass about this guy."

"I just don't feel we'll have done our job if I don't go down there and check things out with the people who are closest to it."

She put down her glass and leaned across the granite slab with raised eyebrows. "Yeah, except you don't know anything about mining, or Africa, or how to do anything other than take a quick look around over dinner and drinks with a few people you've been set up with. You heard Rogers. All the experts have looked at it, and everyone involved is eager to get this deal done."

The air in the kitchen was filled with the scent of fresh soap and shampoo. He turned on his stool to concentrate his eyes on the harbor. "I'm not terribly comfortable arguing about this with you wrapped in a wet towel."

"Tough. I need to cool off."

"This isn't a big deal," he said. "I don't need to know a lot about mining. The point is that this is where Henry operates, and that's where he's made friends and enemies. I'll start pulling on some threads and see if anything unravels. We came up empty with his former investors and the guys in the hedge funds. But that info was years old. We need current intel. In this case, we might have to turn over some rocks, literally. When we've done that, then I'll be satisfied that he doesn't have some clever tricks in his bag that help him get over on Rogers and take off for the wild jungles of Africa where no one can get to him."

She threw open her arms. "What's wrong with the phone and videoconferencing? And you don't even know what the hell you're looking to find."

McBain finished his glass and put it down. He stood across from her and leaned onto the island. "I'm surprised at you. I'll be gone for a week at most, stirring the pot and asking questions. What is this all about, Boston?"

She folded her arms again and shuffled her feet.

"I haven't done this before, Boozy."

"Done what?"

"This is your world, not mine. The only reason I agreed to take this job was because you were comfortable with it. I've never worked in a corporation or an investment bank. Blowing smoke at a party is one thing. There are a bunch of meetings coming up to go over the deal material. I was counting on you being there to take the lead."

She wandered over to the balcony door.

McBain stared at her wet shoulders, puzzled. "We've worked on things separately before."

"Not like this," she said. "Not like this. Investments are one thing, spreadsheets and calculations and interviews. I can do an investigation of a portfolio in my sleep. But sitting in a fancy boardroom with a bunch of experienced bankers and lawyers and successful executives? They've been doing this for years and have degrees from Harvard and Stanford and someplace in Switzerland. I never finished my second year of college."

He smiled at her and took off his baseball cap.

"Boston, we've been doing this long enough that you and I both know what credentials are worth. You're gifted at math, and you know how to value a stock and a company almost as well as me now. You've seen the work those guys do, and you know yours is just as good if not better. You know accounting cold, especially if the numbers don't make sense, mining business or no. Don't forget, you'll have Rogers and his people at your fingertips anytime you need expertise on the companies or mining or anything else. Having them there for support is much more important than anything I could tell you. As for the meetings, just take some notes and nod politely in agreement at the right time and leave the heavy lifting to the HRT team. We've been under the radar up to now, and nobody expects us to play a major part in the negotiations. If anything comes up, you and I can talk about it anytime, day or night."

She stood by the table of photographs and fiddled with several.

"It's just that . . . it's always better when we work together on cases. I should be able to go with you. What if you get into trouble? A nosy American like you stalking guys in the mining business could probably use someone to watch his back."

"I wish you could, but it's a moot point. You don't have time to get the right shots for a trip to Africa from your doctor. And do you have a passport yet?"

"No."

"Then get one, please."

"You know I can't possibly get one in time to go with you," she said.

"No, but next time you'll have it, and we can go together, which I would much prefer for many reasons." He smiled at her. "Besides, how am I going to take you to Paris without one? Tell you what: You get a passport, and I'll give up smoking."

She eyed him skeptically.

He spread his hands apart. "It's a twofer. We both benefit. How can you say no to that? You're doing it for us."

The redhead bit her lip. "Bastard."

"That's why you love me." He stood up and approached her with open arms. "C'mon now, give me a hug."

She straight-armed him with a curl of her lip, grabbing her towel with the other hand. "You'll get a hug when you come back and beat your best time."

"Can't blame a guy for trying." He smiled and poured himself more wine.

"How long do you think it'll take?" she said.

"I don't think we have much time," he said. "You heard Rogers. The board wants this wrapped up. Unless we can find some reason to block or slow down the rush to close, they're not going to give us too much room to snoop around anyway. I figure if I can't find anything down there, I'll be back in a week to ten days."

"Fine." Boston spun around and went into her bedroom to get dressed.

McBain sat back down at the counter. "It's amazing how many things a woman can communicate with that one little word," he said. He yelled into the bedroom. "Let's talk about the division of labor while I'm away."

She shouted back. "As usual, you're leaving me with the grunt work while you race off to interview people over drinks. I don't see that we have much of a choice."

"Not true," he said. "I've already downloaded most of the key documents I want to look over and ask questions about, including the term sheet. I have no intention of abandoning you to do the paper chase on your own. I'll call you from South Africa every day to talk about any issues I find when I report in. You can focus on finishing your valuation model with input from Rogers and his people and shoot me any questions that come to mind, especially about Henry and Africa. In fact, I may have even more information for your analysis after I grill some of the mining industry experts down there. I'll also send you copies of any important documentation from the government agencies in South Africa and Angola that we don't have yet after I talk to the Brazilians. You can run them by Rogers."

"OK," she said. Then, after another minute: "By the way, who do you know in South Africa who can get you in to government offices or Henry's competitors?"

"My friend Gina," he mumbled with his glass at his mouth.

"Who?"

There was no sense dodging it. He counted on her not remembering—a fool's hope. "I said, my friend Gina."

Boston sauntered out of the bedroom in jeans and a white cotton shirt, drying her hair with the towel. She stopped and looked at the ceiling. "Gina. Why does that name ring a bell? Do I know . . .?"

She dropped her towel, and the memories returned. Her eyes narrowed and centered on McBain's as she put her hands on her hips and leaned forward. "Wait, do you mean Gina Ferrari? That blonde whore you were screwing during our first year in business together? Melissa's so-called friend? Shit, the ink wasn't dry on your divorce before that bitch was up here sniffing around. What the hell does she have to do with this?"

"Gina is pretty high up in corporate public relations and events for a media management company in Cape Town. You may not like her, but she knows the business culture and landscape across southern Africa."

"How convenient for us."

"Now who's the one who's making this personal?"

"This is different," she said, jabbing her finger at him. "I have good reason to make this personal, and you know it. She treated me like dirt and never missed a chance to let me know how sophisticated and worldly she and Melissa and your whole circle of model and business friends were. Now you're jetting off on safari with your old flame. Meanwhile, I'm back here sitting in a conference room full of hostile lawyers and bankers."

"Gina was never a flame. That's not what this is about. Like it or not, she can help us get to the right people in the shortest amount of time. She has the connections."

"How do you know?"

"Because I already talked to her, and she's lining them up."

"Of course you did," Boston said. "When were you going to bring me into the conversation?"

"As soon as you started talking to me again," he said. "I was originally planning on doing some interviews by phone—with you. But after our meeting with Rogers, I knew the surest way to get our answers was to go down there."

"And now I'm wondering whose idea that was." Boston stared at him and raised a thin eyebrow. "This isn't just a little travel junket so you can get some vacation in, is it?"

"You know me better than that, Boston. When I'm on a job, I don't mix the two. This is business, and Gina can help. She knows a lot of people in southern Africa."

Boston snorted. "Yeah, I'll bet she does."

"Anyway, I've booked a flight on Emirates in two days out of Logan. I'll be back in a week, tops."

"What's Emirates?"

"Another good reason for you to get a passport," he said with a smile. "Your kind of people, first-class all the way. Maybe when this is over, we'll book a first-class flight to Paris like I promised, just so you can break in your new passport and experience it."

Boston swept up her towel from the floor and smiled a Grinchy smile at her partner. "Guess again, McBain. When this case is over, we've got a stack of folders to get started on. Maybe you better consider this your vacation after all. Enjoy your time with your good friend Gina."

ELEVEN

When you have money you always have friends. If people think there is a chance you can make them lots of money, your new friends accumulate like bees around a honeycomb. Boston O'Daniel was suddenly a very popular queen bee. As she visited hedge funds and mutual funds around the city digging for information, word spread around the community of investors and research analysts that she had close ties to HR Tech and the founder and largest shareholder, having been hired personally to close the deal.

Numbers can be dangerous, especially in the hands of experts like accountants and investment bankers. But, as McBain had reminded her, she was an expert, too, and the more time she spent with Rogers and the deal team assisting HR Technologies, the more clearly she saw and the more she understood. Boston went over the internal HR accounts with their finance staff and senior managers again and again until she had memorized the links between their businesses and the financial statements. Then she went over the valuation with the finance director and the board's investment bankers until she had it down cold and knew where AFR's offer was coming from. They even conceded a couple of faulty assumptions in their financial modeling that Boston had identified that helped strengthen their argument for a higher price for HRT shares.

During the day, she spent hours with Harold Rogers and his finance people learning the ins and outs of their accounting and how they valued their business. After her initial meetings with the contacts Rogers had recommended, her phone began to buzz with an increasing number of invitations for lunch, dinner and, drinks from money managers, brokers, and private investors who wanted in on the AFR deal—one way or another. As the voice mails, emails, and text messages accumulated, Boston was shocked. Given his many contacts and his track record in New York, McBain had always handled the connections with the industry. The young detective had to come to grips with people reaching out to wine and dine her for the first time—the real bread and butter of finance.

But Boston had always been a quick study. Over late-night drinks with investors or reading on the treadmill, Boston learned about the mining industry and the players. She figured out the important details she needed to gain from her new friends and soaked up information along with each cocktail. Unlike Rogers and his team, many of the money managers and research analysts in the city had been analyzing the rare earth industry and Rodney Henry's trajectory for years. Most knew the finer points of the growing demand for each mineral and the rest of the major players in the hunt for the new source of riches around the world. Some of them had even made money with Henry before and wanted in again. In contrast to the deep well of resentment their information gathering had produced thus far, the more sharklike among these investors seemed eager to get in on what they called a new gold rush with full awareness of Henry's history.

As she learned about him, Boston learned about the mining industry and the most important parts of closing a deal. Her new friends also provided examples of similar mergers in the past that led her down new paths of discovery and saved her days' worth of research. That helped her focus on the crucial elements of the negotiations and the critical documents in the data room. One thing was clear. The commodities business was something new and different to her experience. The people in it were different from other kinds of investors she had come to know over the past four years, and she struggled to understand why. McBain had tried to explain it to her before he left, finally settling on an example she understood quite well—precious stones. There is something special about the business of valuing and trading real tangible things that you can hold in your hand, that come out of the earth and find their way into not just the mind, but the eye, the soul, or the heart. Something different from the abstract nature of stock portfolios or a hot high-tech or social media stock. The people were strange, the prices volatile, and the trends hard to predict with any reliability. She felt a kinship grow as she discovered that many of those in the commodities trading business were blue-collar people who loved numbers and math. They were risk takers, comfortable living on the edge and taking long chances for big payoffs. That's what made it harder to be good at and lost so many smart people money. Odd, she thought, since grain and precious gems had been as desirable in Cleopatra's court as they were today. And from iron to gold to oil, Boston discovered that the secrets of commodities trading and the adventurers who ruled that world had paralleled the rise of civilization and fueled the wealth of empires throughout human history well before that.

These rare earth things were different. In and of themselves, they were simple rocks and dirt. But through the alchemy of modern chemistry, they became part and parcel of the special products that people needed, wanted, had to have. Boston followed thread after thread of online research building up the map of the elements. She had always hated science classes but, until now, had felt little cause for regret at her lack of interest and bad grades. Now, she cursed it again and concentrated on learning about the periodic table of elements and how these new rare earth metals were put to use creating immense value. She needed an accelerated education, so every expert whose name appeared more than once in the literature received an email or phone call, sometimes at inconvenient times of the night.

As she mapped the rocks and earths on sheets of paper and index cards, she listed the various commercial products that they helped create, some of which she owned, and wrote the associated mineral on a note. She would memorize them by snapping pictures and cataloging the results. Since there were no military bases near the city, Boston also made a point of printing out pictures of jet fighters and tanks and other pieces of hardware that made the Pentagon a party with keen interest in the rare earths production business.

Boston saw the plan as it emerged in front of her. Once he married up the HR Tech science with his contracts around the world, Henry would become the world's newest commodity billionaire. And he would control the critical resources needed by the defense industry and irreplaceable consumer products that were flying off the shelves. In a way, he would own the future. No wonder everyone was so hot for Henry.

If there was that much money for the taking, it made her wonder who he was competing against. She learned names like Anglo-American, BHP Billiton, Rio Tinto, Trafigura, and Glencore. As she also learned about the African end and the massive Angola project in Moxico Province, Boston spent more time with Harold Rogers and his research staff, learning about the project development process and the challenges of making such a long-shot dream a reality. Rogers went over the steps in the process that he had laid out that day in their office, but in more intricate detail. Gradually, she came to understand the importance of the project and the competition Henry had been up against. In everything she had read about the rare earths business, the word *China* came up again and again.

It seemed that China was the main source for a majority of the currently known deposits and production of many of the most prized rare earths. Boston read stories going back over the past two decades about the quest for more, always more. Nobody liked the fact that they were dependent on China: not the Japanese, who had been boycotted; or the manufacturers of hot electronic products; or the American and European defense industries, which wanted more secure sources of critical production materials. So the search was on across the globe, and when prices rose, the digging continued in far-flung locations from Canada to Australia to Kazakhstan to . . . Africa. Africa had been a logical choice since so much of the world's wealth of resources was already coming from there: gold from South Africa, copper from Zambia, diamonds from West Africa, and oil from Angola or Nigeria.

And where the world's resources were, China was to be found. Driven by the insatiable need to feed their economic engine, the Chinese had found their way to Africa decades ago to secure a steady flow of Africa's mineral wealth. In exchange for loans and development, the Chinese had begun to extract and send back mountains of resources. The sea lanes between Africa and China were a veritable conveyer belt of freighters.

Boston learned one other thing that had attracted the Chinese companies to Africa. Their dominance of rare earth mining and production at home had come at a price. The extraction and production techniques used to unearth and process rare earth metals for their factories at the great rare earth city of Bayan Obo were relatively cheap to engineer but had produced a horrible cost in environmental pollution. Boston read and heard tales about rivers of toxic waste and clouds of poison spreading over the communities in China where these factories were located and where their workers toiled. Economic growth was all, but China's rising middle and upper classes were beginning to grumble about the unexpected fallout from these processers.

In Africa, where governments were desperate for jobs and growth at any cost, there was often little objection to such methods. Indeed, in many cases, the governments were either ignorant of the side effects from the processes or had little to worry about in terms of dissenting opinions from the public.

Boston leaned back in her chair in the office and thought about the Angola project and its importance to closing the deal. Somehow, Henry had outmaneuvered the Chinese for the project, and according to her new friends, the Chinese were all over Angola. Maybe their companies didn't have to play by the rules, but Africa's Future Resources didn't have that luxury. They had to obey labor and environmental laws in South Africa and other Western countries where they operated.

Didn't they?

Boston recalled Harold Rogers's lecture about the sequence of events that every project underwent, from exploration to final production, and thought about one thing. Then she got on her computer and logged into the data room for the AFR deal. She was still searching there a half hour later when a large, older man in the uniform of a police captain, with thinning red hair and the face of a boxer, walked through the front door.

"Hey, I've been texting you for fifteen minutes," he said. "Didn't you hear anything?"

She looked up, startled. "Oh, sorry, Dad. I've been so absorbed by this search that I didn't realize I still had the phone on vibrate." She went around the desk and hugged his barrel chest. "What are you doing here?"

"What am I doing here?" He pointed to his watch. "We're going to the range today, don't you remember? You haven't been for three weeks, and we agreed last weekend that today was good."

Boston slapped the side of her head. "Damn, I forgot. I'm so immersed in this deal and learning about this stuff that I completely zoned out." She looked at the stack of pictures and files on her desk. "Can we reschedule for next . . . ?"

Tom O'Daniel crossed his arms and gave her the hairy eyeball. "No, we cannot reschedule. I organized my day around this, and we haven't seen each other for weeks." He looked at the piles of paper and research reports on the desk as well. "Besides, from the looks of you—and that—you need a break. Now grab your guns and get moving. Traffic is already a bear."

She started to object, but he raised his hand to silence her protests.

"You need some fresh air to take your mind off this stuff for a while. But if you absolutely want to keep working, you can fill me in and bounce your ideas or questions off me. Unless it's something I don't want to know about, as usual. Let's go spend some time around real metal."

She laughed. "I wouldn't call a firing range 'fresh air,' but I get the point."

During the short drive to the range, Boston sketched out the highlights of their assignment. Her father expressed polite interest but seemed more impressed that she and McBain were doing what he termed "respectable work" for a change.

For the next hour, there was no chance to talk about the deal. The thunder of the police firing range did clear Boston's mind, but it demanded absolute focus. There were only a few officers at the range, so Tom and Boston O'Daniel were each able to practice with several of their handguns. She was ordinarily a better shot than her father, but he was right—her lack of practice and distraction with the case had numbed her edge, at least at first. Boston ran through several magazines with her Glock, then switched over to the Beretta. Her father took a break from his shooting and watched her go through another magazine. He reloaded his weapon and handed it to her.

"Here, try my new toy," he shouted.

She took off her headgear and looked it over. "What is it?"

"A new Walther."

"What are you, James Bond, now?" She hefted it and looked unimpressed. "Kind of small, isn't it? Especially for a guy your size."

"Designed for concealed carry. Less recoil, nice and smooth. If you're good and stay out of trouble the rest of the year, maybe I'll get you one for Christmas."

She turned it over in her hands. "Hmm, I really like something with a bit more kick."

"Yeah, I know, because you're a tough guy. But it has plenty of stopping power, believe me. You can always use something special for the right occasion. The Glock doesn't really go with formal wear."

They put their ear protectors back on, and Boston gave the Walther a try. It took her more than a few rounds to adjust to the smaller gun and lighter recoil, and that, plus her lack of practice, produced a disappointed grimace when she handed it back to her dad.

"OK, I guess."

He laughed at her. "Don't be such a big iron snob. If it's good enough for James Bond, it's good enough for you. Think of it as another one of your designer accessories."

She stuck her tongue out and made a face at him. "Ha ha. You think you're so funny."

Tom O'Daniel was pleased with himself. "Heh, well if you're done here, let's grab a beer and a snack at Doyle's, and you can tell me more about your case."

They drove to Doyle's Café in Jamaica Plain and sat at the bar for lunch. Captain O'Daniel tried to appear interested as his daughter expounded on her newfound favorite subject. His eyes glazed over when she brought up the names of the rare earths themselves, but he seemed impressed with her enthusiasm when she started rattling off the names of the elements together with the end products.

"You sound like quite an expert, kid," he said. "I thought you hated this stuff."

She finished her cheeseburger and washed it down with Sam Adams. "I do. Or at least, I did. But you've got to admit it's a little fascinating, right? I mean, all these things we use every day and take for granted. They wouldn't be able to run without these crummy little rocks and dirt from Africa or China. This phone, my Shelby, the equipment in jet fighters and batteries— so many things we wouldn't have today without these obscure metals."

"I'm more impressed that you two are doing normal, honest work," he said.

"Don't start, Dad."

He grabbed some fries. "I'm only saying, this sounds like real financial professional stuff, the kind of thing you should be doing. The kind of thing I thought you'd be doing when you started this business with McBain four years ago. Little did I know . . . "

Boston poured her beer and threw him a nasty look. "Look, this is a one-time thing we're doing as a favor to Dave Thomas because the pay is pretty good. When this one is over, it's back to business as usual. We've got a long list of prospects and plenty of scams to unearth. Sorry to disappoint you."

The captain pushed back his empty plate and shook his head.

"You can never disappoint me."

"That's not what you said six years ago."

"That was different. I was trying . . . " He sighed and looked at the ceiling, muttering something in the name of Jesus. "Can we not argue about the old times, please? Or about McBain again? I'm trying to say I'm proud of you. And that it sounds like you've learned a lot about the financial business.

By the way, where is your lesser half? If this job is so important, why isn't he burning the midnight oil in the office with you?"

Boston ordered another beer from Frank the bartender and ground her teeth before answering.

"Africa."

"What about it?"

"That's where McBain is. In Africa, meeting with some people and doing some investigating for our client . . . or so I hope."

"What the hell does McBain know about Africa? Where in Africa?"

Boston stabbed at a couple of fries and shoved them in her mouth. "South Africa. A city called Cape Town. I guess he used to go there a few years ago with the ex. He knows . . . some people."

Tom O'Daniel smirked and took a sip of his pint. "Gee, I hope he doesn't get eaten by a lion or something."

"That's not funny, Dad."

"Just kidding. Well, it's not like he's going out into the bush, right?" her father said. "Other than the crime and poverty, I hear Cape Town is a nice place. Good fishing near there. And surfing, if you ignore the great whites. Say, does McBain surf?"

At the mention of surfing, Boston bit her lip. "He had better not be surfing. He's supposed to be performing some due diligence for our client with some mining execs and government people. He'll be back in a week."

The captain waved to Frank for another round. "So why did he have to go to Africa to do that? They don't have teleconference in South Africa?"

"Sometimes it's better to do these interviews face to face. You can pick up more signals and maybe follow up with a lead right away. Especially with the distance and time zones."

"You don't sound convinced."

"This guy Henry has a lot of contacts and friends down there. McBain wanted to get the background on him firsthand. Dammit. I bit my lip."

Her father read her expression and nodded. "From what little you've told me, this guy Henry sounds like he could be trouble, all right. But a big wheel like that has probably made a reputation for himself in the business anyway. I don't see why your partner couldn't do his digging from the States. I'll bet he's sneaking in a couple of days of R and R for himself on the beach."

Boston nearly pulled the shot glass out of Frank's hand as he set it down and had it turned upside down on the bar in two seconds. Her father raised his eyebrows and stared. "I was just kidding," he said. "Take it easy. I'm sure McBain is all business. He knows how important this is."

"He'd better."

Tom O'Daniel sipped his beer and waited.

After thirty seconds of silence: "Sometimes I just don't get him, Dad."

"Sometimes? What is it this time?"

"He could have done the interviews from the States. Maybe we might have missed a couple things, but there's probably nothing to find over there anyway. This is a straight-up corporate merger. Tough negotiations, but it's not like our usual jobs where we are pretty confident somebody's been ripped off. There are tons of other bankers and lawyers and accountants on our side looking at this offer. But for some reason, McBain has a bug up his ass about this guy Henry. And it's not even like Henry's one of the Wall Street types that he loves to hate. From what we've found out, he's a poor boy made good, beating the Ivy Leaguers at their own game. I thought McBain would give him some credit for that. Not trust, that's not what we do, but respect. Instead, it's like he's on some kind of crusade to nail the guy whether he's committed some crime or not. I don't get it.

"Based on all the work we've done, this should be an open-and-shut case.

But there's something about this guy Henry that got under McBain's skin in a way I've never seen before."

Tom took another pull and toyed with his shot. "I don't know, but I can take a guess. This guy sounds different. McBain has a nasty streak when it comes to Wall Street and rich investment types. Can't really blame him, considering how his marriage ended. But you can see when he taunts and mocks these guys to their faces, he's entirely comfortable with the fact that he despises most of them. Looks down on them. That's because he knows the game and that they aren't really worth much outside their own universe.

"This Henry sounds different. I've seen guys like him before. So have you, for that matter. From what you've told me, nobody handed him anything; he did it his own way. With Henry, you could strip away everything he's got, and he'd just start building it again. He's a hard man. Most of these white-collar types, you send them to jail for a night, and they'd be shitting their pants, crying for their mommy and singing to the DA by morning. This guy, I'm guessing you could send him to a maximum-security prison, and he'd kill the first guy to try and touch him and be running the joint like a miner's union boss in no time. He's not afraid of hard work or pain. All McBain's mockery and contempt are meaningless to him. He doesn't care or take offense because it's not what defines him. And that scares McBain for some reason. You'll have to ask him why."

TWELVE

He was standing on the edge of a steep cliff, on the Zimbabwe side of the border looking north, one hand resting against the bark of a gnarled pine. McBain squinted hard against a hot blue sky and gazed across the chasm. The thunder of Victoria Falls filled his eyes and ears, a cool spray of moisture caressing skin roasted in the African sun. His gaze followed column after column of cascading white foam as it plunged over the side of the rocks in the distance, tumbling hundreds of feet in an eternal crescendo of sight and sound as it hammered into the river below, molding the rock and earth as it had for thousands of years. The falls spread as far as the eye could see, and in the canyon below, a rainbow pierced the gauzy air, so close to him he felt he could fill his lungs with color. He reached out to touch it and closed his eyes. Suddenly, he was falling toward the water, sinking as if already weighed down with soaking wet clothes.

As he fell, the roar softened, and the pitch changed and became rushing wind that lifted him slowly out of the dream. McBain blinked and raised himself up from his flat bed seat, then stretched and opened the sliding divider of his first-class compartment. By the time he returned from washing up, the flight attendant, dark and exotic in her red Emirates hat and white veil, had rearranged his seat, collected the empties from his minibar, and delivered breakfast. A short time later, she leaned across him and pointed out the window.

Far below the aircraft, drenched in sunlight, McBain saw it rise up in the distance, a collision of mountain and ocean that pointed like a rocky finger to the end of the world: the Cape of Good Hope. It was a strangely optimistic name for a continent with so many troubles, rippling relentlessly through the years up and down the length and breadth of Africa for centuries. It was the end and the beginning of Africa.

There was Table Mountain, flanked by the Devil's Peak and the Lion's Head, the majestic backdrop of cliffs for the white houses and office buildings scattered along the shoreline, climbing the slopes or curving down to the beaches. The Dutch had called it Cape Town, but to his mind, there should have been a more glamorous name for the city on the edge of the continent where humanity got its start. Perhaps for the Zulu there was, but then they might have a different view of history.

As they descended and circled around Table Bay and the Cape, McBain observed below them what seemed like a small invasion fleet—container ships, tankers, and freighters approaching the coast or parked just offshore waiting to take on or offload cargo. He recalled Rodney Henry's talk about Africa and the future. As he surveyed the warm beauty of the coastline curving around from the Atlantic to the Indian Ocean, the investigator himself was overcome by the siren song of hope, not just for his mission but for the people below him. Hope wasn't something he put much stock in. But maybe it could be different this time.

Some things hadn't changed. McBain waited ten minutes in the line at customs. He pulled his passport out of his khaki pants and handed it under the glass to the young black woman in uniform at the computer.

"What is the reason for your trip?" she asked. "Business or pleasure?"

"Always a little of both," the investigator said. "I should be here about a week on business, financial consulting. And cram in as much holiday as possible. About two weeks tops."

His wide tourist smile drew a blank face, a brusque stamp, and a wave of the hand. Not an unusual experience at passport control anywhere, but McBain took it as an indication of how well his visit would be received by the rest of his hosts.

The doors to the main terminal swung open, and it took only a few seconds for McBain's eyes to locate the suntanned honey blonde in a crisp tan business suit and big Chanel sunglasses behind the railing. Gina had cut her hair short, and her bangs swept over her forehead, a good shape for her face.

She pushed up her shades and gave him an "it's been years" kiss hello, all the while measuring him with her hands like a piece of beef at a butcher's market. "You're looking good, McBain," Gina said, holding him at arm's length and giving him the once over with sapphire eyes. "You've been working out again. Nice improvement from last time."

The lilt of her South African accent resurrected dormant memories of his past visits to Cape Town. "Thanks. You don't look so bad yourself, Gina. I love the short hair. You should still be modeling."

"I do a gig now and then to keep my hand in, and my body. But the money's much better doing PR in the corporate world, love."

"These four years have been good to you. My partner's been pushing me to watch my health and get in shape. I've cut back on the smoking to almost nothing."

"Partner, huh? I hope you mean your business partner. You haven't gone fag on me, have you?"

"Not likely," he said. "You remember Boston O'Daniel. I was just starting an investigation agency with her four years ago when you and I were seeing each other."

Gina took a step back, and her jaw dropped. "The red-haired juvenile delinquent . . . you still work with her? Oh, come on, McBain. You deserve better than some poor girl psycho. What's the story: she's a tiger in bed?"

"Boston and I are business partners, Gina. I'm not sleeping with her."

She threw up her hands and shook her head. "That's even worse. Christ, you were married to a goddess. Melissa speaks five languages and could have been a Victoria's Secret Angel. I could understand you tossing me aside for her, but the redhead . . . Does she even have a real name?"

"Thanks. You want to remind me how that worked out while you're at it? I was so grateful when Mel and her lawyer bent me over. Best sex I ever had."

"OK, I'm sorry. Melissa was wrong, and I told her so. You know that. Don't change the subject."

McBain grabbed the handle of his bag, and they started walking. "I know you and Boston didn't get along before, and you didn't like her. But you'd be surprised how much she's changed since then. She's certainly no juvenile delinquent, and she's got more style than most of the women I know."

Gina smirked as they walked toward the exit. "So what, you performed some kind of Pygmalion routine on the flower girl? Big deal. I guarantee you she's still the bar brawler I saw back then. The street cat doesn't change her tabby stripes. I'll bet you I could taunt Eliza Doolittle out of her nice clothes and have her swinging at me in three minutes."

"Lay off, Gina. We run a very successful business these days, and she's a damn good partner. That's why I'm here. I told you over the phone—this isn't a social call."

Gina batted her blue eyes and pouted. "It's not?"

McBain threw his arm around her waist. "Well . . . it's not just a social call. I need your help."

"So you said last week. No worries, darling. I took a couple of days off from work, though in my line, when you're socializing, it's never really a day off. I've lined up a couple of meetings with clients and friends to get you started here in Cape Town. Tomorrow, we'll schedule some calls with people in Joburg and Pretoria. Maybe you'll be able to score a few more tonight."

As they emerged from the terminal building, McBain recoiled at the heat and blazing African sun. Gina hailed her driver on her cell phone.

"Tonight? Are we meeting people tonight?"

"Of course," she said. "Your timing is suspiciously impeccable, as always. It turns out a couple of the men I wanted you to meet will be at the contest tonight."

McBain put his hands on his hips. "Contest?"

"Oh, don't worry. You'll like this contest. You're going to be my date at the Southern Africa Final of the Elite Model Competition. You do still like models, don't you? Girls, I mean."

McBain used his lips to establish his bone fides. A black Range Rover came racing up.

"I do now," he said. "So you've got a few contacts lined up for this event tonight. Anything else I need to know about this contest?"

"Just that it involves lots of corporate and government power brokers in the country, young model wannabees, free caviar, and alcohol. You do still drink, don't you? Or is that part of your new workout regimen Eliza has you on?" Gina glanced at her watch. "It's just after one. I figured since you just arrived and we've got a few hours to kill, we could go find a drink now—that is, if you're up to it. Unless you can think of something else to do."

McBain looked at his watch, then settled into the back seat and her exotic blue eyes. "I'm a master at multitasking. Besides, as a great man once said,

'It's five o'clock somewhere.'"

There's something to be said for an event that is deliberately held for the purpose of looking at beautiful girls. Actually, there's quite a lot to be said for it, and McBain was running over the list in his head as he sipped his drink. Once upon a time he had commented to a friend after one too many that it was possible to tire of being around beautiful women. But then, not unlike many other people, he had said and done a lot of stupid things in New York City.

Tonight, however, he was thinking that the best thing about a modeling contest was that, in New York, Paris, Beijing, or Africa, it attracted many influential and powerful people.

As he had in the past, McBain enjoyed the contest itself. Part beauty pageant, part fashion show, and part musical extravaganza, the theater had been packed and loud. The throb of the relentlessly enthusiastic singers and DJs had taken him back to New York and happier times, but they left his emotions drifting between nostalgia and bitterness. He tried to focus on the girls on the runway and feel some sympathy at their first time under the glare of an adult public spotlight. They were probably sixteen on average, made up and pressured way beyond any rational reason for girls who should have been sitting in the movies with their friends or a nervous sixteen-year-old boy, instead of being gawked at with barely anything on by men and women who should know better. Like Mel had always said, it was a hell of a business.

But hey, everyone has dreams. Some realize there is a price and start paying it earlier than most. He raised his glass: "Good luck, girls. I hope for your sake you don't make it."

Afterward, the exclusive reception was held in a large hall adjacent to the auditorium.

For the first hour, he watched Gina work the crowd. He imagined this must be what Boston felt like when she watched Tom Brady play football. Jeez, the woman should have been negotiating peace in the Middle East. If McBain was a Mack truck entering a conversation circle, she was a ballerina. Gina spoke English, Afrikaans, Zulu, Xhosa, Ndebele, and a handful of European languages—all of them well. On her game, she was liquid charisma with men and women alike, from senior government ministers to corporate and banking titans of every race. She massaged egos with the skill and grace of a geisha: the power brokers, their wives and mistresses, their acolytes and objects of desire.

McBain spent the time mingling and chatting with several men Gina felt would put him on the road to learning more about Rodney Henry and his history in Africa. All of them were older veterans, both of the mining business and the apartheid years. The investigator learned a lot in those conversations, both about Henry and about old habits dying hard.

As one senior gold mining executive walked away, Gina finished introducing a couple to one another and sidled up next to him at the bar. "What do you think so far?"

"It's as good a show as many of the ones we went to in New York. The theater was packed. The runway, the music, the presentation and staging— flawless. My compliments to the producers. How many people?"

"Probably two thousand at the contest, maybe five hundred here at the reception." She sipped her champagne. "I see you met Mr. Van Ardness," she said. "Charming, isn't he?"

McBain raised his cocktail and eyed the crowd. "He may have the old apartheid mentality, but he's impressively nonracial in his taste when it comes to the girls. He's a little too into the models, if you ask me."

With a curl of her lip, Gina looked around them and nodded. "A lot of them are. That's why they're here. Fishing."

"Christ, Gina. This isn't the Victoria's Secret fashion show. These girls are just starting out. Don't they know most of these kids aren't even eighteen yet?"

"Of course they know. That's the appeal for some of them."

"Sick."

She hooked his arm and raised her champagne glass. "Goodness, look at the white knight on his charger. Careful, a slip of heroic morality is showing. Next thing you know, the old McBain will rear his gentle head."

"That would be tragic," he said. "So let's order another drink and send that bastard back where he belongs." He lifted his empty glass to the barman. "OK, who's next?"

Gina surveyed the crowd and the dance floor, then looked up at McBain and pulled on his arm. "Hey."

"Yes?"

"Shall we dance?" she asked.

A shadow passed across his face, and he looked at the ceiling lights as he listened to the cadence of the song. "I don't dance."

She shook her head. "If you say so. OK, here comes Maurice de Graff. You'll like him. He's only here because his thirty-year-old trophy wife is socially obsessed. He has forgotten more about mining in southern Africa than most people ever knew. He hates almost everyone, but he's smart and driven—your kind of people. His family left Zimbabwe decades ago. At the time, they were some of the most prominent miners in the country. But they saw the handwriting on the wall. They cashed out before they got carried out, if you know what I mean."

McBain reached for his new martini. "I do. Smart guy. My kind of man—bitter."

"As I said."

She glided forward and air-kissed a sixtyish man in a tuxedo with a face the texture of a gravel pit. Maurice de Graff wasn't a big man, but he was solid as a piece of stone from one of his quarries. Hard eyes scanned the American from under bushy black brows.

"Maurice, this is Mr. McBain from the US. I was hoping you'd have a few minutes to chat with him before Stacey grabs you again," Gina said.

He grunted. "Stacey is busy with the designer from Dior." He took McBain's hand and shook once. "What are you? Another fashion poof or interior decorator?"

McBain took a sip and smiled. "Not really qualified for either of those. I'm here doing some work to look over the acquisition of a company by a man you might know of: Rodney Henry. He's acquiring a company to help develop some new mining assets he's working in Eastern Angola."

"Tell your boss I said he's a piece of shit," de Graff said. His tone was less violent than his eyes.

"He's not my boss," McBain said, "but I'll be happy to give him that message. Actually, I'm here to investigate him for some due diligence on the deal he's pitching. I'm working for the other guy, and I'm trying to dig up some dirt of my own."

De Graff grunted and surveyed McBain with a less hostile but suspicious grimace. He eyed the investigator over the rim of his glass of whiskey as he finished it at the same time as he raised his right arm for the barman. Quite a feat, in McBain's experience.

Gina pressed the older man's arm. "I'll let you two talk while I mingle." She flitted away.

De Graff looked him up and down, and the barman delivered a drink for each of them.

"So," the older man said, "what's your opinion of Henry?"

McBain nursed his cocktail. "Based on what I've got so far, I'm inclined to agree with your succinct evaluation. But I'm trying to remain open minded while I collect more detailed background information. After all, this is business, not personal. And my client stands to end up pretty well off. What can you tell me?"

"You want my advice? Tell your man not to sell."

"He may not have that option."

"In that case, watch his back, take his cut, and get the hell away from Henry the first chance he gets while he's still got some cash and his balls."

"That the voice of experience or a jealous competitor, Mr. de Graff?"

"Neither," he said. "I'm very familiar with Henry's mining project in Angola. My family owns a large tract of land in northern Rhodesia, what you call Zimbabwe, not far from there. Henry leased mining rights on it from the government, despite the fact that he knew it was ours."

McBain didn't know a lot of local history, but he knew enough to realize he was on tender ground. "Who is your quarrel with Mr. de Graff, Henry or the government of Zimbabwe?"

"They're both my enemies, McBain," he said. "And I'm not stupid. But you Americans don't seem to think more than a couple years ahead. My family owned that land for decades before it was taken from us without payment, and by rights, we still do. When the current government stops wrecking the country and opens it up to foreign investment, our rights will be valuable again. And they'll need our experience more than ever. We're not going anywhere, and we have lots of staying power."

McBain nodded. "In the meantime, they leased it to Henry and AFR for possible development at some point. So you have no legal recourse to stop his deals. What can you tell me about the potential value of the mining rights in the Angola/Congo project, not just your land?"

De Graff reached over the bar and topped up his glass with whiskey himself. The barman scowled but stayed back. "Well," he said," I know value to the Rand in iron ore, copper, and palladium. But as to what Henry's discovered, nobody knows."

"What do you mean, nobody knows? It's already valued in the market."

The bushy black eyebrows smirked at him over the rim of the whiskey glass. "What do you do for a living, McBain? Because you don't know shit about mining."

McBain smiled. "According to what I'm told, I generally ask annoying questions and make trouble for people. I don't know shit about mining, but I'm anxious to learn. Particularly about rare earths and strategic minerals."

The older man coughed and sneered. "The market is valuing the mines at what they think Henry has found. So far, the samples and assessments all say it has the potential to be big. Maybe they're right. With demand growing the way it is and these new technologies, new finds are cropping up all over the world, in places that couldn't be reached before, even back in your country. So, voila, lots of mines and regions that were supposed to be all mined out now appear to have potential for new finds, including your rare earth metals. And the mining engineers are learning more every year. Southern Africa is rich in minerals like cobalt, copper, gold, iron, platinum, and other ores that could indicate a motherload of those elements—in theory. All I know is production, and nobody is producing anything yet. So I'll wait and see."

"What about all these analysts and inspectors and journalists telling us it's the next big thing?"

De Graff jabbed at McBain's chest with his glass. "You believe who you want. I've been in this business fifty years, and I know what it takes to get something out of the ground and turn a profit. I also know that country. Henry's project is way out in the middle of nowhere in Moxico in eastern Angola, with hardly any way to get sizeable volumes out in the near future and no infrastructure for hundreds of miles. The closest towns of any size with roads and rail are Kolwezi and Lubumbashi, in the Democratic Republic of the Congo. I'll believe it when I see delivery." He finished his whiskey and leaned over, but the barman had the whiskey bottle ready and topped him off. "And when the time comes, I'll sue Henry for every last ounce of anything that comes out of my family's property."

McBain thought for a moment of his meeting with Henry at the reception. "Did you discuss your family's rights with Henry at all?"

De Graff looked at McBain and smiled. "He told me to go fuck myself. That my family had no rights, and we could rot in hell. We were the past; he was the future."

McBain was skeptical. "I met Henry. I don't think—"

"That's what he said, word for word. Don't be fooled by Henry's polished front, McBain. He may wear custom-tailored suits from London and have lots of rich friends, but in his bones, he's a miner. When miners talk to each other, they're very upfront, and he's as vulgar as any of us. And we are all ruthless sons of bitches when it comes to the land. At the end of the day, we crawl out of a hole in the ground. Remember that."

● ● ●

JET LAG IS A terrible ordeal. Lying awake at four in the morning in a distant land is a tedious experience for anyone. McBain was willing to suffer through it with a physical thirty-five-year-old blonde lying on his chest, but part of him worried that he didn't feel worse than he did after five martinis. He considered the possibility that he might have a drinking problem. As always, the sober part of his brain was already calculating what he needed to do next to sniff out the truth about Henry and figure out who he had to meet here in Africa who could help him uncover the scheme, whatever it was. Part of him felt guilty about what he had told his partner and at the thought of Boston sweating over the details of the numbers, as she would be about now. He didn't like feeling guilty, and he didn't like thinking about his partner when he was in bed with another woman.

But then there was the blonde. She stirred and pulled him tighter. He wrapped his arms around her, running his fingers through her hair when he saw her eyes open.

"How are the girls?" he said. "How's everybody?"

Gina laughed. "Your girls are all good. They're all working and busy. Candice just popped out a beautiful baby boy, and she looks like she could do a shoot tomorrow."

He kissed her and smiled his first genuine nostalgic smile. "Wonderful. Great to hear. I miss them all."

The hotel room was quiet but for the hum of air conditioning.

"A million lira for your thoughts." she said.

"Turkish or Italian?" he said. He kissed her.

"I don't think the Italians use lira anymore."

"Stick around. They will," he said.

"Always the cynic." She smiled and ran her fingers across his face. "Did you get what you wanted tonight?'

His fingers followed the curve of her back and rested on her thigh. "And then some."

"Thanks," Gina said. "I really meant your dirt-digging expedition. You certainly had enough time and conversation to find out something about your guy Henry."

McBain frowned. "He's not my guy. He's the other guy. And I certainly did find out more about him. As I suspected, it looks like Henry's made a lot of enemies down here. Almost as many as he made on Wall Street. A guy like that isn't likely to be playing fair with my man. I think I'll have to do some more mining of my own in the next couple days."

Gina rolled over and pushed back the covers. The air conditioning could barely keep up with the two of them. "From what I overheard," she said, "he also has some powerful friends around here too. And I can tell you that means something."

"Like what?"

"That Henry has spread a lot of money around buying support. If this deal you're in on is so big, there are going to be quite a few hands out that are going to profit from it. And that means he has friends and partners who have a vested interest in seeing it done. That's how it works down here. You might want to tread carefully over the next couple of days until you find out who some of them are."

"I don't care about them. My job is to make sure my client isn't getting screwed when this goes down. Any friend of Henry's who's planning on making money off my man that way had better watch out if he's in on that."

Gina shook her head and blew out a breath. "The people who stand to make millions off of this project are well connected, and they aren't going to like it if they find out you're here sniffing around, trying to torpedo the deal. If Henry is threatened, they might feel threatened, and you'll end up with more trouble than information."

"I've got a gut feeling about this guy," McBain said. "Maybe it's the contrast between the nasty things I've heard about him and the tailored suits and polished manner, but I think he's up to something here. My client is a smart guy, but Henry wants what he has bad, and he might think Rogers is soft enough that he can take what he wants easily. My hunch is that Henry would try to grab his company and take it from him for nothing, just to prove he could. If that's the case, I'm not going to let that happen, even if I have to smear Henry in public to stop it."

Gina rolled over to lean on an elbow and stared at him for a few seconds. "You were never this mean when we were in New York. What happened to you?"

"You know what happened, Gina. You had a front-row seat."

She sighed and lifted her head. "Melissa was over five years ago. You've got to let it go."

"I have let it go."

Gina shook her head. "Really? Then why are you so different from the guy we all loved in New York?"

He looked at the ceiling fan. "I'm the same guy. Just a little more beat up with a lot more mileage. Maybe I've spent too much time in the financial sewers over the past four years."

Her eyes interrogated him. "You drink more in one night now than you did in a week. You don't talk about books or music or any of the other things you used to like. You're just now getting back in shape. No one blamed you for the deep dive after the way it all played out. But I thought the bitterness from back then would fade. I know you were treated like shit, but you've got to move on. Melissa did. Hell, we've all got bruises. You're too young to be this spent. It's been too long."

"Spent? That's not what you said an hour ago."

Gina swept her fingers around his shoulders and through his hair. "Don't get me wrong. I like the wild animal that suddenly appeared in Boston. I just wish the guy who taught us all how to tango and dance the polka to *The King and I* and made us laugh with bad French poetry was still there. Can't I have both?"

McBain stretched and looked for his cigarettes. He lit one. She pulled him back and took it from his lips, gazing at him through the smoke ring she blew.

"I guess not," Gina said.

"Sorry," he said. "It's a Jekyll and Hyde thing. But permanent."

She shrugged. "OK. Well, did the new cynical McBain find out anything else he needed tonight? Anything concrete you can use to follow up over the next few days?"

He nodded and massaged the back of her neck. "He certainly did. He found out he needs to ask more questions and keep pushing. This guy Henry has lots of enemies. Even worse, like you said, he has lots of friends. He worked a lot of angles to get these contracts and that land. From what de Graff told me, there are a lot of moving parts and hands involved in getting this project to happen. Here in South Africa, in Angola, and even in the States. That means he's paid off a lot of the right people, in business and in those governments. It also means those people probably stand to benefit a great deal from Henry's business, like you said."

She shrugged and pushed away her bangs. "That's no surprise. That's how it works here. A lot of palms out. But doesn't that mean your man stands to gain big too?"

"Maybe so," he said. "But I took this job even before I knew anything about Henry or his history. I want to make sure my client doesn't end up on the list of people who got in Henry's way on his road to his billions. That's why I want to find out more from the other people who are on Henry's good side, maybe in some of those meetings you set up over the next couple days. I'll have to think about my approach to this. I think you're right about that.

Pissing people off may be a mistake in these circumstances. Maybe if they think I'm here to help the deal get done, they'll be happy to talk to me."

"And what if they're not happy to talk to you? What if they get suspicious and think you are trying to threaten his deal and their payoff?"

He took the cigarette back from her and inhaled, then sighed. "Then I guess I'll just have to use my magical charms to make everyone believe I'm one of the team."

She moved her hand down his body. "In that case, any more of that magic left in this wand . . . Mr. Hyde?"

THIRTEEN

Under any circumstances other than those that had landed her in this situation, Boston O'Daniel would have been bored senseless into sitting back in her chair and catching up on her badly needed sleep. As it was, she followed the ebb and flow of the deal negotiations hour after hour on the edge of her seat, listening intently as the lawyers and bankers for both HR Technologies and AFR made financial points or reeled off details of clauses or agreements or proposals. For the most part, she remained silent, maintaining a posture of quiet deference to the senior HR Tech team members, just as McBain had suggested. She was careful to respond or comment only on those areas she felt comfortable with, chiefly the financial forecasts and valuation of the offer for the company.

There were thirty people sitting at a long conference table in the offices of AFR's leading law firm, high above the Boston harbor with a view of the Financial District and the distant islands. They had been there most of the afternoon, engaged in the back and forth of minor points and the tedious language in many of the documents. The young detective observed at some point that much of the conversation seemed focused on who in management would have what position after the acquisition was completed or on who would own how much of the resulting company's shares.

As the hours ticked by, however, Boston was quietly asking herself why no one else had raised the question about the document she had failed to find in the data room. From everything she had learned, this was a critical final step in the approval of the Angola project and, therefore, this deal.

Maybe she was wrong—this was her first exposure to an actual merger deal in the mining business. Then again, it wouldn't be the first time she had identified a potential problem in the small print.

Several executives were glancing at their watches, and Boston looked down at the meeting agenda in her binder. Time was running out at this critical session. Perhaps at the next meeting, she would bring it up. She could ask Rogers about it first.

Todd Mortimer stacked his sheets of paper with fanfare. "I don't see any other items on the agenda, so let's adjourn for the day and . . . yes?"

She couldn't stop herself. Boston's hand was in the air again. "I'm sorry, but I do have one other question about the document list."

Mortimer, half-raised from his chair, glowered impatiently and looked at his watch as he sat again. "What is it?"

She wasn't certain about this. It was probably nothing. No one else had found it important enough to bother with. Boston hesitated, glanced at a couple of people around the table. Twenty-nine faces waited in the silent hum of corporate air filters for her to speak.

"Just another minor point, probably," she said. She straightened in her chair, pushed up her glasses, and ticked a last item on her legal pad with her pen. "I went through all the foreign government documentation required for approval again last night. It seemed pretty complete, but when I matched it against the initial requirements checklist, the environmental impact approval from the government of Angola didn't seem to be there."

Mortimer wheeled on the short Rolex banker to his right. Rolex took only a second to pull the checklist out of his folder, along with another two-page document, and hand it to Mortimer. "Here it is," he said, smiling deliciously at Boston.

She looked over at the first page. "Um, no. I know we received the overall approval from the Angolan Ministry of Mining that says it was done. But according to the guidelines for project and merger approval I've read, we need an actual sign-off from the Angolan minister in charge of environmental affairs on an environmental impact assessment. I didn't see that or the EIA itself anywhere. We need it to ensure AFR can proceed legally and without risk of delay. If we don't have—"

Mortimer leaned back in his chair and laughed. "So what you're saying is the approval of the number-one guy in the country isn't good enough for you. We need some flunky three layers down to come back from a long lunch break and sign a piece of paper that's already moved past him. Am I hearing you right?"

"I suppose—"

The investment banker edged forward with glinting teeth of confidence. He glanced at Rodney Henry, sitting silently at the head of the conference table, then back at Boston.

"Look, Red. I don't know how much experience you have in doing deals around here, but it's clear you don't know much about how business is done in Africa. Here's how the politics works over there: You make connections at the highest level you can, build a relationship, make a deal, then go to work. You don't wait for some nobody's signature on a piece of paper. Do you even know the guy's name who heads the environmental agency that you claim didn't approve this? No? I didn't think so. You know what? I don't either. That's because it's not important. He's not important. You're talking about holding things up for a technicality. That's why your piece of paper isn't in the file. Sometime a year or two from now, when the mine is in full production and AFR stock has tripled, his successor or somebody else will find that nine-hundred-page report in a desk somewhere, look at it, then toss it back in the file cabinet. Like this."

He picked up his copy of the documents and threw them onto the middle of the conference table in front of her with a thud. Mortimer's smirk would have filled two seats by itself. Twenty-eight people in the room chuckled along.

It took all the self-control she had for Boston to hold her head high. Of course, he was right. She cursed herself for her naivety and stupidity. It was a rookie error that anyone used to working in corporate M&A in Africa wouldn't have made. Relieved that the meeting was over, she organized her papers, removed her glasses, and looked up toward the head of the table.

The only other person in the room who wasn't laughing was staring at her. She opened her mouth to apologize, then snapped it shut. There was nothing she could say. The game was over.

His hard eyes held hers for a few seconds as the laughter died away, and for a moment, she thought she detected something akin to curiosity in his gaze. Then he reached forward to the speakerphone on the boardroom table and hit the button. He dialed a number quickly, and after two rings, a woman's voice answered.

"Mr. Mitchell's office."

"Mr. Henry for Mr. Mitchell."

The conference room fell silent.

After five seconds, a gregarious voice sang out from the speaker. "Rod, what can I do for you?"

"Charles, I'm sitting in the due diligence review with the teams from our side and HR Tech. We seem to have a potential problem here that could hold up this deal."

The temperature in the room dropped below freezing.

"We've discovered that the final Angolan environmental impact assessment hasn't been received. Without explicit legal approval and environmental clearance, the Moxico project could be delayed for months, if not longer. We've got to have these particular approvals and documents from all four African governments involved in ironclad form, or else we're as vulnerable to government red tape or contract disruption as those other cases we've seen. Or worse. We can't risk having our rights voided. Remember what happened to First Quantum in the Democratic Republic of the Congo."

"I do, very well," Mitchell said. "Not the kind of loose end we need. Sorry for the oversight, Rod. I'll take care of it."

"Thank you, Charles."

Henry looked down the table.

"Oh, and Charles, if Mr. Mortimer is still working at your firm tomorrow morning, you're out of the deal. Am I clear?"

Brief silence, then: "Sure, Rod. It's done. Anything else?"

"Thanks, Charles, that's it. See you for dinner tomorrow night."

Henry shut off the speaker and addressed the group in a baritone that gripped everyone at the table by the throat.

"I want everyone in this room to understand something. This project is going to go through several layers of final government approval, even after the board of HRT votes to go ahead. If anything—I repeat, anything—comes up to delay or sink it that should have been discovered during this review process, I promise you the one who screws it up is going to find out what it is like to work at the bottom of the real mines instead of your metaphorical hard labor on the Street. Ms. O'Daniel has identified a potential roadblock. Fix it."

He rose and left the conference room, followed a moment later by a procession of bankers, lawyers, and executives, who tumbled after one another and scampered down the hall as soon as they were through the doorway.

All except Todd Mortimer, his face a red mask of shock and hatred, glaring at Boston O'Daniel as he stalked out of the room.

Boston sat alone at the table, looking out over the distance, not seeing the surrounding buildings or harbor. She waited until she had her breathing under control, took a swallow of water, then got up and left.

• • •

BOSTON LEFT THE office building and bolted to the gym. She spent the better part of an hour trying to work off her anger, first on the speed bag, then the heavy bag, then working with a master black belt on strikes to an opponent's joints and holds attacking pressure points from her Brazilian jiu-jitsu training. At first, her fury blazed up, but under the sensei's steady hand, she was able to direct her blows and control her emotions. It wasn't easy to focus. She was angry with Mortimer for trying to embarrass her, angry with the rest of the bankers and lawyers for laughing at her, and angry with Henry for defending her. Most of all, she was angry with McBain for not being there, for leaving her vulnerable in that room full of people who didn't think she belonged among them.

The October evening was coming on, and the gym became too crowded to allow her the solitude she needed. Boston was still energized and burning a slow burn, but the workout had helped. She grabbed her gym bag and decided to run back to the apartment to finish off her workout, climbing the slope to the Bunker Hill Monument first. Stuffing her dress clothes into the bag, she walked out of the building and into the streets of Charlestown in her sports top and gym shorts, grumbling to herself with her mind focused on the meeting and the turn of events. Her head was down looking into the bag, and she was just about to break into a jog when they started to pass her.

"Yo, Tits, what's happening?"

She spun around. There were three young punks with lots of attitude and no class looking her up and down. They were in jeans, flannel, and hoodies—local guys from the other side of the hill in Charlestown on their way to or from the latest beer.

"What's going on, baby?" The leader, the guy with the biggest mouth, arms, and ego to fuel. "It's your lucky day. Let's get some drinks and have some fun."

Boston kept walking past them, but the second man with the bad facial hair and too many snake tattoos grabbed the strap on her gym bag. "Whoa, hottie, what's the rush?"

The strap ripped out of his hand so fast he took a step back.

"Fuck you, asshole." Boston didn't shout it. She leveled her voice and her eyes. Her stance was already alert, her body on automatic, already calculating her response. "Keep your hands off my shit."

The three looked at each other, and the leader stepped forward. "What's your problem, bitch? We're talking nice to you and offering to buy you drinks, and you go cursing. Why don't you show some fucking respect?"

That was the wrong word at the wrong time. She sneered. "Respect? For you losers? I don't see anything to respect in front of me. And I didn't hear anything to respect either. You think that's talking nice to a woman? Yeah, I guess maybe you would, considering the kind of girl who would spend any time with you and consider that foul-mouthed shit a compliment. Tell you what—why don't you boys take it on to the next bar, buy each other some drinks, then go home and fuck each other."

The three of them looked at one another wide eyed in growing anger, as if no one—no woman—had ever talked to them this way. As if any bitch ever would get away with it. The leader spat on the ground at Boston's feet and came at her, slowly at first, then faster as he reached out to grab her arm.

He might have been fast, but to Boston's eye, he moved like molasses. His fingers had barely touched her skin as she dropped her gym bag and found the pressure point on his wrist. The agony was instant and intense, and the punk screamed as he dropped to his knees. Boston released his arm and was ready for the fist from the second man she saw coming at her face. He missed and started to fall toward her, so she took his momentum and seized his arm and elbow, spinning him around and to the ground. As he struggled to get up, she kicked him in the groin and turned to meet the third attacker, who had been hanging back. He was the smallest of the three, but he was in a fight with his friends and had drunk plenty of courage. Too much, in fact. He had expected his two friends to have beaten her to the ground by now, so he reacted slowly and more out of pride than any tactical sense.

"Biiitch!" He charged at her and tried to tackle her. Boston used his wild charge against him and, at the last minute, dropped low and swept her leg in an arc to take his knees out from under him. He fell face first onto the sidewalk and started to sputter blood from his mouth.

Boston's vision picked the leader up just as his good fingers grabbed her arm, and his weakened hand grabbed her throat. His face was so close, the air in her nostrils stank of whiskey. But only for a second. He thought he was getting her pinned to the red-brick wall next to the sidewalk. What he got was a knee to the balls. His grip loosened, and Boston reversed their positions against the bricks and got the distance she needed. Her hands worked as fast as they ever had in the gym. A double blow to his stomach, then a strike to his throat, then three blows to the side of his face with her fists that sent his head hammering against the wall with an audible crack.

He was barely standing; she was half lifting him up, and she pulled her arm back again as she prepared to drive his nose into his skull with the heel of her hand. A split second before her reflexes delivered the strike, her mind cleared, and sense returned. She realized that such a blow would probably kill him.

She released his neck, and he slumped to the ground bleeding and half-conscious. Boston stepped back and looked at the other two, writhing on the pavement, and at the blood on the sidewalk. The whole fight had taken less than thirty seconds, and though the adrenaline was pumping, she was barely breathing hard. Her head was clear and her vision sharp. The sounds of the neighborhood and distant car horns returned to her ears. After another few seconds, Boston picked up her gym bag and, with one last farewell kick to the stomach of the goateed attacker as he started to rise, walked back to the harbor at a brisk pace.

Boston went home and stood in the shower for a long time. The shower is a private place. Standing under a stream of hot water, no one can see your tears. Not even you.

FOURTEEN

It was morning in South Africa. McBain was waiting outside the entrance to the majestic Victoria and Alfred Hotel by the seaside, retracing memories of past visits to Cape Town, of breakfasts by the sea in chic cafes, of art galleries, and white beaches with fashion models, penguins, and surfboards. He had once been happy here, but for the life of him he couldn't bring himself to smile as he recalled the reasons why. How was it possible that seven years ago now seemed like a lifetime? Although he had changed, the view and weather had not. The sky was still a beautiful azure, if slightly overcast, with strips of cloud that seemed to graze the tops of the mountains to the east. As always, there was no threat of rain.

Gina pulled up promptly at nine in her car to take them on their first series of visits in Cape Town. She drove her own Land Rover so they could have some privacy to talk about the old times and McBain's plan for the next three days. She looked him over as he got in, dressed in khaki suit, powder blue shirt, and safari hat.

"I'm surprised you aren't wearing a pith helmet," she said.

"I couldn't find one."

She sighed and shook her head. "I have a feeling this is going to be a long couple days. OK, let's go. We have to finish up quickly here in Cape Town today. Then it's up to Johannesburg for tomorrow, and on to Pretoria the next day to a couple government offices and your consulting company."

McBain scanned his list. There was a lot of ground to cover in only a short time. Gina had assembled a host of contacts that included mining company executives, bankers, investors, and government ministers. Most of them would be friendly toward AFR and Henry, with a vested interest in seeing the Angola project go forward and the AFR/HR Tech deal succeed. McBain would have preferred to start with the money men—the bankers and investors—but they would be up in Joburg. It was always good to start with the source of the money to see how it had all evolved, who the players were, who had been edged out, and where the cash flowed. Instead, they would begin by interviewing well-connected businessmen from the social circle in Cape Town. Henry had relocated his headquarters and African residence to Cape Town in the last year, and the South African business community was small. And people liked to talk, about both their friends and their enemies.

McBain liked to listen. He had been conducting due diligence well before he became a detective and long enough that he knew the right questions to ask. He liked having Gina along with him to remind him to act the good cop and steer him around local society without making too many waves, at least unintentionally. Boston usually played that role and kept his biases in check, along with his tendency to insult when provoked. Gina was skilled and diplomatic enough to help manage that. And she had the advantage of having known McBain for a long time and seen him at his ugliest, so she could gauge his temperature while steering him around confrontation.

As they traveled around De Waterkant and through the old town full of galleries, it took all the focus he could muster for McBain to concentrate on the job and not the old days. It might have been his imagination or just coincidence that some of the offices and streets they visited seemed to be in neighborhoods that he and Melissa had seen with Gina and her crowd years ago. With the timeless African sunshine blazing down, it was as if he had never left.

Partly because of this, he was happy to start talking about Henry with their list of contacts, and throughout the morning, they interviewed a number of mining executives who were spending the weekend in Cape Town. Around one o'clock, they lunched with a retired consultant at one of the more popular cafes with a view of the beach. They sat outside at a ceramic table shaded by a blue-and-white umbrella, surrounded by casual locals in no hurry to be anywhere soon. Tourists maneuvered to avoid the occasional beggar loitering near the edge of the terrace.

McBain had expected to find men who were friends of Henry and more than a few enemies. What he had not expected was the near-universal agreement of these grizzled South African businessmen on one thing: Henry was crazy and wasting his time.

"Why do you say that?" McBain asked Hans de Witte after they had ordered lunch. He was a bright, clever industry hand who liked to share his experience at an expensive restaurant over meals provided by someone else. He had retired from the mining business with most of his white hair intact, but he knew most of the people and all the major players in South Africa and throughout the region. And unlike Maurice De Graff, he had no grudges to bear.

De Witte smirked the veteran's smirk and shook his head. "Look, I know your man Henry is smart. A lot of you Americans are smart, and you've got the money and arrogance to prove it. But like so many foreigners who show up here, he seems to think he knows something none of us obstinate natives do. Or that he is sniffing some kind of wind of change. Do you want to know how many Englishmen or Indians or Chinese I've heard that from in my lifetime? After a few years, a lot of money, and hard lessons, they lose the romance and find out what it's really like to do business here."

Fiddling with his gin and tonic, McBain laughed lightly. "I can't really argue that one with you. It's a failing a lot of us have. Incurable optimism lashed to boundless faith in humanity." He ignored Gina's smile. "On the other hand, I've met Henry, and he doesn't strike me as the rose-colored-glasses type. Or a humanitarian, for that matter. There must be some sound reason he's gambling on this Angola project."

The South African shrugged and sipped his white wine. "Punting is certainly an accurate term for what he's doing," he said. "Most people who prospect for new veins are more conservative where they search. For instance, they revive old sites that might have been played out long ago or have potential with new mining technologies. Or else they have experience and a long history of relationships in Africa. What he's trying to do in Angola is just plain crazy, and I'm not sure he knows what he's up against."

"I don't know. They tell me Henry has a pretty good track record."

"Maybe up to this point," de Witte said. "But when people mine in the Democratic Republic of the Congo, it's in places that are already mapped out and accessible by road or rail. Henry seems to think he's found some kind of mother lode in the middle of nowhere. While it's always possible, it isn't likely."

"Well, the Chinese were bidding against him. They're not exactly ignorant of this kind of thing."

"The Chinese have a lot of money to throw around, and they consider Angola theirs. I personally think they were just being territorial. Or, if you like, *imperial*. Either way, they don't have any more idea about what's out there than he does. Or how to get it out. They just don't care for the idea of any competition."

McBain thought about that. "That's certainly a problem. But if he is right, and he marries up AFR with my client's technology company, he could be able to pull it off. At least getting it out of the ground. The estimates he's throwing around have everybody's mouth watering."

The consultant smiled again. "Sure, for the sake of argument, anything could be there. Africa's rich in minerals, and that is unexplored territory close to the copper belt. I hear the initial assessments and samples are encouraging. As far as your rare earth exploration goes, I've heard about lots of promising theoretical discoveries, from Afghanistan to the ocean off the coast of Japan. But here's the thing: assuming you are right, how do you find it, get it out of the ground, process it, and transport enough of it from the middle of nowhere to the point where it can be used? And it has to be cost effective at market prices. Moxico has almost no developed infrastructure to support the logistics. It all has to be built out or re-built, and that takes time and costs money." De Witte paused and tilted his glass so that the remaining wine flashed in the sun. For a moment, a wistful longing replaced the cynicism in his eyes, and a smile creased his lips. "On the other hand, if Henry is right, it will be massive . . . What is that old expression? Fortune favors the bold."

"Henry doesn't seem to have any shortage of money."

"Ha. That's for certain, McBain. But then, that's what bankers are for, no?"

McBain was taking a liking to the South African. He felt a gentle tap of Gina's foot against his ankle. She poured more wine into de Witte's glass.

"Hans," she said, "is that the general consensus of your friends? That Henry's wasting his time and the bankers' money? It's hard to believe the project would have gotten this far without some kind of support and idea of his prospects for success."

"Thank you, G," he said with a grin. "He does have his fans here, mostly the bankers and investors in Johannesburg. They know a big fish when they see one. For the bankers, as long as they think they can manage the flow of cash to the project and get paid back, they're happy to fight over access to Henry. Some investors are betting on Henry's track record. And, of course, the Angolans seem quite taken with him. Why wouldn't they be? He's promising them the world, and if he strikes the jackpot, the ruling families there will be twice as rich as they already are. It seems to me that, for them, there is plenty of upside and little downside. As far as they are concerned, AFR can spend fifty years prospecting out there."

Gina laughed. "Ever the cynic, Hans. Have you been back recently?"

"To Angola? No, certainly not. They seem more interested in the oil business these days than in mining. Plus, times are a little harder now, and people are squeezing their money for paid advice."

They paused while the rest of their lunch arrived, an array of greens, fish, and local grains. They devoted themselves to their meal for a few minutes in silence. McBain ran through his mental checklist.

"Hans, you sound pretty skeptical about his prospects for getting the goods out of the mine. Have you ever been to that part of the country?"

"Moxico Province?" De Witte shook his head and winced. "Not a chance. AFR's project is so far east, it is close to the borders of the DRC and Zambia. That's why I keep telling you he's bonkers. Nobody has tried to develop anything there for decades, even after the war ended. That was Savimbi's territory. He and UNITA controlled the diamond trade in that part of the country during the civil war. With all the fighting over the years, the roads and trains and everything else just decayed or got blasted to hell and gone. The closest town of any kind is half a day's drive away through rough terrain. It's pretty lawless. You can encounter roving gangs armed to the teeth who have nothing to do with politics. Not to mention there must have been a million land mines spread all over the place. Not my cup of tea, thanks. I've felt safer in the Congo."

They worked their way through lunch as de Witte discussed the political situation and economics of Angola and the rest of southern Africa. After listening intently, McBain leaned in and broached a sensitive subject.

"Hans, you mentioned something about knowing how to do business here. If the traditional boys like Anglo and BHP have a lock on the mining business in southern Africa, how was it that Henry was able to cut them out and win the bid for the rights to develop the project there?"

"Old resentments, I imagine." The South African swirled the wine around in his glass and raised it to examine it as the sun lit up the golden streams.

McBain pressed on. "And the Chinese?"

De Witte grinned. "New resentments, perhaps. No one is quite sure. It was quite a feat and surprised everyone."

Gina smiled. "But you have your suspicions," she said.

"Always, my dear girl. You know how things work in Luanda as well as I do. I'm sure our man Henry made it worth their while. On the other hand, some of the ruling clique in Angola are quite smart. Maybe they were sending the Chinese a not-so-subtle message: Don't think you can take us for granted. That's the trouble with corruption; sometimes they don't stay bought. And after a number of years having them here, I think some of the glamor has worn off of the Sino-African romance. So perhaps AFR is just being used as leverage. Maybe they think they've found a new cash machine. Who knows? My guess is that it is some combination of the two. The terms of the arrangement are pretty closely held."

McBain swallowed and dabbed at his mouth with the cloth napkin. "Whatever we can say about Rodney Henry, he certainly isn't naïve, no matter what corner of the world he's playing in. My guess is he played the angle you are talking about, and he greased the skids, as we say in the States. Although there are laws against that sort of thing."

De Witte chuckled. "Oh? Are there? Now who is being naïve, my friend? Developed countries can pass all the laws they like. As I said, Africa does business its own way, and people in power are always going to get paid." He smirked again. "Maybe even more than once if they are truly clever. And in Angola, some have made it an art form. There are a lot of oil companies operating up there, and everyone seems satisfied with the results to one degree or another."

Gina nodded. "If I remember correctly, AFR also has a somewhat complicated structure and may not be subject to all the laws written in the US or UK."

"That's very true," de Witte said. "And while South Africa is also a party to international agreements outlawing payoffs, there are so many moving parts to these contracts that there are quasi-legal ways to—how shall I put it?—share profits. Frankly, for these large development projects, there are so many stages where money changes hands that it is nearly impossible to track anything but blatant and clumsy bribery incidents. Oh, the banks and investors make sure they control the cash flows and get paid back. But as long as the local officials are on board and everyone is happy, deals get done. Let's face it, McBain. I'm sure you've read about problems with government corruption, even here in South Africa. For reasons Gina or I could explain, the Angolans are world class. From the ruling families to the average bureaucrat, it's simply a part of life there."

McBain was beginning to feel he was on the scent of something. "So Henry could have just bribed the Angolans and other officials to muscle out the competition. And the other governments in the deal as well. That could jeopardize the final project approval and the merger, couldn't it? If I could prove it?"

Gina moved uneasily in her chair and frowned at him.

But de Witte laughed heartily and attacked his dessert. "As I've tried to explain, it is undoubtedly more complicated than that, and done much more subtly, through slush funds or payoffs to the right local officials. Or maybe, as I've suggested, he simply offered them a bigger cut of anything he found there; an underground mountain of rare earth minerals just waiting to be harvested."

"But what if—?"

"My dear McBain, do you know how many American and European oil companies compete for Angolan and Nigerian oil contracts? And they have to operate under those international laws you mention, as well as strict environmental scrutiny. No, I think it is much more likely that your friend Henry just thinks he has discovered the new pot of gold and was willing to cut deals with the right people for the rights. And as I've said before, it's my opinion that he is going to be leaving in a few years much the poorer for his African education." He waved at the waiter for another bottle. "Who knows? Maybe he'll make it. But perhaps I'm misunderstanding. Based on what you told me about your client, don't you want Henry to succeed?"

McBain observed Gina's instructive expression, then raised his glass. "Of course, Hans. I guess I'm just making sure things are locked down with the project so the deal gets closed in my client's best interest. Here's to the project's success. And to Africa's future."

They finished lunch and McBain picked up the check along with three other phone numbers of contacts in the mining industry that the detective could call for other opinions. Then he and Gina made two other appointments before heading back to the hotel, where their bags were waiting for the trip to the airport and their South African Airways flight to Johannesburg. Airport security was mercifully and strangely less frustrating than in America, and McBain and Gina spent the two-hour flight assessing the day's results and planning for the next stages.

FIFTEEN

Johannesburg has been the financial and business capital of Africa for as long as anyone can remember. It is strategically placed in the northeast of South Africa, and the business community there thinks of themselves as central to all business on the continent, or indeed as a bridge between Europe and South Asia. Although global air travel and the end of the apartheid era changed much of that, the bankers in Johannesburg still use their expertise and local regulations to maintain a stranglehold on all dealmaking in the southern half of the continent. White, black, or mixed race, the investing and banking cartel in positions of power use their relationships from South Africa to the Congo to ensure they have at least a piece of every important transaction that appears.

McBain and Gina started their calls early, with a breakfast meeting at their hotel with eager investors, all anxious to hear about the impending marriage of AFR and HR Tech. For these meetings, McBain dispensed with the safari hat and became Wall Street again, wearing a gray suit, powder-blue shirt, and buy-side attitude. At last he was back in his strike zone. The detective soon found out, as Boston had, that everyone wanted to be the new best friend of Rodney Henry and the expanding commodities juggernaut that was AFR. The reasons became even clearer during the first few visits that he and Gina paid to the bankers at Standard Bank and NedBank. Henry was, as de Witte had suggested, a big fish to all of them. New opportunities are rare in a place with well-developed businesses, closed circles, and histories such as mining or energy, and Henry had come storming in a few years ago with an aggressive and successful money-making reputation.

And there was something else that had surprised them. Unlike other babes in the woods who showed up in Africa without relationships, Henry had clearly done his homework. Building off his career on Wall Street, Henry had needed no special help with political contacts in Africa—he was already well connected. A man who had Washington on his side found doors opening up across the continent as his search expanded for unexplored tracts with potential for rare earth mining. He didn't need their network of local contacts. He was getting access at the highest levels.

He did, however, need their money and expertise. International bankers from London, New York, and Tokyo were circling AFR, looking for ways to edge their way into his Africa play along with his other geographies. The South African bankers had been more than eager to assist Henry with any opportunities and, with his reputation for big wins, more than willing to finance him along the way to glory at the right price. With so many eager suitors lusting after the new kid on the African block, McBain had no trouble finding answers to his questions. Working with the questions the miners had given him, he dove in headfirst, looking for answers on AFR and on Henry.

In the afternoon, Gina had arranged a meeting with a senior vice president at ABSA, the lead bank in the current stage of financing for AFR's project in Angola. When she and McBain arrived at the bank's headquarters, she emphasized that Octavius Morton was an old hand and no one's fool, and he was determined that if AFR was going to grow in southern Africa, it was going to do so in partnership with ABSA and nobody else. They entered a palatial office on the highest floor of the bank and were greeted by a tall and elegant banker with silver hair and chiseled features, impeccably dressed with an air of reserve. It was very clear from the scale of the office and the African sculptures decorating the walls and pedestals that Morton held a position at the top of the financial world in South Africa. This suggested to McBain that he was exactly the kind of man he needed to talk to.

Back on her A game, Gina introduced McBain and exchanged pleasantries with Morton for a few minutes before letting the detective set the tone for his inquiries. McBain was determined to take her words of caution to heart, especially given how stunningly professional she looked in her white skirt, black blazer, and pearl earrings. They seated themselves in Edwardian arm-chairs across from a wide desk carved from a massive oak taken from the distant highlands. The chairs seemed designed for discomfort, to suggest a visitor keep their time to the brief period allotted by the executive. The rich leather couch and armchairs on the far side of the room were reserved for paying clients.

"I appreciate your time, Mr. Morton," he began. "I realize that a man in your position must have a busy schedule."

The banker crossed his legs with his hands folded in his lap. He smiled a polite acknowledgment. "I'm always available to make time for important friends of ABSA, Mr. McBain. I was informed you were here to help with the closing of the merger our client Africa's Future Resources is expecting to finalize. Anything I can do to expedite the transaction is my pleasure, given our critical role in financing the Angolan project."

McBain mirrored the banker's smile and crossed his own legs. "Exactly so," he said. "I'm working for the company that AFR is on the verge of acquiring, for the founder of that company, to be precise. He's obviously quite pleased with the potential merger and is looking forward to closing the deal soon. He's asked me to come down and 'kick the tires,' as we say in America. Ask a few questions, check out relationships, speak to a few people who are well informed about the company and the legal system down here, make sure everyone is quite comfortable with the details of the transaction and the track record of AFR in the region. A formality, really."

"I see." Morton smiled and nodded. "And are you a banker, Mr. McBain, or a lawyer?"

"Neither, really. I worked on Wall Street for a time, but now I consult on merger due diligence and finance with my partner. I've been in South Africa before, but I haven't really worked in finance here, so I'd appreciate any insights you have on the complexities involved in closing this deal, and in particular on AFR and the Angola project. I understand its virgin territory up there, so I'm interested to hear your opinion on the potential for Henry's venture."

The banker spread his hands and leaned back in his chair.

"My opinion is that there is great potential in this project. And in that entire area. The potential to develop a sustainable source of wealth that benefits not only AFR but the entire region. If the results of the surveys to date stand up to the test of early development and sampling, the opening of a new frontier in rare earth mining represents the kind of find that may be as historical as the discovery of oil in the Middle East, Alaska, or the North Sea. Think about the opportunities for economic growth and development throughout southern Africa. For investments in business growth. In communities. I firmly believe that; otherwise I would not have been so persistent in leading this financing."

McBain nodded along in agreement, recognizing the script. "I agree. I've become a big fan of Mr. Henry in a short period of time, based on everything I've learned. But I'll admit this project management business and long-term development is all a little intimidating to an old Wall Street trader. How did you get comfortable with the financing? It is, as you say, early stages of development."

Morton steepled his fingers and condescended in the style of a college professor.

"I built my career on project financing throughout southern Africa, Mr. McBain. I have a track record of success in identifying promising opportunities like this while approaching them in a methodical manner that safeguards the capital of the bank and investors. I can assure you that each stage of the project and associated financing has been managed with the utmost professionalism. Like you, we believe in thorough due diligence. At no point have funds from our banking consortium been dispensed without adequate research and controls and a thorough risk assessment."

McBain drew another card. "I have no doubt. Have you been to the project site in Angola yourself?"

Morton shook his head while brushing imaginary dust from his pant leg. "That's not where we add our value, sir. A few of my bankers have been out there to perform a cursory check on the facilities as the project has progressed through the initial milestones. They checked on the status of the mine and the equipment that's been deployed thus far to ensure that there are no irregularities. But most of the site work has been done by the project managers and mining consultants who were selected. And they are all at the top of their field. Let me explain the process."

McBain drew a small notebook and pen from his jacket pocket. The banker ran through the project development steps that Harold Rogers had described in detail in McBain's conference room, though he took care to emphasize the importance of ABSA's role at each stage and ability to approve or deny funding based on the bank's evaluation of progress.

The investigator took some notes as he followed along, nodding as he wrote while thinking about weak spots in the chain. "It sounds like you have a firm grip on the project, Mr. Morton. And on the risks." McBain cleared his throat. "I should mention that I spoke to a number of people here who consider this project a bit of a long shot, chiefly due to Mr. Henry's relative inexperience in Africa and the somewhat remote location of the dig. They suggested that AFR may be in over their head in their enthusiasm for big finds in rare earth mining, even with my client's new technology."

The corner of Morton's mouth went up as he listened, his eyes focused on the wall of his office that was covered with photographs of mining projects in South Africa and shelves of framed tombstones of successful deals he had arranged.

"Let me guess. These people wouldn't happen to be current or former executives in the mining industry, would they?"

His gaze turned to the detective, who shrugged sheepishly.

"Yes, I thought they might. Mining in Africa is a very insular world, Mr. McBain. AFR beat out quite a few local conglomerates to acquire the rights to mine that area, not to mention other locations. As a relative newcomer and outsider, Mr. Henry has generated quite a bit of anger and jealousy in that community. I, of all people, understand that anger and have had to manage a fair bit of it directed at myself. After all, ABSA does business with almost all these companies. But at the end of the day, the governments of Angola, Zambia, and the DRC made their choice, and it was AFR. I try to emphasize to our other clients that there's room enough for everyone, especially in new territory."

"AFR is a fairly new entrant to these parts, Mr. Morton. Have you done much business with Henry before this? I've talked to people in New York about his successful career in the commodities business. What's his track record down here? I'm sure you wouldn't go out on a limb for some untried foreign company. Have you made money with him before?"

"I'm pleased to say that I've been able to help AFR and Mr. Henry build a growing portfolio across southern Africa in the past three years. We've financed several small acquisitions that have allowed AFR to build up its staff with mining expertise and accelerate their timetable for acquiring mining rights and planning by several years. That's another reason I'm quite confident in the company's ability and prospects."

McBain tapped his notepad with his pen as if lost in thought. "Hmm. Forgive me asking, but any of them hostile or unwanted? Any dissatisfied customers from the investment side? Aside from maybe some of those mining execs you mentioned." He smiled.

Morton smiled back, showing some teeth. "Hardly. Quite the opposite, in fact. Mr. Henry has been quite generous in his offers. His intention has always been to build a strong company with the most skilled people, and the owners and employees were more than happy to sell and become part of a larger company, especially one with an expanding future, if you'll pardon the pun. It's another sign that Rodney Henry is in this for the long haul. I'm certain your client will be quite satisfied." The banker examined his polished nails. "And as to the skepticism regarding the Moxico project, I can tell you without violating any confidences that I've had advanced discussions with both AFR and the government of Angola on long-term development of the infrastructure of that province. Plans are already well advanced to speed up the construction of transportation in the region, or should I say reconstruction? Yet another source of jobs and opportunity that Mr. Henry and AFR have helped advance."

McBain closed his notebook and glanced at Gina, then smiled at the banker. "What a guy," he said. "Sounds like you've been very thorough, Mr.

Morton. You and your people know your business. No doubts or reservations? They tell me that's quite the frontier up there, and jealous or not, I don't mind telling you they make a convincing case for the risks."

Octavius Morton uncrossed his legs and leaned forward on his forearms, a look of utmost seriousness on his face. "I assure you, Mr. McBain, and please assure your client, ABSA is here to help manage those risks in the most prudent and professional way. That's one of the many reasons Rodney Henry chose us to partner with. Risk is our business."

They shook hands and departed. When they were downstairs waiting for their driver, McBain finally exhaled and rolled his eyes. "Could you believe that guy? Quite a salesman. You'd think he and Henry were married the way he quoted from the team playbook."

Gina leaned in and kissed him on the cheek. "Imagine someone in banking blowing smoke to get a deal done. I'm sure you've never done that, my dear."

McBain slid his sunglasses into place and smirked. "Yes, gorgeous, but I like to think I was at least a little more subtle and less self-congratulatory when I did it."

"Yes, we'd like to think that, wouldn't we? Meanwhile, after two days, it's about as you expected; the miners have one take and the bankers and investors another. Learn anything new up there?"

He glanced at his notebook full of useless scribbles. "Nothing I'm happy about or that surprises me. I knew Henry was smart and that the money guys would be supportive. Looks like he's been planning a long game here in Africa and around the world. Henry's that rare creature: a Wall Street pro with a long-term view. He doesn't care about pissing off competitors. He wants the whole market, not just here but in as many places as he can buy into. What I didn't figure on was the political angle. He seems to be playing hardball there, too, and I'm not sure how he has done it. I'm just beginning to think about that part of the game."

Gina nodded and scanned her smartphone. "I tried to tell you from the beginning. He's got lots of friends who stand to benefit. Not just the bankers. That's how it's done here." She scrolled down the screen. "That's why I've set you up with some meetings with the ministries in Pretoria tomorrow." She looked at her watch. "We have some time. Ready for an early drink?"

McBain ripped a page out of his notebook and handed it to Gina. "Not quite yet," he said. "One more call to make. This isn't too far, is it?"

She looked at the address and shrugged. "We can get there quickly, depending on traffic. Do we have an appointment?"

Their black BMW rolled up.

"Yes," McBain said. "I called the guy and set it up before we left Cape Town. I'm really looking forward to this one."

"Robert Shawn. Who is he?"

McBain opened the door for her. "One of Henry's biggest cheerleaders."

Gina gave the driver the address and said it would take about thirty minutes to find the offices of *The Rare Investor* in the town of Sandton, a wealthy area outside Johannesburg proper. McBain had once stayed not far from the office in an expensive guest house while his ex had been shopping in the equally expensive shopping center of Sandton City.

The vehicle wound its way through the side streets to avoid afternoon traffic, taking them down well-paved lanes in wooded neighborhoods. The foliage was punctuated in places by high stone walls topped with barbed wire and cameras or security posts at the closed gates of forbidden driveways. The security teams at such entryways lounged in chairs or stood mute as they observed the cars and trucks go by. They seemed both bored and unfriendly. The faded beige or white walls bore none of the charm of Cape Town or Miami. McBain scanned each of them as the car rolled by or stopped for traffic.

"It's different now," McBain said. "Or is it just my imagination? Maybe I was just happier before and didn't notice. The barbed wire and security, the poverty and crowds of young men, the news stories. This area used to be a more cheerful place."

Gina gazed out at a long granite wall with a crest of spikes and barbed wire and shrugged in indifference. "Maybe. It's been six years since you were last here. I can't recall when things started to seem bad. Six years? Ten? It has occurred to me that the crime in some places just gets worse each year. Good economy, bad economy—it doesn't seem to matter. Lots of things are getting worse.

"Some of the crimes you read about are so horrendous you can't believe they really happened. New politicians make promises about change, but the government gets more corrupt than ever each round. I know because I see it firsthand. The police are overwhelmed or demoralized because there aren't nearly enough of them to combat the theft and murder; they are underequipped and underpaid. It's sad really, but even worse is that too many people just want to pretend it's OK to live this way and that somehow it will get better."

McBain searched her face for emotion. Resignation didn't sit well with some people, but that was all there was.

"I remember," she said, "when I was a child growing up in Cape Town, back when Mandela was first released, and it felt like the country would come together and put the past behind us. There was the poverty and racism, of course, and a lot of hard feelings on both sides. But for a while, there was the sense that it could be fixed, and that South Africa was meant for better times." She laughed once. "It's almost funny now to hear people talk about this guy Henry and Africa's future and all the good things that will come from this. If I hadn't lived in this country most of my life, I might believe it myself."

"Sorry to hear that, Gina. Everyone always spoke so hopefully about the future." He glanced out the window at another high brick wall topped by barbed wire as they passed a gate. "You wouldn't have guessed it at the contest and reception the other night."

Gina smiled ruefully. "Yes, you wouldn't think so. But times like that get fewer and farther between. It almost has that fin de siècle feel to it. I often imagine this is what it was like in Vienna and Moscow around 1914." She looked over at him and grabbed his hand. "I certainly hope not. I love so much about South Africa. I'm trying to be optimistic while I consider my options."

"For example?"

She pushed at her blonde hair and smiled. "I have quite a few contacts in the Middle East. A number of them have suggested Dubai could use a woman with my many talents."

McBain laughed. "Peace in the Middle East in my time. Who would have thought it?" She laughed back. He held up his right hand and counted. "On the other hand, I always thought of you as a London or Paris or Rome girl. You just thrive in Europe."

Her eyes sparkled at him. "You never know. I might want to give Boston a shot. It has its charms."

He threw his head back. "That's not what you said four years ago when you visited. You spent every weekend there working to get me to come back to my senses, and New York City."

"Can't blame a girl for trying. And I still might try to save you from yourself . . . and Eliza."

Before he could respond, the car turned left and accelerated through an intersection. They saw the retail kingdom of Sandton City on their right as the car wound its way into a turn and toward a small commercial building a few hundred yards farther. The driver swung into the parking lot and pulled into a space to wait.

McBain and Gina entered the lobby and glanced up at a camera as he pushed a button for the office of *The Rare Investor*. The gate buzzed open, and they took a small elevator up to the third floor. The office was not large but had room for two metal writing desks, file cabinets along one wall, and tables full of computer and television equipment along the other. Afternoon sunlight angled through the blinds. An air conditioner hummed, but the air held the faint aroma of cigarette smoke. Robert Shawn was seated at one of the desks, stretched back in a modern ergonomic chair on wheels, dressed in jeans and a black cashmere turtleneck, with dress shoes and no socks. McBain reckoned him to be in his early thirties by his thinning dishwater-blond hair.

He rose and gave McBain one of those modern handshakes that people his age used to prove their cool.

"Mr. McBain, I presume," he said. "And who is your friend?" He failed to hide his admiration. "I'm Robert Shawn, African editor in chief of *The Rare Investor*. You can call me Robert. How are you, Ms. . . .?"

Gina extended her hand in the old-fashioned style and managed an icy smile. "The name is Ferrari, Mr. Shawn. Gina Ferrari. English, Mr. Shawn? Near London, I would guess."

McBain meandered over to the windows while he assessed the office.

Not exactly *Forbes*, but then this was a small and specialized sector of the investment and mining industry. And Sandton was a pricey neighborhood.

"Thanks for taking the time to see us, Mr. Shawn," he said.

"Robert. Please."

The investigator smiled politely. "Robert. Thanks. And my friends call me McBain."

The journalist chuckled and sat back down behind his desk. "Nice touch, McBain," he said. "So, McBain and Ferrari, consultants. One from the US and one South African. You mentioned on the phone that you were here working to help close the deal for AFR and that you had a few questions. How can I help?"

"I'm trying to do a little last-minute due diligence for my client, the founder of HR Tech, to help him get comfortable with a few details before they sign. I've been reading up on rare earth minerals in the past few weeks, including all your back pieces on AFR, rare earths in this region, and the Moxico project. And, of course, Rodney Henry. It seems you're the man to come to if I want to find out anything on the subject."

Shawn threw his arms open. "That I am, McBain. That I am. Rare earths are a new and exciting field for both miners and investors. *The Rare Investor* covers the industry and the markets around the world, and I've helped make the company the leading publication in the industry, especially in Africa. Other news outlets may keep you up to speed with precious metals and other mining news, but if you want the best information on investing in rare earth mining and development, I'm your man."

McBain pulled up a metal chair across from Shawn, while Gina hovered around the television, watching the news with an ear tipped in their direction.

"Sounds like I came to the right place, Robert," the detective said. "How did you come to be the expert? You an ex-industry man yourself?"

Shawn grinned. "Hell, no. I've been a journalist my whole life. Graduated from university in England and fell into it naturally in London. I worked for the *Financial Times* for a while and became interested in investing. While I was there, I got onto their companies desk and started covering the commodities business, then the mining sector. A couple of years ago, I had the idea of focusing on the rare earths industry because it was a less-developed niche field in investing and mining. I guess the timing was right, because in the last couple years, I've built up a pretty good following for the publication."

McBain smiled and nodded. "I'll say. From what I've seen, you've put out some top pieces on the industry. Not to mention making some good investment picks. You even seem to have had a couple of scoops. Nice work."

"Thanks," he said. "I like to think it's about to become one of the more exciting parts of the investment world. Thanks to the Green Revolution and consumer technology, demand for new sources of metals is growing by leaps and bounds."

Gina walked over to the desk and sat down, crossing her legs. "And how is it that you ended up in Johannesburg, Robert?" she asked.

Shawn sat up and leaned forward on his desk, winding up his pitch. "Very simple, Gina," he said. "I did my homework and saw where the Chinese were going and what they were after. You might not be aware of it, but China is the world leader in the mining and development of rare earth minerals. And they want to keep it that way. I figured if they were into Africa in a big way for everything else, it was only a matter of time before they hit the jackpot here too. They want to make sure they're the only game in town when it comes to certain critical rare earths." Here, he raised an eyebrow and delivered an elegant pause. "And they were, before Rod Henry and Africa's Future Resources set up shop."

McBain smiled and took his opening. "Yes, so I've heard," he said. "I gather from a couple of your pieces that you've met Henry in person a few times. What's your take on him?"

Shawn nodded. "He's an impressive man, with an equally impressive background. I'm not surprised he was one of the first to see the opportunity in rare earths. With his track record in the banking and investment business, it was clear he was going to be one of the first movers to spot what the Chinese were up to. The wonder is that nobody else seemed to be aware of what was going on, even as the world became more dependent on rare earth metals from China. And I think he may just have beaten them at their game."

"Here in Africa, you mean?"

"No, I mean all over the world," Shawn said. He eyed McBain with a little smirk. "If you've learned anything about Rod Henry and AFR in this deal, you know Africa is just the beginning. He's acquired rights to some of the most promising locations in the world, and with your client's processing technology, he's going to be one of the biggest names in the future of mining on this planet." He leaned back again. "And maybe beyond."

McBain glanced at the ashtray on the journalist's desk. "Mind if I smoke, Robert?"

Shawn shrugged and pulled out a pack of Marlboro Reds. He took one in his mouth and offered the pack to McBain, who used his own metal lighter to light up. He stared at the journalist for a few seconds, then exhaled.

"You seem to have a lot of insight into Henry and AFR, Robert. In reading through your back articles, I noticed that you were able to get some pretty exclusive access to Henry. Nobody else in your end of the business seems to have been able to interview him even once. From what I've discovered, he's a pretty private person. How were you able to get close to him?"

Shawn took a drag and rocked back and forth in his chair while he talked. "Because Rod Henry and I are of the same mind when it comes to the potential for rare earths development and the future."

"Well, it certainly hasn't hurt your career any," McBain said. "And the good press hasn't hurt his. They say timing is everything. How did you come to meet Henry in the first place?"

The journalist paused as he looked at the ceiling for a moment, then over at Gina's poker face. "It was at one of those investing conferences in London," he said. "You know, where they bring together all the big players from the corporate and investment side, the analysts and geological experts and financial journalists. I was with the *FT* at the time, but I was thinking about striking out on my own to research rare earth investing. I met Rod Henry during one of the presentations, and we hit it off. You know, great minds think alike and all that."

"Yes," McBain said and nodded. "I do know. Very fortuitous that, especially considering that he's notoriously closed mouthed when it comes to interviews. You seem to be the only one he's talked to at length about AFR and his strategy. Again, nice work."

Shawn tilted his head and examined McBain.

"He explained it to me once, McBain. He told me he didn't really care for most journalists but felt he owed it to his shareholders and customers to make sure the world was accurately informed about what AFR was trying to accomplish. That there was something bigger involved than just another mining company."

"Yes, I'll bet. I can certainly see the advantage in that, especially given Henry's track record on Wall Street."

"I'm not sure what you mean."

The air in the room was getting thicker despite the air conditioner.

McBain smiled lightly. "Oh, come on, Robert. You've done your research on Henry. You must know about his reputation from Wall Street and some of the accusations."

The journalist stubbed out his cigarette and snorted. "I know about his reputation for success at everything he does. And I know some people were jealous of that success. Were, and are." He looked at McBain with a raised eyebrow.

McBain glanced at Gina for a moment; she got up and drifted away from the desk again. He drew on his cigarette and crossed his legs as he evaluated Shawn. The air conditioner hummed on, and the news on the wide-screen television sounded a little louder.

"Fair enough," he said. "I'm sure the Chinese are jealous that he beat them in their own territory and at their game. You're the expert. How do you think that happened?"

Shawn smiled with that little know-it-all glint in his eye. "Because Rod Henry is smart and focused, and he knew how important it was to the governments and people of this region that they were the ones who would benefit from his investment. Not the outsiders for a change." The journalist leaned back as he lit another cigarette. "And I don't mind saying that I might have lent him the benefit of my experience down here in how to approach people and what their complaints have been."

"Well, then," McBain said. "Since this is your terrain and you know how the game is played, maybe you can put my mind at ease—and that of my client."

"About what?" Shawn said.

"You haven't heard of anything shady in connection with the deal, have you? You know, related to the Foreign Corrupt Practices Act, things like that?"

Shawn stared at him and drew on his cigarette. "No."

"Just checking," McBain said. "Part of my due diligence, you know. Speaking of which, have you been up to the project site in Angola?"

The journalist coughed out a laugh. "Why would I do that, McBain? I'm a journalist, not a mining engineer. I've talked to everyone who has been there, from executives at AFR to the consultants and the bankers and the people at the Department of Mining here in South Africa. I've talked to geologists and mining analysts at the top investment firms in the world. I've even talked to the chief minister in charge of foreign investment in Angola. What possible point would there be in a journalist going to Moxico to visit the project?"

McBain shrugged and inhaled the last of his cigarette before leaning forward and snuffing it out in the ashtray.

"I don't know—sense of adventure, maybe. Develop some real street credibility with the readers and analysts. Check out the sight for signs of progress or trouble. Just some basic due diligence."

Shawn shook his head slowly. "I don't like wasting my time, McBain. I talk to the experts in their field, and investors rely on my expertise in mine. I synthesize the information from those experts and relay it to the world so people can make their own judgments."

By now, the room had filled with cigarette smoke as the two men stared at one another silently. McBain had a strong gut feeling about this reporter and his relationship with Henry. A series of car horns blaring in the street outside broke the silence.

"By the way, another standard question from my old Wall Street days. You happen to have any vested interest in AFR or any of Henry's other investments? Own any stock? You know, back where I come from, analysts and reporters are required to note in their pieces if they have any positions in the company they are writing about."

Robert Shawn rose and looked at his watch. "As I just said, McBain, I don't like wasting my time. I'm not sure what you're after with those kind of questions, but I've got better things to do. Good afternoon."

"Ever go to any of Henry's parties in London or Cape Town?"

Gina swept by and took McBain by the arm as Shawn gritted his teeth and began to color.

"Thank you for your time, Mr. Shawn," she said and opened the door.

McBain looked the journalist up and down, enjoying seeing his pale face redden.

"Yes, thanks, Robert," he said. Then a little corner of his mouth went up. "It's certainly been educational."

They went out.

Shawn lit another cigarette and walked over to the window. As he watched the pair get into the vehicle and leave the parking lot, he pulled his phone out of his pocket and dialed.

●　●　●

MCBAIN AND GINA returned to their hotel in Johannesburg to change, then went out to dinner at a nearby restaurant. They lingered over wine when the meal was done, talking about Gina's travels throughout Africa and the Middle East. She had regained her spirits, but McBain became quieter as he mulled over the information from the day. The sparring with Robert Shawn had briefly improved his mood, but the more he thought about the journalist and his timely career change and investment picks, the more something began to gnaw at his insides. He let it stew while he and Gina reminisced about old friends and happier days. McBain made a mental note to check in with Dee Dee to discuss his suspicions about Shawn as soon as he returned to Boston.

"Karen sold her jewelry business and moved to Morocco," Gina said. "She comes back to visit her family in Durban once in a while or takes her kids to Kruger so they can see the animals in the wild."

McBain focused on her again. "Why Morocco?"

"Because it's close to Spain, and Karen loves Spain. You haven't been listening."

He shook his head to throw off the cobwebs and pushed his wine-glass away.

"Yes, I have," he said. "Sorry. I think maybe the jet lag is catching up to me, so I'm missing a few beats. Yes, I do remember that Karen loved Spain. I would hope so; her husband is Spanish, right?"

"Ex-husband now."

McBain grunted. "Yeah, lots of that going around, I hear."

Gina took a sip of Chablis. "Switching gears again, what was up with Shawn today? You haven't talked about it since we left his office."

"What did you think of him?" he asked.

"He comes across as quite taken with himself, and I sensed an undercurrent of sleaze, but nothing nefarious. I got the feeling straightaway that you went in there looking to discover something about Henry. Or to pick a fight."

"Sharp as always." He swished the wine around in his glass but didn't drink any. "Just a gut instinct I wanted to check out. His stories about Henry and AFR have an odd tint to them that made me want to check him out personally. Most of them read like some analysts or news items I've read that bend toward enthusiasm for their subject, not objectivity."

She smiled at him. "On the other hand, some people might suggest you've become a little too much the cynic over the past few years. And, in this case, let's not forget you are out to prove that Henry is up to something with your client."

"True. But that doesn't mean I'm wrong."

"I would never suggest that, darling," Gina said. "And I didn't like Shawn either. But so far, after two days of meetings with dozens of people, I have to point out that there is little indication from anyone that this is anything other than a brilliant deal that will benefit your client tremendously and, of course, Mr. Henry. As I keep telling you, a lot of people down here have a vested financial interest in supporting him. I'd have to say Shawn is one of them."

McBain frowned and looked around the room.

"You could be right. Maybe it's the timing of Shawn's miraculous epiphany about rare earth investment opportunities and his acquaintance with Henry. From what I read, he's been acting more as Henry's damn wingman than an objective analyst. I think he's bought and paid for."

"He's not an analyst, is he, love? He's a reporter. His job is to sell news and build up his reputation. So what if he got a few hot tips from Rodney Henry along the way? One hand washes the other and all that. That doesn't make it the crime of the century."

"I suppose not," McBain said, cracking a smile. "Stop using logic on me."

The blonde leaned forward on her folded hands. "When you are this tired, you're easy pickings," she said. "Have another drink so I can take advantage of you."

The investigator pushed his chair back from the table. "For once, I think I'm going to pass and have a light night. Between the last couple of nights drinking, the jet lag, and your appetites, I think I'll be out like a light in thirty minutes anyway, so you can take advantage of me all you want. Let's call it a night. It's getting a little late anyway, and we have to get up early and drive to Pretoria for our last leg."

McBain paid the tab, and they were on their way out the door when Gina saw a couple of important clients at the bar.

"I'll be up in a few minutes," she said. "So feel free to collapse. And do go straight across the street to the hotel. No wandering around for a smoke and a walk to think. It's dark now and might be getting a little dangerous, even in this neighborhood."

McBain kissed her and left the restaurant. He scanned the street and buildings in the area, then crossed the street at the traffic light and strolled the hundred yards to their hotel. He didn't light up until he was just outside the entrance and within sight of the hotel valet. He thought about Shawn and Henry and the things Dee Dee had always told them about financial journalism. Them. His partner. He looked at his watch, tossed his cigarette on the asphalt, and rushed to get upstairs. He would make his call to Boston short and just fill her in on the highlights of the day's meetings.

The tenth floor of the hotel was quiet though it was not that late. So even as he inserted the key card into his lock, his senses told him something was wrong. The lights were on in the room, and he could hear rustling in the bedroom through the open doorway from the main suite. McBain's sudden rush of fear and anger flushed the weariness out of his system, but as he focused on the sounds from the bedroom, he was not alert enough to notice the young black man in the corner to his right, bent down next to the writing desk, trying to open McBain's briefcase. The man stood and shouted something, and the investigator spun to his right.

"Who the hell are you?" McBain yelled. "And what the fuck are you doing in my room?"

The man shouted again and threw the briefcase at McBain's face. He grabbed it just as the other thin young man came rushing at him. He was not large, but he had a head of steam heading for the door and caught McBain off balance with a shove. The first man drove into McBain's side as he followed his accomplice out, knocking him over the sofa and into the glass coffee table.

"Shit!"

McBain cursed again and again as he disentangled himself from the furniture and wobbled to his feet, kicking away the sofa. He wiped his forehead where he had hit the table, and his hand came away bloody.

"Goddammit."

He ran to the door and scanned the hallway, but they were gone. McBain put his hand to his head and felt more blood. He went into the bathroom to check the damage and quickly grabbed a washcloth and put it over the cut, then dialed the front desk. After a few rings, the desk clerk answered.

"This is Mr. McBain in ten oh four. I just walked into two men trying to rob my room. If you see them running through the lobby, grab them. One of them had a red soccer-type shirt on and jeans."

"Yessir, I'll tell security now. I haven't seen anyone dressed like that this evening yet. I'll send someone right up."

He hung up just as Gina came in through the open door. "Hey, I thought I told you to keep—"

"Check the bedroom, Gina," McBain said. "Two guys were just in here, and I didn't see if they had anything in their hands when they left. One guy was trying to get into my briefcase."

"McBain, your head. You're bleeding."

"Yeah, I got sucker punched and hit the table."

Gina examined his head, determined the cut was not deep, and cleaned it up in the bathroom with a small first aid kit.

When hotel security arrived, McBain and Gina went through their things and determined that nothing was missing. The bedroom was a pile of tossed clothing and bedding from the closets and drawers, but, being a local, Gina had locked everything of importance in the hotel safe. McBain had not left anything of value in the room except his briefcase with his laptop, a rookie mistake, but at least he had left the case locked. If the thieves had just taken it or he had come back to the room a few minutes later, he would have been screwed.

Gina berated the security man for a few minutes in Zulu, after which he looked apologetic and shaken. McBain found the minibar and downed a mini–Ketel One as he sat on the sofa with his adrenaline returning to normal. When the hotel man left, Gina came and sat next to him, sipping a vodka as well.

"He said that this is the third break-in this month. Says we got away luckier than the last couple. I told him I expect better from a hotel that calls itself luxury. How does your head feel now?"

He ground some ice in his teeth. "Bad, but not as much as my pride. I'm pissed and offended. I've never been robbed before or walked in on someone trying to rob me. It was pretty unnerving. I guess I'm lucky they weren't armed."

Gina pushed his hair back. The bandage seemed to have worked.

"Yes," she said. "Though they usually aren't since they count on guests not being in their room most of the time. But you never know. They probably took one look at the size of you and decided to bolt. I guess it looks like it was a good idea to pass on the extra drinks for a change. Sorry I wasn't right behind you with my mace. What an end to the day."

He sighed and finished his drink. "I should probably phone Boston before I call an end to this day."

"Oh, come on," Gina said. "If you get started on what just happened with her, you'll be up for another hour. What happened to an early night? Why don't you fill her in tomorrow from Pretoria? You'll have more information by then anyway."

McBain thought about it. He normally reported in at this point in the day, but Gina was right. Boston would keep him on the phone getting all the details of the incident. He nodded and looked at his shirt and blazer grazed with streaks of his blood.

"You're right. I'll give her a call tomorrow. Right now, I want to get out of these clothes and try to sleep."

She stood up and triple-locked the front door with the security locks, then strolled to the bedroom doorway and unbuttoned her blouse.

"So," she said. "How's that adrenaline level feeling now?"

He looked at Gina sideways and started to smile again.

SIXTEEN

They left Johannesburg in the morning after breakfast, strong coffee, and aspirin. Gina rented a Mercedes SUV, drove up the M1 to the Ben Schoeman Highway, and followed it northeast to Pretoria. The sky was a cloudless blue, and the sun burned hot in October, the beginning of summer in Africa. McBain had never made this trip before, and he was fascinated at the change from the city. On some stretches of the highway, suburban communities and strip malls dotted the landscape. But the more distance they put between themselves and Johannesburg, the more empty the countryside appeared, with the road intermittently broken by overpasses or turnoffs that led to distant hills sprinkled with farms at the end of dirt roads on the horizon.

Gina left the radio off and described parts of the country as they sped north. McBain scanned the verdant hills and stands of trees that stood out in stark green contrast to what he had viewed from the air between Cape Town and Johannesburg. In places, the rail line out of the city paralleled the highway, and the trains and traffic heading for the capital gave the area a European feel. The empty spaces left McBain thinking about the American Midwest, except that the greens seemed brighter somehow, nourished by the winter rains. McBain found it quite beautiful in places and recalled why he had enjoyed coming to South Africa. The beaches and the game parks, the vast open-air spaces and wildlife. The sense of hope for the future that Gina had spoken of in passing the day before. He wanted to believe that this countryside was in the same place that parts of America had been a hundred years ago. There was that raw beauty that he had seen again approaching Cape Town three days before, a natural and unspoiled landscape that held off the encroaching advance of men even as it tempted dreamers with a sense of possibility, the false promise of preserving a long-gone past.

"We should be in Pretoria in about twenty minutes more," Gina said. "We have appointments with the Ministry of Mineral Resources, the Ministry of Finance, and the Ministry of Trade and Industry, just as you requested. Though I'm not sure what you expect to find out from them that you haven't learned from the others."

"Maybe nothing," McBain said. "But it's worth a shot. If Henry has allies anywhere, I'm beginning to suspect they may be in the government. From what you and the others have explained to me, they are the gatekeepers whose palms you have to grease to get high-level approvals. We can just probe a little and see if anything emerges. Assuming we finish up by three o'clock, we'll be able to connect with the offices of Coutinho and Company here last. I've called their office and reserved an hour with our client's main contact. They should be able to give us the latest on developments up in Angola and the progress on final due diligence at the mine and tell me if they have any doubts about the operation or deal. Then we can get back to Johannesburg in time for cocktail hour and dinner."

Gina glanced at him with admonition.

"Just remember," she said, "what I told you. These are senior government people, not investment bankers in New York. They have a heightened sense of importance about their position and won't understand or take lightly your usual banter and methods. You better phrase things carefully and not insult anyone. They can take offense easily, so be sensitive to how you approach some of your questions."

McBain focused on the names of the ministers in his notebook. "Got it."

"A couple of them are also valuable contacts for me, and I don't want the relationships damaged."

"Understood."

"Robert Shawn was one thing, and you had your fun, but please be cautious in Pretoria. *Capiche?*"

McBain's eyes widened, and he looked up at Gina with a start. "Don't worry. I understand. I'll behave. Just please don't use that expression again."

After a sharp look from Gina, McBain opted to leave his safari hat in the car. She introduced him to the ministers of the first two agencies with a brief comment on the reason for their visit. The men they met at the Ministries of Finance and then Mineral Resources were gracious but not particularly friendly. They were dignified and emanated an air of gravity laced with impatience. They answered McBain's questions deliberately but with a measured reluctance that indicated they were surprised there was anything left to discuss about AFR or the project in Angola.

McBain hoped for some kind of speed bump from the Minister of Finance, a tall, middle-aged man of Indian descent who was well spoken but took his time answering questions. He confirmed the financial and regulatory information McBain reviewed and assured the investigator that AFR's finances and local acquisitions had been thoroughly vetted and audited by proper legal and accounting firms. The company showed no sign of stress or overleverage and was growing at a healthy pace. McBain probed gingerly around his chief area of interest—disgruntled investors and business partners. In South Africa at least, it seemed Henry's financial house was in order and there had been no complaints. As the bankers had suggested, if anything, local investors and small business owners who had sold to him were quite satisfied and overcompensated.

The Minister of Mineral Resources discussed the history of Henry and the growth of Africa's Future Resources since they had first arrived in South Africa. He noted that new entrants were welcome in the country as a counterweight to the traditional mining giants with their legacy from the apartheid days. As a foreigner, Henry had been respectful of the needs of the communities and peoples of the provinces where his businesses were located. He had been scrupulous in his dealings with the government about both regulations and growing the company with an environmentally and socially aware approach and had shown great patience with the approval process, surprising for an American banker. The minister expounded at length on his hope that Henry would build on his success in Angola by prospecting soon in South Africa, where there had historically been significant finds of rare earth deposits. McBain thanked him for his time.

The detective kept tapping his notebook against his side as they left the second meeting. He was coming to the end of his African investigation with nothing to show for it, nothing to indicate anything suspicious about the Angolan venture other than the likely and entirely common expectation for some back-door payoffs to government officials. But as Hans de Witte had explained to him, any such arrangements were likely to be difficult to prove, and time was not an ally. And, as Boston would retort, big deal. As long as it didn't affect Harold Rogers's payday there was no reason for people to care.

McBain looked at his watch. "We still on time?"

Gina lit two cigarettes as they walked around the corner to their last meeting on Meintjies Street and handed him one. "Yes, the entrance is just here. Right on time by my mark. Minister Mbomani will be expecting us in a few minutes. We'll probably have to wait outside his office for the cust omary heel clicking that he puts visitors through, but it seems like you're running out of new questions anyway, so we should be able to keep it short and make up the time to get to your consultants by three."

McBain nodded. "What do you know about Mbomani? Is he a regular contact?"

Gina shook her head. "No, I've only met him once. I know he's old-school ruling party, with connections going back to the old days before Mandela got out. He's from one of the townships near Johannesburg. He's come a long way for a former revolutionary. The Ministry of Trade and Industry has a lot to say about business in the entire region, so he should be up to speed on your deal."

They were greeted formally by the minister's private secretary but, in fact, waited only a few minutes before being shown into the office. The colonial-style room expanded into a colonial-size office toward the far end, where an aging but substantial official rose from behind a massive desk. Minister Mbomani greeted the visitors with a warm smile and open arms. Surveying his plus-size blue suit, graying hair, and round face, McBain had a hard time envisioning the man as a scrawny little freedom fighter in the bush. He was a pleasant change from the severe officials at the other two agencies.

After they were seated, a pretty young woman arrived with tea for the three of them. Mbomani waved her away with a hand and looked at the business card McBain had given him.

"McBain and Partners, Financial Consultants. Boston, Massachusetts, USA. You are a long way from home." He smiled at the investigator. "So, you mentioned you have some questions about Africa's Future Resources, Mr. McBain. What can I tell you?"

McBain sipped his tea and thought about what else he might possibly ask this man that he had not discussed with the others. "Just your views on a couple of questions. I represent a party to the deal that Mr. Henry and AFR are about to close, and I'm trying to finish up a few final questions before I go home. Ms. Ferrari tells me that you are an important man to know in the business world down here in South Africa, and well informed. I wanted to get your views on the buying company, AFR, so I can put my client's mind at rest."

Minister Mbomani listened with his hands resting on his lap, nodding as the detective spoke. "Yes, I am well informed, Mr. McBain. Very well informed, indeed."

He was quiet for about half a minute.

McBain said, "And your views—?"

"My view is that this merger is a wonderful opportunity for AFR to grow their business and begin to explore new territory for resource development in southern Africa. I have reviewed and approved this cross-border trans-action because many people will benefit from the projects that AFR will pursue. People here in South Africa, and in Angola, and in the DRC and Zambia. There will be new jobs and new businesses. And I think your client will benefit from an association with Mr. Henry and AFR. I think he will benefit in many ways. In fact, the only people I can think of who may not be in favor of this project or the acquisition of your client's company by AFR are Mr. Henry's competitors. He has enemies here, you know. And do they not say that one can take the measure of a man by the enemies he makes?"

"I hadn't heard that one," McBain said. "But I suppose it can be true."

All the while Mbomani spoke, he never stopped smiling. In fact, he seemed to enjoy talking about the subject. McBain glanced at Gina, who sat there holding her cup, poker faced and listening intently. She did not look comfortable.

"It is true," the minister said. "I have been watching people sabotage their competitors here for twenty years and more, sometimes to protect their monopoly position and sometimes just out of spite. They try to stop change, stop the future. And they can be very clever at finding ways to undermine progress. They may spread lies to keep a deal from happening. Sometimes they just want to see someone fail."

McBain nodded. "I've seen that in the States too."

Mbomani sipped his tea and pointed to a picture on his wall. The picture had been taken in the wilderness with a backdrop of a small village of huts with thatched roofs and showed a group of young men standing in the dirt in mismatched clothing, jeans, knee-length shorts and green or khaki shirts, some holding machetes or guns or torches.

"In the old days, when I was in the bush, we would reward our enemies with a necklace."

McBain chuckled. These old-timers had some strange warrior customs. "That was very generous of you, sir. Where I come from, we just try to reward them with unemployment."

He glanced at Gina to laugh along with her. Gina was not laughing or smiling. She was slowly stirring her tea with a spoon. Her face was a mask as she stared straight ahead at the minister.

The minister sighed. "Sometimes I miss the old days. Things were so much simpler. Solutions to problems were easy." He shrugged and looked at McBain. "Now we have the law and the courts and the papers that dispense justice slowly, if ever. Justice was quicker then." Mbomani leaned his bulk forward onto the deck, and his smile melted away as he took the investigator's gaze. "At any rate, back to your questions, Mr. McBain. I hope that you are truly looking out for your client and trying to help us all with progress. Are you, Mr. McBain? Or are you one of those who just like to see others fail, who want to see AFR fail?"

The windows rattled faintly as a tractor trailer passed the building. McBain placed his cup on the side table at his elbow and cleared his throat. "Minister, I assure you that I'm only here to look after the best interests of my client and make sure he gets a fair shake from this transaction. And, to reassure you, he is looking forward to—"

"That is a good thing," Mbomani said. "because I was beginning to wonder about the purpose of your visit. As I said, I am very well informed. And from some of the questions that I am told you have been asking for three days, some people are beginning to talk."

McBain crossed his legs and took a breath. "What do these people say?"

The minister's lip stuck out, and he took a bit of a biscuit while he stared at McBain. "They say that you are interested in finding out bad things about Mr. Henry and AFR. They say you are asking about illegal activities and bad deals in the past. To me, that sounds like someone who does not want this deal to succeed. It sounds like someone who is looking for a reason to end the deal or to make trouble. Is that what you want?"

McBain fought his most basic instinct and shook his head. Finally, he said, "I think some people may have misinterpreted their discussions with me, Minister. Where I come from, we do the most thorough investigation we can to make sure our client's deal gets done, and he or she benefits. It's called due diligence."

Mbomani toyed with another biscuit, pulling it apart piece by piece with his large fingers. "I see."

"In this case I'm happy to say that my three days of discussions will go some way toward reassuring my client that this is, as you say, a great deal, and I've found no reason for him to have second thoughts."

Mbomani leaned back again and steepled his hands. At last, he pushed himself up from his chair. "That is good to hear, Mr. McBain. We need more friends here in South Africa, not enemies. I hope our conversation has been helpful for your client. And you. You will be leaving South Africa after today, yes?"

McBain understood that the meeting was over. He stood and buttoned his jacket, straightening his tie. "Yes, Minister. I think I've learned everything I can here. My plan is to leave South Africa as soon as possible." He nodded. "Thank you for your time."

Gina led the way out two steps ahead of him and had a cigarette lit before they were out the front door. McBain waited until they were on the sidewalk. She was tense as she turned to him, her blue eyes on fire.

"Well, that didn't go quite as I expected," McBain said.

"Shit." Gina almost yelled it. She squinted at the sun and heat and put her sunglasses on.

"What's the matter?' he said. "I thought I behaved OK. The guy didn't even let me ask questions. You seem antsy."

She shook her head. "Mbomani must really be tied in. I didn't realize he had that kind of a network. Some of the people you've been talking to must have started connecting. I thought maybe we would have had more time to finish up without people sharing, but this deal must be really hot."

McBain glanced up at the building and thought for a minute. Mbomani could have talked to anyone. Gina said the business world was small here. It looked like the government world was as well. Henry had a lot of friends down here, and after three days, it had become obvious nobody was interested in rocking the boat. Even the finance and investment people who had been friendly and informative had looked at him oddly when he started asking the hard questions about Henry's background and potential violations or negative news.

"Yeah, it's hot, all right," he said. "I wonder who he heard from. I thought I was behaving myself pretty well here. That's what I get for playing nice. It's pretty clear Henry's got him in his pocket too. Who knows who else?"

Gina pulled him into the shade and took off her sunglasses so that he could see her eyes. They were deadly serious. "McBain, the necklace he was talking about wasn't a piece of jewelry. It's a ritual from the bad days. When people like him wanted to punish enemies, especially people they thought were informers to the government, they captured and beat them. Then they stood them up and dropped automobile tires around them until they were up to their neck, and the prisoner couldn't move. Then the tires were soaked in gasoline and set on fire."

"Jesus, you're not—"

"They would dance around the victim while he screamed, the black smoke of the burning tires melting into the body. They called it a necklace." She crushed her cigarette under her shoe. "All that talk about the old days? Whether he really thinks you're looking to blow up Henry's deal or not, Mbomani was sending you a message. Don't."

The laugh died in his throat as he watched Gina's face. "Come on, Gina. That stuff was all in the past. The guy is not some revolutionary anymore. He's a government minister."

Her smirk dripped with cynicism again. "And you think that makes him *less* dangerous?"

McBain finished his cigarette and looked around them, then up and down the street. "Let's get to the car and find where Coutinho's office is," he said. "Sounds like I should finish up and get back to Johannesburg to the hotel." The hotel. "And now I'm beginning to have second thoughts about our break-in last night. Looks like I should plan on getting out of South Africa soon."

"Yes," Gina said and smirked. "That occurred to me as well. Let's go."

• • •

THEY ENTERED THE offices of Coutinho and Company and found a Mr. Suarez awaiting them. He was a mining engineer by trade and introduced himself as the general manager of the Brazilian company's African operations. He was from Brazil but spoke English well. McBain greeted him politely but hoped that the company's role as an independent party to the Angola excavation would help avoid any tension in this meeting at least. Not that the investigator expected to learn anything about Henry from Mr. Suarez or his people. They had no part in AFR's financial operations and had been hired to review the mineral potential of the site in Angola.

The general manager provided McBain with copies of several reports on the Moxico project's history and early assessments to take back with him. McBain didn't expect to understand anything in the reports, but he would forward them to Boston to have HR Tech translate the results. He paged through them, glancing at rows of data with chemical symbols and percentages. When the manager was finished explaining the basic findings of the report, McBain smiled and nodded. He looked around the office, then paged through his notebook.

Suarez looked back and forth between McBain and Gina. "Is there anything more specific I can tell you about the project?"

Gina glanced over at McBain.

"I suppose not," McBain said. He looked up from his notes. "Sounds very promising from everything I'm told."

Suarez nodded. "Yes, very promising. We are just awaiting the final results from our leading geologist at the site in Moxico to send back to the various parties."

"Oh yeah," McBain said. He looked at his notes again. "Weren't you supposed to receive it already? What seems to be the holdup?"

The manager shifted in his seat and looked embarrassed. "I'm afraid there's been a little delay. Our office in Luanda has not heard back from our senior geologist at the Moxico site for over a month. They tried to contact him. Now it seems that there have been—ah, how do I say this?—some reports from the camp about potential irregularities on the part of our man."

"Irregularities?" McBain asked.

"Actually, some accusations of unprofessional behavior on his part." Suarez shrugged. "I'm afraid I don't have more detail. The office there is reluctant to provide us with more information until there is some kind of proof. Mr. Neto is one of our most promising young mineralogists. He is a local from Angola and is both smart and inquisitive. It is hard for me to imagine him being unprofessional. He always struck me as somewhat shy, even religious. But given the deadline and pressure for our report by the parties to your merger deal, I am sending a man up to Luanda tomorrow to get some answers from the office there."

McBain smiled. "Well, I understand the site is a long way from civilization and deep into Angola. Lots of people find themselves straying or going crazy after a time isolated in the jungle. Ever read Joseph Conrad?"

"I am afraid I have not."

Gina tapped his elbow. "McBain, we should probably finish up and let Mr. Suarez return to his work so he can finish up for the day."

McBain nodded. He was out of time. "Well, never mind. Have you been to the project site yourself, Mr. Suarez? What did you think?"

The manager nodded with enthusiasm. "Oh yes. Many times. I was there from the early days with Mr. Henry and his team from AFR that did the initial exploration."

"Henry has been to the site?" McBain asked. He could feel his blood rising.

"Certainly. Almost routinely in the first stages. I have been there with him myself a few times, most recently this past August. As I said in the report, the results look promising for significant finds of neodymium, dysprosium, lanthanum, cobalt, and a variety of other important minerals, even rhodium. If early testing is confirmed, as I am sure it will be at this point, we could be looking at veins of ore that stretch across eastern Angola into the DRC and Zambia. This is completely unexplored territory, but given the history of rare earths in those countries and in South Africa, the find could be exceptionally large."

McBain tapped his notebook with his pen and nodded. "Yes, so everyone keeps telling me." His throat was tight, and his head was beginning to throb again. He thought about the break in at the hotel and about Mbomani's veiled threat. He had talked to many people in South Africa with different views and found out nothing of consequence. Boston was right. Harold Rogers stood to become a very rich man. And everything he had learned in the last few days about Rodney Henry and his influence just made him dislike the man all the more.

Gina stood up to go.

"You say you have a man going up to Angola tomorrow?" McBain asked Suarez.

"Yes, tomorrow around noon, leaving from Johannesburg."

McBain took a deep breath and forced himself to do it. Gina was not going to be happy. Nor was Boston.

"I'd like to go to Luanda to meet with your team there," McBain said. Gina raised her eyebrows at him but said nothing. "Can you set me up with

THE STUFF THAT DREAMS ARE MADE OF | 189

some people? Maybe your man Neto will have surfaced by the time I get there. I'd sure like to talk to him."

"Well, I suppose so," Mr. Suarez said. "I'll make the call and tell them you're coming. It will take some doing on short notice, but we will talk to some people here in Pretoria and help you get your visa expedited as well. I know time is an issue on this deal. Let me know if we can do anything else for you."

Once they were out in front of the building, Gina stopped.

"Luanda, eh? That's a bit farther than I expected you to want to go. What's this all about? I thought you said you were done."

McBain felt stupid. He didn't know why he had said it; it had just come out. He didn't have any new questions to ask or leads to follow. He just had to go as far as Luanda. Maybe the lost guy would turn up, and he could put his vague concerns to rest for Rogers's sake.

"I came this far," he said. "I figure I might as well talk to the people in Luanda who are working for Rogers. Maybe a few government people there, too, since Angola is the key country on this deal. Hey, since some people seem so eager to see me leave the country, I might as well oblige them. You know anybody there you can put me in touch with? It should only be a couple days, and I can get back here to spend some more time with you before I fly home. Once Coutinho's final report gets sent, the signing will just be a formality, so there's no rush."

Gina shook her head. "What am I going to do with you? You're such a diplomatic disaster on your own even when you're not trying to offend people. No, I don't think you can be trusted to go there by yourself."

She really was beautiful, her skin glowing bronze in the afternoon sun. He kissed her. "You don't have to do this, Gina. You can just give me the name of a good hotel and a couple phone numbers."

She grabbed him by his jacket. "Fat chance, Yank. You've already proved you can be a loose cannon here in South Africa. Two days in Angola alone, and you'd ignite another regional war. The only way to make sure you get back here in one piece is for me to go with you. I'll take you to Luanda and try to help keep you from making too many more enemies, to use Mbomani's words. In your case, that seems to be a full-time job for any girl."

SEVENTEEN

The deal teams were spending the afternoon reviewing the document checklists yet again to confirm that all materials critical to the approval of the Moxico project and merger agreement were signed, sealed, and delivered by the right people, the residual of Boston's discovery two days before. After the first half hour, Boston stopped making any effort to ask a question or venture an opinion. Other than the occasional voice that asked for a file or uttered a one-word response to an issue, the conference room remained so silent that she longed for those periods when the hum of industrial air conditioning lent background to the session.

It wasn't just the bankers from Whitney, Mitchell. It was clear that everyone on the AFR team resented her bitterly. Even the HR Tech group seemed to imply from their attitudes that she had spoiled what had been a party mood of mutual bonhomie.

Well, she thought, the hell with them. They could take their attitude and shove it, then kiss her ass. She was good at what she did, and she had been right. Even Henry had known that. If it cost Mortimer his job, so what? He wasn't going to starve. That was his own fault, not hers. She wasn't looking for friends on this job. She had protected her client and made it more likely the deal would not fail. Screw them. Like McBain had said once about this business: You want a friend, get a dog.

Just after seven, the AFR team left, making clear the session was over, no matter how many questions she still had. The HR Tech people looked at each other and shrugged. Nodding to Boston, they left as well. She sat at the conference table for two more hours, doing calculations on her spread-sheets and checking off the last of the to-do list for the day until a woman knocked on the glass door. She recognized the administrator for the floor.

"We're closing up the rooms for cleaning, Ms. O'Daniel. If you could finish up, we'd appreciate it."

Boston nodded and thanked her. She closed down her laptop and began packing up her briefcase but was fixated on some deal notes when she heard the knock again.

"I'm sorry. I'm leaving now." She gathered her folders into her arms and dumped the last of them into her briefcase, then looked up. "I—"

"Good evening, Ms. O'Daniel." Rodney Henry was standing just inside the door, white shirtsleeves rolled up on his forearms.

"Oh, good evening, Mr. Henry. I didn't realize anyone else was still here."

A corner of his mouth went up. "Did you think you were the only one with a midnight-oil ethic on this deal?"

Boston put her glasses on and closed her briefcase after several tries. She stood up and straightened her blazer. "No, no, of course not. I didn't mean that. It's just that the other team members left. I thought perhaps everyone else had gone on to dinner somewhere."

He folded his arms over his Hermes tie. "I would think a team dinner would involve the whole team."

Her eyes cast about the table, making sure she had all her things. She took a second to compose herself before she replied. "Maybe your people and their bankers needed to get together and discuss some proprietary issues without the other side around."

"Perhaps I should speak to my management team to emphasize what I meant about us all working together to close this merger without any fur-ther issue. It would be unfortunate if anyone let personal feelings create an impediment to finalizing the last details as efficiently as possible. I thought I had made that clear the other day. To everyone."

"I'm sure that's not necessary," she said. "Everyone is getting anxious as we get closer. Things are a little tense. No one wants to make any mistakes."

"Someone already did," Henry said. "But thanks to you, we've taken care of that problem. If I have to speak to the new Whitney team leader about professionalism, I will."

"I don't need anyone to defend me." Her voice was more defiant than she intended.

Henry raised an eyebrow, then shook his head once. "I didn't defend you the other day. I supported you. I defended the project, my company, and my deal. There's a big difference. You did your job, and so did I. So what's the problem?"

Boston gripped her briefcase handle a little tighter and prepared to leave. That sense of uncertainty gnawed at her again, and she struggled to understand the boundaries of corporate etiquette.

"They all hate me for getting Todd Mortimer fired."

Henry stared at her with interest, and she feared for a few moments that she was being too bold.

"Whitney, Mitchell is a competent firm," he said, "but Mortimer was stupid, and he let his arrogance get in the way of the work. All he cared about was the deal closing, not the long-term impacts of my project. He was focused on getting headlines and getting paid when he should have had his eyes on the important details to the very end, no matter how obscure or boring. I fired him to give the rest of them that message." He looked her in the eye again. "You got caught in the fallout from that, but so what? I'm guessing you're tough enough to take it and still do your job."

Boston raised her head and felt a rush of blood to her face. "I am."

She could tell from his steady gaze and silence that he was judging her. But it was not judgment in the same manner as the others. He was evaluating her, and it was more unnerving than the simple rejection of the bankers and lawyers. After a few more moments, she picked up her briefcase and handbag from the table and moved to get by him to leave.

"I should get home. Thank you for your support."

Henry looked at her hands holding her briefcase and bag. "Those are some pretty nasty cuts and bruises on your hands. They look fresh. I don't recall your having those the other day."

She had forgotten to put on her gloves and glanced down at her battered fingers and knuckles while she thought fast. "Oh. Nothing serious. Just an accident working around the apartment. I'm fixing a problem with a wall. They're fine."

As she passed close by him, his eyes narrowed and focused on hers. "You've got a lot of anger in you, Ms. O'Daniel."

Boston stopped in her tracks, shocked by Henry's breach of an unspoken professional barrier. Yet, in a way, he was renewing the conversation they had started that night at the Mandarin.

"That's fine in some ways," Henry said. "Anger can be a useful thing and a powerful driving force in life, if managed properly. You have the potential to be tremendously successful at anything you do. Don't let your anger get in the way of that. Find a way to make it work for you."

Her eyes engaged his. "I'm just sick of the attitude I get from people like them."

"Why should you care?" Henry asked. "You're better than they are. Don't you know that?"

Boston was taken aback, but for just a moment. She felt her face heat up.

"Yes, I know it," she said. "And it still doesn't make a bit of difference. They can be as incompetent and make as many mistakes as they want. But they'll always have the secret handshake that gets them the job and keeps them where they are, regardless. Guys like Mortimer will land on their feet. People like me have to prove ourselves again and again, always have to be more than perfect. And at the end of the interview, it will always be thanks, but the job's already been assigned; the position is already filled. Filled by someone who had the right credentials and connections from Mom and Dad's club. By the Mortimers of the world, no matter how many mistakes they make."

Henry's face displayed indifference as he shrugged. "You're right—most of the time." Then a calm confidence came over his expression. "But there are exceptions for people who have the brains, guts, and determination not to be beaten by that game. Not to be intimidated or ever quit. And I'm living proof. Maybe you are too."

He strolled over to the conference table and leaned against it.

"They're like dumb animals running on instinct or breeding," Henry said. "They're drones. They care more about the appearances of being important and smart, the trappings of the job, like town cars, homes, and meals on expense accounts. That's where you have an edge. You care about the work, the quality of what you do and give to people who hire you. You proved that when you took a risk and challenged Mortimer at the meeting. It would have been the easiest thing in the world for you to let that go and assume somebody else had it covered. I'm guessing something inside you just couldn't let it go. That threatens them. So they look for weakness and try to ostracize you from the tribe. Their natural weapon is credentials, and they can sense when someone is vulnerable on that front. Degrees from the right schools. Name dropping their connections. Important companies they've worked for or exclusive vacation spots. Shallow accomplishments that are mere ticket punching from the time they were children.

"That's why they're afraid of me. Not just because I'm rich. Most of them have been around money all their lives. They know where I come from and that they mean nothing to me. It's not armor, and it's not contempt. I simply don't care about the things they value, and that frightens and confuses them because they're faced with truth and doubt for the first time in their lives. I focus on my own success and my results. I became who I am because my clients saw what I did for them, with a little help from my own sense of self-promotion. Someday, if you learn to look at them that way, you'll have the same attitude and the same freedom from doubt and from caring.

"The most rewarding thing at the end of the day is the feeling that you have done something of worth. For all the rottenness and monotony of this business, once in a while you can say that you've actually created something no one else could, something that can grow and add value to many lives. That's what Harold Rogers has done, and that's what I've done. Together, I think we can make a huge difference. I don't pretend I don't want to make a lot of money on this deal. But at some point, the money means less than the achievement of launching something that will grow. And that means even more in Africa than it does here."

She bit her lip and thought of McBain's parting words about getting a passport. For a moment, a picture of him and Gina Ferrari flashed into her mind. "Uh, I'm sure. But I wouldn't know first hand. I've never been."

He nodded.

"Then that's something to look forward to, isn't it?"

"It's another world, literally," Henry said. "In many ways, Africa is what I said at the reception that night—the future."

He looked at his watch and stood to go.

"Well, I can do at least one thing to ensure my whole team gets together to relax for a few moments in harmony. I'm throwing a party out on my yacht this weekend for everyone—AFR, HR Tech, the bankers and lawyers. It's docked at Nantucket. Make sure you and your partner are there."

Nantucket. Her spirits rose, and she lit up for a moment. Then her face fell, and she pursed her lips. She thought about it. She couldn't believe she was saying this.

"Ah, that's very generous of you, but I can't."

"Why not?" From the sound of his voice she could tell he was a man who was not accustomed to hearing the word no, especially from minions her age.

"I . . . uh . . . I'm sorry, but I have other plans. I'm sorry, but I really can't cancel on short notice." Boston felt both uneasy and disappointed, but she just couldn't back out.

After half a minute, he nodded. "I see. I suppose I can understand. I've had a busy social calendar myself from time to time."

Suddenly, a light bulb went off in her head, and she smiled. "Oh no. It's not a date," she said. "It's just that the Head of the Charles is this weekend. I go every year. Otherwise, I would love—"

"The Head of the Charles. What's that?" Henry asked.

Boston's eyes widened, and she forgot herself again. "You've never heard of the Head of the Charles?"

Henry shook his head. "I'm afraid not. Is it important?"

Boston opened her arms in amazement, her briefcase in one hand and her handbag in another.

"The Head of the Charles is only the most famous and important rowing regatta in the world. I go every year with some of the other girls from Boston College to root for the BC boats. I rowed when I was there, and we never miss it. I'm surprised you've never heard of it, you a sailing man and all."

"I'm not a sailing man," he said. "I just own a yacht. I grew up in the mountains and served in the army. So I don't know anything about sailing. Or rowing."

Boston looked at the door and blushed. "I just assumed. I apologize. And thank you for the invitation. I appreciate it, and I really love Nantucket, but I couldn't possibly desert the girls."

"But I'd be interested in learning," he said.

"Learning?"

"About rowing. About this Head of the Charles race."

"Of course," she said. "I'd be happy to describe—"

"Perhaps I could accompany you to the race," Henry said.

Boston thought perhaps she had misheard him. "The race? This weekend?"

"Yes, if it wouldn't be too much of an intrusion on your time with your friends. I'd like to observe the race in person as it happens with an expert. You can explain it to me that way. That's how I learn best."

She wasn't easily flustered, but this was the last thing she'd expected. "Um, certainly, but . . . I thought you just said you were having a party for the teams on your yacht . . . and . . ."

Henry had that confident look on his face again. "Oh, the party will go on, with or without me. As I said before, I do what I want. And now what I want is to learn something new." He looked at her with softer eyes. "If you're willing, that is."

There was only one thing to say. "All right." Unable to think of any way out of it, her thoughts and emotions colliding, Boston turned to go and almost walked into the wall.

Before she could recover and leave, Henry walked over. "I can have my driver pick you up and drop us wherever you like to meet your friends and watch the races. What time on Saturday morning?"

She straightened her glasses and glanced at her watch to stall for time to think. She didn't want the car picking her up at her apartment. "I have a busy morning since I'm going to be at the regatta all day. How about I just meet you in the lobby of your hotel at nine and we go over from there?"

He extended his hand again as he had at the reception. She took it again, just as firmly, bruises and all.

"I look forward to it," he said. "Good night, Ms. O'Daniel."

"Good night, Mr. Henry."

Boston rode down in the elevator, dazed from what had just happened, and walked across the building lobby with a slow and steady bearing, puzzled yet confident, the anger toward the others dissipated. This was a strange turn of events. She thought back to that first impression of Henry. Yes, a very serious predator indeed.

EIGHTEEN

For the past hundred years, there has been nothing in the world like oil money. Not finance, not gold, not technology, and not the lottery. A country awash in money from limitless oil and gas resources is high on a head-spinning, high-rolling jones that can last as long as the black gold keeps pumping out of the ground at the right price—a high that feels like it will last forever, until the day it doesn't.

Gina leaned back in the limo and smiled. "No one in the civilized world has any idea where on earth Luanda is. And it's the most expensive place to live on the planet—that's what oil money does."

McBain learned all this and more from Gina as they took a Mercedes from Quatro de Fevereiro Airport to their hotel. The EPIC SANA Hotel was one of the best in the city and one of the few five-star hotels in all of Africa. Luanda was a densely packed urban landscape perched on the western coast of Africa at the edge of the Atlantic Ocean, the seat of government and energy wealth in the country, opening its arms as the car inched along. Coming into view, the city's skyline rose up along the Marginal, the coastal strip on the Bay of Luanda, raised up into the future by cranes that pulled it farther aloft into modern glass and steel visions, built with equipment from some of the most powerful names in global construction.

But it was the contrast that stunned him the most. Every country McBain had ever been to in the Middle East had some level of prosperity. The road into Dubai from the international airport struck the visitor with the sheer scale of the wealth, a city built on the sand from nothing. The disparity in income was well hidden from visitors.

Angola was different.

Until they came to the center of the city, the sight of the desperate poverty on the outskirts of Luanda was staggering. Even compared with the townships and ghettos in South Africa, in some areas it was repellant. The ranks of tin shacks and lean-tos fell away in disorderly patterns as far from the highway as he could see. Rivers of mud and still water meandered through the dilapidated sections of each sprawling heap of what must surely have been called homes. The windows of the car were sealed tightly, and McBain could only imagine the stench filling the air for miles. His eyes took in the horror of each . . . what? Village? And he tried to imagine the thousands of people they passed by in the limo. The boys and young men dressed in sports jerseys and ripped blue jeans or corduroys, the women in loose-fitting dresses or sleeveless blouses and dark skirts that fell to their bare feet or sandals. From the highway and behind the tinted glass, their faces were indiscernible. There were slivers of smoke rising into the air, and fires burning here and there from piles of trash or rusted metal drums, the only residual of oil wealth that McBain could see on the horizon.

Gina ignored it and fixed her eyes on her phone, as he imagined everyone did who was ingrained to the sight all over Africa. McBain was silent for most of the way. He had been to Cape Town and Johannesburg and the shanties surrounding each. He had seen African poverty, or thought he had. But this was somehow more unnerving. He had little to say until they reached the heart of the modern, growing city of Luanda.

"Oil money? What oil money? I don't understand. I know the townships in South Africa, but this . . . there's no oil money here. What . . . what are all these people doing here, Gina, living in this hell? I keep hearing from Henry and everyone else how rich Angola is. Oil, gas, forests, minerals. The country is huge. These people look more like refugees. I've never seen anything like this in an oil power."

Gina nodded and glanced past him out the window. "Good catch, McBain. In a way, they still are refugees. They call these areas the *musseques*. And they are some of the most horrible places I have ever seen. In most ways, more horrible than the rural areas, which are very poor. What do you know about Angola and history?"

He shrugged. "Not much, sorry to say, other than the recent economic story I've done some research on for this job."

She sighed and lit a cigarette, glancing at the driver for a moment. "These people are refugees, or children of refugees. From thirty years of civil war and centuries of abuse. The fighting started the minute the Portuguese pulled out in 1975, although the Angolans were fighting for independence for a decade before that. The Portos left in a hurry, almost all of them, and what they didn't take with them, they damaged or destroyed. After that, different tribal and political factions went at each other to try and grab power, and it lasted thirty years. Times being what they were with the Cold War and colonial history and all that, both sides teamed up with a major power who supplied them at various times with guns and money."

"You're quite a student of history. I don't think I ever heard you talk about it."

"It's family history, really, but it's helpful to know if you want to do business here. My father and uncle used to be in the South African army years ago. The army backed the group called UNITA and a man named Jonas Savimbi. The main enemy was the MPLA, who got money, weapons, and troops from the Soviet Union, East Germany, and Cuba. That's one of the reasons the fighting went on for so long and was so fierce. It was real warfare, with sieges, artillery, and bombing of towns. Dad didn't talk about it much, but my uncle did, and I overheard some things when they got drunk telling war stories and thought nobody was around. They say the war saw the biggest tank battle since World War Two at Cueno Carnavale in the southwest. Though they've cleaned up part of the wreckage around Luanda, you can see burned-out tanks and trucks in some places and along most highways in the parts of the country where the fighting was heaviest. Both sides laid millions of land mines throughout Angola, and there are still places where it's dangerous to go where they haven't been cleared."

"Jesus. I guess that's why we passed so many smashed and burned cars on our way in."

Gina smiled at him. "Not really. Most of those are a sign that the country has progressed to the point where you're in more danger now of dying from a traffic accident in speeding cars rather than getting shot. Although there's still some risk of that too."

McBain drank from his bottle of water as they turned down a wide boulevard lined with modern buildings and more under construction. "Some kind of progress. Looks like all the oil booty I've heard tell about isn't getting spread around that much, especially to those people we passed on the way in. I wonder if it would have been different if the Marxist side had won the war."

He was taken aback when Gina smirked at him. "They did."

"What? You mean . . .?"

She shook her head. "I've been telling you that you have a lot to learn about this place, McBain. Yes, the side the Russians backed did finally win the civil war, after Savimbi was killed in 2002 somewhere out in Moxico Province, where Henry's mine is located. But, as you can see, the peace hasn't brought much prosperity. You see, Angola is run by a very narrow minority of families who are part of the ruling clique. They have elections, but the current president doesn't have much to worry about. I've worked with some of them and met a few more. That's how we got you a visa so fast. That and the fact that throwing AFR's name around here seems to ring the right bells. By the way, you owe me five thousand US.

"Strange how in some ways time stands still here. Did you know Angola was one of the centers of the slave trade over the years? The Portuguese worked with some of the locals here and, over time, sent four million slaves across the Atlantic to Brazil and the Americas. The Portuguese were different from the Dutch and English who came to South Africa. From what I've read, they sent their absolute worst to Africa, to Angola and Mozambique, criminals or worse than criminals. At any rate, nothing really changed when slavery was outlawed. They just called it servitude or some such lie, but for the people outside of power, things didn't really change. So why should it change now? It's like the ruling class that threw out the Portos and won the war just inherited their contempt for the masses. Then they decided to keep most of the country's wealth for themselves, although the government has made an effort to promote projects that create jobs and education and get some of these refugees to move farther away from Luanda. If this guy Henry is as corrupt as you think, he'd be a natural fit to work with the government here. They're his kind of people. And the cynicism that corruption creates has trickled down into every corner of society here.

"That's how Africa is, McBain, I keep telling you. On the other hand, maybe Henry is legit and is thinking about promoting progress and capitalism here. There's an old saying around here: In Africa, only foreigners care about the poor. From what I've heard the last few days, Henry's project is just the kind of development the government here is looking for."

Gina heaved a sigh as they approached the hotel and spoke to the driver in Portuguese. Then she turned to McBain. "You know what the strange but cruel thing is?"

McBain shook his head and put out his cigarette in the ashtray.

"The price of oil and gold and diamonds goes up and down, but it never matters to any of those people in the *musseques*. Only the ruling class cares. It will probably be the same with this big strike from the mine."

The driver dropped them at the hotel a few minutes later. The EPIC SANA Hotel was a luxurious place, an expensive destination in one of the priciest cities in the world. One of McBain's great pleasures in life had always been checking into exclusive hotels. Not this time. The drive past the *musseque* stayed with him, the sight of it forced deeper by the note of inevitability and hopelessness of what Gina had said about the past and present. The contrast between the billboards, designer shops, and expensive cars, the signs of wealth here in the center of Luanda and the hotel, set against the squalor of those people living in poverty from which there was no escape infiltrated McBain's senses. For reasons he could not nail down he felt ashamed to be a part of this deal. Those people didn't seem to know about hopes or dreams of wealth to come. If Gina was right about the past, if oil money had left them like this, then what were the chances of the people dwelling in those slums ever seeing the benefit of mineral wealth?

At any rate, they would not be in Luanda long. Given the speed with which word had traveled in South Africa, McBain agreed with Gina that they should plan on gleaning whatever information they could as quickly as possible from her contacts at dinner that night, then meet with the Minister of Mineral Resources and Petroleum and the people from Coutinho and Company the next day before heading back to Cape Town. McBain would be careful to be overly friendly and radiate positive energy about AFR and the

Angola project in order to avoid suspicion when they met with the minister.

"You need to take extra care here, McBain," she said as they dressed for dinner. "Angolans, in particular officials, are not usually welcoming toward foreigners in any case."

He glanced at her in the mirror while adjusting his tie in the hallway. "You mean even more unfriendly than threatening to burn me alive in gasoline-soaked tires?"

"Pay attention. You saw at the airport that this place is different. As a rule, they don't trust foreigners, maybe because of their history, maybe because other countries have always interfered in their affairs, whatever. I'm just telling you to be prepared for a level of hostility that you didn't encounter in South Africa. Doing business here is difficult for that reason alone. So I doubt you'll find the minister responsive to any probing questions, even with your charm in impressing him with how much of a team player you are."

McBain grunted and looked at his reflection in the mirror. "Well, somehow, Henry managed to charm them into a deal and beat out the competition."

"Henry's got money and political connections. Not to mention time and patience. You don't."

McBain didn't need any reminders of all the things that Rodney Henry had that he didn't. The knowledge that the Angolan deal and HR Tech merger seemed to be the beginning of something beyond even the success the man had known so far gnawed at him every time he heard it afresh. There was nothing he could do to stop it, and for the sake of his client, he shouldn't even be thinking along those lines. It was time to make sure any loose ends were tied up and ensure there was no risk to the deal so Harold Rogers could take home the prize. Angola was the final stop.

"OK, Gina," he said. "We'll collect what intel we can from your friends, make nice with the minister, then see if our missing geologist has shown up or sent word back to Coutinho's office yet." He turned around. "How do I look—? Whoa."

Gina emerged from the bedroom suite in a sleeveless gold blouse and white silk pants, adorned with diamond earrings and pendant. McBain tried to whistle. "Maybe I should just shut up and let you do all the talking—tonight and tomorrow."

She walked over and kissed him. "I'll take that as a compliment, shall I?"

They were picked up at six o'clock by the car sent by their host for the evening, a senior vice president for Total, the French energy giant with a significant presence in Angola in the form of a number of offshore oil fields being developed to come online and begin production in the next year. The SUV navigated the long curve around the harbor and onto the Ilha do Cabo, a sweeping arm of land that curled out into the Atlantic and hosted the most expensive and fashionable bars, clubs, and restaurants in the city. McBain and Gina ascended the stairs to a terrace at L'Atlantique, one of the most sought-after dinner spots favored by the European expatriate community. As the hostess showed them to their table, McBain took in the view of the firefly skyline of Luanda to the east that glowed brighter opposite a flaming red sun setting over the ocean to the west.

When he caught up with Gina, she was air-kissing three fashionably dressed gentlemen at a round table in the finest corner of the terrace. She introduced Pierre de Botton, along with an executive from Royal Dutch Shell and another from BP. For the first thirty minutes, Gina and the three men caught up on old times while McBain asked the occasional polite question about life in Luanda and sipped his drink. He soon sensed that it seemed important not to bring up the subject of wives.

At de Botton's suggestion, they ordered prawns and spiced rice dishes as appetizers while they talked. As the waiter walked away, the Frenchman smiled at McBain. "So, Monsieur McBain, Gina tells us that you are involved with Monsieur Henry and AFR. Lucky you."

McBain grinned back and surveyed the faces of the three men. "Well, that's one way of putting it, *mes amis*. At least on a short-term basis and not for much longer. My client is getting in bed with Henry, to coin a phrase, and I'm just here doing some last-minute checks to make sure the deal goes well for all parties concerned."

Ralph Stephens, a lean, redheaded Englishman who had been in Angola the longest with Royal Dutch Shell, smirked as he glanced sideways at the other oil men. "Well, if he's getting into bed with Rodney Henry, he better make sure he sleeps on his back."

The other men laughed. Gina chuckled lightly. McBain felt the tug of a fish nibbling at a hook. But after Pretoria, he wanted to make sure he wasn't the fish. He shrugged in indifference.

"Hopefully, it will all go well. From everything I've learned so far, the people I've talked to think highly of Henry and the projects he has underway here in Africa. They seem to believe my client is getting in on the ground floor of something big. I haven't heard anything yet that makes me think any different."

A gentle tug on the line. While the three gentlemen laughed, he looked over at Gina, who smiled and sipped her champagne.

"It will no doubt be fine," Stephens said. "As long as your man takes his money and does his part. Henry's not a man I would want to get lost in the Angolan jungle with. He's a pretty tough bird."

"Have you done business with him, Ralph?" Gina said.

"Me? No, but I met him once. And those of us who have been around

Angola a few years were certainly interested and impressed at the way he made a big splash and managed to secure those mining licenses."

Pierre de Botton poured himself and Gina more Veuve Clicquot as he spoke. "Not to mention all those trips he took out to the bush when the surveys and excavations were just starting. Pretty big balls for an American investor. Rumor here has it that he might come from a mining background."

McBain drained his martini glass. "Yeah, I heard that too." Even the people who did not like or trust Henry seemed to admire him. He dabbed at his mouth with his napkin. "By the way, we'll be paying a visit to the Minister of Mineral Resources tomorrow. Given your positions, I expect you all know people there. Should I ask him about the process Henry used to obtain those mining rights, or do you gentlemen have any thoughts? You've all been here long enough to know the real story. I don't want to come across as an ignorant American."

Gina waved her hand. "Really, McBain, I'm not sure we have to get into talk about boring negotiations."

Stephens finished slicing up a prawn and raised his knife. "No, Gina," he said. "It's a pointed question and one we were all curious about for a while. When Henry first landed the deal to explore out in Moxico, everyone wondered how he had beat out the Chinese. We Europeans have a lock on the oil business here, but the rest of the big business in Angola has mostly gone to Chinese companies for some time. It was quite a trick to pull off."

McBain signaled to the waiter while he watched the Englishman.

"I think the timing was right," de Botton said. "Henry had made his reputation as a comer in the strategic and rare earth minerals business. He had lots of connections, and the Angolans knew he was buying up rights in promising places around the world. Plus, he has some friends in

Washington, and that didn't hurt. And frankly, Moxico is so remote that nothing was happening out there anyway. So he probably made a deal that promised the government all upside with no risk and little cost to them."

"That's right," said Stephens. "If it pays off, I'm sure there will be benefits for certain people here in Luanda, with enough spread around from here to the border. On that front, I believe he was quite clever in making certain commitments to put money into that part of the country and create local jobs for Angolans. That's a bit of a sore spot around here when it comes to the Chinese. Lots of loans and projects, but they mostly bring in their own labor. That's why you will see so many Chinese laborers and construction workers up and down the coast. To some extent, we are guilty of the same behavior. But at least in our case, the government sees the need for highly skilled labor. We try to hire and train local staff when we can."

McBain's drink arrived. He thanked the waiter and looked at Stephens. "If it pays off? The way I hear it, that project's a blockbuster sure thing in the end."

The three oil men chuckled as one. Pierre de Botton raised his glass and said, "You'll have to excuse us, Monsieur McBain. We are all old oil veterans."

"Yes," said Stephens. "We and our companies have done well over time, but we've learned to approach these large, long-term projects with a healthy portion of persistence sprinkled with a layer of caution, if not skepticism. Time will tell. I will say this: I'm no geologist, but that part of the continent is so rich, I think he's bound to stumble into something big out there. I mean, just look at the news—South Africa, Tanzania, Malawi. With the new technologies they are bringing to bear, the mining companies are probing for new veins everywhere. And the market is hungry for as much as they can find."

Gina coughed and signaled the headwaiter. "With that said, I'm starving. Let's order again, shall we?" Her diamonds sparkled in the candlelight as she smiled at McBain in satisfaction.

NINETEEN

"**G**ood morning, Mr. McBain, and welcome to Angola."

Alejandro Silva was a tall man and, McBain thought, looking at his goatee and sharp black eyes, quite distinguished for a mining professional. He had envisioned them all looking like the South Africans he had met, burly and hard. The company director's command of English was solid as well, a trait McBain had found common in most of these expatriates on his prior trips to Africa.

"Thank you for meeting with us on such short notice, Mr. Silva. Your colleague, Mr. Suarez, in Pretoria was generous to set up this sudden trip for me, and I appreciate your time."

McBain and Gina took seats on the sofa across from a mahogany coffee table under a wall of windows overlooking the highway along the Marginal ten stories below as it curved northward. The blinds were slanted open, and the morning light fell on the table as Mr. Silva's assistant placed a tray of coffee and hot croissants between the magazines. Silva took a seat across from them and placed a folder on the table. He poured steaming coffee into their cups and pointed to the cream and sugar on the tray.

"It is my pleasure, Mr. McBain, Ms. Ferrari," he said. "Yes, Mr. Suarez mentioned that it was a matter of some urgency that we meet in order to help finalize the reports needed for the merger teams in America. How can I help?"

McBain stirred his coffee with a spoon and wondered what else remained to be asked. He focused on the things Boston had discussed with him over the past few nights. The most important result now was to make sure their client was getting a fair shake and a fair price.

"Now that we are getting near closing," he said, "maybe you can tell me something about your company's part in all this and what you think the potential is for this project . . . and this merger."

Silva smiled for the first time and seemed pleased to be able to speak to his company's strengths. He described Coutinho and Company's background in Brazil and its important role in discovering and supporting some of the major rare earth finds in Cabeco do Cachorro in the northwest part of that country near the Amazon. As he warmed to the subject he spoke of meeting Harold Rogers and the excitement that had rippled through the mining industry and his own company as they worked together on the geological and satellite data and the initial technology trials to advance the exploration and development phases of the project. He was looking forward to being able to deploy some of the new search and separation technologies in Moxico.

"I was out there fairly early in the project," Silva said. "Our teams worked with Mr. Henry and AFR's mining crew soon after the initial excavations had gone down several layers and started producing samples for the trial assessments. We were quite excited about the density of the samples they had discovered, and our next few rounds of testing supported the findings."

Gina sipped her coffee and smiled at the director. "We were having dinner with some gentlemen who suggested anything is possible out in that part of the continent, Mr. Silva. What are your thoughts on the project?"

Silva reached over and opened the folder he had placed on the table. He drew out several pages of graphs and numbers and handed copies of the sheets to McBain and Gina. McBain feigned interest and understanding of what he was looking at, barely able to make anything out beyond some of the symbols from the chart of chemical elements he had briefly studied back in Boston before the flight.

"We don't want to waste your time," he said. "Perhaps you could just summarize for us."

"Of course. These columns indicate the type and number of minerals that showed up in the surveys at different levels of the dig, along with their potential density and percentage of purity, as well as the likelihood of their being found in significant quantities to warrant further exploration and development. I presume Harold Rogers has briefed you on the processes involved with mineral identification, extraction, and separation. These columns here indicate our initial expectations for the size of each find. Our estimates, which I must say we consider conservative, confirm that the project could expect to develop fairly large groupings of key minerals such as niobium, tantalum, neodymium, dysprosium, and others. Of course, you know that that region is a supplier of much of the world's tantalum already, not to mention rich deposits of coltan ore, cobalt, and copper."

"Of course." McBain nodded.

"So that was not a surprise, really. What has surprised us is not just the potential for some of these other minerals but the—how shall I say this in English?—the thickness of the amounts in the earth's crust that the samples suggest. As you know, often these so-called rare earths are not rare at all, easily found but in small amounts. Moxico and the region near the border look to be exceptional by these standards. It means that, over time, the project could produce substantial quantities of these minerals for extraction and processing at high grades and at reasonable cost. And if the new separation and processing technologies that HR Tech is working on prove successful in their trials here, it would raise the rate of production and the value of the combined company by quite a bit."

McBain nodded along as he scanned the pages. "Great news," he said at last. He exhaled loudly and examined the names of the minerals. Then he thought of something Boston had mentioned. "About the processing piece—do you have any lingering concerns about environmental issues impacting the operation? We've heard of some problems in other places—for example, China."

Silva shook his head. "Not really. Although that is not really for us to say. We can identify the types of minerals and likely quantities, but the separation element of the production process is not something we are involved in. That will be in the hands of AFR."

"But you have an opinion based on your work with the other people on the project? Not to mention your company's expertise around the world."

He did have an opinion. Silva spent fifteen minutes discussing the history of mining developments and pollution from rare earth processing plants in China and Brazil. He made clear that this was different. He coughed into his hand.

"That's less likely with this project, Mr. McBain. One of the . . . ahem . . . unfortunate side effects of the long civil war here is that that part of Angola is sparsely populated. In this case, it is also an advantage. Although there are a few local villages close to the AFR site, the fact that much of the population has not yet returned after decades of conflict turns out to be a positive thing for once. The same might be said for the animal population as well, I'm afraid."

McBain placed his cup back on the table. "Even the animals?"

The director shrugged. "Many species were devastated. Some of them are coming back to the area faster than others."

Gina nodded. "Yes, I understand many of the most rare animals such as the antelope and big cats were killed in the fighting or as food. One hopes they find a way to recover over time."

McBain looked over the pages again. The deal was looking more prom-ising than ever. He finished his coffee and looked up at Silva.

"This all sounds pretty solid, Mr. Silva," he said. "I'm just curious what the holdup has been on finalizing your report to the Boards of HR Tech and AFR. Have you heard from your man out there yet?"

Silva leaned back in his chair and looked uncomfortable as he folded his hands.

"No," he said. "It's unfortunate that this seems to be the one unpleasant development in the middle of all this."

"What seems to be the problem?" McBain said. "I thought your work was just about finished."

"Yes, it was to have been completed weeks ago." Silva stroked his goatee for a moment and was hesitant with his words. McBain sensed it wasn't because of his English. "You see, our leading geologist seems to have gone missing prior to submitting the final report on the last samples in the mine. It has taken longer than expected to make up for the loss."

McBain filled his own coffee cup and glanced at Gina while refilling hers. "Yes," he said, "your man in Pretoria hinted about some problems. Is this unusual?"

"Oh, certainly," Silva said. "Coutinho has the highest reputation in this industry, and we pride ourselves on the quality of our staff and work. It is unheard of for one of our men to abandon his position. Frankly, Daniel Neto would have been the last person on our staff I would have expected this to happen to. He is . . . was one of our very finest young geologists and the most talented Angolan we employed. Very, um—what is the English expression?—up and coming. At least, that is what we thought before . . ."

Gina looked concerned and poured the director more coffee. "Before what, Mr. Silva?"

Silva steepled his fingers and cleared his throat. He avoided looking at Gina as he replied. "A few months ago, we started receiving reports from the head of mining on the project. He told us that he was no longer happy with the quality of the work that Daniel was doing, that it was not up to their expectations and was putting the project schedule at risk. He also informed us that Daniel was missing work occasionally, apparently because he was spending more of his time with some of the girls at a nearby village. I found it hard to believe at first, but at last, our business manager on site confessed to me that it was true. He had not wanted to confirm it, hoping that it would be a brief episode, and Daniel would return to his old ways and help us finish our part of the project. But he suggested that the reports about the girls were true and that there was drinking involved. He couldn't explain it and guaranteed me he was doing his best to smooth things over with the project managers and AFR's head of mining. He told me that when he confronted Daniel about it, he became angry and threatened to start lying about the project. And now he seems to have disappeared without informing anyone. They simply can't find him."

McBain looked at Gina, who shrugged and waved the comments aside with a hand. "I'm sorry to hear that. Perhaps he will turn up. But with the work almost done, you should not feel this reflects poorly on your company."

McBain's eyes were focused on his coffee while he stirred it and listened. An idea was forming in his head, one he didn't like. The rational part of his brain was fighting to stay in charge, but the new thought was surging up from inside his guts.

"You're right, Mr. Silva," he said. "That is an unfortunate turn of events.

218 | RILEY MASTERS

But I think we can all agree that this survey has to get filed so we can all make our final reports and close the deal for Harold Rogers and his board. Have you found a way to proceed without Mr. Neto yet?"

The director's demeanor brightened at the chance to assuage McBain's concerns. "Yes, Mr. McBain, we have. Just yesterday, we received an envelope from our manager out there on the project site with Neto's last results. I have looked at them and will be making a special trip out to the site starting tomorrow to review the final assessments from the mine surveys and bring back ore and soil samples from inside the mine. The rest of my team here is already working on the write-up and we should be able to present the results to everyone as soon as I return. They look most promising, I can tell you."

McBain smiled at the director and avoided looking at Gina. A battle was taking place in his heart and head between his years of professional judgment and the thing that had appeared that first night he met Henry at the Mandarin. The thing that had gnawed away at him and was now consuming more and more of his ego with every day and every conversation he had had since arriving in Africa. He would not put a name on it, but he knew that it was strong enough to overcome the fear that was numbing his stomach when he said . . .

"Mind if I tag along?"

Gina looked straight at him with eyes wide as saucers and alarm written all over her face.

Mr. Silva looked confused. He leaned forward. "I am sorry, Mr. McBain. My English is not very good. I do not understand. Tag along?"

"Yes, go with you," McBain said. "On your trip out to the AFR project."

Gina coughed into her hand, but McBain ignored her and stared at the director.

Silva straightened up in his chair and stroked his goatee while his eyes narrowed. It took him a few seconds to respond. "That would be highly unusual," he said.

"But not impossible."

Gina reached across the sofa and put a firm hand on McBain's arm. "Really, McBain, I think we've asked quite a bit from Mr. Silva and his company in the past few days. I'm not sure what—"

McBain didn't dare look back at her. He half smiled at Silva with his most charming deal-closing curl of the lip.

"I presume you only plan to be out there for a few days at most, right?" he said. "A quick run to pick up the materials and then back to Luanda. And I imagine it isn't the first time a special guest or banker has been out to the mine to make a casual visit and look around. And after all, I'm already in Angola. How much harder would it be to arrange an extra passage for someone who is part of the big deal?"

The director frowned and tapped his fingers on his lap.

"Yes, well, permits could possibly be arranged. And it is true I am only going to the mine itself for two days. But are you certain? The trip itself is long and quite trying. There is a flight east and then a small company plane to the closest airport in Cazombo, but after that, the drive is long and uncomfortable. And in October, the rains have begun to come more often, and if the dirt roads become muddy it could take much longer. Or we could be stuck on the road at night. And there can be dangers at times."

McBain sipped at his cold coffee and put on a serious face. He could still feel Gina's hand exerting pressure on his other forearm.

"How long are we talking about?" McBain asked.

Silva shrugged. "Probably seven or eight days if all goes well. I assure you it will be quite uncomfortable, Mr. McBain. And unnecessary. Why would you want to go to Moxico?"

That was the question, wasn't it? There wasn't a good answer for anyone.

"Well, if it's important enough for you to take the time to go out there to finalize the report, and the report is important to finalizing the deal, I'm certain I can afford to take the time."

"Yes, but I assure you—"

"Come on," McBain said. "It will make me look good in front of our client if I make the trip. Plus I haven't had a vacation in a long time. It's not as if I'm the first American to go all the way out there."

Silva looked at his watch and seemed to absorb the fact that McBain would probably stay in the office until he agreed. At last he stood up and sighed. "Very well, sir" he said. "If you are certain you want to do this, I'll see what I can do about some quick permits with the local authorities. Let me make a few calls this morning."

McBain grinned as he rose and extended his hand. "Thank you, Mr. Silva. You have no idea how important this is to me. Perhaps we can even find out more about your man Neto while we're there."

Mr. Silva shook his head as McBain gripped his hand. "I am sure I do not understand. Please call me later this afternoon, and I will inform you about the flight arrangements. I will say this: You are a very persistent man, Mr. McBain."

McBain glanced at Gina's stern face as he headed for the door.

"So I've been told."

• • •

WITH NO TRAFFIC, the drive would have taken ten minutes. But in Luanda, drivers seemed to know only frenetic speed or glacial progress, and at this time of the late morning, the road along the Marginal was packed and loud.

The car crawled along the road as it swung past Luanda Bay and headed to the Ministry of Mineral Resources. This gave Gina plenty of time to let off steam about what she thought of McBain's brainstorm.

"What possessed you to ask Silva that? What could you possibly hope to accomplish by going out to the mine?"

McBain was already having second thoughts about his idea. He was unsure why he had blurted it out and did not have an answer for Gina. Which meant he had about ten hours to come up with a really good story for this evening's conversation with his partner. But as the seconds ticked by, the thing that had taken control of his gut was whispering in his ear that he would regret it if he backed out now. He threw up his hands.

"I really don't think it's that big a deal, Gina. It's not like I'm striking off by myself into the bush. This guy is a pro. I'm sure over the past year or two, dozens of banker types have gone out there to look around. This is the twenty-first century. I'm not going all *Heart of Darkness* here."

The blue eyes stared him down. "That's not the point. Silva was right—there is no point. You're spending a week, best case, roughing it to go out to take a look at a big hole in the ground and follow him around without getting in the way. This man Neto is gone—probably gone bonkers from the isolation and taken up with some village girls. You couldn't even read the file he gave us. Once again, what do you hope to accomplish with this?"

McBain looked out at the coast. "Maybe it's like I told Silva: I just want to tell the client I went all the way. And I've never been to a place that far out on the frontier. After all these weeks of reading about this stuff, going to meeting after meeting with all these miners and bankers, and hearing about the future of Africa, I'd like to actually see the real side of it, not just the numbers and stacks of papers."

Gina folded her arms and stared straight ahead. "You're on your own now, you know. I can't go with you. And I wouldn't even if I had the time. I have a meeting with a client here this afternoon after our visit with the minister. How do you think I'm swinging some of these expenses as business related? And then I have to get back to Cape Town tomorrow."

"I know, Gina. I want to do this on my own."

"And a whole week or more. Here I thought you were coming back to take some time in South Africa before you went home. After all the meetings we've been to this week and the time I took off from work."

She looked at him sideways, folder her arms and pouted. McBain reached out and put his hand on her crossed arm.

"I do appreciate everything you've done. And I promise I'll spend another few days at least in Cape Town before I head back. The deal should be about done by then anyway, so I should be able to swing it with the client."

Gina tapped the driver and asked him to stop in Portuguese. She looked at McBain and smiled. "Fine," she said, and got out of the car.

They ate lunch at the Café Paris next to the ministry building and went up to see Minister Azevedo at two o'clock. As they exited the elevator on the fifth floor of the ministry building, Gina gave McBain her usual reminder about Angolan sensitivities and his diplomacy.

"No worries, Gina," he said. "I thought of a new plan."

• • •

AFTER A LONG wait, the door to Minister Azevedo's office opened and they were shown in to see a severe man wearing an expensive tailored suit and red tie. Gina expressed their gratitude for their audience in Portuguese, while McBain put on his most polite but restrained Wall Street sales demeanor. Given the lateness of the hour, he was eager to finish the meeting and get ready for the next day. But he also needed to know he wouldn't be experiencing any surprises along the lines of South Africa and thought that the best way to ensure that was to be a team player. Of course, the best way to do that was to lie.

"Thank you for seeing us right away, sir," he said. "I'd like to express Mr. Henry's personal appreciation for your time. He sent me on this last-minute trip so I could ease my client's mind about the success of the project. Mr. Henry spoke very highly of the Ministry of Mineral Resources and your work in helping to finalize this venture."

Minister Azevedo did not exactly smile, but satisfaction was evident in his expression.

"Quite so," he said. "And how can I be of assistance to Mr. Henry now and ease your client's mind, as you say?"

McBain leaned back in his chair in a casual posture. "Mr. Henry has asked me to take a quick trip out to the mining site along with Mr. Silva of Coutinho and Company in order to have a firsthand look at the development and the region around the mine. I was hoping that you could provide me with any assistance in obtaining local permits given the short notice."

The minister cast his eyes down on some paperwork on his desk for a moment. McBain could not see what he was reading but hoped it wasn't a warning from someone in Pretoria. He looked at Gina, who smiled in a noncommittal way. But after a minute, the minister merely signed the document and looked up.

"Of course," he said. "Anything to assist Mr. Henry." Then he leaned forward on his desk, his fingers folded. "But why do you want to go to Moxico? Are you a geologist or a miner?"

McBain smiled and threw open his hands. "May I be honest, Minister?"

Gina edged forward in her chair.

"Please do."

"It is a personal favor for Harold Rogers, the founder of HR Tech. Mr. Rogers is—how shall I phrase this?—a very progressive-minded businessman and concerned about the environment. As a man who has worked most of his life in natural resource exploration, he has come to feel very strongly that the projects his company takes on both help local communities and are developed with an eye toward care for the environment, especially in countries such as Angola that have areas that are unspoiled by decades of techniques that often lead to destruction of the region and population. I know we all have confidence that this is just the beginning of major developments in the region that will occur over years. Everyone has heard the stories from Bayan Obo in China and other places about the damage that was done by rare earths mining and processing. And I'm sure you could speak of things I am not even aware of in Africa."

The minister nodded and leaned back in his seat as McBain spoke.

"So, you see," McBain said, "Rogers wants to ensure that you and your government are satisfied with the plans for development of the Moxico region over the years, both during the mining stage and then when the new mineral processing begins. He wants you to have the utmost confidence in his technology, as does Mr. Henry. My visit is partly to assess that you are being treated fairly from that perspective."

"That is very generous of Senor Rogers," Azevedo said. "You may assure him that the people of Angola are quite satisfied with the arrangements that have been agreed to. A number of discussions have already been held about long-term development in the country that will be possible because of the project. The people of that region are already beginning to benefit, and others who moved from there to Luanda and other cities may be able to return to their tribal lands."

He made some notes on a pad. "I will approve. My office can help with the paperwork for your trip. But please make sure you are escorted at all times, Mr. McBain. The environment, as you call it, can be difficult for strangers. Someday we hope it will be easier, but today, I would advise you to stay close to the mining staff and listen to what they tell you."

"I certainly will. Thank you, Minister." They stood to go. "Ah, there was one other item, sir. I understood from the office in Boston that there was something about a study that they were waiting to receive."

"Yes," Azevedo said. "I had heard. The environmental impact assessment for the project. I looked into it this morning, and it is almost final. After it reaches my desk and I review it, the EIA will be signed by the Minister of the Environment and then several others. We expect to have it sent out in a week or less."

"Wonderful news," McBain said. "Shall we go, Gina? I have to buy some clothes and gear if I'm heading out to Moxico."

Gina glanced at her watch. "All right, but we should hurry. We've taken up enough of the minister's time, and I have to rush to another meeting."

Minister Azevedo held up his hand and picked up the phone. He spoke a few sentences in Portuguese and hung up. He scribbled on a notepad and handed the sheet to McBain.

"No need to hurry yourself, Ms. Ferrari," Azevedo said. "Here, Mr. McBain. A driver will be waiting for you in the lobby. He can take you to a few of these shops and then back to your hotel. You can take your time and find what you need without inconveniencing Ms. Ferrari. I am sure we would all prefer you not try to take a taxi at this time of day."

McBain glanced at Gina, who nodded. "Thank you, Minister Azevedo," she said. "I was informed you were very gracious, as well as distinguished."

"I appreciate the help, sir," McBain said. "I promise to report to Mr. Henry and Harold Rogers how much assistance you have been to us all. Good day."

Gina expressed their appreciation in Portuguese, then reached into her large Chanel shoulder bag and handed the minister an envelope. He pulled out what looked like two tickets to an event and smiled at her. *"Obrigado,* Ms. Ferrari."

She smiled and shook his hand. *"Por nada."*

In the entryway to the building, a driver was waiting. Gina engaged him in Portuguese for a few minutes, then turned to McBain.

"OK, you're set. His name is Alfonso, and he'll take you to a couple of those stores on your list. He speaks a little English, but try to stick to the basics. Tell him when you've finished, and he'll take you back to the SANA. I'll be a few hours and I'll meet you there. Don't stop off for any drinks until you get to the hotel. Got it?"

McBain saluted and kissed her on the cheek. "Yes, ma'am. I have to behave if I'm going up the river."

She shook her head and left.

The investigator looked at his driver and his list. "Alfonso, I am McBain."

Alfonso nodded and inhaled slowly. He did not seem pleased with his assignment. He turned and led the way to a black Mercedes parked at the bottom of the steps without speaking.

The next two hours went by fast. The traffic less so, which eased McBain's concern about the broken seat belt in the back of the car. They stopped at three stores before McBain was satisfied that he had the right size khaki pants, blue cotton shirts, safari jacket, and sweater for the outback if the temperature dropped. Mr. Silva had made clear that they would not be camping out, at least not intentionally, but McBain also purchased a flashlight, compass, and small metal whistle, tools from a childhood forgotten.

He jumped into the Mercedes and said to the driver, "OK, Alfonso, all finished. *Finito.* Back to the SANA Hotel."

Alfonso looked at his watch and growled. "Late. Traffic now bad. Hurry." The driver made a quick phone call on his cell phone. He shifted into gear, and the car took off like a shot from the storefront. "Short cut," he said as they accelerated.

The side streets were so convoluted that for the first time in a while, he thought kindly of the colonial-era maze of narrow, one-way streets in Beacon Hill and the North End back in Boston. But Alfonso was focused on the road ahead and seemed confident in the way city taxi drivers do as he sped through intersections. McBain had tried to follow the topography of the city during their shopping expedition and saw vaguely that they were close to the coast and not far from the hotel. When they finally caught up to traffic, he could see familiar skyscrapers just ahead.

They crawled for another five minutes. Alfonso checked his watch again, and then his mirrors.

"Are we almost there?" McBain asked as he watched the driver squirm in his seat.

The driver turned and looked at him. "Almost SANA." His eyes darted past McBain to check the traffic in the lane next to them.

The Mercedes first nudged into the other lane, then jumped across the oncoming traffic into an empty, narrow street as horns blared. Alfonso accelerated down the street and toward the next intersection, where he made a sharp right turn, McBain hanging on to the handle over the car door in desperation.

"Ha," the driver grunted.

"Nice work, Alfon—"

McBain heard the driver's shout and snapped his head around as the white Toyota pickup filled the car window and his field of vision with horn blaring at high speed. His body tensed as the truck smashed the Mercedes at an angle that lifted it up over the curb and rolled it. The inside of the car spun, and McBain flailed his arms and legs searching for something to brace himself while they rolled completely over once, then again down the street until they came to a stop upside down in a hissing, rocking slide, with the pickup lodged against one side.

McBain lay flat on his back on what had been the ceiling of the Mercedes and looked up at the back seat. His head ached with a dull, painful throb and echoed with spinning memories of the Toyota, and his vision was blurry with blood trickling from his brow. He could hear one of the horns continue to blare, or was it a car alarm? Through the haze of sound, he waited for something. He couldn't remember what or why he was here. He dimly smelled car exhaust, motor oil, and steaming hot water from a busted radiator, and for a moment, he thought about burning alive. He reached up and felt his jaw with one hand, then his teeth. Finally he closed his eyes and drifted his way past the pain into unconsciousness.

TWENTY

McBain reclined in an armchair by the hotel window, gazing out at the orange ball falling into the Atlantic Ocean, holding a highball glass loaded with vodka and ice against his head for the second time in four days. Gina had liberated him from the hospital after confirming that his injuries were limited to a number of superficial cuts to the head and scalp and minor bruises. They had decided to order room service and have a quiet night in order to rest up for the travel day tomorrow. After a hot shower, McBain put on a robe, laid out his new clothes, and sat taking in the calm beauty of the African sunset while thinking about how he was going to break the news to his partner about his road trip.

"Having second thoughts about tomorrow?" Gina asked.

McBain looked over at the blonde with the tan legs lounging on the sofa in his blue linen shirt with a drink in her hand. "Not a chance," he said. "Especially after this."

Gina winced. "Come on, McBain. You're not going to keep insisting this was an attempt on your life, are you? I have told you a couple of times, traffic accidents are a constant nightmare here. Hell, the minister himself even called you up to apologize for his driver."

"Yes, so he said." McBain took a sip and put the glass back against his forehead. "By the way, did he mention how Alfonso is? I don't remember anything after we got rammed."

"Worse off than you. He has a fractured skull and some broken bones. Seems he took the brunt of the impact on his side of the car. And that's another thing. You think Azevedo or somebody in his employ would have tried to kill one of their own people? If they had wanted you hurt, he could have just dumped you in an alley somewhere and had you knifed."

McBain peered down through the twilight at the street and the headlights of the traffic below. He supposed that it didn't make sense. But he was feeling more than a little paranoid after the last few days. On the other hand, this was not Boston; it was Africa. He thought through the meetings they had been to and the subtle undertones of the conversations.

"OK, so maybe it wasn't Azevedo. Maybe it was somebody else. Remember how fast Mbomani got word I was snooping around? He could have found out we were coming here yesterday and made some phone calls. For that matter, who knows who Silva or Azevedo might have contacted to arrange my permits? I suppose it was just a coincidence that the driver of the Toyota that hit us disappeared and left his truck there. If he was hired to hit my car, there's no way they are going to find out who paid him."

"I think those blows to the head are making you a little too crazy," Gina said. "On the other hand, maybe it wasn't the best strategy in the world to walk in there lying to him about how Henry sent you after all. So yes, in theory, there could be some conspiracy, but it is also not uncommon for people who cause accidents here to just take off and leave their car, especially when it might be obvious he just hit a government vehicle."

McBain sulked until dinner arrived. They ate fresh fish from the Atlantic and curried rice and drank French burgundy while they talked about McBain's trip to the east and the date he would return to Cape Town. After room service removed the trays, Gina filled her wineglass and smiled at him.

"I'm going to take a quick shower while you call Eliza and explain to her where you are going next and why. Much as I would enjoy a good laugh listening in."

McBain listed his arguments in bullet points on a sheet of notepaper while he took another drink of courage. Then he dialed Boston at her desk in the office. She picked up on the first ring.

"You're late," Boston said. "It must be nearly eleven there."

"Yes, just after," he said. "It's been a pretty full day. Sorry. How are you doing?"

"The same, more or less. We're getting close. Still lots to do." She was quiet for a few seconds. "So how's your buddy Gina?"

"She's fine. She's been a great help to us. She's just leaving now."

"Did Eliza sell any flowers today?" Gina asked.

"What?" Boston said. "What was that about flowers?"

"I told her how hard you're working on this. Gina says remember to take time out to smell the flowers."

The blonde laughed as she put the wine back in the ice bucket and unbuttoned her shirt.

"I'm sure," Boston said. "Tell the whore she better get her shots."

McBain turned to Gina and put his hand over the phone. "She wishes you well."

Gina smirked, held up two fingers at the phone in a traditional English salute that was not V for victory, and carried her wine into the bathroom.

He gave Boston a report of the conversations he had had with the oil men, the consulting firm, and the minister, letting her know that the environmental impact assessment that she had identified as missing was in its final stages of preparation. She updated McBain on the progress in negotiations and confirmed that they were close on the final price to be paid by AFR for HR Technology. She didn't mention the cold shoulder she had been receiving from the others or the Head of the Charles. Boston also confirmed that Rogers had heard from Coutinho and Company that they were preparing the final report to be submitted on the assessment of the Moxico project. McBain swallowed another mouthful of vodka and jumped.

"Yes, I spoke with a Mr. Silva today in their office here, and he confirmed that his people are writing it up. They received some analysis from the site, and he's pretty pleased overall. He's flying out to the project tomorrow to collect the final samples and review the site himself. It seems their man out there has not turned up yet, and he's going to find out what happened. It sounds more than a little suspicious to me as well, the way he just went to pieces and disappeared."

"Well," Boston said, "be that as it may, it looks like your African quest to find something wrong with the deal and project have come up empty. Just as I suspected it would. When are you getting back?"

McBain turned his back to the bathroom as he heard the shower start. "The thing is, Boston, while I haven't heard anything concrete from anyone, some odd things have been happening here. Henry's definitely spread the money around and greased a lot of palms. While I don't think there's anything to torpedo the deal with HR Tech here, I've got a gut instinct. And there's been some trouble since I started asking questions."

"Like that's something different for us." Boston was quiet, and he could envision her mind working. "What do you mean, 'trouble'?"

McBain told her about the break-in at the hotel, the veiled threat by the minister in Pretoria, and finally about the accident. "Except that I'm not totally convinced it was an accident."

She exploded over the phone. "Then the sooner you get the hell out of there, the better, McBain. When's your flight?"

"The thing is," he said, "I'm not coming right back. Between these incidents and what I've heard about the disappearance of this guy Neto out there, I want to ask a few more questions and poke around a little more."

"Questions? You have talked to dozens of people. Who else is there? What else is there left to ask? And just suppose you're right, and today's traffic accident wasn't an accident. You keep pissing people off for no reason, and they might kill you. Get out of there!"

McBain took a sip and a deep breath and said it.

"I am getting out of Luanda," he said. "I'm going out to the project site with Silva, the manager from Coutinho, tomorrow. We will be out there for about a week or so round trip, checking on his man and getting the final materials for the report to Rogers. I'll be back after that, about ten days all told, based on what Silva told me."

The phone was quiet, and McBain could almost hear Boston's temperature rising based on the sound of her breathing. He let her take her time, and when she spoke again, her voice was steady with anger, but also with a trace of nervousness. Or fear.

"This doesn't make any sense," Boston said. "Why are you doing this? You haven't found anything to support your suspicions. You just won't let it go that I was right."

"I agree that you were right. Absolutely. At this point, we can confirm to Rogers that there is no reason not to go ahead with the deal. From what I've found out here, he is going to be a very rich man and head of a major global rare earth mining company. I just need to do this one last thing. I've never been out in that kind of undeveloped wilderness before, and I want to see the real thing for a change. I've come this far already. It's just one more leg. I'm sure Silva wouldn't let me go if he thought it was too risky. Hell, Henry has been there plenty of times."

"Listen to me, Boozy," she said. Her voice was quieter now and full of the soft persuasion of someone who was afraid. Of someone who was trying to carefully talk someone down off a ledge. "I've done a lot of research on that part of the country over the past few weeks. They fought wars there not long ago. The place is wild, and there are diseases there that they don't even have cures for. It's still a dangerous place. Just because there is a mine there with some security people doesn't make it safe. That's their world. You're not goddamn Indiana Jones. You're an out-of-shape guy from the city. You don't belong there. What are you trying to prove?"

There was the question; there was the thing. And he found the courage to try to answer his partner without lying. He had promised he would never lie to her.

"I'm not sure at this point. I think I'm trying to prove I'm as tough as he is."

McBain could tell from the icy silence that she understood and that she knew that he was going regardless of what she said.

Boston's voice trembled on the other end of the phone. "This was supposed to be a simple due diligence. Remember? You said that in Dave's office. Now it's become an obsession for you. You've made it personal, despite what we always said. You've got no business going out to the mine. It's a dangerous place under normal circumstances and a different planet from everything we know. And from what you've said, you're making people uncomfortable and angry, threatening their payoffs. That isn't our world, Boozy. Come back. Please."

"Boston, I'm just going to check out the dig, and I'll be back soon. Don't worry." The phone went quiet. "Boston?"

"Fine," she yelled. "Do what you want. Go ahead and get yourself killed. See if I care. You like it there so much, as far as I'm concerned, you can just stay!"

The line went dead.

• • •

GINA TOOK MCBAIN to the airport the following morning. Before she left him with Silva to take her flight back to South Africa, she pulled him aside. "What is it about this guy, McBain? You are chasing a phantom to the ends of the earth to see if he's dirty. You could do that from South Africa. Even Luanda is the frontier for a guy like you. But you're traveling across hundreds of miles of empty wilderness to the border to a mining camp without even knowing what you're looking for. Dozens of experts have been out there and checked out the place. For once, Eliza is right. What the hell are you doing?"

McBain lit a cigarette and looked out the plate-glass window past the runway to the horizon, a distant green and brown haze receding to the distant and forbidding east. The entire left side of his body hurt. "I don't like the feel of these little accidents I've been having. Maybe because everybody I talk to either envies or fears him so much. Maybe because my partner admires him."

She shook her head. "So you're jealous."

"Of course not."

"Jesus, this is just some macho competition to you? You're fighting over her?"

"That's ridiculous, Gina," McBain said. "There's no competition. This is just a job to her, to both of us. There's nothing to fight over, except maybe that I'm right, and she is wrong."

TWENTY-ONE

The crowd stood on the Boston University Bridge over the Charles River, scanning the water flowing to the southeast toward the harbor. They could see the Massachusetts Avenue Bridge spanning the broad expanse of the Charles in the distance, and beyond that, the city shining in the bright morning sun. In the foreground of that bridge, an array of four- and eight-person boats circled around or sped down the river, gathered like an ancient Greek fleet marshaling for battle. A cold breeze carried the calls of the announcer from the starting line at the Boston University Boathouse to the throngs of people lining the banks of the Charles or waiting on the BU Bridge.

"MIT crew, you are approaching the starting line . . . Ready . . . aaaand *row*! Rochester, space it out a little . . . That's better . . . You are on the course, aaaand *row*!"

The crowd on the bridge was well represented by alums from many schools, among them Boston College. It was coat-and-boot weather, and everyone was bundled up against the chill wind blowing down the Charles from the northwest with the promise of autumn and the threat of winter in the not-too-distant future. Boston was dressed in jeans and boots with a tight-fitting gold sweater under her maroon and gold BC crew jacket, her hair mingling in the wind with her scarf. Rodney Henry stood at her side wearing a brown bomber jacket with a shearling collar and gray wool dress pants, listening to her explain the art and science of competitive sculling.

She pointed out the style and method in the rowers as the four- and eight-person racing shells passed gracefully under the crowded bridge, guided by shouts of the coxswain, while Henry followed along intently and absorbed each detail as the boats went by. There came a brief spell between races. Boston pointed to the next flotilla of boats gathering in two columns in the distance beyond the boathouse.

"The Women's Championship Eights will be up next, one of the races I used to row. The Boston College boat will be in that group."

Henry pulled off his sunglasses and gazed at the boats. "What attracted you to this sport to begin with, Ms. O'Daniel?"

Boston closed her eyes for a moment and took a deep breath of autumn. "The quiet, for one thing, particularly if you are out on the river in the early morning. The chance to just lay it all out there in synchronized rhythm with a team without a crowd of people screaming at you or intruding on the beauty of the surroundings. Whenever I was in a boat with eight or four people, or just by myself, there was always a sense of solitude when you reached that point where it was just the wind and water and your muscles on automatic. Even if you weren't competing against other teams, you could compete with yourself. It's a great way to get out your frustrations in a Zen kind of way. At BC, my friends said it was one of my best subjects."

Several of Boston's friends from her college days stood nearby, hovering around a small folding table that Henry's driver had set up to hold a sizeable buffet of hot coffee and chocolate, bagels, muffins, and pastries. They glanced over on occasion and chatted among themselves in low voices but kept their distance while enjoying the hospitality. The driver returned from time to time with another container to keep the coffee hot.

"What else did you study besides rowing?"

"Mostly finance. I didn't actually do all that well in college with most subjects. Couldn't stand science courses or English. Most classes just bored

me. But I found out I had a knack for math and accounting; it just came second nature to me. So I excelled at that and made it through some advanced
classes, and next thing you know, I was interested in numbers and markets
and simulated investing and valuations. But other than that, I had a hard
time staying focused. I was pretty much a so-so student in areas I wasn't
interested in. Plus my extracurricular activities got in the way occasionally.
My parents were not happy with how I was spending their money. So I got
the job at the body shop to help pay my own way and stay out of trouble."

"Did it work?"

She laughed. "Not much."

"Perhaps, but you were better off for it," Henry said. "It sounds to me
like you were on a road to becoming a self-made person. Finance, math,
and work in a garage. Some might suggest you were setting out to prove
yourself in a man's world. That might also apply to knocking down walls
by yourself in your apartment."

Boston looked down at her hands. "Maybe. But sometimes there's a price
to pay for being different."

"True." Henry smiled. "But with your looks and style, very few people
probably ever notice your hands."

"Thank you."

"And I can understand your interest in wearing glasses when you don't
really need them. I'm sure you want to be admired for your brains and
skills, not your looks. It also helps distract people from your nose."

She reached up and touched the bridge of her nose. "Guess it's hard not
to notice. Yes, I got careless once in the garage and walked into a car that
was up off the ground. I do feel self-conscious about it, though, so I use
the glasses to hide it."

"You certainly are accident prone," Henry said, then he shook his head once. "Look. I did some boxing in my early years, Ms. O'Daniel. I know what a broken nose looks like. Not to mention your hands. What kind of sparring do you do?"

She shrugged and counted on her fingers. "Bujutsu, Krav Maga, some mixed martial arts. The occasional boxing at the gym I go to. I've been training for about four and a half years. I did a lot of fighting before that . . . informally."

Henry chuckled. "Let me guess: a bit of a wild child in your teens?"

"That's an understatement. It's a wonder my father never locked me up. He did his best to keep me out of trouble."

"That's a father's job, whatever his profession."

"He said once I was always trying to prove something. I just couldn't figure out what it was or to who. It didn't help being the youngest and having four overachieving sisters to follow. Maybe I was just trying to get attention as a tomboy since they were all so accomplished and ladylike. But you know all the movies and songs make it sound very glamorous when it's the small-town preacher's daughter, rebelling and all. Not so much when your dad's a city cop."

Henry nodded as he looked into the distance. "You still think you have something to prove. To yourself and to them. But you don't. I know. I was there twenty years ago when I got to New York. Angry all the time. Hungry. Resentful, even as I worked my way up and made more money than my father ever knew existed. More than the men who owned the mines ever imagined being worth. I had that chip on my shoulder that you have, except yours is more like a large block of carbon that's waiting to become a diamond."

She laughed despite herself. "That's good. Do you use that a lot with women?"

He didn't smile. "No. It wouldn't be appropriate for anyone else. It just came to me thinking of you."

She glanced at him sideways, and a corner of her mouth went up. "Thanks. I think."

Before he could speak again, Boston pointed to the starting line. "Here they come—the eights. Get ready, girls!" Her friends drew closer to the rail and started to yell as the boats approached. The crowd on the bridge was getting louder as the first boat from the University of Pennsylvania surged forward and picked up speed.

"UPenn, you are on the course. Have a good race, ladies."

The cheering grew as the skulls approached and passed under the old stone railroad bridge and the BU Bridge, with the local schools drawing the loudest calls. Finally, they heard the announcement:

"Boston College, you are approaching the line. Aaand row! You are on the course, ladies. Have a good race."

The boat was nearing the bridges, all eight rowers moving with machine-like rhythm in the morning air. Boston and her friends were hooting and screaming encouragement at the top of their lungs.

"Go, Tessa! Yeah!"

"Row, row, Mallory!"

"Woot woot, let's go, Lilly, pull!"

"Go, BC, go!"

They could just hear the voice of the coxswain calling out to the rowers as the boat passed under them, the BC fans yelling as they leaned over the rail to call out and urge on their friends. The boat knifed through the arch and headed up the Charles toward Harvard and the finish line, miles away.

The crowd continued to cheer as the rest of the sculls in the Women's Championship Eights cruised under the arches. As each approached, Boston pointed out several style points to Henry in the eight-woman crews. After five more minutes, the last of those sculls came through. The announcer reported over the breeze that the next race would begin in ten minutes. Boston refilled her coffee mug and Henry's from the hot urn and returned to the railing. They enjoyed the quiet for a moment. She pointed to the city skyline in the distance. The morning sun was still rising and had broken through the moving cloud cover to illuminate the cityscape in dazzling light. "Beautiful, isn't it?"

Henry followed the line of her finger, then looked at her. "Yes, it certainly is."

"As much as I'd like to travel," she said, "I can't really imagine living anywhere else."

Henry nodded. "I have to admit, Boston is unlike anything I've seen before, unique in its own way. And I've traveled quite a bit."

"It's the best sports town in the world. Dad is always ribbing us about growing up with winning teams and titles in baseball, hockey, and football. Says us youngsters can't imagine The Curse, or not having a team that can get to the Super Bowl each year." Boston bit her lip and looked a bit sheepish. "By the way, you don't happen to know the man who owns the Red Sox, do you? I was hoping to score some box seats for the World Series this week."

"John Henry? Yes, I know him. Quite the commodities trader. Sorry, he's no relation." He smiled slightly. "I'll see what we can do about the tickets."

Out of the corner of her eye, she saw her friends trying to get her attention. When she looked up, they waved as they walked toward the city side of the river. Jillian yelled out, "We're heading up to the finish line, then to the hospitality tents. Goodbye, Mr. Henry. Thanks so much for the hot coffee and breakfast. Boston, we'll see you at the tents."

Henry smiled and nodded, then turned toward her and leaned on the railing, sipping his coffee. "I imagine Boston is not your given name," Henry said. "May I ask what it is?"

She pulled out her sunglasses but didn't put them on. "People always ask how I got my nickname, but I've gone by it so long, I hardly ever use my other name. Maybe I got tired of hearing my parents yell it so often. At any rate, it's my little secret, and I don't really give it out." She gave him a smile. "I'm guessing you're a private person, I'm sure you understand."

Henry nodded. "Yes, quite. On the other hand, that can't stop me from hazarding a guess about the reason for your nickname." He folded his arms. "Well, since I've seen a couple sides of you so far, I think you are very much like your city. For starters, you're classic full-blooded Irish, with all the complications born of a root tough core and the soul of a poet. And, like your city, you are full of contradictions, both old-world Yankee sophistication and blue-collar grit. You can be as unpredictable as the New England weather. I've heard people in this town are very close and hard to get to know, at least the ones who grew up here or planted roots long ago. That's probably true in your case too. When a person is out to prove something to everyone, they don't tolerate intrusions or open up too deeply to cavalier relationships. And you are both focused and clever, with a Boston Irishman's eye for the opportunity."

Boston took all this in with growing amazement. Henry seemed not only sincere but eloquent. She was becoming a little embarrassed. "Maybe I was just a big fan of the band from the seventies."

Henry shook his head again slowly. "Not a chance. Too simple and uncomplicated. And that's not you." He eyed her closely. "I think I'll just keep guessing. I will get it eventually before this deal is closed."

The redhead saw her opening and took a chance. "What about you? It's a pretty unusual man who spends so much time asking a strange woman about her life, especially when he's as accomplished as you. I'm not sure I'm comfortable sharing on a one-way basis. Or are we still strictly business when it comes to that?"

"That's not unreasonable," Henry said. "What would you like to know?"

"What did you do in college, besides box?"

"I took courses related to geology, mining, and engineering. I had a knack for math and problem-solving, but I still had to work hard to do well. I'm afraid I wasn't quite the social dynamo that you were. Of course, college in Blacksburg doesn't have all the distractions that the big city does, so it was easier to focus. On the other hand, like you, I had some things to prove at that age, so fights outside the gym were not uncommon for me either.

"So no time to be a ladies' man, huh?"

"Only one lady," he said. "We met there, and I never dated after that. I had neither the time nor the desire to see anyone else."

Boston took a pull of her mug. "In my experience, that's pretty impressive for a college man. She must have been something special."

Henry gazed off at the skyline for a moment, then looked back at her. "She was. After graduation, she became my wife. She passed away at a young age."

"I'm sorry."

He continued speaking about his coursework and graduation, then his time in the army and travels overseas. Boston asked him about the different countries he had visited from time to time, being careful not to interrupt. When he spoke of his career, she asked probing questions about the climb up the ladder of the financial business. His answers were frank but not revealing.

"I've read a couple of articles about you," she said. "They make it sound like it was easy. Was it?"

Henry looked downstream to the gathering boats, though it seemed to Boston he was somewhere else.

"They made it sound easy because that's the branding message I wanted them to spread. I was very focused on the business and becoming successful as a Wall Street investment banker, but I had also observed that there were many among my peers who worked just as hard and were just as smart. What they didn't have was the confidence and the knack for marketing themselves. As you have observed, brains and hard work only get you so far in this competitive field. Connections and self-promotion can also be useful, but when you marry up all those things with an absolute will to succeed, you can stand out from a crowd."

She waited for him to mention the second wife as the cries floated across the water from the boathouse calling for the next race.

"But there is one element that is critical to rapid success, that makes the difference between the ones who rocket to the top quickly and those who might take their time getting to the executive offices.

"What's that?"

Boston was watching him intently now, no longer bothering with the race. He downed his coffee, then took her cup from her and refilled them both at the table before returning.

"The same thing that counts for rapid success in technology or any other business. An eye for the details and the ability to see an opportunity before others, coupled with a vision of the future. And sometimes that means the willingness to take risks. Although if you have done your homework and have confidence in your vision, the risks might be far lower than others think they are."

She smiled and pushed her hair aside. "You mean those reports I read? You mean rare earths and Africa?"

Henry shrugged. "Those could be two examples. In the case of rare earth metals and mining, I didn't think the future was all that difficult to see and was surprised I didn't have more competition. Fortunately for me, most of my competitors do not look at the world the way I do and are focused on making short-term money in well-known securities like stocks, bonds, or hedge fund strategies, or they ride the commodity cycle up or down. Which can make you a lot of money, as you know."

Boston nodded. "But you watched the Chinese, and you detected the trends in green investments and technology early on and did your research and began to realize how important these minerals were going to be to everyday products someday, like the electric car and the smartphone."

Henry raised an eyebrow, then smiled at her. "Or the defense industry. You know your industry, Boston O'Daniel."

She fixed her scarf inside her jacket and avoided his eye by glancing downstream for a moment.

"I'm no specialist," she said. "But I am a fast learner, and I have to admit this fascinates me like nothing I've seen in a long time. I'm still playing catch-up on all the minerals and possibilities, but I can sort of see your vision."

"I know you can," Henry said. "Because I know from your catch the other day that you have that same keen eye that the best of us have for the key detail in an ocean of unimportant information. Plus you added value with your catch, and you showed guts by standing up when it would have been just as easy for you to let it go and assume it was meaningless. As I said, that can make all the difference, recognizing when something is important and seizing the moment."

He took another sip of coffee as the breeze picked up and the new race began. "And that is why we are doing this deal. I recognized the broader potential of HRT's new technology when it was early stage, even before they did. I put it together with the rare earths trend and the dominance of the Chinese. I had already begun investing in sites around the world and signing contracts with production companies and governments for locations with promising potential. And as you said, I find rare earths minerals fascinating. I'm glad you do as well."

Boston reached up to touch her emerald pendant and smiled. "I do, but I'll confess I'm still more interested in the old-fashioned minerals, like rubies, sapphires, and diamonds. I hear they have quite a few of those in Africa too."

Henry leaned on the railing of the bridge. "Yes, but that's a very small club and an industry that is both dominated and played out by companies like Anglo-American. Some people still chase those prospects, but the prices ebb and flow with recessions and supply. I found there was much more room to explore the boring stones the scientists were excited about. Riskier but, as they say, the greater the risk, the greater the return. Don't you agree?"

She nodded, then thought of one of the other features of the deal that she had been curious about. "Speaking of risk, I was wondering about some of the performance clauses that could affect the merger, in particular related to the ability of the new HR technology to perform as planned. I know they are standard language to some extent, but given how geographically challenging the Angola project could be, it seems awfully dangerous to HR's prospects."

Henry shrugged. "Yes, they are standard breakup clauses, and there are cash penalties involved for termination. But I've already thoroughly reviewed the technology Harold Rogers has developed and talked to companies in the oil and gas business that use his systems. I would not have gone ahead with the proposal if I had any doubts about HRT coming through. On the other hand, you are right there is substantial risk in going ahead, but not necessarily to HRT."

Boston was puzzled. "I'm not sure what you mean."

Rodney Henry smiled and turned to look at her.

"It's natural you would have looked at it from your client's perspective. But the fact of the matter is the clauses run both ways. Much of the risk arises for AFR if we fail to perform or hit certain targets. And my company's stock price will get hammered in the market if it turns out we can't capitalize on this technology and achieve the savings and delivery timetables everyone expects. A lot of people are betting against us because the Angola project is so remote, just like other properties we own and plan to develop. And the fact is that we are charting new territory here both geographically and commercially. Much of the technology has not been used in this way before, and there is a great deal of risk, as you suggest. And if you read them from my perspective, certain covenants favor HRT in this area if the mines do not perform. So, you see, if this all falls apart because I can't make it work, HRT would still remain independent and able to sell their technology and systems to our competitors and other users, as well as receive a cash breakup fee. While we would be set back years in our development plans for rare earths."

The detective nodded in apparent understanding. "I see," she said. In fact, she did see in a new way for the first time, and it troubled her. She just smiled and said, "But as you said, I'm sure everything will work smoothly. Rogers also has the utmost confidence in the prospects for the new company."

"I know he does," said Henry. "And I share his confidence. That's why I made a decision last night that may make your job easier. Or perhaps harder. I've already spoken to Harold, and he's accepted.

"Accepted what?" Boston asked casually. She concealed the alarm that was rising and felt again the nervousness of the neophyte in the corporate world.

"I'm going to step aside after the deal closes. This will effectively become as much a technology company as a commodity company. I'm more of a strategist and dealmaker. Rogers will become CEO of the combined company."

She could not conceal her surprise this time. "Wow. I'm shocked. I have to admit, I didn't see that possibility coming. That's very generous of you."

"I don't know about generous. It's certainly the right thing for AFR. If the Angola project succeeds as well as we expect, our new CEO will have his hands full building an empire. It's only because I know Rogers has already built and run a successful company that I have confidence he can do it as well as I can. And, of course, I will still be involved in strategic decisions and working with customers and governments."

This news was so unexpected, Boston's head was reeling from a rush of new thoughts, and she needed time to process. She was once again out of her depth and wishing McBain was here to provide his experience. Boston needed to call him as soon as possible.

"Well, I suppose that's wonderful news," she said. "Looks like the deal should be wrapped up on schedule then. That's great." She glanced at her watch, then looked downriver to the boathouse. "On that note, I really should be going. I promised the girls I would join them up the river at Harvard at the alumni tents." She paused. "Would you like to come?'

Henry shook his head. Boston was relieved.

"That's gracious of you, but I think I've imposed enough on your time with your friends. And I do have a party to get to. The helicopter is standing by."

"I quite understand. Thank you for joining us this morning and for bringing breakfast. It's certainly been enlightening. And thank you for your kind words and encouragement."

Henry nodded and signaled to the driver to come and collect the table and remains of the breakfast spread. Then he looked at Boston with purpose.

"Well, to emphasize my belief that you are already that gem, I'd like to extend an invitation to you to accompany me to next week's charity fundraiser for Africa. We're hosting it with several others at the Boston Public Library on Saturday to raise money for health and education to fund clinics and vocational schools and training programs in the countries in that region. We're putting the arm on Boston's leading mutual funds, hedge funds, and venture capital community, along with the blue bloods in your town. Giving them a chance to put their money where their socially conscious mouths are."

Boston raised her thin eyebrows. "I hardly think it would be appropriate for me to go to a social event with you as your date, Mr. Henry."

"Quite right," he said. "You would be going as part of the deal team and Harold's representative to see firsthand the commitment of our company—and the new CEO, I might add—to the community. As our company is one of the sponsors of the event, I don't think there would be anything inappropriate if you attended. We can arrive separately if that would make you feel more comfortable. And, of course, your partner, Mr. McBain, is invited as well."

Boston turned for a moment and thought about what Dee Dee had said. Briefly, her thoughts flew to McBain in Africa. Then she thought of him and Gina Ferrari traveling together and of their argument on the phone and his latest act of stupidity. She folded her arms and turned back to Henry.

"No, that won't be necessary. I'd be happy to go as part of the team and represent my partner. After all, the deal is almost ready to be signed. Thank you for the invitation. And I'd be honored to arrive with you as your guest."

TWENTY-TWO

McBain held his hands in the air. For the second time this year, he was looking down the barrel of a gun pointed at his chest, fighting to control the cold knot of fear gnawing at his stomach. For some reason, this time he was more shaken, perhaps because it was an AK-47, and the skinny kid holding it did not look any older than fifteen and did not speak any English. The investigator kept looking from face to face, listening to the guide from Coutinho speaking to the half-dozen men and boys surrounding the open-air 4x4. He could not discern any sign of humanity, only mistrust and hostility. For the first time in two days, he felt deep in his bones that The Thing had led him into a trap and that this trip had been a horrible mistake.

The flight from Luanda to Luena, the capital of Moxico Province, had revealed stunning views from the air. McBain saw the panoramic majesty of nature unfold before him as the dense urban crowds of Luanda and the surrounding areas had given way to grasslands and tree-lined slopes. The greens were smattered by open stretches of brown savannah broken by narrow roads and brown and gray regions of short grasses and collections and houses or squat concrete and brick buildings that made up villages and small towns. Soon enough, the land rose up to the central plateau of Angola, even more sparsely populated and breathtakingly beautiful. The trees began to resemble a primeval forest rather than a jungle, and the land rose into tree-lined cliffs bisected in places by white foam and rushing water. By the time the Air Angola flight landed at the city of Luena, 750 miles east of the capital, McBain felt as if he had passed through several different countries and a time portal. It was hard to believe that a civil war had devastated the land.

After a few hours at Luena Airport, McBain and Silva had boarded a small private plane that belonged to Africa's Future Resources and flown nearly two hundred miles farther to Cazombo, a town east of the vast wilderness of Cameia National Park. The scope of the forest was impressive, and the two-engine plane passed over it at five thousand feet. McBain had seen waterfalls and fast-running rivers, and he questioned the director about wildlife and the return of birds to the park. Silva had only shrugged and mused that time would tell. He admitted that although it was a national park, visitors would be slow to return and that foreigners were either unaware of the beauty of the country out here or were not welcomed by the authorities. When the trees began to thin out, Silva had pointed down to the eastern border of the park as they passed over the great Zambezi River, widening ever still as it wound its way toward Zambia on the long journey to Victoria Falls and Zimbabwe, then on to Mozambique. The director had informed him that the river flowed into Angola not far from the mining project but assured him that the environmental studies had confirmed that the waters would remain undisturbed by the production when it ramped up.

Given the late hour of their arrival, they stayed the night at a small hotel in Cazombo. The contrast of the simple rooms and limited services was stark compared to what McBain had experienced in Luanda and South Africa. At dinner, they had eaten a meal of roast chicken, rice, and corn, and McBain noticed that the people in town stared at Silva and himself as oddities from a foreign land.

The two men woke at sunrise the following morning to get an early start. They met Ramon, their guide, a gregarious local Angolan who had made the drive dozens of times and knew the uncertain roads well. Silva had insisted on the six o'clock departure.

"It is four or five hours on the road to Caianda," Ramon said, "and then another two perhaps to where we take the dirt road north, about one hundred and twenty miles' distance from here and close to the border of Zambia. Then another twenty miles to the site, but the trail is somewhat treacherous there, even after clearing work in places. I called ahead by satellite phone to let them know we were coming. We should be there by midafternoon, but all depends on the weather. Let us see how our luck is today."

McBain could tell from the heat and humidity that their luck was already questionable. The guide left the top of the Mercedes four-wheel-drive vehicle down but told them to be prepared to put it up quickly. The clouds on the western horizon were menacing even in the dawn light. They initially made good time on the unpaved road to Caianda but stopped after two hours to raise the roof on the vehicle. The temperature was close to eighty Fahrenheit; it was humid; and soon enough, cloudbursts passed over, turning the road to mud in spots. The rain had stopped when, just outside their destination, they passed a body lying by the side of the road. The corpse had jeans but no shirt, and a cloud of flies buzzed around the torso. The man's arms had been cut off and were lying on his chest.

McBain looked at the back of Ramon's head.

Without taking his eyes off the road, their driver said, "Thief." He did not slow down.

They reached the town and purchased more fuel for the Mercedes, then pushed on as quickly as they could through passing storms that forced them to slow down. The unpaved road had turned into a slalom of potholes in places, and the vehicle skidded along, slowing to a crawl now and then.

At one point along the way, McBain asked Silva, "What about land mines?"

The driver had looked at him and smiled before answering in broken English. "We stay on the road."

Progress had been slow, but at least the sun had come out. With the vehicle stewing them in the heat, they took the top down again at the juncture with the dirt road north. At four o'clock in the afternoon, they were late but looked to make it soon.

Then the burst of fire from an automatic weapon had ripped the quiet of the trail. Two men stood on the dirt path, and four other bodies rose from the grass on either side of the Mercedes.

Now, as the sun burned through the late afternoon clouds, McBain's eyes blinked away the sweat from the heat and fear. He didn't dare move his hands down to his face, and his shirt collar was soaked. He shook his head every minute or so and used the opportunity to take in the sight of their captors without meeting their eyes. Their clothing was a mixture of jeans, cotton shirts, worn khaki, and camouflage. They did not have the sharp professional appearance of the soldiers he had seen in Luanda. Ramon remained calm as he spoke to the leader in what must have been a local dialect. The man dressed like a guerilla and wore an army cap, and though he was not loud, he spoke in a commanding voice and pointed to the vehicle, then the ground, with his weapon. At last he shouted, and the others joined him, urging the riders out of the Mercedes with guns raised to their line of sight. Ramon nodded at the leader and whispered to Mr. Silva.

At last, Silva said, "We have to get out of the truck."

The three men moved slowly and then stood close together a few feet from the vehicle. The leader of the group barked an order, and the three youngest moved to cover the prisoners while the leader and two older men tore into the equipment bags and backpacks in the truck to examine what they had.

254 | RILEY MASTERS

McBain's legs were getting weak as the fear spread throughout his body. He was having trouble holding his arms away from his sides. His tongue was dry, but he had to know. He spoke to Silva in a low voice. "What do they want? What are they going to do with us?"

The director was also losing the cool he had maintained. His voice was strained as he responded without looking at McBain. "They are taking the truck and the supplies in it."

The investigator saw him glance at the ones throwing packs on the ground and opening them, then back at the three gunmen with their rifles leveled at them. McBain saw that their faces now resembled smug teenagers the world over who knew their victims are helpless to stop them.

"I hope then they will just go," Silva said. McBain didn't like the way he said it. He glanced at the driver. Ramon's face was a mask of sweat and fear.

No one said anything for another minute. Then the leader came over and stood next to his three young killers, his own weapon resting on his shoulder as if it was a baseball bat. His face was expressionless. Finally, he shouted at Ramon and motioned with his empty hand toward the grasses and scrub trees beyond the road. The driver glanced that way, then began to talk rapidly to the leader. The man shouted back at him.

Ramon stepped forward with pleading in his voice and hands extended. Suddenly, the AK-47 in the hands of the youngest gang member exploded with a burst into his chest and stomach. McBain and Silva trembled in shock and terror as Ramon collapsed backward into the dirt.

The leader now looked at the two of them and gestured with his hands again for them to turn around and start walking. With no other choice, McBain slowly turned, then closed his eyes and began to put one foot in front of the other. His mind was a collision of thoughts that grasped at hope and excuses, rationalization and terror, that searched for something to say to a man who did not even speak his language that would save his stupid life. The seconds were endless, and he was so near to fainting from the heat and resignation that he stumbled and . . .

Two shots rang out, and he fell to the ground, waiting, but could feel nothing. He rolled over to look at Silva and stared up into a scene of confusion. Only then did he recognize that the sound had come from some distance from the truck. He saw the leader of the gang leaning against the vehicle, and as McBain watched, two of his older men started firing their rifles up the dirt road. Another dozen shots echoed from the distance, and he heard rounds glancing off the vehicle even as he saw the head of another of the men blossom into a bloody pulp. More shots hit the ground next to the jeep, and suddenly, the brave teenagers were running for the cover of the scrub brush, tossing their guns aside in their fear and haste. The last of the gang held on to his weapon but hobbled off in the opposite direction. McBain was watching the body of the leader slump to the ground beside the front tire when two more bullets hit him and shook his body. His head fell to the side, and he stopped moving.

McBain rose to his knees and used his sleeve to wipe away dirt and sweat from his face. Silva was kneeling over Ramon, his hands on the guide's bloody shirt. The investigator looked around him: at the vanishing backs of the gang, at the body of the leader and the other gunman lying dead by the side of the truck along with half their bags, and finally at the blue sky and clouds and sun. He was still breathing, even if very fast to fuel his pounding heart. The trail was quiet except for the growing roar of engines in low gear approaching from the north. In another long minute, two vehicles cleared the trees fifty feet from the Mercedes.

McBain did not know who they were, didn't know if they brought even worse than what he had been through; all he saw was the cavalry riding in. The small white Toyota trucks carried a dozen disciplined-looking men in camouflage uniforms, with full web gear and Belgian FN assault rifles, half of them with scopes. As they pulled to a stop near the Mercedes, some of the men scanned the bush for any sign of the remaining gang members while others jumped from the trucks to check the bodies. McBain's gaze was fixed on the man in plain brown army fatigues and BDU patrol cap who emerged from the cab of a truck and walked up to him with eyes fixed on his own dirt-streaked face. The weathered features were Mediterranean and exuded the poise of a commander. He glanced over at the unmoving body of the driver on the ground and Mr. Silva, who was sobbing into his hand. McBain spoke no Portuguese, and when he opened his mouth to say thank you in some language that he knew he could not speak, his lips and tongue were as dry as the grasses. The officer, if that was what he was—he had no insignia—extended his hand and spoke in accented English.

"You must be Mr. McBain."

• • •

THE MINING CAMP emerged behind a metal-and-barbed-wire fence as they came out of the trees around a curve in the dirt road. Shafts of green grass were beginning to rise higher on either side of the road now that the soil had tasted the beginning of the rainy season. The grasses ran back from the trail almost a hundred yards before giving way to the scrub brush and trees of the forest. The sun was passing west into the remains of the streaking clouds as the small convoy wound its way solemnly through the gate.

It had taken over an hour to make the trip back. Some of the men had repacked the Mercedes four-wheeler with the bags and equipment thrown on the ground, and they had loaded the body of the slain guide into one of their trucks. McBain and Silva sat silently in the back seat behind the head of the AFR security force, Mr. Machado. He had apologized for being late to meet them, but the camp had only just heard about the presence of the gang in their region. The three vehicles had moved up the dirt road at a steady pace, with their weapons and eyes pointed toward the trees. They left the two bullet-riddled bodies of the gang members behind for nature to deal with.

Now that he had arrived at his final destination, McBain took in the view of the project with little interest, his eyes glancing off the excavating machines and metal structures that made up the sprawling camp, briefly leaping over the lip of the great pit. The adrenaline had drained away, and the early start and toll of the day hung on his body like weights. The security team showed the visitors to a small gray hut with a tin roof, where they unloaded their gear and pointed to the shower area. As he stood under the hot water and wiped the dried mud from his face and arms, McBain watched Silva wash the blood of the courageous Ramon from his hands. The director did not speak much as they ate a quiet meal of chicken and rice. There would be time for that tomorrow. McBain fell asleep listening to the quiet, his only thought that he had reached the place he had needed to be, wondering if it was worth it.

He slept hard but not well. The investigator woke suddenly to the light and sound. The sun and work crews rose early in Eastern Angola. He found fresh khakis and a white shirt in his pack and joined Silva in the dining hall for a breakfast of scrambled eggs, cheese, and slices of English bacon. The director was more talkative but somber.

"I have to go over the reports today," Silva said. "I will catalog the last rock samples to take back to Luanda with us. I am sorry we cannot stay longer, but things have changed now. The camp has made arrangements. I have to take Ramon's body back with us to Luena, where the company will take over. We will leave tomorrow morning, weather permitting. Today you can either stay here with me as I look at the data or wander around the camp."

McBain nodded and finished a cup of coffee.

"I'd better leave you to your work, Mr. Silva. I've come a long way to see this place, so I think I'll just walk around and see what a real mining project looks like. Maybe talk to the camp manager and Machado if they aren't too busy."

The day was clear and warm. The African sun burned hot, but with the rains gone for now, there was little humidity. McBain walked around the camp until he found the main offices. He was trying to find someone who spoke English when Mr. Machado and a short, balding black man in beige pants and a short-sleeved white shirt and red tie called out to him. Machado introduced Mr. Soko as the general manager of the project and most important AFR representative in the country.

The two men offered to show McBain around the camp. As they walked, Mr. Soko described in detail the operations that had been developed over the past few years and the different stages of exploration and development that the investigator had heard about. McBain asked him questions about the potential of the mine and the environmental issues that Boston had talked about. The manager was meticulous in his description of the mining work that had been done and the measures that had been taken to ensure that any environmental impact would be limited.

"The pit is not that deep," Soko said. "All the mining work we will do is underground." He pointed to an area on the western edge of the camp that looked like the beginning of a construction site. "When the processing facilities are in place, they will be the most up-to-date technology that the rare earth industry has in order to reduce any toxic waste from the minerals. Our mining and processing will mean safer working conditions for both the miners and the local population. That is one of our advantages. Not to mention the size and quality of the rare earths treasure we are standing on top of."

The manager waved to a group of miners in beige or blue overalls as he walked by them. The men were standing around and smoking or drinking cans of soda. They nodded to the manager and security chief but looked at McBain as if he were an animal in a zoo. He guessed that they did not get many visitors around here and assumed he was just another banker.

"Yes," McBain said as the three of them stopped near the edge of the pit. "I've heard a great deal about the potential of this project. That's why everyone I talk to in America or here in Africa is so positive. I understand Mr. Silva is looking over the last results to take back with us. A pity about that Daniel Neto guy, but I guess otherwise, I wouldn't be here."

The manager and Machado both nodded.

"That was very unfortunate," Soko said. "Neto was such a good worker for so long, and then he just seemed to come apart. We still do not know what happened to him. One day, he was here, and the next morning, he was gone. Such a shame."

McBain nodded in agreement, then raised his head as he noticed the group of workmen that they had just passed. They had stopped talking, and one of them, a large middle-aged miner in beige coveralls, was staring blankly at him. There was no anger in the look but what seemed to McBain to be interest. He opened his mouth to ask Soko about it, but the manager was looking at his watch.

"I am sorry, but I must get back to work," Soko said as he shook McBain's hand. "Lots to do, especially since I have to make arrangements for your transportation back and the body of your guide, may he rest in peace."

"Thank you, Mr. Soko. You have been very generous with your time and answering my questions. I'll be sure to mention you to Mr. Henry when I get back to the States."

As Soko walked away, Machado stopped and put a kindly hand on Mc-Bain's arm in a confidential gesture. "Mr. McBain, since you have come so far on behalf of Mr. Henry and Mr. Rogers, would you like to see the work with your own eyes? Would you like to go into the mine?"

McBain glanced down into the vast pit and back at Machado. "Is that allowed?"

The security man looked around them and shrugged. "Why not? The camp was warned about potential sabotage or attempts to disrupt operations in order to stop the project. We have stopped work for a few days, so there are no crews below. We will not interfere with any mining, and besides . . ." He elbowed McBain conspiratorially. "I am the head of security."

"So is it safe to go into the mine?"

Machado laughed. "Of course. I have to do a walk-through of several sections myself in a few minutes to inspect and check on security. You are welcome to join me or not. It is perfectly safe." He smiled at McBain. "Would you like to see the future?"

McBain only took a few moments to decide as he gazed around at the vast project, the equipment, the winding road down into the pit, and the blue sky above. "I'd love to," he said. "After all, that's what I came for. Let me just grab my gear."

"Very well. But do not bring too much. We will not be down long. Join me here in fifteen minutes, and we will ride down into the pit."

McBain jogged back to the hut. He rummaged through his khaki backpack and pulled out everything but his notebook and emergency equipment: the whistle, compass, flashlight, cigarette lighter, matches, and phone, which he had switched off days ago. He was halfway out the door when a familiar nagging voice in his head lectured him, and he grabbed a liter bottle of water and threw it in the bag.

Machado drove the Toyota down around the pit and parked in front of an elevator cage that marked the entry point. McBain saw several yellow trucks parked nearby loaded with gravel, dirt, or boulders, the real-life versions of those toys scattered around living rooms all over the world. The security chief handed McBain a miner's hard hat with a lamp on the front and put on his own as he opened the gate to the elevator. The investigator saw he was wearing dark-brown coveralls and a yellow-and-black security vest.

"Do I need any special gear other than the hat?" he asked.

Machado shook his head. "No, we will not be long, and there is no work going on now. The tunnels are safe. Just stay close to me at all times. It is dirty, but you have good boots."

McBain took a deep breath as the cage door clicked, and Machado threw a switch. With a jolt, the elevator began to descend. The ride was slow, and McBain guessed that the trip down was several hundred feet at least. Silva had told him that most rare earths are baked into the earth's crust fairly close to the surface. McBain kept breathing steadily as he watched the light above disappear and the rocks that slipped by grow dimmer and slicker.

When the elevator slowed and stopped at the bottom, the security chief shoved aside the gate, and they emerged into a wide antechamber of rock, lit by several lamps. Digging equipment and crates were stacked along the walls awaiting the return of the crews. Machado grabbed an orange safety vest and gave it to McBain.

"Here you are, sir, in case it makes you feel safer. There is our path."

He started down a sloping tunnel that led into the bowels of the mine. McBain put on the vest and slung his backpack over one shoulder as he hurried to catch up. The air was thick but not terribly cold at this level. The two men moved along the tunnel at a brisk pace, following a string of lights that appeared every hundred feet fixed to the walls or ceiling.

Machado talked about the digging every so often as he stopped to look at pieces of equipment or timbers that supported and braced places in the roof or rock walls.

"These areas are very solid. The upper sections of the dig are really the assembly areas for workers and equipment. We will get to the real mining areas in due time."

McBain wondered how much farther down they would go. As they descended the tunnel, it narrowed in spots, and in those places, the air and silence became thick and uncomfortable. His nerves were becoming more sensitive as they continued on. The investigator was not claustrophobic, but he had never been this far underground before. He felt the need to hear sound.

"Wow," he said. "These tunnels don't look anything like those ones the dwarfs built in those *Lord of the Rings* movies. Is it going to get much narrower ahead?"

Machado turned. "It will in places. I am not sure what you mean about dwarfs, but some of our miners are fairly small men. It is useful sometimes in these early parts of the digging."

McBain realized that not everyone knew about American movies. He looked Machado over, realizing for the first time how large the man was relative to the workers and other security men at the camp.

The tunnel did widen out at last and, in another minute, flattened and presented them with three separate branches to follow. Machado led them to the right. In another few minutes, there was another split and they took a left turn. Now the ground sloped downward sharply, and they had to watch their footing on loose rocks. In the light of one bulb, McBain saw lines drawn on the wall with arrows pointing to holes.

"What are those lines for?"

The security chief tapped the wall. "Diagrams for explosives. Don't worry, all the materials were moved out of the mine when we stopped work." He looked at his watch. "Let's keep moving. We are almost at the end, and then we will go no farther."

But they kept moving for more time than McBain expected and took several more turns right and left before finally stopping not far from the entrance to another branching of the tunnel. The front of the tunnel was blocked off with a rope that had a sign in several languages, including English. OFF LIMITS. Only Authorized Personnel Beyond This Point.

Machado turned on his flashlight and shined the beam down into the dark for a minute. Then he retraced his steps and scanned the dirt and rock wall before smiling and patting it with his hand. He grabbed a handful of the wall and held it up to McBain as he shook his head.

"Amazing, is it not? Men come down here to blast and dig for what appears to be nothing but simple rock and earth. Poor men mostly in caves like this all over the world. They bring it up, and then it turns into something that other men value."

McBain walked over and touched the rock himself. "Yes. The stuff that dreams are made of."

They were looking at the face of the rock when they saw it tremble at the same time the echo of an explosion came rolling up from the off-limits tunnel behind them. The stream of lights lining the roof above them flickered on and off for several seconds. McBain looked at them and then back at the security man. Machado was staring down into the tunnel that ran to the cordoned-off area of the mine. After half a minute the rolling thunder of the explosion faded to silence.

"Stay here," Machado said. He slipped under the rope, and as he began to walk down the tunnel with his flashlight held in front of him, he turned to McBain. "Do not move. I will be back; wait for me."

McBain checked his watch and saw that it was almost three in the afternoon somewhere above them. He watched Machado's shape and beam of light disappear around a corner as the tunnel turned. The second hand on his watch now sounded like a clock in the night as the time crawled by. When he looked at his watch again, only three minutes had passed.

"Hey! Machado!" No response. "Find anything?"

McBain's barely recovered nerves were beginning to fray again as the silence itself was suffocating until . . . Another explosion, this one much closer than the last, shook the walls, and dust drifted down from the ceiling past the lights. Then two more.

And then the lights went out.

McBain's headlamp was on, but the glow from his hard hat extended only a short distance. The investigator froze in place. "Machado!"

As the reverberations echoed and died away, he heard nothing. There were no more explosions. For another minute, it was utterly silent. There was no sound except for McBain's boots shuffling slowly across the rock-strewn floor. When he stopped moving, he did hear a sound, one that made his flesh start to crawl. The sound was coming up from the tunnel below the turn where the security man had vanished. It sounded like . . . laughter.

McBain took a deep breath. "Machado, is that you?"

The voice laughed again, a little louder. And as his blood began to freeze, McBain recognized the voice as a harsh whisper began to carry up from the dark.

"I think I found the problem, Mr. McBain," Machado said. His voice hung there for a minute, then he said, "The problem is you."

McBain looked back up the tunnel they had descended and began to sweat. He noticed the cold, dank feel of the tunnel and felt the pitch black begin to close in as if it were a physical presence.

"What are you talking about, Machado? Come on, let's get out of here."

The unnerving voice chuckled again. McBain could not judge how near or far it was. And now it came up to him in Machado's broken English from below.

"You ask many questions. Questions about the future. I think you will have plenty of time to figure out the answers to your questions. All the time in the world. I think that the future does not include you, Mr. McBain."

McBain took a few wobbly steps back up the tunnel. He wondered if he could remember the way back, if he could outrun the security man in this maze that he knew like the back of his hand. He doubted it. Was Machado going to just shoot him and dispose of the body down here? How could he explain that? Wait . . . What had he said . . . ? Plenty of time . . .

The last laugh was louder. "You know, at least Neto was eaten quickly by the crocs. Down here, the rats may take days with you, after you are exhausted, starving, and unable to move but still alive. You will not even have the strength to scream. But you will want to."

The last sounds McBain heard were as spectral and horrifying as anything he had ever experienced in the total blackness of night, floating up in a mocking hiss.

"Who's hungry . . .?"

TWENTY-THREE

The door to the office opened, and two men wandered in. They were dressed in off-the-rack suits with white shirts and rep ties that were mostly hidden beneath their overcoats. Boston had seen them approaching in the small camera hidden in the hallway, so she was seated behind the main desk facing the doorway, her blazer on, hair tied back, and hands folded on her large oak desk. They did not dress like successful financial types yet had the appearance of the office worker or bureaucrat. They were not hard enough to be experienced cops and too stiff to be investors related to her current job. As they crossed the carpeting, she judged them to be government men. They exuded the vague air of a few serious and self-important types she had met through Dave Thomas but lacked the relaxed confidence of those FBI agents she knew from family gatherings.

They were something new, and that put her on her guard. Her eyes measured them as they approached, both middle aged, one Caucasian and one Asian. They were trim but not rugged. They were not potential clients, and she sensed trouble. Bureaucratic trouble. She wondered if she had done their taxes properly this year.

They stopped behind the armchairs in front of her desk and waited for her to smile or extend an invitation to sit. Boston did not smile.

"Good afternoon, Ms. O'Daniel," the Asian man said. "May we sit down?"

"That depends," she said, looking from one to another. "You don't have an appointment with us, and we're very busy. What can I do for you?"

"I'm Mr. Kim, and this is Mr. Jackson. We work for the United States government and would like to talk to you about an important business matter."

"That being?"

"Something you are currently working on," Mr. Jackson said.

Boston didn't like their looks already, but her face remained emotionless. She had a Glock in the drawer and a lawyer on speed dial.

"I don't discuss my clients' business, gentlemen. Not with strangers and not without an introduction from a client, even if they say they are from the government."

Mr. Kim looked at his associate, then sternly down at Boston. "I'm afraid we have to insist since this is a matter of national security."

She held his eye and said nothing. It was clear what they were about and that they were not from the IRS. "My partner isn't here right now."

"We know," Jackson said. "He's in Africa. Luanda, Angola, to be exact."

So there it was. McBain. He had kicked over the hornet's nest.

Boston glanced at her computer monitor and locked it dark. "You have identification?" she asked.

The two men reached into their jackets and held up folded IDs. Boston reached out both hands and beckoned with her fingers. They handed over the documents so she could examine them, holding them up straight and keeping the men in her line of sight.

Mr. Kim was a special agent and Mr. Jackson a senior research analyst. Their faces matched their pictures. Boston guessed that they had not had to hide their smiles for the official photos. She handed them back.

"Please sit down, gents. Maybe you can start by telling me what the Department of Strategic Threat Assessment does." But she already knew. The clouds were both parting and gathering.

Mr. Jackson pulled off his overcoat and threw it on to the back of the armchair as he sat.

"Ms. O'Daniel," he said, "we are not at liberty to discuss the nature of what we do. However, we can say that the government in general and the Defense Department in particular take a great interest in the upcoming merger of Africa's Future Resources and HR Tech. As an arm of the government that conducts research into the international availability of crucial mineral resources for the country, we work with private sector companies when necessary to advance those ventures that help long-term access to important regions of the world that can provide our country with secure sources of those minerals."

"Such as AFR," she said.

"Exactly," Kim said.

"OK, so what does that have to do with us?"

"We know that you and Mr. McBain have been investigating AFR and asking probing questions about Rodney Henry. You were hired by Harold Rogers of HR Tech."

Boston leaned back in her chair and shrugged. "Yes, it's called due diligence. Based on your identification and what you just described, I would think you would be familiar with it."

The two looked at each other. They were clearly used to a more civil tone salted with deference to their credentials.

Jackson crossed his legs and got comfortable in an interrogator kind of way.

"We're quite familiar with due diligence," he said. "But from what we've heard over the past few weeks, you and your partner have been asking the kind of questions that seem to go beyond financial and corporate research. Some of our reports on them suggest they go beyond the boundaries of due diligence into personal matters and innuendo with regard to Henry's background and possible illegal activity."

"Your . . . reports? I didn't realize you were a part of this transaction. Reports from who?"

"Never mind that," Kim said. "As we stated, we have taken a keen interest in the success of this merger and the African projects. We've done our own research into Mr. Henry's background and are satisfied that there is nothing significant there to warrant holding up the conclusion of the transaction. There are a number of private and government agencies that are awaiting the final signing, and we don't want anything to jeopardize that now by raising issues that cause concern in Africa. I don't know what you think you are doing, but—"

Boston smirked at the pair. "What we're doing, as you say, Mr. Kim, is what we were hired for. We may not be big important G-men, guarding against global threats, but we have a job to do too. We're just a couple of working stiffs trying to make a buck, and a client is paying us to make sure he's getting a good deal and not the shaft. If McBain is asking questions in Africa, or if I ask them here, it's with that goal in mind and no other. We're not being paid by AFR. We are being paid by HR Tech, and until the deal closes, Harold Rogers is the only person I'm concerned with and accountable to. If AFR is on the level, everything will go fine."

The two men bristled at her tone.

"Do you have any idea how important this merger is to this country? How vital AFR will be?" Jackson asked.

"Some. I've done my research."

"Well, do some more. There's a report produced by the US Geological Survey and the Defense Department that goes into great detail about the importance of strategic minerals and rare earths to this country."

"I know. I've read it."

"What do you mean, you've read it?" Jackson said.

Boston reached down into her drawer and pulled out a large stack of paper. She dropped it on her desk like a brick. There were dozens of little colored tabs attached to pages throughout the document.

"Twice."

Jackson uncrossed his legs and shifted forward in the chair uncomfortably. Boston guessed that he had something to do with the document.

"Then you know what we're dealing with here—the importance of AFR to the supply of strategic minerals to our defense industry. The latest tech and weapons depend upon the US having a reliable supply of scores of critical metals that we are completely dependent on foreign countries to provide us. Vital and irreplaceable components in fighter jets, missile technology, laser sights, submarine propulsion systems, armor for tanks, night-vision gear, the latest magnetic rail guns and space launch capabilities. I could go on and on. Right now, our military imports almost all the critical minerals and parts we need from overseas. America doesn't even have the mining operations or production facilities to supply our own air force and navy. If you've read the report, you understand how bad the situation is, how dependent we are on China and Russia for so many of these minerals and processed metals, and how absolutely vital it is that we address this crisis now."

"AFR is the key, Ms. O'Daniel." Kim weighed in. "They have mining rights in key locations around the world. Once they marry up with HR Tech, refine the technology and processes for production, and ramp up development, it changes the game and gives us a fighting chance to close the gap and even move toward becoming independent. And in the not-too-distant future, maybe become the dominant mineral power in the world." He jammed his fist down on the arm of the chair.

Boston watched and listened impassively, her hands folded on the desk.

"I understand all those things, gentlemen," she said. "So what's the problem? From everything I've reviewed and based on what I know, it looks like the transaction is going to close within the next few weeks. My client will be a major shareholder in your favorite company and a rich man and, based on what you've said, with an even richer future. He's happy, you're happy, and we're happy. I still don't understand why you're even sitting here."

Kim leaned forward and jabbed a finger toward her. "Because the deal isn't done yet, and from what we're hearing from our confidential sources, your partner is rocking the boat with all sorts of baseless allegations about corruption and payoffs and unhappy investors. Word has spread to some of our country's friends in the highest circles of government down there, and it's making some people uncomfortable."

"Don't you and your partner realize," Jackson said, "how sensitive this whole complex deal is? If anything stops this merger and cross-border project from going forward, the whole thing is likely to turn around on us and land right in the lap of the Chinese. They're all over the region down there and just waiting for AFR to fail. Waiting for an opening to take over the rights to that find."

Boston glanced at some of the colonial paintings on the office wall and thought about some of her last conversations with McBain about the region before speaking.

"I don't know what due diligence is like in your field, but we have to be absolutely thorough for our client. I'm sure you are as familiar as we are with business methods in Africa and some of the shadier operators and accusations against certain commodities firms. If McBain is asking tough questions, it's because he wants this deal to be as clean as possible and above reproach with the locals. He wouldn't—"

Special Agent Kim tensed up. "We already told you we gave AFR a clean bill of health. Your partner is making waves for no reason, and it has to stop. Call him and tell him to cease and desist."

"He's doing his job." Her eyes narrowed. "And from what I've heard, he's well aware that some people are uncomfortable. Hopefully for no reason."

Jackson glared at her. "His job is over. Your job is over. Finish up, pack it up, and tell your client your work is done, and it's all golden. We will take legal action if we have to."

Boston's short fuse was lit. She was out of her chair and leaned forward with her fists on the desk like the head of a Wall Street trading department. "Nobody walks into my business and tells me how to do my job, asshole. You can come back with all the paperwork you can generate. Until then, get the hell out of my office!"

Kim and Jackson rose from their chairs and took a step forward, their patience at an end. Kim's bureaucratic exterior was broken, and he was almost shouting.

"We could have you arrested on suspicion of acting as an agent for a foreign power—"

The slamming door behind them rocked the room.

"Not in my town, you piece of shit," Tom O'Daniel said.

The two men spun around in shock and saw the police captain in his blue uniform drawn up to his full height. His eyes were blazing with a cold rage that wilted them by the second, and his frame grew larger as he strode closer and closer with his finger pointed like a knife.

"You come to my city and threaten a private citizen with a baseless ac-cusation of a federal crime? I'll have you in a jail cell waiting for days for the US Attorney to show up with indictments. And if you get off, you'll never walk by an officer in this town again without thinking twice. You understand me?"

The two men were silently sweating as they stepped around the chairs. Jackson picked up his overcoat and glanced at his partner.

"In that case, you heard Ms. O'Daniel," Tom said. "Get the hell out of her office." They gave the captain a wide berth as they headed for the door. "And don't give me cause to call my friends at the Justice Department."

The two men hurried on their way, closing the door behind them. Boston came around from behind her desk and locked the door. She walked up to her father and hugged him.

"Anybody ever tell you that you have excellent timing?" she said.

He kissed the top of her head. "Once or twice. Want to tell me what that was about?"

She let go of her father and exhaled heavily. "I'll give you one guess."

Tom O'Daniel frowned. "McBain." He shook his head. "So much for an easy, legit corporate job."

TWENTY-FOUR

Boston got a call from Dee Dee early the following morning, suggesting they meet for lunch at Joe's American by the waterfront. "Bring a good foul-weather coat," she had said. "I think there's a front moving through."

The investigator worked at her apartment in the morning, then walked from Charlestown across the bridge and through the North End over to the restaurant. When she arrived at the door of Joe's, her friend was standing there holding a shopping bag.

"I picked us up some sandwiches so we could eat and talk," Dee Dee said. "Let's take a stroll and find someplace to sit."

They walked across Christopher Columbus Park toward the Long Wharf. Boston was a bit puzzled by Dee's small talk about the weather and her staff issues when there were so many more pressing things to sort out now. She also kept walking past the empty benches in the park. "Nah, not there. I know a better spot."

They finally reached the wharf and walked along it until they came to a small floating dock with a speedboat tied up to it with two large outboard engines idling quietly. Dee Dee climbed down into the boat.

Boston laughed. "Really? Isn't it a bit chilly to have lunch outside?"

A tall young black man in jeans and a blue windbreaker came up from the cabin under the wheel. Boston recognized him as one of Dee Dee's teenaged sons. "Ben? I didn't realize you could drive a boat. How are you?"

He smiled and looked at his mother. "Hi, Ms. O'Daniel. It's a loaner, sorry to say. Mom borrowed it to give me some practice."

"OK, let's go, Benjamin," Dee Dee said. "Jump in, Boston. I thought we might chat and take a short tour of the Harbor Islands while we eat. It's been awhile since I got out of the office and on the water. Even in this weather, the view is great. How are your sea legs?"

Boston leaped into the boat, fell into a seat in the back, and tied her hair back in a ponytail. Benjamin cast off and taxied away from the dock. Dee Dee stood next to her son for a couple of minutes as they pulled away from the waterfront. Boston noticed that her eyes kept scanning the wharf, not the path in front of the boat. After a short time, they had navigated the ferry area and found the channel away from the docks and out to the broader harbor. Dee Dee told him to open it up, and the dual Mercury engines came alive with a roar while the boat reared its head and headed to the islands on the horizon. Then she came back and sat next to Boston with the shopping bag.

"Now we can eat," she said. They would have to shout to hear each other over the noise of the powerful motors.

Boston laughed and dug into the bag. "Yeah, but wouldn't it be easier to talk back at the office or in the restaurant."

Dee Dee zipped up her forest-green rain slicker and frowned. "Sure. Also easier to listen. Maybe even for people who want to listen from a truck not far away. I've used this routine before to meet people. I feel like it's a better way to put distance between yourself and potential snoops of any kind. And the noise from the engines is a great scrambler, too, for anything but the most sophisticated tools."

Boston looked her in the eye and listened to the screaming engines. She realized what the newspaper editor was talking about. She turned and gazed at the receding shoreline. She had casually mentioned her visitors from the day before to Dee Dee on the phone that morning.

"You don't really think . . . ?"

The older woman shrugged and shouted over the sound and spray. "I don't know. What I didn't tell you on the phone was that I received a visit from Mr. Kim and Mr. Jackson the day before you. I didn't like their tone and told them I had no information for them. And I told them that the AFR acquisition of HR Tech is a big financial news story, so any questions I ask are fair game. But they seemed very persistent and very interested in you and McBain and what your angle was. I should have known they would go directly to your office at some point. Plus, I've received a couple of calls from certain politicians in DC in the past few days, talking about the importance of the deal. Maybe I'm being overly cautious taking our conversation out to sea, but when people start throwing around terms like *Defense Department* and *national security*, I tend to watch my back. I have no idea what capabilities they have or what authority they have. We both know abuses have happened before too. So for now, I'm going to be careful about what we talk about on the phone or in places that can be monitored from a van on the street that looks like it's a harmless electrician at work."

Boston shivered a little and pulled up the collar of her red Helly Hansen sailing jacket. "Sonuvabitch," she said. "I should have thought of that."

The boat sped on, and the skies filled with the power of jet engines climbing to altitude as they passed Logan Airport on the left and headed farther out. Boston filled in her friend on the visit from the government men and the tense end to their questioning, clenching her hands when she described their threats and her father's abrupt entrance.

After several minutes, Benjamin throttled back a little as the speedboat neared Spectacle Island, and Boston could hear the anger in her own voice more clearly in the wind.

"I still don't see what they are so afraid of. Even if, for some strange, reason this Angola project gets delayed or killed, the merger will still happen. If this mining deal doesn't go down, AFR has plenty of other opportunities. But from everything I've learned, it's like I said to the two of them. It's almost done."

Dee Dee nodded, pulled out a Styrofoam container, and started to eat a turkey sandwich.

"I think I understand. I've been doing a lot of research on the whole REE thing. That's why I think I landed on the DoD's radar. And I learned a bit more from Kim and Jackson than they intended to let on. I believe this whole deal is about much more than you and I or McBain understand. It's not just about the minerals. It's about the whole food chain."

"What do you mean, the food chain?" Boston said.

Dee Dee stretched out her legs and took in the view of Spectacle Island as the boat rounded the shore. "The reason this merger is so important to the government is that they have bigger plans for their partnership with AFR than we know. Plans for making AFR something huge globally and vital to American interests and security."

Boston shook her head. "I already know about the importance of rare earths and the Chinese hammerlock on the supply and production. I told them that."

"There's more," Dee Dee said. "Much more. The minerals are just the beginning. But here's the problem. There are plenty of minerals around the world, and new discoveries are made every year. Eventually more supply will be discovered that China doesn't own or control. And I think the Chinese know that. That's why, over the decades, they have done everything possible to make sure that they control the whole processing chain. I can tell you for a fact that there are massive reserves of strategic minerals right here in the continental US. But it doesn't matter where you find the minerals because they have to be processed into useable metals. Then those metals have to be made into components. And, in many cases, there is only one place on earth with the processing and industrial and metallurgical plants and infrastructure for you to send those minerals to be turned into real parts and products—China.

"From what I've found out, there has been a deliberate economic strategy by their government for decades to buy up and transfer the manufacturing technology from the US and other countries back to China. Over the past couple decades, they have even purchased American companies, then shut down the American operations and transferred the production facilities to China, allegedly due to cost efficiencies. Maybe that was true, but the end result was that what processing and manufacturing capabilities this country had in rare earths and strategic minerals production has almost completely disappeared. In some cases, like many of these green energy companies that are completely dependent on components produced from rare earths, they have insisted on a quid pro quo that requires the parts to be produced in China. And the end user doesn't really have any choice."

Boston took it all in, finally understanding parts of the USGS report and aspects of HR Tech's operations that had not made a great deal of sense before. And some of the more obscure and closely guarded information about small parts of that company were beginning to add up.

"I believe," Dee Dee said, "that the government intends to work with Henry to rebuild that capability here. They plan to create a company that is completely vertically integrated, from extracting the minerals to processing them into metals to producing the critical parts that go into everything from defense technologies to computers and microelectronics to renewable energy production. I've studied up on your employer HR Tech as well. I could be off, but my guess is that they have a couple of skunk works departments that are off the radar working with the government on the processing and production points in the chain. The plan is so sensitive that they have to keep it secret and prepare to build it under the radar, testing and developing the new processing technologies and production rollout quietly so no one gets wind of it, especially their Chinese competitors."

Boston kept listening intently, spellbound as the tumblers fell into place, and the implications for the new company and its potential value began to run through her brain. Dee Dee was on the same track. The boat hummed along toward Georges Island at a steady pace.

"Just think," Dee Dee said. "If even some of the new production technology works, and they get the cooperation of the government and a consortium of defense or technology firms that are edging to get out from dependence on the Chinese, this will be massive. Sure, it could take five to ten years, but so what? Remember how it seemed like one minute people thought of Amazon as selling books, and the next thing they were worth a trillion dollars and reaching into every corner of the economy? That could happen here. Except we're not talking about e-books and food and getting your stuff two days earlier for a bit less money. We're talking about national defense and every critical component that goes into scientific and green energy development. That's why HR Tech is so critical to AFR. And most of the market doesn't even realize it yet."

Dee Dee's arms were flying around as the excitement and sense of future possibilities poured out of her. Boston closed her eyes to the spray from the harbor and thought. She had been watching the prices of the two stocks for days, and something now seemed strange.

"Well," she shouted, "something's happening with the price of AFR's stock. I've been trying to nail down an independent valuation, and at this point, with anybody else out of the running for HR Tech and the deal having passed most hurdles, the price shouldn't be moving around that much. But it has been. So somebody seems to know something."

"Yes, I've seen that too. Any ideas?"

"Not at the moment," Boston said. "But I'm going to make a couple of calls."

"What does McBain say?" Dee Dee asked.

"Beats me." Boston folded her arms over her jacket. "He hasn't had time to check in while he's on safari. My guess is he's probably dicking around with his blonde slut. He's off running around the bush, in more ways than one. I don't doubt he's just about forgotten about this case . . . and me."

"You haven't heard from him for a couple days?"

Boston told her friend about the last phone call with McBain in Luanda and their fight about his plan to go out to Moxico and the project site, finishing with: "The idiot."

"Are you worried?" Dee Dee said, sitting up in her chair.

"He didn't seem to be. Why should I?"

"Because he's your partner, and you two care about each other."

"That's what I thought, too, Dee," Boston said. "But he didn't seem interested in listening to me anymore and getting his ass back here to Boston. In fact, one of the few things we agreed on was that his trip was a waste, there was nothing to suggest Rogers is going to get shafted, the deal is going to get signed, and Henry is just a businessman building what could be an important company just like you described a couple minutes ago. McBain just has something to prove by going out into the jungle. Like maybe he's as tough as Henry."

Dee Dee raised her eyebrows. Benjamin banked the boat to the left to head back to the city at a steady pace.

"Sounds like you've reached some conclusions about Henry yourself in the past few weeks," Dee Dee said.

"Some," Boston said. "I've learned a few things about him while we've worked together. I mean the different teams."

Dee Dee nodded. "Have you managed to get close to him at all? Find out anything that isn't in the public record?"

Boston could see Dee Dee was watching her closely and guessing some things. She decided to tell her about the Head of the Charles, some of the conversations with Henry, and the invitation to the gala the coming weekend. She did not share her feelings about any of this. She knew she didn't have to. Dee Dee had been a friend and mentor for four years.

As she spoke, her friend remained quiet. Finally, Dee Dee put the remains of her sandwich in a plastic bag and placed it in the shopping bag. She pulled out an accordion folder tied closed and handed it to the investigator.

"You sound pretty confident that the deal is almost closed," Dee Dee said, "and that your client will be in a pretty good position. It seems Henry is just what you said before: a tough businessman looking to build an empire. Nothing wrong with that, that's for sure. He could be the next Jeff Bezos or Bill Gates."

Boston pushed loose strands of hair away. "Based on what you're telling me, you could be right. What's in the folder?"

"Just a little last-minute research. I did some more digging and pulled up a few cases of fraud or accusations of corruption or investment scams in the mining business over the past few decades. Look the files over. Maybe they'll give you a sense of finality that you've covered every angle for your client." She leaned over and put her hand on Boston's arm. "You're almost there. The case is almost over. Believe me, I can understand. From what you're telling me, you have been able to get close and learn a lot about Henry that has helped your client and built a solid foundation for your conclusions. And God knows, I can see how the more he knows about you, the more he would be drawn to you and confide in you—any man would. It sounds like you are dancing around the edges of a new world. Powerful men have a strong attraction, a pull. It's as much a law of physics as gravity. Have fun at the gala, but be careful. You told McBain he was making it personal, losing his objectivity. Just make sure the same thing doesn't happen to you."

Boston looked at the clouds gathering as Benjamin slowed the boat after passing the airport again. She held on to the accordion folder and fought against the truth of what her friend was saying, knowing that Dee had said out loud things that she had not even allowed herself to believe were happening.

She exhaled loudly. "This case may be almost over, but in some ways, it is getting more bizarre by the minute. Between this news of yours and the movement in the stock price, now I don't know who is doing what. Up to now, we've always assumed we were just dealing with HR Tech and AFR. Now I have to find out if there are other players out there trying to wreck this deal. Hell, I don't even know if I can trust my own client." She gritted her teeth. "And, of course, my partner picks a fine time to run off on safari to test his manhood. This would be much easier to investigate if he was around."

At last, Benjamin throttled back the engines as they drifted toward the dock at the Long Wharf. Boston began checking the wharf again for unwelcome attention or suspicious vans. Dee Dee smiled at her and took her hand.

"I don't know what McBain is up to, but don't be too hard on him. Any man would be jealous and competitive of a man as rich and successful as Rodney Henry. And remember this: Your partner would never have left you to do this if he did not have absolute confidence that you could handle anything that came up without him. You'll figure something out.

"As your dad and I always taught you, when you're stumped it often comes down to asking a single question. You've been over the details and the paperwork with a fine-tooth comb. You know all the important players. If it is somehow a setup and, for any reason, the deal collapses—"

Boston stopped twisting her ponytail and looked up. "In any criminal investigation where the suspect is not immediately known, the first question to ask is "Who would have the most to gain?"

Dee Dee Franklin smiled proudly. "As someone once said, 'That, Detective, is the right question.'"

TWENTY-FIVE

Boston took the Orange Line to the Back Bay Station and walked down Clarendon Street to her office on Tremont Street, arriving just as a light rain started to fall on the square. While on the T, she thought through her options. If there were new players to consider as the last days counted down to closure, time was not her ally. The deal had to close soon, and McBain had reported that the environmental approval would be coming from Angola in the next week. She had to think fast and decide what information she needed and where she could find help on short notice until her pigheaded partner emerged from the wilds of Africa.

The first thing she did after throwing her bag on her desk was to take out the surveillance detection devices that McBain had insisted on purchasing a few months ago after the Baker case had been closed. She methodically swept the office for hidden electronic cameras and bugs, then checked the phones, mentally kicking herself for not being suspicious enough before her meeting with Dee Dee. *Sure, nice easy legit corporate job.* She was never going to get caught out making assumptions like that again. Lesson learned.

When she was finished, Boston locked the front door and went into McBain's office. She sat at the desk and made notes on a legal pad to sketch out what needed to be done. Some things were out of her control, but she still had access to the data room and as much information on AFR and HR Tech as she needed, not to mention Dee Dee's research team. The key thing she needed help with was market information, and for that, the investigator had to find experience that she didn't have.

Boston pulled over McBain's old-fashioned Rolodex, grateful once again for his random technophobia. Her partner defended his old habit of relying on paper by saying he was afraid of losing his information or leaving it in the hands of some tech giant. Now she smiled as she paged through the cards, meticulously catalogued by professional function or expertise of each person—Managing Partner, Equity Trading . . . Senior Vice President, Fixed Income Portfolio Management . . . Executive Vice President, Mergers and Acquisitions . . . Emerging Markets Analyst . . . Head of Foreign Exchange Trading . . . There were hundreds of them, with little notes scrawled on the sides. McBain's version of Facebook friends. But some were marked with an asterisk in the upper-right corner. McBain had pointed these out and explained to her that these were the people they could trust in a pinch: traders, money managers, and bankers who were both tied in to the informal information network that undergirded every transaction and could be relied on to dig out hard-to-find truths behind market movements and keep their mouths shut about it at the same time.

These were the cards Boston pulled out and considered. There were maybe two dozen that might fit her needs. She evaluated each of them in turn for their expertise and position. She shuffled them like playing cards and looked at them again and again. Finally, her eyes landed on one that had a small difference from the others. A dollar sign was written next to the name. Boston had a gut feeling. She looked at the phone number and glanced at her watch.

It was almost ten at night when she picked up the phone. She looked at it for a few seconds, thinking about Dee Dee's comments. She decided to chance it and dialed the number at the Investment Bank of Singapore. It rang twice.

"Equity Derivatives. Raj here."

Boston cleared her throat. How to introduce herself . . .?

"McBain, you asshole," the voice said. "You don't call me for three months. What do you want now? I knew I should have looked at the number before I picked up."

"Hello," Boston began. "My name is O'Daniel. I work with Mr. McBain."

The line was quiet for a minute. Boston could hear phones and voices in the background. Trading room voices.

"Boston O'Daniel?" he said.

"Yes, McBain might have mentioned me. He's out of town at the moment, and I was hoping you could help me with some information. It's kind of urgent. I know—"

"He might have mentioned your name once or twice," Raj said. "On the other hand, how do I know this is really Boston O'Daniel? McBain is always careful. If he's not there to vouch for you . . ."

Boston frowned and tapped the Rolodex card with a pencil.

"I'm not sure how I can prove it to you if you don't know from the phone number. Maybe there's something about McBain I can tell you. But he hasn't really mentioned you before. I'm having a problem with something, a case we're both working on, and I found your name in his Rolodex. It has an asterisk on it, so I thought maybe you could help us."

"Probably because he owes me money."

Boston looked at the dollar sign. "Maybe he just thinks highly of you as a reference, Mr. Ganatra."

"It's pronounced *Ginatra*, rhymes with Sinatra."

"Mr. Ganatra, I know you're busy, but if I could—"

"McBain did mention you before. But he left me a private combination code for times like this. What is it?"

"Um . . . combination code? Just a minute." She hesitated, scanning the card and desk and starting to panic as the seconds rolled by, wondering what her partner could possibly have used as a—

Her eyes fell on a picture on a side table of the two of them dancing close together in formal wear at her sister's wedding. Suddenly a thought crossed her mind: *He wouldn't.*

She said slowly, "Thirty-four . . . twenty-four . . . thirty—"

"Wrong," Raj replied. He barely had the word out.

"Wait!" She pulled a length of hair into a red mustache and hid her smile. *McBain, you're such a jerk.* "No, it's thirty-six . . . twenty-four . . . thirty-five."

"Correct," Raj said. "And you can call me Raj. You know, maybe we should do this by videoconference before I—"

It was getting late. "Come on, Raj! I need help fast. McBain is out of pocket."

"OK, Boston, what can I help you with? And where is your asshole partner with my money? Something better not happen to him before he pays me."

Boston took a deep breath. McBain trusted Raj, so she would too.

"We're working due diligence on a job you may have heard of, the AFR acquisition of HR Technologies. McBain is in Africa doing some investigating, and he's out of touch. I can't reach him. I don't know where he is. All I know is something funny is going on with the price of the AFR stock, and I need help finding out what's behind it."

As concisely as she was able, Boston gave Raj all the background she could on the two companies, carefully avoiding any violation of confidence or nonpublic information.

"Yes, I've heard about the deal," Raj said. "But I thought it was all over, so I haven't been watching the stock. Hmm. But you're right. At this point, if there are no other players that you're aware of, the stock should not be trading far from the expected valuation. The prices should be tightly locked in, not ticking up or down. The only time that happens is if maybe somebody knows something. Someone inside the deal."

"That's what I'm beginning to wonder about, Raj. But so far, everyone involved here or at the major houses is so in love with this that it's like it's all over but the champagne."

"Hold on . . . What?" Raj started talking into another phone for a minute. Boston heard some shouting in the background. She knew the Asian markets were in full swing and moving with news. After another moment, Raj came back on.

"OK, Boston, I'll do some research and see if I can sniff out anything from the Asian or Middle Eastern market centers. If the other bidders have dropped out and the deal is a nice friendly merger, the price of AFR stock shouldn't move on anything other than some additional info or rumor of a competing bid."

"No, it shouldn't. Can you find out if something is happening behind the scenes? And keep it quiet, will you? I'm getting the sense that this is dynamite and that certain important people are getting sensitive about some of the questions McBain and I are asking. I screened for bugs, but this line may be tapped."

"Is that so?" Raj said. "Well, if that's the case: Fuck you, assholes! Boston, I'll get back to you as soon as I can. Give me at least a few days. And when your partner decides to resurface, tell him he owes me even more for this."

"Thanks a lot, Raj. And please hurry. I've got to know if there is some kind of trouble brewing that we are blind to. We're running out of time."

TWENTY-SIX

His body rigid with fear, Boozy McBain waited. The mine was silent and, outside the range of his headlamp, pitch black. The investigator dropped to one knee and let his pulse and breathing steady. After ten minutes or so, there was still no sign that his executioner was close at hand. McBain had to think, starting with how to retrace his steps. Machado had left him here to die, but that didn't mean the security man was not lurking somewhere back up the tunnels with a pickax or knife in order to have a little fun with his victim. He thought about those last words and shivered involuntarily in the damp mine air. If this sadist had watched a man being eaten alive, what wouldn't he do for his own pleasure? Crocodiles. Poor Daniel Neto.

Now that he knew what had become of Neto, McBain was certain that someone had been telling lies about the young geologist and that he had to have been killed for a reason—a reason having to do with this mine. And in his stupidity and egotism, he had walked right into a trap himself.

But he couldn't afford to think about that. Neto was dead, and he was still alive, at least for now. He had to get out of here. Based on experience, the investigator had tried to pay attention and make sense of the route they had taken and the different turns, but that had been through a tunnel with a string of lights and a guide he had trusted. Now, he was alone in the dark with almost no resources. McBain looked in his pack and did a quick inventory. Aside from the light on his helmet, he had a flashlight, a lighter and some matches for his cigarettes, his phone that could be used as a flashlight if he turned it on, a compass, and his liter of water, still untouched. No food. And nothing to use as a weapon.

McBain stood up and looked at the wall and ceiling. The wire string of lights was a good path to follow. He started back up the way they had come, walking slowly with his hand touching the wall on the right, trying to make as little noise as possible on the gravel-strewn floor of the tunnel. The headlamp did not throw off enough light to see more than a few feet ahead, but that was enough for now. Every few minutes, he stopped and listened, but the thick underground air remained deathly quiet. The lights had been in different places, given the width or narrowness of the tunnel—sometimes on the wall within reach, but more often strung along the ceiling. McBain raised his head from time to time, even as he moved along the wall to check the wire. After a few minutes, an opening came into view on the right. This was where they had entered this part of the mine; he knew that much.

The investigator stopped and stepped away from the gaping hole even as he moved in front of it, ready to defend himself as best he could. McBain reached into his pack for the flashlight and shone it into the tunnel. No sign of Machado. He moved into the opening and felt his way forward again. With his ears and eyes alert, he worked to remember the next turn. There had been several before the final tunnel, and he struggled to focus his memory on how far they had gone down one stretch and the direction they had branched off and do it in reverse, hoping he had not missed or ignored an opening. Continuing to work his way along the wall, he tried to move more quickly as he scanned for an opening on the left side of this tunnel. He made an effort to adjust his pace to match that of the journey down so he might guess the time right. After what seemed like fifteen minutes, he had not seen the turn, so he kept walking. In another few minutes, the tunnel curved left, and he turned on the flashlight. There it was; he had made it to the second turn.

Yes, this seemed right; this stretch was a bit narrower. McBain had only managed about ten minutes more when he realized that the lamp on his hard hat was not as bright as before. He took it off.

"Shit. I thought these things were supposed to last for days."

He put it back on and walked faster. In another ten minutes, the light had faded completely.

McBain pulled out the flashlight and kept moving. The time stretched on as he searched for turns and took them, trying to limit his use of the light but afraid of missing a turn that he was expecting. Finally, he found a part where the tunnel sloped down instead of rising or running level. Fear gripped him again. He did not recall going uphill at any time. He stopped to think, then retraced his steps to the last turning point. There he stopped. His empty stomach was telling him how long it had been since he had eaten. Worse, his body screamed for a drink. To shut them up, he pulled out the water bottle and drank a long sip. He had to ration the water if he had any hope at all of surviving until he found a way out or someone came for him. His legs were rubbery. He sank to the ground and shone the light on his watch, then turned it off. It was eleven o'clock at night.

Hunger and thirst woke him. For a moment, McBain was not sure he was awake. Lying on the hard ground, he had drifted in and out of consciousness laced with uncomfortable dreams or nightmares. He shook his head and sat up, feeling for the light in the blackness. His watch read seven now. Fighting the rising panic, McBain realized he had to keep moving while his strength and mind lasted. He focused his thoughts and started to feel his way forward again. To keep away the dark and fear, he started to retrace not only his steps, but also his investigation since he had arrived in Africa and started asking questions.

Machado had sounded certain McBain was going to die down here. Was the tunnel sealed off somehow by the explosions? He hoped not. He could only hope the bastard counted on him getting lost. But in any case, Machado would have left himself a way out. He had to find it. But would no one come looking for him? Machado would have thought of that, too—made up a story of some kind. Or maybe he didn't have to. Maybe they were all in on it: the camp manager, most of the employees, even Silva. But why would they want to kill him? He had not found out anything and, for the past few days at least, had stopped asking probing questions. Now it seemed pretty simple. There had to be something here no outsider was supposed to see or know. But what? He had asked questions and had looked around.

After what felt like an hour, he found another turn and took it.

There were lots of tunnels down here and some equipment scattered here and there but not a lot of obvious development underground. How deep had they gone in the elevator alone—six hundred feet? More? He didn't know much about mines, except what he had read whenever there was some kind of disaster, like those miners in Chile. They had been much farther below the surface and had survived, but how could he stay alive until someone found him, if someone found him? How long? A trained miner might be able to endure it for weeks, with food and some water, but not someone with no experience being underground in the dark. His nerves were already feeling the strain of stress in an unknown environment reduced to only a few feet of a beam of light.

In his mind, McBain kept seeing those movies. This was nothing like the goddamned hobbit movies or dwarf mines. This was the real thing.

Dirty, narrow, smelly, and dark. More like a big rabbit or weasel hole. This was real mining, with men working shifts down here to dig the coal for furnaces or for jewelers to make the platinum, gold, or silver that people wear. With his strength failing, McBain had to take occasional breaks, fighting the urge to take more than a mouthful of water every few hours. Even awake now, his head was getting fuzzy, his concentration scattered. The hunger and thirst kept robbing his train of thought. Hobbit movie . . . dwarfs . . . mines . . . gold, silver, and precious stones.

Harold Rogers had talked about the mines to the east and north. He had said that many of the discoveries of rare earths had been made not far from other deposits. De Graff had mentioned new finds were taking place in areas that were supposed to be barren. The copper belt in Zambia was not far. What else? Henry had gone on and on about Angola's potential, as had the oil men in Luanda. Silva and the people at Coutinho had added something else. A rich country, with oil, natural gas, timber, rare earths, and other strategic minerals. The civil war that lasted for decades had been about control of territory. This particular territory—Moxico Province. Gina and others had talked about the fighting here: This was where that guy Savimbi had died. Was it possible that there was more here than the expected rare earth minerals, some other kind of rare strategic mineral? McBain stopped and sank to the floor of the tunnel again.

There was another mine. There had to be. That's what the off-limits signs and warnings that he had seen earlier had been about. In digging for rare earths, maybe Henry had hit the mother lode. McBain struggled to recall the most priceless of the elements Rogers had named that they might find out here in virgin territory.

If, by some chance, there was another mine, another vein that could be developed secretly nearby without anyone knowing, someone could divert the find and run a parallel operation that could be worth billions more. Gold, uranium, rhodium, who knows what or how much? A guy as smart as Henry could use his contacts and operation to develop a separate set of books, and the investors in AFR would never know anything about it. Now some of it made sense too. All the knowing smiles when McBain had started asking about corruption and the description of ways around it. Working out deals with everyone, even Angolan officials. Of course.

Maybe I was on the right track after all.

Daniel Neto had been a smart young geologist. The young man must have discovered it and been killed for it. And now, he would be as well, as punishment for not getting the message. Did Henry know about it—know he was here? Sure, he did. As soon as he had walked out of the encounter in Pretoria, he should have realized it. Word travels fast, Gina had said. McBain had thrown around Henry's name quite a bit, especially in Luanda. Of course, someone would have reported back to him and let him know McBain was snooping around asking tough questions, questions about corruption and bribery and back room deals to shaft investors. Suddenly, something else made sense: the escalating string of incidents, from the hotel break-in to the car crash, had been intended to send him a message, one he had ignored at his peril. And fool that he was, he just kept coming, all the way to the mine itself, no doubt convincing them that he knew more than he did. All of a sudden, a memory surged up from weeks ago when they had first met at the event.

Have you ever killed a man, Mr. McBain?

Of course, Henry had. McBain now knew he was the kind of man who would kill someone just for sport, even from a distance. Machado was just his blunt instrument. He was probably laughing even now.

"Henry, you son of a bitch."

Even as he said it, McBain could feel the dryness in his mouth. He rubbed his lips and tasted the dirt.

And that was when a small part of him said it was fine with that, that he had it coming anyway, and that he would welcome it.

McBain growled, slapped his face, and struggled to his feet again. The fight was not over yet. He moved on, switching the light on and off hour after hour, glancing up to the string of dead light bulbs like a lifeline in an ocean of dirt and rock. The fight was not over, but he was losing it with each passing hour. He would come to a dead end and have to retrace his steps or would find there was no string of lights to follow. The hours crawled by, and he was losing concentration and strength. He had to take more frequent breaks and sit while his legs rested, nursing his hope and his water.

Each time he woke sitting against the wall or lying on the hard ground, the investigator had to remind himself which side of the tunnel he was on and the way he had come. It was easy to get confused, even when he stuck to the lights as a landmark. His sense of smell was heightened, but there was little to inhale down here in the stagnant air, aside from the dirt and occasional whiff of oil or gasoline. Without the light, there was nothing to see, and for the most part, there was no sound. On those rare occasions when his ear did detect something, he did not have to wonder what it was; he had been in the New York City subway system often enough to recognize it. He tried to think of it as a sign that he was getting closer to the surface.

McBain kept moving and taking turns into tunnels if they seemed to go up, for all the good his disorientation did him. Sometimes he fell asleep despite the thirst and hunger. After one episode, he woke with a start. He checked his watch by lighting a match; he saw that it was four o'clock. But was it morning or night? He struggled to his feet again. How long had he been down here? He felt the wall and clicked the flashlight on and off again, just long enough to realize that it was beginning to lose power. McBain rubbed his forehead and his aching face.

This much stubble takes me about three days to grow. And if it's been that long, either the tunnel is closed, or no one is coming.

He kept stumbling along and licking his lips. At least this stretch of the tunnel seemed to be a kind of upslope. Progress was agonizing, but he kept going, even as that vile little voice inside his head resurrected itself again—that this was a fitting end. It tried to get him to stop putting one foot in front of the other, to give up, but he would not. He took a small drink from the bottle; there was not much left anyway, a few swallows. Now the voice was taunting him, joking that he had gone a whole week since his last cocktail, back at the hotel in Luanda. That was the longest stretch in six years, since Mel had walked out on him for that rich asshole. And since that night a year later when he had met Boston.

That had been a hell of a night. It had changed everything for him.

And with that, he sank to his knees at the mercy of that admonishing voice.

The flashlight refused to respond, so he used a match to check the time, then sat against the wall as the voice cut through the disorientation to lecture him on his faults and tell him that this was penance before the final sentence for what he had done that night and five years of sins. McBain fought back by remembering the happier times and who he had been before Melissa had left him. He was not a bad guy.

But he had changed, and since then, he had done some bad things, even for a good cause. He had never been able to forget or forgive or find that person he had been. It had been a search just as futile as this one to find a way back to the entrance to the mine. But this time, he did not have five years, and this penance would not result in redemption. Inside, McBain was crying, but his eyes could shed no tears. He growled again and shook his head to beat back the thought of giving up. Then he took a deep breath and prepared to try one last time on his hands and knees.

Something smelled different to him. What was it? It was an effort to clear his mind, push past the weakness, and focus his thoughts. He pushed himself up against the wall of the tunnel and looked left, then right, and sniffed the air. There was the scent of gasoline and oil and damp wood. And there was another thing. The air was not as thick. There was a trace of clean air. With his mind drifting and concentration difficult, he could not be certain.

McBain raised his body up by pulling at the earthen wall and a wooden brace. He stumbled forward up the slope; yes, it was rising. His feet were made of lead, but he kept going. He no longer kept track of time, but as he made progress, he now sensed that, among the odors of the mine, some kind of fresh air was stronger in his nostrils. That scent that he had first experienced during the rainy trip to the mining camp, who knew how long ago? He dug into his pocket for his phone and powered it on again, hoping there was something left. With fuzzy vision, he found the flashlight function and shone it ahead.

Up ahead in the distance, the light glinted off something. Maybe it was the rock wall of the tunnel. As he came closer, he felt the ground tilt at a higher angle, and he remembered the initial sharp descent into the mine. As the light reflected off man-made objects, he dared to hope again, and this time it was rewarded. As a chamber opened, the tunnel wall suddenly fell away, and he lost his balance and stumbled to the ground, but with the fading light of the phone, he saw the miners' equipment stacked against the wall around the entrance to the elevator to the surface. Adrenaline gave him a short burst of energy, and he crawled to the boxes and began to go through them one by one looking for more light . . . a radio . . . some food . . . a water bottle . . .

And found nothing but mining gear and tools.

Holding the phone's light out, he found the cage door and flung it open. There was no elevator. Machado must have left it at the top. McBain didn't care what awaited him up there. He slammed the gate and pressed the button to bring it down to take him to the surface, and . . . nothing happened. It ticked and ticked every time. There was no power.

It had taken days, but against all odds, he had found his way back to the only means of escape, only to find it as much of a dead end as a rock wall. Of course. Machado would have left nothing to chance.

McBain stepped away from the gate, sinking to the ground in the dark. Even the flashlight in the phone was fading now. He crawled to a stack of boxes to rest against them and watch the last of the light evaporate. His final struggle was with himself to accept his death. His mouth was a desert, his stomach well past starvation as his body devoured itself. But at least now there was no point in crawling any farther. There was no place left to go. He felt his body sag as his will to live began to collapse.

Hey, as graves go, this is a pretty expensive one. So I got that going for me.

I can't remember the last time I went this long without a drink. What a way to die out . . . I mean, dry out.

McBain tasted the last sip of water, his tongue savoring the final drops with greater reverence than the most priceless wine. The bottle was empty. He sat there with the blackness closing in while time lost all meaning.

Just remember, you wouldn't have made it this far if she hadn't lectured you about carrying the water.

With a parched mouth, he had almost no voice left. "I don't want to die in a hole in the dark."

Well, you should have thought of that before you left Boston.

If the light had been strong enough, he would have realized he was smiling as he thought of her. His confused thoughts leaped from memory to memory as he accepted that he was going to die, but his acceptance helped him focus now on how lucky he had been to have her as a friend and partner for almost five years. And what a five years it had been. She had grown and blossomed from the tough-talking townie he had met in a bar into a consummate professional woman. Gina was wrong about that. The change had been amazing to watch and be a part of. Maybe he had even helped. That had been one good thing. Watching her attack this job and a new kind of work, he had often wanted to tell her how sharp and quick she was and how many options she had if she ever wanted to give up this ugly business of shaking down scam artists, shady brokers, and Ponzi schemers. Listening to her reports over the past few weeks on the phone had been a pleasure and a revelation. He should have told her. But he understood enough to know that he didn't want to, didn't want her leaving him for something better.

She asked you not to leave her.

I shouldn't have left her.

You didn't leave her that night. And you should not have left her this time.

She had been right all through this job, especially when she told him he never should have gone to Africa or out to the mine. What a shame she would never get to hear him admit it. She would have enjoyed that.

I wonder how she will take the news when they tell her. I wonder if they will ever dig me out of this hole and give me a real grave. Or if I will just disappear like Daniel Neto.

Not that she needed him now. She would be OK without him. Hell, fucking Henry was going to get his way, so she would take home a nice paycheck from Rogers. Maybe even a bonus when they finally discovered McBain's corpse. That was something too. Whatever secrets he was being buried with—Henry's or his own—she was the only thing that mattered now.

She had grown. Gotten better and smarter and tougher than him even. As she had said herself a few months ago, she didn't need him to protect her anymore. And she was right. She would find a new partner or a new line of work. Maybe she'd convince Dave to join her after all, now that the troublemaker was gone. They'd make a good team.

He had been so lucky to have her. Luck. He searched under his shirt and pulled out the medallion that he had hung around his neck since Luanda— her lucky medallion. He took it from around his neck. With no light, he just felt the metal with his thumb, moving it slowly along the edges of the gold number 7, then the handles and the sheaths of the two crossed cavalry sabers. McBain began to drift off, and his head jerked as it fell. With no strength left, he leaned over and lay with his back against the elevator cage. He guessed that when he fell asleep now, it would be the last time. Not wanting to let go of the medallion, he reached into his shirt pocket with two fingers and took out the picture of Boston that he had brought along. He could not see it, but that was all right. He had memorized it long ago.

"I'm not going to die alone in the dark. I have my partner with me."

Closed or open, there was nothing to see with his eyes that was not captured in his head or heart already. McBain slid lower onto the ground, too depleted to sit up. He lay down on the rough dirt with his head on the elevator shaft cage door. With the air from the surface flowing down now, it was cold, and he was so thirsty. His tired hand closed around the medallion. His lips were cracked and his throat dry, but he had to try to speak the words aloud to have them mean anything.

"I'm sorry I left you to handle this alone. I love you, Meghan."

As his consciousness collapsed with silent intensity, McBain looked up the elevator shaft, and the small part of him that remained realized that all the stories and movies were true: You do see a light at the very end of the tunnel.

TWENTY-SEVEN

The ritual silence of the library had been suspended for the evening. The credenzas of books in the vast lobby had been rolled away and replaced by small gatherings of men and women in black tie and evening gowns, with the crowd punctuated by cocktail tables and alcoves of bartenders. The chattering of society friends at a fundraiser was a murmuring undertone to the strings, woodwinds, and horns that filled the cavernous entry and front hall of the granite slab of the Johnson Building of the Boston Public Library with an autumn serenade of classical music. The walls of windows looking out on Boylston Street were lit with red and green in accordance with the theme of the night: Africa.

By eight o'clock, the space of Boylston Hall was filling up, and the waiters patrolling the floor with trays of hors d'oeuvres were cycling through a little faster. As more people, arrived the hosts and hostesses encouraged them to explore the sections on the upper floors and in the back. Many were directed to the older McKim Building through the courtyard, lured with a glass of champagne or wine and the rare warm evening in late October. A dance floor had been sectioned off under the grand staircase for those inclined to indulge their taste in swaying to Mozart and Vivaldi. The staircase itself rose up on both sides of DeFerarri Hall to the second floor, draped for the evening in soft red and green cloth, the steps lit strategically with candles to enhance the dimmed lighting. The steps met at the top in a balcony overlooking the dance floor and entryway that formed the entrance to the rows of fiction books and reading tables in the rear of the building.

Most people opted to mingle or observe. Boston being what it is, and the nature of fundraisers being what it is, many of those circulating in the room knew one another. The African-themed evening was dedicated to raising awareness of, and significant funding for, the Sub-Saharan Africa Health Initiative, a new organization that would be directing funds to social projects throughout southern Africa for clean water, health clinics, and medical training. The organization's sponsors had already raised a substantial sum of money from Boston's finest and were hosting the event to thank the contributors and provide them with a chance to speak to some of the professionals who would be putting their funds to use in South Africa, Mozambique, Tanzania, Zambia, and other countries, including Angola.

At the same time, social season was about gossip, so as people strolled around to the strains of Chopin and Bach, the soaring hall also buzzed with air kisses and laughter as friends and frenemies exchanged greetings and news. Some, of course, acknowledged the irony of the evening.

"Hello, Martha," Mrs. Jenkins called out. "I was hoping I'd see you here. Is Charles with you?"

"Yes, he's looking for the bar and one of his partners. I thought I'd wait for the drinks to come to me." Martha Patterson looked around. "I have to admit, Tracy, I feel a trifle odd tonight. Don't you think it's strange to be wearing black tie at an event with a theme of poverty?"

Tracy took a sip of her champagne and placed it on the cocktail table next to them. "Maybe, but the event is to raise money for a good cause. And frankly, it would be more offensive if someone tried to dress us in native costume as a posture. We are who we are, Martha. Sending money to people who can help is something. Better than just another party for the season. And Harvard doesn't need more of your money."

"I suppose you're right, Tracy." A waiter stopped by the ladies with a tray of chardonnay, and they liberated two glasses. "I hope they raise quite a bit. The place is really filling up." Martha scanned the entrance as the doors parted, and several couples walked in. Her glass was halfway to her lips when her hand stopped. "Is that . . . ?"

Tracy Jenkins put her hand on her friend's arm. "It certainly is. One of the men of the hour—Rodney Henry."

"I've never met him," Martha said. "I've seen pictures, but he's more imposing in person. And who is that on his arm?"

Tracy shook her head. "The redhead? I don't recognize her, so she must be from out of town. She's stunning. Is she wearing—?"

"Yes. The Winston Cluster."

As Boston entered Boylston Hall, she took in the sights and sounds of her first black-tie social event. She paced herself with Rodney Henry's deliberate entrance and kept her free hand hooked lightly inside his extended elbow. Her smile was soft with composure, but as they strolled farther into the room to the sounds of classical strings from the orchestra, her nerves began to tingle. More and more of the couples or islands of guests were turning to stare at Henry and . . . her.

The past three days had been a frenzy of preparation as the panic of what Boston had agreed to overtook her. She had attended several stylish weddings, but never anything like a black-tie fundraiser with a room packed with some of the city's wealthiest and oldest families. Since none of her friends traveled in these circles, she had placed a frantic call to Christina Baker, one of their former clients who lived in Beacon Hill, to ask for guidance. Boston had called on several of her favorite stores and shopping friends to find just the right dress and shoes and barely managed to secure an appointment on Newbury Street a few hours before to get her hair and makeup done. Her Tiffany solitaire diamond earrings and tennis bracelet she had chosen herself; however, Henry had asked her to allow him to bring a special necklace that he had borrowed for the evening.

Now, as she drifted slowly into the center of the room, 195 marquise and pear-shaped diamonds draped around her throat were ablaze with light from the candles and chandeliers, as if drawing power from them by the force of gravity. Her fiery auburn hair cascaded down her back, exposing the necklace in all its splendor. The black strapless Oscar de la Renta tulle gown curved around her body, then flared into a skirt of feathery gauze down to her black Christian Louboutin Pigalles, their classic red soles mirroring her hair and Chanel Pirate lipstick.

As they moved forward, Henry began to acknowledge one or two people who raised their glasses to him. Boston observed that he was not particularly friendly but smiled politely in a formal, businesslike manner. She was grateful for the slow pace as it gave her room to scan the crowd and their surroundings, both to take in the elegance of the occasion and to steel her nerves for any encounters. The library itself was familiar to her from previous visits, but few of the faces were, and those only from local periodicals. That was a good thing, for while she had prepared her story and the reason for her presence ahead of this night, she feared encountering former clients who might wish to discuss her usual business in front of Henry.

The only real test came when they stopped near the entrance to DeFerarri Hall and the grand staircase, and three couples engaged Henry just as they intercepted a waiter with a tray of glasses and a chilled bottle of Moet champagne. As he handed her a glass, Henry introduced her to Mr. and Mrs. Horowitz and Mr. and Mrs. Thomason. Mrs. Horowitz, in turn, introduced her friends the Parkers to Rodney Henry. Mrs. Parker, a tall blonde woman in a cobalt-blue gown, shook Henry's hand and then stared as she took Boston's.

"Excuse me, Ms. O'Daniel," Mrs. Parker asked, "but have we met? You look somewhat familiar."

Boston smiled lightly and shook her head while laughing inside. "I don't think so, Mrs. Parker. But I work in the financial business here in Boston, so perhaps we might have had reason to run into one another on business of some kind or another. Where do you live?"

"Beacon Street, of course."

Boston tilted her head as if in thought. "Well, it's a small town. Perhaps we just passed each other in the Public Garden. It is a pleasure to meet you."

As they moved on toward the courtyard, Henry glanced over at her. "Care to tell me what that smug look is about?"

She sipped her champagne. "Maybe later. My, but sometimes, a nice glass of champagne tastes better than at others." She looked around. "Aside from meeting people, exactly what are you expected to do here tonight? I think you said you already donated to the fund, so no one should be asking you for more money."

Henry pointed to some of the exhibits of materials at tables scattered throughout the hall.

"Education, to some degree," he said. "While many people here have donated money, they don't really appreciate the places it is going or the great need. They know vaguely it is a good cause, but several of us who set up this event tonight would like to provide more information and firsthand accounts of the situation on the ground in communities and rural areas in Africa. Maybe make it more tangible to some of them so they get involved on a more frequent basis. There are tables set up in different parts of the library with brochures manned by people to help explain where the money is going."

They started in the world languages area and worked their way around the different sections so Henry could meet and greet people and steer them to staff members and tables representing African countries or topics, from health care to small-craft training programs. For an hour or so, Henry spoke at each station about the work being done and talked to guests about specific countries and needs. When he was engaged with a contributor, Boston hovered nearby and absorbed the details about each country she had memorized at the large map on the conference table in her office, from the landlocked Lesotho to the rain forests of Mozambique and impoverished rural villages of Zimbabwe. When he expounded to one white-haired couple on the challenges of Angola in the aftermath of the long civil war and the damage wrought to both people and rare animals by land mines, she listened with focused intensity.

At one point, they stopped at one of the bar stations and ordered another glass. Boston almost leaned on the bar with her elbow but caught herself.

"Still, it seems weird to me," she said to Henry. "I'm not one of these people, but I'm a little uncomfortable with the atmosphere as I look at some of the brochures and hear you and some of your nonprofit people talk about the need. Maybe if I had the kind of money to donate, my conscience would feel better."

Henry stared at her and raised his glass to touch hers for a moment. "Then you feel exactly as you should," he said. "We should all feel that way, and I'm sure most here do. They are good people for the most part. Their hearts are in the right places, and they're making a difference in the only way they can. So are my people in AFR. So are you."

She looked at him.

"There's no reason to feel guilt if you're doing whatever you can in your power to make things better. That's why I've built AFR into a global organization. We operate in many parts of the world where we can create a better place for people by developing resources and communities together. That's the thing I want these people to come away with tonight. The need is vast, and not just for one night. The more they understand the good things we can do, the more committed they might be over time."

She noticed an undertone of passion in his voice that she had only heard once, in the conference room that afternoon when she had uncovered the mistake. He was observing the crowd again.

"In the long term, we can do so much," he said. "As we grow this company around the world, we'll make our mistakes, even as we learn how to get better with Harold Rogers's technology. But as it all comes together, the potential will be unlimited."

She was beginning to understand some of what he had explained about his style of marketing and how he had become so successful. Boston took her eyes off Henry and gazed around the room. Tonight, that potential certainly did seem within reach, in the middle of all the success and wealth and committed donors. She reached up, realizing as her hand touched the necklace that she was still drawing attention from many an envious eye of the women in the room. She touched Henry on the arm.

"Have you seen the courtyard before?" she said.

"No, I didn't realize there was one."

"Yes, the courtyard is on the way to the older McKim Building. I could use some air, then I'll show you around that wing. It's older, and it's unique. I've been a couple times."

Boston led the way out up a few steps and through the doorway into the courtyard. The night air was cool on her shoulders, but not uncomfortable. The stone-arched walkway on three sides of the courtyard was scattered with benches and small cocktail tables. The air hummed with chatter and the clink of glasses and forks on plates. Boston raised her dress as she stepped carefully down to lead Henry over to the fountain and the small sculpture in the middle of the courtyard.

"I think it's bronze," she said. "I don't know anything about art, but I remember hearing the story about how, when the guy first sculpted it, some of the upright citizens of Boston objected to the sight of a naked woman holding a baby and grapes and appearing to be drinking and dancing." She looked around at the upright citizens at the tables in tuxedos and evening gowns. "Looks like they came around after all."

She noticed that Henry was also evaluating several of the islands of people, and they seemed to be returning his attention. Boston sensed an uneasy familiarity in the way the looks were exchanged. She and Henry walked along the outside of the fountain as they scanned the archways and interior granite walls of the McKim Building, lit up in green and red lighting that somehow appeared less festive and more ominous in this darker enclosed area. The music from the orchestra was audible but faint outside.

"It's quite peaceful out here," Henry said.

"Yes, normally, people come here to think and enjoy the quiet. Not tonight, of course. The courtyard can even be pleasant in the winter covered in snow."

"Let's see more of this building, shall we?" he said.

They climbed back up to the walkway and started toward the entry to the older building. They passed one of the standing tables that Henry had been staring at, with three couples and more than a few empty glasses. He ignored them, but Boston observed that he clearly knew some of them and that his face displayed traces of humor.

One of the men, middle aged and bearded, who wore the weight and look of a drinker, knocked back the last of one and licked his lips. "Well, look who's here. I'm surprised to see you here, Henry. Trying to polish your dirty image by throwing some cash at poor Africans?"

Boston stopped and waited for Henry's reaction. He turned to face the man, took a step closer, and looked him up and down.

"Well, someone had to, Josephson" Henry said. "Since your fund got cleaned out, I'm sure you don't have much to donate to good causes. Get anything out of the bankruptcy court yet? I'm surprised you could afford the price of admission tonight."

His wife was a slender woman in a pale silk gown with platinum-blonde hair. Even in the dim lighting, Boston could see her eyes were full of hate. Mrs. Josephson jutted her jaw out and stared at Henry with a glare of condescension.

"We may have lost some money on those investments," she said, "but others will pay off. And at least we're doing the right thing, and not just for one night."

"Good luck," Henry said. "Maybe at one point in five or ten years, you'll find a green investment that doesn't go under and take your money with it. What is this, four now?"

None of the three couples seemed to take any notice of Boston. They were all focused on Henry and what was clearly their history with him. She stood back, watched, and listened to what she perceived was an on-going battle. A bald man in his thirties with narrow metal glasses leaned forward on the table.

"Our funds are designed for the long term, Henry," he said. "Even if it takes time for us to make money, we are investing for the future of the environment. Unlike you and your mining and fossil fuel operations. And we were successful at getting a couple of university endowments to drop their investments in your companies."

Henry shrugged. "Thanks, Hamilton. Sellers like you just allow me to buy up stock at fire-sale prices. So keep trying." He calmly looked at the couples as he folded his arms. "And now that I think about it, I make money both ways when it comes to people like you. In fact, I count on you."

Mrs. Hamilton put her wineglass down and sneered at Rodney Henry. "I don't know how you can look in the mirror, Henry, with your filthy mining operations destroying the planet. You're despicable."

Against the background of green and red torch lighting in the dark court-yard, with its stone arches and covered walkways, Boston thought her black hair and gown gave her the appearance of a witch preparing to cast a spell.

Henry just pivoted his glance slightly to look at her hand on the wine-glass. "Curious you say that, Emily," he said. "That's a large diamond you have on your finger. Where do you think it came from?"

The woman pulled her hand down and stared at Henry. "I can assure you that this diamond ring is certified as coming from a conflict-free zone and came from a responsible source, if that is what you are inferring."

"How long have you had it?" Henry asked.

"Almost twenty years," she said.

"Then they lied to you. At that time, most of the diamonds in circulation came from Sierra Leone, Angola, and other places in West Africa. They were dug out of the ground by kids who probably didn't live through the next round of fighting and sold on the black market to the diamond merchants in Antwerp. You're wearing a blood diamond. I should know."

Her husband slapped his hand on the table. "So you say. Be that as it may, that's ancient history. Today, what we're investing in is clean, and what you're doing is dirty and exploitative."

Henry turned to Hamilton and the others. "Really? Clean, you say? I know about most of what you invest in. Like I said, I wouldn't be as rich as I am without you. But I wonder if you have any idea of what goes into those clean technologies you're so committed to."

He pointed at Hamilton. "Every time they build a wind farm or a field of solar panels, it requires large amounts of rare earth metals. Those massive wind turbines to generate power that you want to put everywhere except off the coast of your house on Cape Cod? They take tons of neodymium and dysprosium and other minerals that I supply from my mining operations. And those solar panels filling up acres of land out west? They're made with niobium and other alloys that come up out of the ground.

"Josephson, you're a big fan of replacing all those dirty, gas-guzzling cars with electrics and putting the oil companies out of business. Any idea how much cobalt, tantalum, and neodymium that will take? When you get into your Tesla or whatever the hell it is you drive tonight, say a prayer for the tens of thousands of children in the Democratic Republic of the Congo who dug the cobalt out of the ground for your battery. You know, the local miners really like to use the young ones, five and six years old, because they have small hands and can work their way into narrow holes to search for the rocks. Once you've seen what that toxic red dust does to the eyes and lungs of a ten-year-old, you never look at a battery-powered car the same way again.

"And, Dr. Richardson, I know you are an investor in a couple of medical technology companies that are end users of our minerals. Would you like to know what would happen to some of those laser and research products that are so useful for doing precision surgery on patients and pediatric dentistry if the rare earth mining industry shut down operations? You know how many life-saving procedures and pacemakers would not be possible without our products?

Henry glanced down at the table and their phones. "Every one of you has a small computer in your hand that is filled with a dozen bits of rare earths.

Josephson here was a huge advocate of the multibillion-dollar boondoggle in California to build fast maglev bullet trains. If you want those, you have to rely on more neodymium and niobum to build their powerful magnets for the infrastructure than is being processed today. And all the gifts you get for your kids, like three-hundred-dollar headphones, they rely on those little pieces of processed earth, too, to create miniature components. Where's it going to come from?

"But you know what?" Henry said. "You don't know, and you don't want to know. Like everyone else, you just want it at the lowest cost and don't care to learn about the price being paid by someone overseas and out of sight. Then you posture at hating the people who dig it out of the ground to get it for you. Everything that makes your green world possible, from LED lights to heating to stronger and lighter construction materials, comes from men like me who bring the materials to the scientists. Shut down the oil companies and make it all green, right? At least the oil industry uses technology and produces their product with high-paying, skilled jobs. You don't think anything of putting every last coal miner in West Virginia out of a job to make yourselves feel virtuous, but you turn your heads away from the sight of toxic waste in China or Brazil or Africa, where they're not as environmentally conscious as you."

Boston's eyes darted back and forth between Henry and the six people. In the dim light, she could see fingers tensing on glass and teeth clenching. She edged a step closer to the table. Henry's tone remained level, but she could hear an undertone of contempt as he kept grinding down on them.

"Sure, Josephson, you'll protest me, then get into your hybrid car and go to a party. I remember your younger brother from the Wall Street days when he was the man to go to for your coke. Just like all of you now. They would toss out their thousand dollars and snort lines of cocaine or pass around a joint without giving a second thought to the human cost of the drug trade. The violence, poverty, and fear, the death and human trafficking fueled by drug money. By their money. Do they even think for a second about the number of people who died so they can get their high in the comfort of their offices and homes?"

Boston tensed and prepared to move between them, evening gown be damned. She didn't know Henry well enough to know how much restraint he would show if Josephson lunged at him, but she guessed that the damage he might inflict could be quick and severe. The situation was getting personal, and anything could happen. Her natural instincts were setting off an alarm for trouble, and she had to think of a way to defuse it before glass shattered. Black tie or not, the alcohol was in charge now.

Henry paused for a moment, then pulled at a cuff and resumed his placid demeanor as he looked at them all. "But what the hell," he said. "What are a few thousand dead African kids when you're saving the planet? Sacrifices have to be made, eh, comrade?"

Josephson slammed his glass down. "How dare you, you—?"

Boston swept between Henry and the table and put her hand on his arm. "Excuse me, folks," she said. "Mr. Henry, you did promise me a dance when they played a waltz. I believe I hear one now."

Henry turned to ignore the couples. Without another word, he smiled as he took her arm. They exited the courtyard into the light of Boylston Hall to the sound of muttering and left them to stew in their anger.

Boston breathed a sigh of relief as she and Henry reached the edge of the dance floor between the grand staircases. The waltz was a popular one, and three couples had reached the floor and begun to spin. Henry watched them for a moment. "Deftly done, Ms. O'Daniel. In addition to your accounting and finance skills, you clearly have potential in public relations." Henry nodded at the pace. "Strauss is not exactly your style, I imagine, given your age. I enjoy it, though."

Boston smiled up at him. "It's 'The Blue Danube.' Or 'On the Beautiful Blue Danube,' to be exact."

Henry's eyes evaluated her with admiration. "Yes, I know. My second wife was a German countess. I'm impressed that you know it. I suppose you heard it at the movies, perhaps Kubrick's *2001*? I won't press you to dance."

She grasped his hand and led him out. "It's been a couple years, but you lead, and I'm sure it will come back to me. Wait." She had the good sense to pull off her Louboutins and place them next to the wall.

"Aren't you afraid I'll step on your feet?" Henry said.

Her green eyes gazed up at him with a demure expression. "I guess I'll just have to trust you."

They stepped onto the dance floor and turned to face one another. Henry bowed, and she curtsied. He placed one hand on her left shoulder blade, she extended her right hand to join his, and they began to follow the other couples on the floor in the counterclockwise flow. Boston was surprised at how quickly it came back to her, and she guessed that it was not a little due to the fact that her partner knew how to lead skillfully. At first, she was clinging to the mental metronome of "one-two-three, one-two-three" and praying she would not trip, but in less than a minute, the nervousness faded away, and she flowed naturally with the music. The lessons that had been drilled into her hour after hour just a few years ago returned as physical muscle memory, and she was swaying and turning and dipping and twirling in rhythm with Johann Strauss like a movie princess in prewar Vienna. As the orchestra swept seamlessly from the Blue Danube into another waltz and then another that sounded familiar, Boston lost track of time and was aware of only her dance partner, the sound and candlelight from the stairs, and the feeling of belonging to this evening for the first time. At times, she felt she was floating in a dream filled with sound.

With a flourish, the final waltz stopped. They finished, and the audience in the main hall and the crowd lining the entryway, both stairways, and the balcony above all erupted in applause. Immersed in the music and flow of the waltz, she had not noticed that the audience of some of the city's most prominent and distinguished citizens had lined the balcony and staircases on each side and crowded to the edge of the dance floor to watch them sail about. She was suddenly aware that dozens of cameras and phones were clicking away, focused on the two of them.

She curtsied again.

"You waltz magnificently," Henry said, still clapping.

Boston blushed. "Thank you. My partner taught me."

"Mr. McBain? Really? He is a man full of surprises. It is a shame he couldn't join us this evening. I'm certain he would be a pleasure to watch."

"Sometimes. I'm afraid tonight he had other commitments. He sends his regrets."

"I'm sure he does. On the other hand, you will forgive me if I am grateful that his absence gives me a chance to monopolize you tonight. I can tell from the stares that I am a fortunate man to have such a beautiful and graceful dance partner. He's very lucky to have you."

"That's very kind of you to say. I'm afraid I don't get out to many events where I have the chance to practice. You really know what you're doing out there. Thank you."

Henry looked at her with something akin to tenderness and nodded. "No, thank you for coming with me tonight and keeping me in check. And for allowing and supporting the illusion that you were my date for the evening. You are an exceptional woman, you know."

Boston felt her face flush. "Yes, I know." Outwardly, she laughed, but inside, she felt a warm glow spreading. She wanted to believe it, and she needed to hear it, especially this evening. Among these people, she liked hearing it and absorbed it, even as she diverted her eyes from him and looked around and listened to the orchestra. She no longer cared if people watched her with Rodney Henry and enjoyed that they did. In any event, with the excitement of the waltzes ended, the crowd began to thin as cars arrived and the champagne dried up.

"One more dance before we go?" he suggested.

She glanced at her watch. "Of course." She was only a little surprised when she realized the music was at a slower tempo than the waltzes. They danced slowly but formally, close enough to feel the heat from their bodies after twenty minutes of the pace of the waltz. She looked at him from time to time, but her eyes also roamed around the space to take in the sound and sight one last time, Cinderella getting ready to leave the ball. She was watching the staff put out the candles on the stairs that had burned down when the music ended.

"We should go," Henry said. "Shall we walk back to the Mandarin? I can have a driver take you home from there."

She walked over to the wall and picked up her ruby slippers. "Yes, I think it's time we left," Boston said.

• • •

IT WAS FOUR IN the morning, and the bedroom in the penthouse above Boylston Street was quiet. The bed was a king, but they lay close together under the soft sheets, exhausted by the release of tension. Boston let her mind wander, and all it came back to was the impossibility of the entire evening. There were no regrets, just questions, as if she had begun a journey on a road she thought she knew, only to come to an intersection with paths leading in different unknown directions.

She was glad she had limited her drinking tonight. Her mind was clear, more so than her conscience. Although they had put professionalism aside for one night, she knew that she had to complete the job at hand over the next few weeks.

She had her back to him, but Boston knew Henry was still awake by the sound of his breathing and the way his arm curled around her waist. She closed her eyes.

"So this is the life of Rodney Henry," she said. A moment later: "Thanks for giving me a glimpse."

She felt his free hand touch her hair.

"An all-too-rare part, I'm afraid," he said. "And something I would rather not do except under unusual circumstances, like tonight. I am more comfortable at a mining site with my hands full of rocks than among these people. Tonight was quite a distance from where I grew up. No one from the old days would recognize me now."

"Is that why I'm here? Because I remind you of those other places and times and the distance?"

"Perhaps. In some ways, you remind me of happier times, when I was young and hungry and still connected to my past. To my first wife."

Boston thought about the research she had read. "Do I remind you of her?"

He was quiet for a minute, and Boston thought perhaps the topic was off limits. His free hand moved slowly up from her waist until it rested on her throat. The large hand lay there for a moment, the fingers caressing her neck just as the necklace had a short time ago. Then he moved his hand to her hip and kissed her shoulder.

"No," he said. She was almost relieved. And then: "Something worse,

I'm afraid. You remind me of what I wanted her to be, knowing that she never could."

She listened in silent awe and envy as the story emerged, almost in a whisper, and Henry described the love of his life and the inevitable crushing strain on that love as the conflict between relentless ambition and personal happiness corroded and destroyed it in New York. As he finished, she was almost moved to tears.

"I wanted more. The path to real wealth, to make a difference for myself and people like me. But she did not. She thought we had enough. She never left Kentucky, really. Didn't want to. She seemed fine with the army life, but I could tell the traveling started to get to her. After the army, she never got used to New York City. All she really wanted was a house, some children, and a decent living. She never stopped believing we would go back. And I was never going back."

"So you left her?"

"I suppose I did in a way," he said. "She told me I was already gone, so she let me go. I made sure she never had to worry about money. But in the end, all the money in the world did not matter. Two years after the divorce, she found out she had pancreatic cancer. I paid all the medical bills, not that there were many of those. The disease moved too fast. She died quickly. Perhaps of a broken heart, a cancer all its own."

Boston opened her eyes and looked around the penthouse, at the luxurious furniture and bar and silk curtains. She turned her head slightly off the pillow. "What was her name?"

"Lisa. Her name was Lisa. I used to call her Mona Lisa."

The room fell quiet for a time. Boston gazed out the window into the night sky and wondered about her own past and future. She wondered if she would ever have a great love story and if it would end in tragedy or old age. This fairy-tale night was over. The sun would be coming up soon on another day in her life as it was, and this evening had given her much to think about.

"This doesn't change anything. I'm still going to do my job."

"I wouldn't respect you otherwise," he said. "But this deal is going to get done. And when it is over, and your work is complete, I want to have a different conversation."

"Are you offering me a job?" she said.

"No," he said. "Something much more. Something of value. An opportunity. The opportunity to build an empire."

She didn't respond. Instead, she reached down with her rough fingers and intertwined with his larger ones.

"Meghan. My name is Meghan."

TWENTY-EIGHT

The rising sun crested the tops of the trees in the east as a yellow Toyota pickup truck crossed the border and pulled up to the concrete army post and wooden barrier that blocked the dirt and gravel road. In the mist, a burly, middle-aged black man in beige miner's coveralls emerged from the cab and waved to the two soldiers on a porch shaded by a tin roof, calling out to them in their own tribal language. They recognized him immediately and relaxed their posture; few people crossed the border between Angola and the Democratic Republic of the Congo using this obscure road. The big man was welcome, and they casually questioned him about happenings at the mine and what was in the bed of the pickup under several boxes, coils of rope, and a gray tarp. He shrugged and described the usual deliveries. He was making his regular run to Lubumbashi and would be coming back with supplies for the camp in a day or two.

One of the soldiers made a move toward the back of the vehicle, at which point the big man made a show of looking at his watch and withdrew two envelopes from inside his coveralls. That got the soldiers' attention, and with another wave of the hand, the truck proceeded slowly up the dirt road into the DRC.

The trail, for that was all it could be called in some stretches, was rutted and pockmarked but for the most part dry. The morning air remained cool as the sun rose, and the truck bounced along this thin strip in a sea of trees for mile after mile before the driver stopped and got out. He took an old army canteen off the seat and walked to the back of the truck, where he pulled back the edge of the tarp and raised McBain's head up to wake him and force him to take more water.

The investigator sipped at the water that the big man parceled out. He tried to raise himself up but fell back. The miner shook his head and lifted a finger to his lips to signal McBain to remain quiet. He had no strength to even nod but lay his head back down and blinked at the light. He had drifted in and out of consciousness since feeling powerful arms wrap around him, lifting his body, and recalled hearing the whir of the elevator as it rose to the surface. Or perhaps he had only imagined it all and was still dying at the bottom of the mine, dreaming of salvation. His mouth was no longer parched, but his stomach ached with hunger again, so maybe he was alive after all. He hoped he was. Before he fell unconscious, he vowed never to take fresh air and water for granted again.

McBain knew he was alive when the truck finally found a real highway, and the painful bumping along the trail ended. With a smooth, unpaved road, it was easier to drift off to the sound of the tires and the engine as they picked up speed. The miner stopped two or three times to give him water, and then handed him a small plastic container holding a mixture of torn chicken, some corn paste, and spicy rice. Even with an empty belly, it was a struggle to make his mouth work.

When he awoke to the sound of a truck's horn fading in the distance, he took a chance and raised the edge of the tarp to get some fresh air. The white road sign receding in the distance read Kolwezi—10 Kilometers. McBain had no idea how long they had been on the road as he had drifted in and out, but at last, he thought he knew where they were. Now that he felt confident that he was alive, he needed to find out who this man was and where they were going. As his mental faculties returned, McBain realized that his savior was the miner who had stared at him near the rim of the pit when he had mentioned Daniel Neto. So if he had not left him to die, where was he taking him?

McBain looked at his watch to track the time, even if he could not tell the direction they were going. After an hour, the truck slowed, pulled off the road, and stopped. The investigator had to shield his eyes from the high sun as the driver drew the tarp back. The miner motioned for McBain to sit up, then half lifted him from the pile of blankets and boxes to stand on his feet. The rubbery legs almost collapsed when he tried to put weight on them, but the man was ready and supported McBain as he led him to the passenger side of the cab and put him inside. He saw his backpack on the floor and another canteen. As the driver started up the vehicle again, he motioned to the canteen with his hand. McBain stared at him and nodded.

"Thank you." It was all he could think of, and it came out in a strained, throaty gasp.

McBain did not know the man's language or any Portuguese. After they were back on the highway, the quiet driver just looked ahead or checked his mirrors. There was little traffic on the smooth dirt road in either direction in this stretch but for the occasional dump truck or long-haul tractor trailer. They were moving at a good forty to fifty miles an hour on the hard surface, and with the windows down, McBain closed his eyes and let the cool, clean air wash over his filthy face. He opened them and watched the trees and scrub brush lining the road under a clear blue sky. In another few minutes, he had a thought and looked at the driver. The hardened face was round, and he was clean-shaven with little dark hair left from a receding hairline. McBain thought that he could have had a shot with the Patriots when he was younger and that he could still snap him in half-effortlessly.

"Neto," McBain said.

The miner turned his eyes to him. "Neto."

"Yes, Neto. Daniel Neto. Do you know him?"

For a half minute, the eyes narrowed in curiosity, then the man nodded once. His gaze returned to the road and mirrors.

"*Sim*, Neto," he said.

McBain did not know what that meant. But at least now, he knew something. He shut up and let the man drive.

At last, they started to pass more vehicles, cars and SUVs, and random shops and single houses near the highway. The road was now paved in spots and became a highway. Once or twice, the driver stopped and made McBain walk around for a few minutes before returning to the journey. Gradually, the rural scenery gave way to more habitable areas—power stations, worn gray-and-white public buildings, and finally, the beginnings of what McBain determined must be a suburb, with rows of shingled houses and traffic lights.

Then he saw the most amazing thing. There, not one hundred feet back from the highway, was a mobile phone tower and, next to it, a billboard with real advertising for AirTel. God help him—civilization. The investigator was taking another drink when he saw another road sign that read N1 Lubumbashi—20 Km. And he knew from his research and talks with Rogers that Lubumbashi was the mining capital of the copper belt in the DRC, very near the southern border with Zambia.

The thinning line of trees opened, and the city came into view in the form of modern office buildings and colonial-era brick and stone architecture. Before they reached the center of town, the driver slowed and turned off into a housing development. The houses were all one story and made of stone or concrete, most with gated porches and red-shingled roofing. Some had gardens to the side or fencing surrounding the back yards. McBain thought they were maintained with dignity, not littered with the garbage seen in some poor neighborhoods outside major cities. He had no idea if the people had jobs or how much money they made. The homes had the appearance of the working poor and middle class.

The sun was riding west as the Toyota made a left turn and pulled into the driveway of a one-story house painted sky blue, with a wide veranda, a red-tiled roof, and a garden in the back enclosed by a wooden fence with wire mesh protecting it from intruders, either two or four legged. The windows had gates on them. The driver lifted a finger to McBain in a gesture that indicated he should sit tight. The miner walked to the front door, knocked, and stepped back. After a minute, the screen door opened, and McBain saw an elderly woman dressed in a bright-yellow blouse, black pants, and sandals emerge from the house onto the veranda. Her hair was wrapped in orange cloth and the head tilted upward to survey the visitor. As he watched, to McBain's astonishment, the woman opened her arms, and the burly miner hugged her to his body with the most gentle embrace.

The miner spoke to the woman for several minutes and then pointed to McBain sitting in the truck. She turned her eyes on him, and the investigator realized that the miner had brought him to this old woman for a purpose, and he knew that she would determine his fate. When she turned back to the big man, he saw her nod and say something before going back inside the house. The miner came to the driver's side door and gestured for McBain to come out, and he helped him up the veranda and over the threshold of the house.

The woman's home was clean and orderly, and the miner walked McBain through the entryway and into her living room, depositing him on a mustard-colored cotton twill couch littered with pillows patterned with flowers. He sat there and looked around the room while the miner made several trips to the truck and back, bringing in McBain's pack and some boxes and sacks for the woman. The floor was decorated in brightly colored area rugs, and there were several armchairs and a comfortable recliner placed in front of an older flat-screen television. The day was fading fast behind the blinds, but McBain caught sunlight falling on a table in a far corner decorated with old photographs, some of children and growing young faces and others of a large family standing in front of houses or gathered in villages with thatched huts and dirt clearings. On the wall above the table was a newer one, a larger picture of a younger version of the woman standing beside a smiling young graduate holding his parchment like a baton and, next to it, a framed degree of some kind.

As the miner put his last boxes in the entryway, the woman came into the living room with a tray of little bottles of Coca-Cola and glasses for the two men. McBain had not had a Coke without bourbon in it for years, and the taste of carbonation and sugar was bliss itself. He finished his soda, and when he put the glass down, all he could think of to say to this stranger was, "Thank you."

Now that he was slouching here on this Congolese woman's couch, McBain had no idea what was going to happen next or what he could say to her. His only hope was that somehow, he could find a way to get the heck out of the DNC and back to South Africa, then home.

"You are welcome," she said.

His eyes popped open, and he struggled to sit up straight. "You speak English?"

"Yes, I speak English. I learned many years ago. Some days, I get work with the mining companies to use my English."

McBain hardly knew where to start. He looked up at the quiet miner drinking his Coke and staring at him. "Excuse me, but who are you? Who is he, and why did he save me? Where am I, and why am I here?"

She nodded at the big miner. "You are in Lubumbashi, in my house. Joseph brought you here and asked me to help you. He said that the same man who killed my son wanted to kill you because you were asking questions about him. I do not know why he saved you. Joseph and my son were friends. Maybe he thought he was helping Daniel by helping you. He says he thought it must be important if the man was trying to kill you too."

McBain looked from the big man to the woman, then into his glass of ice. "Your son was Daniel Neto."

"Yes."

McBain remembered Machado's chilling words and wondered if she knew how he had died. He hoped not and knew that he was not going to be the one to tell her.

Joseph took his glass to the kitchen and returned to the living room with a shopping bag and a bottle of water. He picked up his backpack and waved his hand to the woman. It was clear he was leaving. They spoke softly together for a few more minutes. Then Mrs. Neto wrapped her arms around the miner, and he started for the door.

"Wait," McBain said. He looked at Mrs. Neto. "Please, how do I thank him?"

She spoke a few words to the big man. He stopped, turned, and nodded once at McBain. Then the miner made a sour face and reached into his pocket. He walked over to him and stretched out his hand, holding something. When the investigator opened his palm, he was stunned to see the man drop the medallion and chain into his hand.

Joseph said a few more words to Mrs. Neto and headed out the door. McBain stared at the tarnished medallion, dumbfounded. Bouncing along in the truck, he had known he would never see it again.

"He says," Mrs. Neto said, "that when he found you on the ground, this was next to your hand. He says it must have been a token of your faith that you were praying to at the end."

Now, as McBain wiped away the dirt from the 7 and the crossed sabers, he realized just how much luck it had brought him. He cleared his throat. "When you see him again, tell him he was right."

She surveyed him for a moment and turned for the kitchen.

"You are hungry. I will make us dinner, and you can get your strength back. While I am cooking, you can wash. Daniel's room is down the hall. He was not as big as you, but maybe you can find something clean to wear in the closet. Tomorrow, you can start to find some way to get out of the country and go wherever you want."

"Thank you, Mrs. Neto."

McBain looked around the immaculate living room and suddenly realized how filthy he must be. He had been too weak to even care about the stench of dirt and sweat he could now smell. He rubbed his face and hair and looked at his clothing.

"I apologize for my appearance. And for bringing dirt into your home. You see, I was trapped—"

"Yes, Joseph told me. He told me that the man tricked you and left you in the mine. He expected you to die. He cut the power and told people that the mine was dangerous. He did not tell them that you were down there, just that it was not safe to go in. But Joseph saw you go into the mine with him and saw him come out alone. He knew. But he had to wait until the security man had gone away before he could turn on the power for the elevator and go into the mine to look for you at night."

Mrs. Neto pointed down the hall. "You will find everything you need in the bathroom. Are you able to walk, or do you need my help?"

McBain pushed himself up. This woman was saving his life. He was damned if he would let her wrap her arms around his filthy clothing and body. He would crawl first. His legs were shaky, but he stood and made them work.

"Thank you. I can find it on my own."

In Daniel Neto's room, the investigator located some brown pants and a blue cotton shirt that he could wear, then stood in the shower for a few minutes, leaning against the wall for support. The pressure was not strong, but he relished the feel as he let the water pour over his head and soak into his face. Afterward, he found a small pair of scissors, a razor, and shaving cream and slowly clipped and scraped away the brown-and-gray whiskers.

Mrs. Neto had prepared a large meal of moambe chicken, beans, rice, and fresh vegetables from her garden, all covered in a spicy red tomato sauce flavored with peanuts. The two sat at a round metal table and ate in silence. McBain focused on every bite and forced himself not to wolf down the food in a few minutes. He thought it the most delicious meal he had ever eaten. The elderly woman ate half her meal slowly and looked out at the growing darkness most of the time. He tried to stay awake, but with his stomach now full, he faded quickly. She took his plate and began to wash the dishes. He tried to help, but she simply said, "You should rest now."

McBain excused himself and found Daniel's room again. He sat on the edge of the bed, exhausted. Before he could fall asleep, he finally broke. He wept unashamedly as, with the hunger and thirst now forgotten, for the first time in days the thought sank in that he was alive.

In the late morning, McBain awoke to find that his own clothes had been washed and dried and were folded on top of the bureau in the room. He dressed and found Mrs. Neto waiting in the kitchen. She pointed to a chair and made him a plate of toast, cheese, mixed nuts, and bananas for breakfast, then boiled water for tea. As he finished eating, she returned with a simple mobile phone. McBain had discovered his own phone in his backpack, but since it had no power and he could not recall Gina's number, he gave her the name of Gina's company in Cape Town. After ten minutes, they were finally able to get through and locate her.

When Gina finally stopped crying, McBain explained to her as quickly as he could what had happened and where he was. She took down the phone number and address and told him she would call back. In thirty minutes, the phone rang again. Mrs. Neto answered and gave the phone to McBain.

"I talked to Hans de Witte," Gina said. "He has connections up there with Anglo and BHP. A man is going to come to the address you gave me tomorrow morning and take you to the airport. You won't have to worry about any paperwork. They will put you on a private plane to Cape Town, and you'll be here by the afternoon. I'll meet you at this end."

"Can we trust de Witte?"

"Yes, I trust him," she said. "But just in case, I didn't give him much information, just that I needed to get somebody out of the DRC quietly. You'll owe him some cash; maybe that will be incentive enough. If I don't see you at the airport on schedule, I'll raise bloody hell right away."

"Got it. Thanks, Gina. Can't wait to see you."

"Just stay put and stay safe. I'll be sick until I see you again. And then I will give you hell. Big kiss."

"Big kiss."

McBain handed the phone back to Mrs. Neto. "Thank you. She said they are sending a man to pick me up tomorrow. I hope you don't mind keeping me for another night. Can I do anything for you while I am here?" He had no idea what a half-starved city boy with minimal household or outdoor skills could help her with, but he was willing to do anything he could.

The old woman shrugged and picked up a pair of gardening gloves and clippers. "You are welcome to stay until they come for you. You should stay inside. The sun is strong here, and you are still weak. Walk around the house if you want to move. There is more tea in the pot."

McBain was enjoying the simple pleasure of a full stomach and clean air. He sat at the table looking out the screen door at Mrs. Neto working in her garden. She moved patiently among the plants and sticks holding up beans and corn, picking out the dead leaves and branches. He guessed that with the rainy season about to start, she would have a sizeable batch of crops in a few weeks. McBain judged her to be more than seventy years old, and she moved with the strength of those working farm mothers, weary but tireless, that he had known growing up as a child in California. Yet her back was straight and her face carved with a dignity that he had seen in the lean upper-class matrons on the Upper East Side and the central districts of Paris, a dignity that preserved a lost past, many burdens, and perhaps tragedy.

He raised himself up and went to the living room, walking around without purpose, other than to force his legs to work, gazing out the barred windows or feeling the texture of fabrics. After a time, he found himself standing and surveying the pictures on the table. Some of them were old, and they showed a large family with a man he presumed was her husband because the man appeared with her several times, with as many as eight children in the frame. He examined the diploma on the wall. The parchment was a degree in mining engineering from the University of Witwatersrand in South Africa, and it had been awarded to Daniel Neto only six years before. McBain stared at the picture next to the diploma of the young man and his mother standing arm in arm beside some trees. Daniel was smiling in his cap and gown, full of hope with a bright future ahead of him. His mother was not smiling, but her eyes shone with pride and joy.

"That was my Daniel on the day he graduated. That was a happy day for him."

McBain turned and saw Mrs. Neto standing in the entrance to the living room. What could he hope to say?

"You should be very proud of Daniel," he said. "Everyone I talked to at his company spoke highly of him. Mr. Silva said he was the finest geologist in the company."

She walked over, stood next to him, and stared at the picture. There was still pride but no joy in her eyes. "He was my youngest, and he was the last."

McBain felt a chill run through his body. "Where are your other children? Your husband?"

She did not speak for a minute. McBain thought perhaps he was being intrusive. He had been deposited as a beggar less than a day before, and now he stood in her home asking questions about her family, about her ghosts.

"Joseph has been like family to us. We have known him for years, and he was a friend to Daniel. He is like us. We are Chokwe people. We grew up in the northeast highlands of Angola for a long time, near Lucapa in the mining country. My father and my husband had jobs even when the Portuguese were still here. For a while, the fighting was far away, but then the war came. We did not take sides, but that did not matter. First my father was killed, then my husband, and then my oldest son. So I left with my other children to come here to Lubumbashi with other Chokwe people.

"We thought we would go home, but the killing went on, and more people kept coming here from Angola. So the years passed, and we made a life here. But there were not many jobs, so most of my children worked for the mining companies. And in this country, there has been much fighting, too, and sickness. One by one my children who worked in the mines got sick from the dust. Two of my boys died in a cave not many years ago. But we needed money. We made sure Daniel went to school. He was smarter than everyone."

Mrs. Neto looked at McBain and waved her hand at the room.

"A few years ago, when he got his job, he gave money to the bank to buy me this house. He said he was working at different mines all the time anyway, so it was better to use the money for us here." She shrugged. "I do not know what will happen now. Joseph brings me some money. I do not ask, but he says it was owed to Daniel. The company that he worked for says they do not know what happened to my son, that he just ran away, so they will send no money. That is not true."

His face flushed with emotion. This woman might live to be a hundred, alone, with only her memories, now that her last child had been taken. Through war and poverty, she had already outlived her husband and all her children. McBain had fought off The Thing. Now he felt angry and ashamed. She had endured far worse and kept on living, preserving her dignity. There was no sign of self-pity in her voice or home.

He said to her, "I don't know what they told you, but the people who killed your son lied about him to his company first. They said Daniel wasn't doing his job. That he was drinking and spending too much time with the local girls."

"Daniel was a good boy," she said. "He did not drink. My son helped the local people. Got them jobs at the mine and helped them get more things from the government. He helped some of the local girls find a doctor. He said that when the mine was working, many more would get jobs. Better jobs than the kind that killed my sons. He said that this time it would be different."

She walked over to a desk on the side of the living room and returned with a battered and mud-smeared manila envelope. She handed it to McBain.

"Joseph would not tell me what happened to Daniel, but I already knew my son was dead. Otherwise, he would not have sent me this. I do not know what it says, but it came from Daniel at the mine two months ago. He sent it to me, but I know he hoped that it would find its way to the right person. Are you that person?"

McBain reached inside and pulled out a stack of pages. They looked like the reports he had seen at Coutinho's offices in Pretoria and Luanda.

"I don't know what it means," McBain said, "but I think that Daniel was trying to get the truth out about something that was going on at the mine. Something they did not want everyone to know. There was something strange going on there when I was underground. That's why they wanted to kill me too. They thought I knew what he knew. Maybe this will help us find out what it is."

She folded her arms and nodded as she continued to stare at his picture.

"My son told me that something was wrong at the mine. He said he did not know what it was but that some people were keeping secrets. He said that he was going to find out because that was his job and because he thought the mine was the beginning of good things for many people. He believed it would bring more jobs and food and schools."

McBain looked at the picture of Daniel Neto again, his face full of that optimism that radiates in a young person who believes that anything is possible, that any wrong can be righted. A strange thing it was that he should have come all this way and through so much to stand in this home beside a soul not unlike his own, who knew in her heart that was not true.

"Maybe he was right. I suspected when I was down there that someone was planning a way to make money out of the dig and not report it."

The old woman turned to face McBain and he to face her.

"That is the way of things here," she said. "Even when the fighting stops, after all the brave talk about who is right, in the end, the powerful take all the wealth for themselves, and the people are left with little or nothing, and the community suffers." She glanced at the face of her son on the wall. "I would tell that to Daniel, and he would smile and say, 'Yes, *Maman*, but for now, there is work.'"

TWENTY-NINE

Boston sat at McBain's desk reading Dee Dee Franklin's files and re-searching the cases further online. She had to know if someone else was involved in trying to sink the AFR project and the merger. Maybe these could provide a clue or at least a thread to pull on. She hoped that Raj would call back soon with some kind of market intel, but for now, these were all she had. Nothing in the data room or her analysis of the market rumors had produced anything so far, other than that AFR had beaten out any number of competitors for the Angolan and other mining rights: the Chinese or Russian government, the big boys in mining, it could be anybody. There had to be at least one person who wasn't too optimistic about the success of the project and AFR. Or knew something nobody else did.

So all afternoon, she paged through the files while wandering around the office with the front door locked or sat in front of her computer, following up on ideas. Every so often, she would find herself mentally diverging on a tangent as she looked at pictures of mines in Africa and researched the big operations there. And then she realized she had the song in her ears again, her head tick-tocking back and forth before she was aware of it.

Diamonds . . . diamonds are a girl's best friend.

That had been a fabulous night, even if it had ended in such an unex-pected fashion. Boston had enjoyed everything, from the dancing to the coy evasiveness in the face of probing questions to the education about the different countries. She bit her lip when she remembered saying goodbye to the Winston Cluster. Even the tense encounter with the investors had sent her blood racing. That had been an educational experience as well. She closed her eyes and tried to imagine the horrible lives of those people in the DRC, those children digging rocks out of the ground with blistered fingers, rocks that would make up electric cars and phones and so many other things.

The thoughts of conflict minerals, as Henry had called them, brought to mind his jab about the woman's diamond ring and the fact that it was made of conflict diamonds. She started browsing the history of these as well, wondering if any of her own stones were from those days. When she found a reference, she made a note to watch the movie *Blood Diamonds* when this job was over.

Boston forced herself to put away thoughts of the gala and precious stones and went back to the files now and then to see if anything else made sense. Dee Dee's choice of cases was interesting, and one or two had crazy twists in how the scam artists had defrauded investors, but none seemed likely possibilities as attempts to disrupt the merger or sabotage AFR's ownership of the project. After another hour, she slapped her hand on the desk in frustration. As smart as she was when it came to accounting and investment fraud, she just didn't know enough about the corporate world to see what else might be happening. Boston picked up her phone and tried McBain again, regardless of the time. It went straight to voice mail. He was either still not back from the mining site yet or . . . She ground her teeth.

"Where the hell are you?"

The twilight was fading outside the office windows, and Boston was getting hungry. She switched on the desk lamp and checked the time. After a few more news stories, she needed a workout and dinner. The investigator smiled and decided to indulge herself for a few more minutes before she left. She started browsing online, once again finding the song in her head. It did not take long for her to find her way to news reports about the mining discoveries in Africa she was looking for.

"Man, those are some big rocks."

Her green eyes lit up as she found one story from just a few years ago:

> Lucara Diamond Corp. has unearthed the largest uncut diamond in recent history in its Karowe mine in Botswana, the Canadian company said on Thursday, beating its own record discovery from November 2015, which it struggled to sell for nearly two years.
>
> The 1,758-carat diamond, larger than a tennis ball, weighs close to 352 grams, Lucara said in a statement. The stone is second in size only to the 3,106-carat Cullinan diamond, recovered in South Africa in 1905.
>
> Lucara's shares rose as much as 11.4 percent to the highest in more than two months, before closing up 6.3 percent at C$1.68. The Toronto stock benchmark ended the day marginally lower. The stone is the latest in a series of high-value recoveries for the Vancouver-based company at Karowe. Since introducing its XRT diamond recovery technology, Lucara has recovered twelve diamonds over 300 carats, the company said, including a 472-carat and a 327-carat diamond in April 2018.
>
> The stone was too big for the company's scanners.

"Larger than a tennis ball. Jaysus." She shook her head. One thousand seven hundred fifty-eight carats. Then her eyes landed on a link to another story. She clicked and scrolled down, and something started to grow in that suspicious corner of her mind.

> An Australian mining firm said that it found the largest diamond ever to be dug up in the southern African nation of Angola. The

gemstone weighs a whopping 404.2 carats. Lucapa Diamond Company, which discovered the 2.75-inch jewel in the northeastern Angolan province of Lunda Norte, said the diamond is the biggest ever to be recovered by an Australian company.

"We're not used to valuing 400-carat diamonds," Miles Kennedy, Lucapa's chairman, told the Australian Broadcasting Corporation, "but if we look at other diamonds of slightly less weight than this, you're looking in the order of $20 million."

The diamond is the world's twenty-seventh largest, according to Lucapa, citing data available on Wikipedia. The previous record-setter for largest diamond discovered in Angola—the so-called Angolan Star—is almost half as massive at 217.4 carats.

Last November, a different mining company, Lucara . . .

Boston's thoughts flipped back to the gala and the booths scattered around the library with maps of different countries meant to educate the guests. Like most of her generation, she had never studied maps or geography. Whenever they needed to know a location, they could just pull up an application on their smartphone. She had only become more familiar with the precise geography of Africa once this job had started and as she studied the maps of the countries of sub-Saharan Africa at the gala. Now, looking at the big picture, she connected the dots—literally.

Boston pushed away from the desk and walked into the conference room. She pulled up their large multicolored map of southern Africa and spread it out on the table. She found a black felt pen and drew circles around the two locations from the internet.

Lucapa, Lunda Norte, Angola. Lucara, Botswana.

With a sinking feeling, she drew a straight line from Botswana to Lucapa in Angola. She tossed the marker on the table and stepped back.

The thin black line traveled from the Karowe mine in Eastern Botswana to Lucapa in Lunda Norte. Boston's eyes narrowed as she followed it and settled on one spot.

Just below Lunda Norte, it cut through the eastern part of Moxico Province, less than a hundred miles to the west of the AFR mining project.

"Shit."

THIRTY

A massive Airbus lifted off the runway as they watched from a table near a bar in the Cape Town airport, the Qatar Airways logo sparkling in the late afternoon sun. McBain scanned the crowded passageway from the corner, his back to the wall. It was the busy time of the day, with whole caravans of luggage passing by in handcarts and trolleys trailed by families scattering across the globe. There were some business travelers and solo adventurers with backpacks, but for the most part, the airport was filled with families headed back to the Middle East or to Europe. McBain was waiting for an Emirates flight that would take him to Dubai and then home, so this terminal had more than its share of Muslim women robed in black with their heads covered, hauling children along in their wake or pushing luggage carts stacked like pyramids.

McBain took a long pull of a cigarette, closed his eyes, leaned his head back, and slowly exhaled.

"Better go slow with that; it's your first one in over a week."

Gina said it lightly, but he could detect the care in her voice. She leaned back in her chair with a cigarette in one hand and a tall gin and tonic in the other, wearing jeans and a white sleeveless blouse, her sunglasses pushed back on her head.

"Yes, you're right," he said. "The first one since I went down in that hole. I ended up leaving the Marlboros in the hut I was staying in, but the matches and lighter came in handy."

"You slept like a log last night. No fun at all," she said with a sigh.

"Sorry. Combination of exhaustion, hunger, and no booze. I'll make it up to you next time."

"I can tell. Your clothes are a lot baggier than when I left you ten days ago."

He patted his stomach. "Yeah, I can feel the difference, believe me. Not the way I would have chosen to lose a few pounds."

She shook the ice in her glass. "Sure you don't want a little one for the road?"

McBain tapped the ash into a tray and shook his head.

"No, I'd better not. This is going to my head already. I went to the trouble to spend ten days sobering up, so I think I'd rather keep my wits about me until this is all over. For now, I don't miss it, and I doubt I'd enjoy it before we finish this job. Either that or I'm scared I'd really tie one on in midair. They might need one of those luggage carts to pour me off the plane."

"After what you've been through these last ten days, I wouldn't blame you. You know, you told me what happened but not why it happened. What is going on there that could possibly make someone try to kill you? What's in that report that made it so valuable that Daniel Neto sent a copy to his mother and got himself killed?"

He shook his head. "I wish I knew. From what little of the geology jargon I can understand, it contains survey results from rock and dirt samples. But there is no summary or conclusion I can make out, and I don't know how to read the data. It's full of mineral symbols, numbers, and ratios."

"You want Hans to take a look?"

McBain inhaled the cigarette again. He wondered how many palms had been greased.

"No," he said. "I like Hans, and I owe him for getting me out of Lubumbashi yesterday, but I don't want to take the chance or the time. I think we should go back to the premise you came up with in Pretoria that we don't know who we can trust. When I get back to the States, I'll make a bunch of copies and turn this over to Rogers and some independent experts. Until then, I'm not going to contact anyone, even Boston. After what happened, I don't want to talk to anyone until I'm out of here. Plus, I don't know what has been going on back home. For all I know, her phone could be tapped."

Gina shrugged. "But why—what's the big secret?"

McBain looked down at his backpack containing the mysterious final report from Daniel Neto. His mind ran through the facts and suppositions that he had had hours to process in the bowels of the mine. He kept seeing that small sign on the rope and the receding tunnel into which Machado had vanished.

"My best guess," he said, "after all our interviews, what we learned, our 'accidents' and the attempt to kill me—they found something big down there that someone is trying to cover up, probably a large vein of valuable strategic minerals. It would make sense, given the geologic history of the region and all the interest in those rights from the US government and the competition."

He chewed on an ice cube and watched another airliner lift off the runway.

"I've been off the board for over a week. I have no idea what's been happening since Machado left me. I barely know what day it is. What's happening with the deal? What happened at the mine? Why wasn't anyone even looking down there? Mrs. Neto told me a couple things she got from Joseph, the guy who saved my life, but otherwise, I'm still stunned."

Gina pulled her chair closer and lowered her voice.

"Right. First of all, the deal is a go. Silva reviewed the survey results and sent the final summary assessment to the companies and bankers. Apparently, negotiations are almost over and terms agreed, and the share-holder votes are in about a week. For now, nobody knows where you are or what happened. I kept it to myself as you asked. When you didn't show after a week, I started to call the Coutinho office in Luanda. I had to leave a threatening message to get Silva to call me back when he finally returned from the camp. He was a bloody mess. He told me what happened on the way to the camp, about your driver getting killed. That guy Machado seems to have terrified everyone. He told Silva you went missing, but he didn't mention you were in the mine and conveyed to him that he should keep his mouth shut for the good of everyone until he contacted him. Silva says he doesn't know what happened, and I don't think he is lying.

"Then Machado disappeared, and the camp started looking for you both. Before he left, he apparently told everyone the mine explosion was sabotage of some kind by an outside party to stop the project, and they're trying to keep it all quiet for now until the deal closes. Silva is frantic. First Neto, and now you. He is afraid to even tell HR Tech. Silva was too scared to say anything until he was safely back in Luanda. Then he called the ministry and AFR's office there, and alarm bells started going off, especially with the deal on the verge of closing. The government and AFR sent people out there to quietly get things under control and find out what was going on.

"By then, Machado had vanished. Now, the theory is that he was the saboteur all along, working to torpedo AFR's contract and that he set the explosives himself. They think he was working for somebody else to destroy AFR's reputation and have the Angolans void the rights so his real employer could move in."

McBain nodded. The killer would have thought of that and given himself as much time as he could to get far away. But . . .

"I can't blame Silva. Machado is terrifying. And until you've been trapped in the wild with an illiterate teenager holding an AK-47 to your head as you watch someone die, you can't understand the effect that kind of fear can have on a man. But Machado could not have been working alone there. There was too much to cover. It must have been an open secret that Neto was killed."

"Probably. Maybe even the project manager too. But the guy had everyone terrorized. It's pretty isolated out there and what he did to Neto must have been a hell of a warning. Everyone is keeping their mouth shut and pointing the finger at him alone."

"I know I'll never forget him. I feel like an idiot. For some reason, I put my normal skepticism aside and trusted him. Lesson learned."

Gina patted him on the leg. "Don't be so hard on yourself, love. You were out of your element and had to trust him. Not to mention the fact that Silva said he saved your lives out there on the trail. And he had a lot of smart mining people fooled."

"I'll bet. But we still don't know if there is something in that off-limits area or if he was just causing trouble. If there was nothing there, he wouldn't have tried to wreck the project."

"Well, it didn't work," she said. "The final report checks out, and the deal is on track to close in about a week. The mine has reopened, and there are new people on the ground."

McBain rubbed his clean-shaven chin. "I think the report they gave Silva at the mine is a fake." He pointed at his bag. "I think this is the real data, and that is why Neto was killed. Whatever is in here was worth killing for."

"But you don't know. It's just a guess. And let's say you are right. This guy Henry is all behind it, and he found a river of gold or uranium or whatever. He's going to cut out his shareholders and pay off a few Angolan officials and keep the rest for himself. You think you can stop it? McBain, this deal is going to get done. It's too big, and too many people are going to benefit. This strategic mineral stuff is massive and global. And Henry is going to be one of the players. And what if you're wrong? What if it's not him? He becomes an even bigger hero as a victim of the Chinese or the majors or whoever is trying to take him out."

He glanced at her. "Maybe that's been his plan all along."

Gina rolled her eyes. "Christ, McBain, I've never seen you so obsessed."

McBain's gaze fixated on his glass of water, filled with melting ice. "Yeah. Dying of thirst and hunger in a pitch-black hole in the earth will do that to you." Seven years ago, he had sat in this airport with his beautiful wife and Gina and a half dozen of their beautiful friends, laughing like young kings and queens, getting ready to board first class, marveling at how wonderful life could be. Today, he realized he had never felt more alive than at that moment in Daniel Neto's bedroom when he had broken down and cried with a full belly, wearing the clothes of a murdered man.

Gina shook her head in exasperation. "McBain, you better understand something. Think about how many people you've talked to, here in South Africa and in Luanda. Everyone who has any vested interest in it wants it to happen. A lot of money is going to be made by a lot of people, especially if you are right, and there is a huge pile of secret money Henry is bringing up. You got a big taste of what it means to threaten that.

"You have an opinion, just that, an opinion from a nobody. A junior geologist who has been accused of poor performance, conflict of interest, and fucking around with the local girls. Staged or not, he's not around to defend himself. If you are right, he has been rotting in the bottom of the river for two months, the poor soul. Who do you think they are going to believe? Be careful. No matter what you think that report says, the deal and this project are going ahead. Too many powerful people want it to happen, maybe even because of what is in that report. Or what is down there. You may live, but you also might sacrifice yourself like Daniel Neto. Remember, if it wasn't for that good Samaritan, you would still be lying in that hole."

Gina strolled to the bar and returned with another gin and tonic.

"Are you going to let Eliza know you're alive?"

"With the time difference, it's only one more day. I'll be there by early afternoon. Besides, it would only stir up a hornet's nest with me isolated on a plane for thirty hours. We need to know what that report means before I start screaming stop. Like you said, everybody wants to see it happen. I've got to have rock-solid proof of what's going on . . . Forget I said that. Maybe you could email her for me just to say I'm fine.

"Ha ha. Sure, darling, that will go over well. Especially for you when you get back. No, thanks." Gina chuckled. "It's safe to say now that you're back here in once piece, but I told you not to go. And I hate to admit it, so did she. Funny how it worked out. You found something after all, although it almost got you killed. We were right, but so were you."

"This is a boarding call for Emirates Flight 370 to Dubai, beginning with our first-class and business-class passengers."

He paid their bill, and they strolled down the terminal to the security gate. McBain looked at Gina as they approached the line. "In addition to what I owe you, I'm going to send you a wire transfer for de Witte. I'm also going to send you one for Mrs. Neto in Lubumbashi."

She smiled at him in surprise. "Are you sure about that?"

"I hope the company does right by her after it all comes out, but in the meantime, I can give her a little peace of mind when it comes to paying her bills. A small price to pay to the woman who saved my life, don't you think?"

"I couldn't agree more." She looked at him, and a corner of her mouth curled up. "There's that knight in shining armor again."

He tried to suppress a smile. "Shut up."

As they joined the line of weary travelers, McBain pushed back her blonde bangs with his free hand and caressed her cheek. "Somehow, 'thanks' seems pathetically inadequate, Gina."

Gina grabbed him and kissed him for a long minute. She took her arms from around him and stood back, looking him over. "Let's just say you owe me. Promise to come back soon. You're still the best kisser I ever met, McBain. Don't waste it on Eliza."

He smiled as he backed away, then blew her a kiss and pulled off his backpack to move up to the security gate.

"I promise. See you around sometime."

"You're damned right you will."

And as he watched her blow him a kiss back, push down her sunglasses, and disappear into the crowd, McBain felt an ache deep inside. And he recognized it as one of those rare moments in life when the heart is overwhelmed by the sudden confluence of memories of an unrecoverable past, feelings of inescapable intensity from the present, and the sense of a door opening to an unknowable future.

McBain took his seat in business class on the Emirates flight. After takeoff, he pushed his seat back and began to think of his next move. And of his partner. He was constantly glancing around, looking at faces to see if anyone was staring at him. He kept his backpack with the document tucked in front of his feet and, for the first time in years, refused a drink from the flight attendant. The detective remained awake and apprehensive for the entire flight to Dubai and only fell asleep when the overhead lights dimmed at 37,000 feet on the plane headed for Boston.

THIRTY-ONE

The red Shelby wove like quicksilver in and out of late-morning traffic on Route 95 as Boston raced to Waltham to meet with Harold Rogers. After ten more minutes, she saw the sign for Exit 26 and attacked the off ramp to the blare of a semi's horn, zipping along Route 117 until she found her way to the technology center of the Northeast. The car made a sharp turn onto Bear Hill Road, and Boston slowed until she saw the sign that marked the entrance to the renovated brick warehouse building that housed HR Technologies.

A professional-looking young Indian woman in a white lab coat was waiting to greet her by the reception desk. She handed Boston an ID badge with her name and picture and showed her the way to Harold Rogers's office on the third floor of the building. The investigator smiled and nodded politely as the scientist described the history of the old textile factory while they climbed a broad metal stairway, even as she gripped her briefcase handle impatiently.

The gentleman rose from his desk and greeted Boston warmly when she entered the room. She observed that the office was laid out for design work, with a number of whiteboards on the walls and transparent plastic drawing boards on wheels behind a long rectangular table covered in sheets of schematics. On the other side of the room, a wall of windows opened onto a wooded park dotted with shallow ponds and fountains sparkling in the morning sunshine.

"Ms. O'Daniel, it is so wonderful to see you again, especially today."

Rogers was wearing blue wool pants, a worn houndstooth tweed blazer, and a broad smile. He was clearly a happy man in his element. He removed his glasses and shook her hand with enthusiasm.

"I am so very glad you called this morning," he said. "We've had several pieces of good news, and I wanted to tell you in person. Please, sit down."

Boston took off her coat and scarf, straightened her jacket, and reined in her nervousness as she sat across from him. "Good news? I, uh—"

"Yes, first of all, my finance team and our bankers have gone through the latest changes you proposed on those projections to adjust the valuation, and I'm happy to say that AFR and their bankers have agreed on a final price, albeit grudgingly, it seems."

"Yes, but if I could—"

He put his glasses back on and looked down at a legal pad with a list of bullet points.

"And I'm also pleased to report that, as of yesterday, Coutinho's office in Angola had forwarded the environmental impact assessment you had identified as missing, signed by the right officials, I'm told. Best of all, they also forwarded those long-awaited final survey results brought back from the mining site in Moxico Province. My team just finished our own analysis this morning and sent up a summary of the results. I can tell you they confirm the quality of the previous samples and are most promising in terms of potential strategic ores and rare earths."

Rogers took off his horn-rimmed glasses, leaned forward on his elbows, and clapped his hands together. "I think we are ready to do a deal."

Boston looked across the desk at a man who appeared ten years younger than that night in September when they first met at the Holiday Lounge. His fears about losing his company had evaporated in newfound enthusiasm for the global potential of the new merged venture, now that it was about to become a reality. As in the conference room weeks ago, she felt like the lone party pooper, raising her own minor concerns now that the cold champagne was about to be opened. They seemed even more trivial in light of this good news that brightened the face and spirits of her client. She suppressed her own anxieties, concentrated her thoughts, and put a smile on her own face.

"That's all very good news, Harold. But I did want to discuss one or two things that still have me concerned at this late date."

"Oh, all right," he said. His face fell a little. "But I thought this was the last of the outstanding items you wanted confirmation on. Have you and Mr. McBain discovered something new about AFR or Mr. Henry? The last report you gave me indicated that you were both satisfied and that he had obtained nothing in the way of negative information in his investigation in Africa."

Boston leaned forward in her chair. "Well, that's just it. I . . . uh . . . well, I haven't heard back from him in over a week. Not since he called from Luanda and told me he was going out to the camp with your consultant. Did they happen to mention him when they sent you the survey results?"

Rogers shrugged. "No, I'm afraid not. After we received the report, I spoke briefly to Mr. Silva from Angola, and he didn't mention Mr. McBain at all. He did say that there had been a small bit of trouble at the mine while he was there but that things were back on track today and that we should not be worried."

Boston's face could not hold the smile. Her eyes narrowed and she sat up. "Trouble?"

"Yes. He was vague and went to great lengths to ease my mind, but I gather it was in the way of some kind of temporary production problems that held up operations for a brief time. He assured me that additional personnel had been sent out there by the company and that the project was back on track and ready for the next stage. He even mentioned that he had seen them laying the groundwork for the new rare earths processing plant we expect to build next year."

She sat back and looked out the window at the treetops for a few moments, trying to weave the pieces together as she fought against a tightening knot in her stomach.

"I wonder," she said. "One of the things I wanted to mention to you is some unusual movement I've seen in the price of AFR stock over the past few weeks. I'm beginning to suspect that perhaps there are other parties who have a vested interest in seeing your deal fail. You say you don't have any detail on these production problems?"

"No, I don't. If you think it's important, perhaps we can reach out to Mr. Silva for more information. We would have to do it quickly. Other parties, you say? Who?"

"I'm not certain yet. I have someone looking into it." She leaned forward and frowned. "By chance, did the survey results show anything unusual, any indication of something significant or new you didn't expect to see?"

Rogers pulled a stack of pages from the top of a pile of folders and put on his glasses again. He shook his head. "Something new? No. I don't see any indication of that. The findings reflect what we expected. Like what?"

"Diamonds."

"Diamonds?"

"Yes, lots of them. I was doing some research on diamonds and that part of Africa and just wondered. Now with the trouble you mention, it occurs to me that someone might have a motive for seeing the project scrapped. Some reason other than just simple competitive jealousy. After all, that area does have some recent history of people fighting over fields of diamonds."

Rogers's mouth hung open for just a moment, then he shook his head and a finger. "No, I can assure you that nothing of that scale has shown up in the years of surveys, sampling, and early development from that mine. Yes, I'm familiar with the geology and history of that region, and it is not out of the realm of possibility that some vein of kimberlite pipes might ultimately be discovered as the mine expands underground, but there has been no sign of it yet."

She rubbed her hands together. None of it made sense, but her instincts were on fire.

"I just feel uncomfortable, Harold. First this movement in the stock price and the appearance of potential competitors, then this trouble at the mine, and McBain still missing. I wonder if we could just hold off on the final vote until he gets back to let us know what he thinks. I have to tell you I'm a little worried. It's not like him to be out of communication as we reach the end of an assignment. Something doesn't feel right. If you could just give us a little more time."

Now Harold Rogers looked worried as well. He took off his glasses, stood, and walked over to the window as he chewed on one of the arms of his plastic frames. He stared out at the tranquil sight of a sunny autumn day for a minute before he turned to her.

"Ms. O'Daniel, if it was up to me, I would do anything you ask. You have done more than add tremendous value to this deal. Aside from the well-deserved payments I will be sending you, you have gone far to relieve my mind about the threat to my company and future. Though I must confess," he said, gesturing to his drafting table, "in some ways I'd rather remain a small engineering company. The idea of becoming chief executive of this global mining conglomerate intimidates me, and I doubt I will be granted much free time to do the thinking and design work that I really enjoy.

"But partly because of those things you have done, everyone is satisfied that the combination of these two companies is a fair deal for all parties. The shareholder votes are scheduled for a week from now, and everyone is excited and anticipating a unanimous vote in favor of merger. The deal has passed every regulatory hurdle or soon will. I cannot in good conscience approach the board now with a few vague suspicions and ask them to wait any longer. We have a fiduciary duty to the shareholders. I'm sure you understand."

Boston stood to go. She had to get back to her desk and keep searching while she waited to hear back from Raj Ganatra. She extended her hand.

"I do understand, Harold. I appreciate you hearing me out."

"Please, when Mr. McBain returns, contact me if he has additional concerns from his trip that have not been brought to light. Something that I can bring to the directors that suggests there may be a problem or that this should not go forward. Otherwise, my hands are tied."

As Boston got back into the Shelby, she slammed the door. *When McBain returns . . .*

She hit the wheel with the heel of her hand. "Dammit, Boozy, where are you?"

THIRTY-TWO

McBain's flight from Dubai landed at Logan Airport around two in the afternoon. He walked out the terminal doors without a coat to the shock of a cold autumn wind that bit hard into his bones after weeks in Africa. Ah, New England in the fall. He stomped his feet until a cab pulled up to the curb. He tossed his two suitcases in the trunk and the sacred backpack on the back seat and climbed in next to it.

"Tremont and Clarendon Streets," he said. "As fast as legally possible."

"Yes, sir," the driver said and hit the gas. He was a thin man but had a cheerful ebony face, Cary Grant sunglasses, and a close-cropped skull. McBain pegged him as central Caribbean.

"Long trip?" the man asked.

"Yeah, very." McBain sank into the cushions.

"Too bad you come back today. Just turned cold last night. They say maybe snow later."

McBain opened the window and inhaled the cold air. "OK by me. Feels pretty refreshing after the heat and sun. I've had enough of Africa for a while."

They stopped behind some traffic, and the driver turned and laughed. "Me too. I am from Nigeria."

. . .

BOSTON WAS ON the office phone in the conference room chasing whatever threads she could think of when she heard the key turn in the door to the front office. She hung up and walked out into the office to find McBain standing in the middle of the room staring at her, his bags dropped by the umbrella stand near the door. For a moment, he just stood there in his travel-worn khaki pants, white linen shirt and hiking boots, wearing a soft smile, saying nothing. He took a deep breath.

"Hi," he said.

"Hi?" she said. "That's all you've got to say to me—hi? Where the fuck have you been?"

"It's a long story."

She put her desk between them, pushed the chair aside, and leaned on her hands the way she had done with the government men.

"Oh, I'm sure it is. A lot longer than the week you told me you would be out of touch. More like that long vacation you've been aching for with your blonde bimbo in South Africa."

He drank in the sight of her, replenishing the mental well of visions from those last minutes in the cave. Tumbling red hair, flashing green eyes, and pent-up passion illuminated the space between them.

"It's not like—"

"I guess with the job almost done you figured a few extra days sunning yourself on the beach in Cape Town with your good friend Gina wouldn't do any harm."

"Not exactly. It's kind of complicated."

"Of course, it's complicated. So complicated that you didn't even have time to call me and tell me you were taking some time off. Because I guess you might know what I would have said."

He chuckled and walked to the desk so he could be closer to her. "If you would calm down and let me explain—"

"You must have had a great time. You can't seem to get that stupid smirk off your face. You do realize how much work I've been doing since you left for the mine, right? You do know that there are some things going on? And that the deal is about to close with the shareholder vote next week?"

"I know." He turned and gestured to the backpack. "I have something in the bag—"

She threw her hands up in the air. "Oooh, a present! He brought me a present from his vacation. You are so thoughtful. Is it a stuffed lion from the gift shop at the airport? Maybe an Emirates Airlines T-shirt?"

"Actually, it's part of that long story. Just give me a minute."

"And wipe that idiotic grin off your face. I'm really angry, and you have a shit load of explaining to do. Leaving me on my own to handle this for three weeks. Three weeks! Do you know what hell I've been through with these people? This long story wouldn't have to do with any quote unquote 'trouble' at the mine that I just heard about, would it?"

"Actually, it does. You see—"

"And you couldn't call me with the clock ticking down to fill me in on something that might have some bearing on the case for our client? It just had to wait until . . . wait a minute." Boston crossed her arms and looked him up and down. "You've lost weight."

He looked down at his baggy shirt, loose around the waist, then back at her. "Yes, that's part of the story too."

She came around from behind the desk and walked up to him, evaluating him from a foot away. "You've lost a lot of weight, especially your gut."

McBain took in the sound, sight, and scent of her, speechless for a moment, fighting to keep the emotion out of his throat and eyes. There was so much he needed to say, but he knew it was important to focus on the case. And so the story poured out of him, starting with the breathtaking flight across the central plateau and national parks of Angola and the long drive across the wilderness until they were confronted by the gang on the trail. His smile faded as he spoke about the killing of Ramon, the seconds waiting for the bullet in the back, and the arrival of the security team. He described the mining camp itself and the state of development of the pit and the facilities, then Machado's invitation and the gradual descent into the bowels of the dig. As he spoke of the explosions, the sudden darkness, and the moment of betrayal by the very man who had saved his life the day before, she shivered as if experiencing it with him. McBain's hands moved as he tried to mimic the slow search along the dirt walls of the tunnels and the loss of time, conveying as best he could the disorientation from fear, thirst, hunger, and the lack of light, finally reaching the elevator cage only to find death waiting. By the time he reached the awakening to salvation and the truck ride with Joseph, he could barely contain his emotions about the macabre killing of Daniel Neto and his gratitude to the big miner for his life.

And of course, by this time, Boston was punching him in the shoulders and chest until suddenly, she had her arms around his neck, showering his cheeks with kisses and tears.

"You idiot . . . you moron . . . you stupid, stubborn . . ."

McBain held his partner as tightly as he ever had, silently thanking Joseph once more as he teared up himself and kissed her hair again and again.

"I told you not to go out there! I told you."

"I know," he said. "I know you did. And you were right. I'm sorry I went. I'm sorry I left you alone back here to handle everything by yourself."

Boston pushed herself away and grabbed a tissue from her desk. You never listen to me," she said, dabbing her cheeks.

McBain wiped his face with his shirt. "That's not true. I do listen to you. This time, it saved my life. If I hadn't grabbed a bottle of water just before I went down into that mine with Machado, I never would have survived long enough for anyone to find me. So thank you."

Boston smiled for the first time and bit her lip.

"Agreeing I was right? Listening to what I tell you? Being down there without food and water for so long really must have affected you. Is this going to be a new you?"

McBain laughed. "We'll see. I blame it on lack of alcohol."

"I should have guessed."

"Speaking of listening to you, it's your turn to fill me in. Where do things stand? You mentioned other things going on."

"Oh, nothing much. Just the Red Sox winning the World Series, that's all."

He frowned. "Yes, I found out on the flight back. Yet another rotten side effect of my bad decision making. Did you get to see any of it?"

She threw him an arched eyebrow. "Unfortunately I was doing the work of two people, so no. Plus it was over in five games out in Los Angeles. Game three was apparently historic. Come on."

Boston led him into the conference room and told him about the visit from the government men, Dee Dee's revelations about the scale of what they were dealing with along with her warnings, the strange movements of AFR's stock price, and the emergence of other players in the game. She rolled out the large map of southern Africa with her black line drawn from Botswana to Angola.

"Something's wrong. This all seems connected to your story about Machado and that 'off limits' section of the mine. I think I know what it means."

"Diamonds," they both said at once.

Boston looked at him and smiled. "You figured it out too."

McBain did a double take and gazed at her in admiration. "Only now looking at this. Up until this moment, I just had some vague idea that it was something extremely valuable. Something worth killing for. How did you know?"

She shook her head and pulled on her emerald pendant. "I don't know. I did some research, and it just kind of makes sense, especially with what you said about the mine. The problem is, how do we prove it?"

McBain left the office and came back with his dirty backpack. He pulled out the battered manila envelope and withdrew the pages.

"This might be able to confirm it for us."

Boston took the pages and glanced through the stack, then handed it back to him. "What is it?"

"This is Daniel Neto's final report with the survey results."

She shook her head. "Can't be. Rogers said that they received the final report from the consulting company and spoke to that guy Silva you went out there with. It confirms the previous findings."

McBain thumbed through the pages and dropped them on the table. "That report is a fake. Ginned up by Machado or somebody else out there working with him. I believe this is the real report. And I think what's inside is the reason Daniel Neto was killed."

"Where did you get it?"

"From his mother in Lubumbashi. She received it in early September. Somehow, he got it out to her before he died. That's why there was such a long delay in getting anything. They had to manufacture a plausible substitute."

Boston sat on the conference table and stared at the map again. "OK," she said, "but who are the notorious 'they'?"

"I'm sure it's Henry," he said.

"Maybe." She folded her arms and stared at the whiteboard on the wall full of diagrams and bullet points of possibilities she had listed there. "I'm not so sure."

"Of course, it's him. It's his mine."

"He is certainly a possibility, but why would he try to sabotage his own project?" She pointed to the wall. "There are other potential players as well: the Chinese, the other mining giants, commodities companies, even Rogers."

McBain frowned. "Our own client?"

"I'll admit it's unlikely, but we have to consider all possibilities, not just Henry. After all, this Brazilian consulting company was hired by Rogers to confirm the findings at the site, and Rogers is now expecting to be the new CEO of AFR, not to mention the breakup clause in the merger agreement if things don't turn out exactly right. I'm just saying."

"I know it's Henry."

"Did this guy Machado finger him?"

McBain shook his head and rubbed his travel stubble. "No, he didn't. But he did say that I was asking too many questions. And most of my questions in South Africa and Angola were about Henry. And I told you about all those accidents."

She nodded and pulled at her necklace again.

"That's all true," she said. "But until we get the results from that report, maybe we should keep an open mind. I've spent some time around him during these discussions the past few weeks. Not to mention the fact that he has everyone lined up behind him to make the deal happen. I'm not sure why he would sabotage this big project or risk his relationships, even for some extra diamonds. We need to take this report to Rogers right away and get it analyzed. While we're at it, we should have a couple copies made and looked at by independent analysts as well, maybe somebody at MIT or one of the investors I met while you were away who can do the job fast. Then we can figure out our next move."

McBain remembered what Gina had said about obsession. He disliked Henry and was certain he had hired Machado, but Boston's professional cool and analysis of the facts and alternatives impressed him. And all at once, he recalled his own thoughts about her in the mine. He realized that with the clear focus of sobriety, he had been more insightful than he knew.

"Maybe you're right," he said.

She smiled at him and twirled a lock of red hair over her lip like a moustache. "Wow, that's twice in one day."

McBain looked at her with his heart full. "You know, when I was down there, I had a lot of time to think. Not just about the case, but near the end, when that didn't seem to matter anymore, about the things that are really important. About my life."

Boston turned and searched his eyes, her mouth half-open. "Boozy, I have to—"

The phone rang four times before she reached over to answer it. She didn't recognize the number but saw it was from overseas. She hit the speaker button. "Hello."

"Boston? Raj here. How are things? Any word from the asshole yet?"

"They've been better, Raj. But thanks for getting back to me so soon."

McBain's mouth dropped open, and he laughed in surprise. He walked closer to the speaker. "Things are fine, Raj," he shouted. "Thanks for asking about me. How are you holding up these days? Making any money?"

"Well, well, well," Raj said. "Look who decided to show up. Yeah, I've got some pretty good trades on now. I have to make up for that money you still owe me. We going to talk about that first before we get down to today's business?"

Boston looked at her partner. "I called Raj a few days ago to get some intel on movements in the price of AFR."

"You came to the right place, Boston," Raj said. "Hey, McBain, where have you been? Out playing around again or on holiday?"

"Just checking out the great outdoors," McBain said. "All part of my new cubicle-free world after I gave up the nine-to-nine grind and the performance reports and the sweating over whether you put your stops and hedges in at the right price. By the way, it's November, Raj. How are those profit-and-loss numbers looking for you as we get close to the holidays? Year-end bonus looking a little light?"

"Very funny for a guy who I heard was AWOL. I look forward to Christmas shopping with that money you're going to send me."

Boston tapped a pen on the conference table and stared at McBain. "If you boys are done, can we get to the matter at hand? Raj, were you able to find out anything?"

They heard a whistling sound come over the line.

"You guys have gotten yourselves into some deep shit. I checked around the markets quietly, like you asked. It took some doing, but I discovered there is somebody making some bets against your boy Henry and AFR. They've been building up short positions over the past few months using anonymous special-purpose vehicles as investment funds."

"So what?" McBain said. "People are making a couple bets against Henry. He's got a lot of enemies. You could probably get hundreds of people to invest in a fund that shorts his stock."

"It's not like that. Somebody has been buying OTC put options. The banks are perfectly willing to write them since everybody on the planet loves the deal and sees nothing but blue skies. But here's the thing, McBain: They're dirt cheap. And it isn't a couple bets. They are large, smart, and well hidden. With different funds going to different big OTC players and hedge funds, like someone who wants to hide the size of their overall positions. Secret and quiet, no names, Boston, that's how we pros do it."

McBain rolled his eyes.

"McBain, here's the odd thing," Raj said. "Another reason they're so cheap—the OTC contracts are all short dated, from three to six months out. With the momentum this deal has, you'd have to be crazy to make that kind of bet in size. Crazy or—"

McBain was nodding. "Or have some kind of inside information that something was going to happen to the deal or the company soon. If, for some reason, this merger cratered or the big project in Angola was a failure, AFR stock would take a beating; you'd make a killing."

"Exactly," Raj said.

"What are you two talking about?" Boston asked. "I know what a put option is. What are these OTC put options? What are they doing?"

McBain scanned the white board and the list of names as he talked it through. "Somebody is sure that something bad is going to happen, and very soon. Probably after the deal gets done, but it must be something that is going to damage AFR in a big way. And they're using customized derivative contracts with individual banks to make bets against the company using these special anonymous shell companies to conceal their identity and distance themselves from whatever that something is. Like Raj said, the bets are cheap because, if nothing happens in the next three to six months, the contracts expire, worthless, like any other option, and you lose all the money you paid for them. This whole sabotage theory is starting to sound more plausible now. And Machado and his friends at the mine were working for whoever it is. Maybe that's the plan. Sabotage the project so that Angola chucks out AFR, make a bundle on a short bet, then walk in to take over the mine and start working the diamonds as well as the rare earths."

Boston ground her teeth and stared at the spot on the map that marked the mining camp.

"Raj," McBain said, "you don't have any idea who it is?"

The voice on the line went a little quieter. "I can't be sure of this, Mc-

Bain, but I have my suspicions. My guess would be it's somebody in China, maybe even the government or one of their big mining conglomerates."

"Why? Could be one of the big boys in Africa or Asia. And it wouldn't be the first time one of the commodities trading firms got caught with their hand on the trigger."

"Sure, maybe," Raj said. "But the funds are all set up as corporate vehicles with mysterious names in Chinese using omnibus accounts. They're spread around in Macau, Hong Kong, Tokyo, and Singapore."

"Mysterious," McBain said. "Like what?"

"Each of them is named after a famous work of art."

"Art?" McBain said. "Isn't that colorful? What kind of art?"

"Hold on." Raj was quiet for a minute, then chuckled when he got back on: "They picked some goodies. Since you are an art fan you probably know them all, but I don't. *Starry Night*, *The Scream*, *Last Supper*, *Massacre of Innocents*, *Irises*, *Sleeping Venus*, *Night Watch*, and—"

"The *Mona Lisa*," Boston said softly. She closed her eyes, turned, and walked to the window.

McBain stared at her back as he finished writing the names.

"Exactly, Boston," Raj said. "I didn't expect you to be an art aficionado too."

The room was still for a few seconds.

"Are you guys still there?" Raj asked.

McBain looked at the wall of names again. "This is interesting, Raj, but it still doesn't get us any closer to finding out who set up the funds. Some of the richest commodities guys I know of are from Europe and have big art collections. It could just as easily be someone in Amsterdam or Zurich as the Chinese."

Boston wheeled and came back to the table. Her eyes focused on the phone. "It's Henry," she said. Her voice was calm but firm.

McBain studied her face. He had seen an iron will reflected in those eyes on previous jobs. Now they were set, full of confidence. "Are you sure?" he asked. "How can you be certain?"

She nodded and sat down. "Just an offhand remark he made once, but I'm sure. It's the kind of thing he would do. He's very clever."

"Why would Henry bet against his own company?" Raj asked. "It doesn't make sense."

McBain's hand hovered over the phone. He watched his partner. Boston said nothing.

"Anything else, Raj?"

"No, that's it, McBain. But whoever it is, you better watch your back. There's some pretty big money on this table."

"Always. Thanks, Raj. You're beautiful. I'll shoot you a wire this week with the money I owe, plus a bonus. Great work."

He hung up and sat next to Boston. She was quiet, her hands resting on the conference table.

"That was smart, calling Raj like that," he said.

"It was a shot in the dark. Lucky for me, you have a good filing system."

McBain gazed at her not just with love but quiet respect. "No, it wasn't. It was solid analysis of the situation with limited information and follow-up with the right contact. There was nothing lucky about it. If I were here, I would have called Raj myself before anyone else."

Boston glanced at him and drummed her fingers on the conference table. "Thanks," she said. "And by the way, you'll notice I managed to dig up this information by phone, without flying to Singapore to meet with Raj."

He threw up his hands. "Point taken. After what I've been through, you'll get no more arguments from me on that count."

McBain stood up and surveyed the room: the whiteboard with the names of companies, bullet points of issues, financial calculations, and a list of important documents that had been finalized for the deal. The table was covered with the map of Africa, with printouts of news stories on diamond mines and major discoveries; notebooks with references to consumer products and medical and industrial technology that were fueling the drive for rare earths and strategic minerals; and a tab-ridden copy of the US Geological Survey report on those same minerals. She had even designed flash cards with pictures of products and the ingredients that were essential to their production.

"On the other hand, I was right," he said.

"What do you mean?"

"You did it all without me. The analysis and valuation, not to mention the meetings with Rogers and his people. The call to Raj, the shell companies, the environmental approval."

She raised an eyebrow at his compliments. "Sounds like you're rationalizing your next trip already."

He pushed back with his palms. "Whoa, no. That adventure in the mine is going to be fresh for a while."

Boston turned to face him, folded her hands in her lap, and crossed her legs. "Speaking of the mine, what did you want to tell me, McBain? You said you did a lot of thinking."

He took a deep breath and decided that the case had to take precedence now. There would be plenty of time to talk afterward.

"It can wait until the case is over." McBain paged through the stack of flash cards. "The problem is we're running out of time. Even when we get this report analyzed and translated, we still have to figure out what's going on. All we've got is this. How do we prove it?"

She stood up and looked McBain in the eye. "We ask him."

He grunted. "Sure, no problem. And just how do we get access to Henry at this point with the discussions over and no time to lose? Besides which, I wouldn't put it past him to have Machado there at his side just waiting for me to show up again now that everyone knows I'm alive."

Without casting a glance his way, Boston left the room and returned a minute later with her holstered Berretta Compact. She secured the weapon behind her back and threw on her Gucci blazer. As McBain rose from his chair and stared at her with a combination of alarm and thirst for vengeance, she reached into her briefcase and pulled out her smartphone. Staring at the map of Moxico Province, she punched the icon for the phone and tapped the name.

THIRTY-THREE

The concierge turned and smiled at Boston as they walked up to him in the lobby of the Mandarin Hotel, she with her designer clothes and leather Louis Vuitton briefcase and he with his dirty backpack and khakis.

"Ms. O'Daniel to see Mr. Henry, please. He's expecting me."

The concierge placed a brief call while casting a jaundiced eye on McBain. "Of course, Ms. O'Daniel. Please go right up to the penthouse."

McBain glanced at her humorless face on the ride up, and a wisecrack died in his throat. He shifted his feet and looked at the reflection of his bedraggled travel clothes. Something was strange.

"That was easier than I expected."

Boston kept her thoughts to herself as they rose to the penthouse floor.

Rodney Henry opened the door to the suite, dressed in a gray pinstripe suit, crisp white shirt, and blue silk tie. He never missed a beat.

"Mr. McBain, you're alive. I'm relieved to see you."

"I'll bet."

Henry turned and beckoned them into the living room. A half-dozen suitcases and travel bags were stacked outside the bedroom.

"Please, come in. You'll have to excuse me. I'm leaving for New York early tomorrow morning and needed to prepare tonight. Ms. O'Daniel did say it was important."

Boston wandered to a dining table and unbuttoned her Burberry trench coat, eyes and ears alert for the presence of anyone else in the apartment.

"We think it might be something you could be interested in. McBain just returned with the results of his trip to Africa."

Henry took in McBain with cool eyes from a distance. "And to think I was not even aware you were in Africa until today."

"I'm sure," McBain said. He shook off his overcoat and tossed it on the leather couch.

Henry evaluated him. "Mr. McBain, you look . . . drawn," he said. "Are you sure you're feeling all right?"

"Three or four days underground will do that to you. Thanks for the thought. I'll live."

"I just heard a few hours ago," Henry said. "I got a call from one of my executives in charge of the mine. They said you had been there, but there was some kind of mix-up during a mine incident after they lost power. The security chief apparently did not tell anyone he was taking you into the mine. When he came up after the explosions, he denied knowing your whereabouts, and no one could locate you when they went searching. No one recalled any sign of you leaving the site. It seems in all the confusion, the mining people assumed you had wandered off into the trees and gotten lost. After Mr. Machado disappeared, someone finally came forward to say that you had gone into the mine with him before the explosion. The camp manager had the mine power switched back on immediately, and they began a search. They are scouring every tunnel and corner of the dig right now. The explosions and attempt on your life were clearly intended to sabotage our project. I am relieved you found your way out. That was very resourceful of you. But I don't understand what you were doing there to begin with."

McBain had no interest in telling him just how he had gotten out. "Just my job. A little on-site investigating in the service of Harold Rogers."

"You should have advised me. I might have been able to make some arrangements to have people meet you. I have some friends down there."

McBain smiled. "So I discovered. In fact, you seem to have a lot of friends down there. And a few enemies too."

Henry smirked and turned away. "As you said, you were in the business. That's no secret to anyone in our profession." He pointed to the bar on the side of the room. "A drink, Mr. McBain? To celebrate your survival."

McBain glanced at the bottles and shook his head. "Thanks. I'll wait until the job is done."

Henry peered at his watch and looked up. "Perhaps your partner did not fill you in. While you were away, the negotiations were completed. The terms have been finalized, and the shareholder votes are next week. Your job is done."

McBain opened his backpack and withdrew the battered manila envelope. He threw the tattered report on the glass coffee table.

"Maybe, but as Boston said, we thought you might want to look over something I brought back from Angola. All the way from your mine, as it turns out. Just like me."

Henry never bothered to glance at the folder. He simply examined his Patek Philippe and ignored the investigators. "I am a busy man, Mr. McBain, and short on time. Do you have a point?"

McBain picked up the folder and removed the frayed pages.

"Yes, I found that time is a precious commodity. It's amazing what you can do with a lot of quiet time to think and no smartphones or internet as distraction. This report helps explain what I was doing at your mine to begin with. It took three weeks and quite a bit of digging—my own kind of digging—but it raises some questions that the directors and investors might want answered before they sign on the dotted line."

"I doubt it," Henry said. "Our project and company have been analyzed, researched, and investigated by governments, banks, law firms, and the best analysts in the world. What could you possibly have in your file that has not been analyzed by the real experts?"

McBain smiled at the jab. "Your real experts never stood at the bottom of that mine, did they? How many of those analysts or experts ever even went to the site since AFR first started prospecting? Few, if any, I'm guessing. I sure as hell know because I asked some of them, including your cheerleader in chief at *The Rare Investor*, along with the rest of the financial press."

McBain thumbed some of the pages. "This report is from the man who used to be the head geologist for that consulting firm that was hired to certify what was down there, Daniel Neto. He wrote it just before he was murdered. I know because Machado told me how he died when the lights went out, and we were standing next to a sign at a sealed-off area at the bottom that said Off Limits. Machado's idea was that I was next, on your orders. He didn't know that the report had gotten out."

Henry's face was impassive. "You're mistaken, McBain. I don't know what this man Machado did or did not do because we cannot locate him. But I will not be held to account for the actions of everyone who works for me. This is a global operation with hundreds of employees and as many outside contractors. Besides, it has become clear that Machado was working for someone else, trying to sabotage the project. His actions can hardly be attributed to AFR or myself."

Henry laughed for a moment as he filled a glass of water at the bar. "I think being trapped below ground has given you some strange ideas. You are not the first amateur to be spooked by being alone in the dark, deep underground. Take it from a miner with long experience. Don't be concerned; the effects will wear off."

"We'll see," McBain said. "We have some independent analysts in the industry looking at copies of Neto's report now. But we have a theory."

Henry leaned back against the bar and folded his arms. "You have a theory. We have a deal. So by all means, have your report analyzed. Coutinho has already delivered their final report on the survey results. Everyone seems to be satisfied except you, McBain. Weeks of searching in Africa, and this is what you come up with? I'm not sure Harold got his money's worth, at least from your side of the partnership."

McBain took a few steps closer to Henry, his eyes dancing for a second off the bottles on the bar. "Our theory is that something else is going on at the bottom of that mine and that something is scheduled to go wrong in the next few months that will put the blame on Rogers after he takes over as CEO. And that you're behind it. And that—"

Henry straightened and turned to face Boston, still standing by the dining table with her eyes fixed on him.

"Meghan, what is this all about?"

Her eyes leaped from Henry to McBain and back. In that instant, she saw her partner reeling, frozen in place with his mouth open, his face a transparent mask of stunned realization and hurt.

Boston forced down her own emotions and moved toward them both to close the distance. Anything could happen now.

"We're here for our client," she said. "There are a number of questions and coincidences that have come out in these last few weeks before the deal, starting with McBain's encounter in the mine. A lot of things don't feel right. This dead geologist, his good named smeared. An off-limits part of the tunnel. Machado. All of McBain's bad luck in Africa. The history of the region. Now two reports from the same site. And suddenly, we find out about some big, anonymous short positions against your stock in Asia with three to six months expiration dates."

Henry tilted his head and shrugged as she finished. "Which all add up to . . . what exactly?"

Boston folded her arms. "We're wondering if you found something else down there."

"Something else?"

McBain shook off his swirling emotions and forced back his questions. "Like diamonds, for instance."

Rodney Henry looked back and forth at them, then stared at McBain. For a moment, the investigators thought they detected an emotion, an opening.

Then Henry laughed, and it was gone. "Diamonds? You can't be serious. You are suggesting we have a secret diamond mine in the middle of our excavation? You really are ill, McBain. And you came back and sold Meghan on this theory? Hell, I can't wait to share this one with our directors at the vote next week."

He turned his gaze on Boston and shook his head.

"It's a theory," McBain said, his face reddening at Henry's focus on his partner. "But it makes sense, given all the trouble to smear and eliminate Daniel Neto. With the history of the region and the fact that it's never been deep mined before, I wouldn't be surprised to find out you struck a big new pipe of diamonds or gold. Running a parallel operation way out there would be child's play for you. All you'd have to do is pay off the right people in Angola and the DNC. I just haven't figured out how you were going to shaft Rogers and make money shorting your own stock. Let's see if this report confirms our theory."

Henry shrugged, and a corner of his mouth rose. "I have no idea what is in there," he said. "But it seems it was written by a missing employee who we know had personal issues, not to mention problems with our company, perhaps in league with Machado, who we know is guilty of sabotage, himself in league with an outside party. Whatever is in there is likely a forgery, created to damage our relations with the Angolan government or sink our deal, probably in connection with those short sellers you talked about. Either way, it is his word against a number of reputable specialists who have a series of reliable geological reports from the mine confirming the find. So go ahead, have your report analyzed. I doubt very much that it will show any sign of your diamond mine down there. Good luck and goodbye."

McBain stood speechless as Henry finished and walked over to the window to stare out at the city. He looked at his partner as he stepped toward his coat, then glanced at her again.

Boston was not moving. She was watching Henry's back with a curiously calm look in her eyes. Over the past few weeks, she had observed Henry under different circumstances. From the meet and greet upstairs in the Mandarin to the boardroom with the executives and then the confrontation at the gala, he had always displayed a steely reserve and control, a command of the situation. The one thing she had never seen on his face was a sense of relief. Until now.

Boston walked to the dining table and opened her leather briefcase. She rummaged through the half-dozen files from Dee Dee Franklin that she had researched. Pulling one from the rest, she came back to the chairs beside the coffee table and tossed it down on the glass next to Daniel Neto's report.

"You're right," she said. "My guess is the report won't show anything about diamonds. In fact, it probably won't show much of anything, least of all a mother lode of rare earths. But maybe you want to glance through that before you say anything else."

Both men came closer to the coffee table. McBain looked at the beige cover of the file. It said only BRE-X.

He glanced at it, then at her. "What is it?"

"An obscure piece of financial history," she said as she locked eyes with Rodney Henry. "Except for people in the mining business. It's about a company called Bre-X Minerals."

McBain looked at his partner in confusion, then at Henry, then at the folder. It was like being at the end of a long poker game. Boston was playing like a woman who had the winning hand.

Henry inhaled slowly but said nothing as he surveyed her with his own poker face.

"It's quite a story really, McBain," she said, eye to eye with Henry as they stood a few feet apart. "With lots of pieces that may sound familiar. Claims of a new find of gold deep in the jungles of Borneo, Indonesia, reportedly more massive than anything ever seen. Stock price soars, and the company goes from a penny stock to a six-billion-dollar valuation almost overnight. Major players and governments interested. Financial press and auditors give it a clean bill of health. But then things start to come apart. The people in charge in Indonesia want their cut; they bring the big boys in, and things don't look quite as rosy as they were led to believe. Suddenly, the geologist who was behind the original discovery falls out of a helicopter on the way to the dig. A year later, the investor who brought others to the table dies of a brain aneurysm."

She glanced at McBain then back at Henry.

"Why, you ask? It turns out that the two hundred million ounces of gold allegedly there for the taking didn't really exist. The geologist had been lacing the core samples at the site with shavings from his gold wedding ring before he sent them off for examination—salting, they call it. When he ran out of ring, he bought gold dust from some local miners who were panning for it the old-fashioned way. When the big company got there and did their own sampling in the lab, they found squat. The price of Bre-X stock dropped faster than a rock. Since the geologist wasn't around, the investigation determined he went there thinking he had found a pile of gold, got an investor or two to support him, then found out there was no pot of gold at the end of the rainbow. Of course, that hadn't stopped him and the others from cashing out a few million dollars when the stock was hot. Hell, there are even rumors they threw a dead body out of that chopper, and the geologist is still alive somewhere, living off his profits."

"That's quite a story, Meghan," Henry said. "Yes, everyone in our business is familiar with Bre-X. But it is hardly relevant here."

Boston's face creased as she tilted her head. "So you won't mind if we take our crazy theory to the financial press or the SEC tomorrow?"

McBain moved close to his partner. "There is one difference at least," he said. "They were all small fry trying to make a big score. In this case, you had all the information and control, from the beginning to now. And you decided to profit from it. Your stock was already near the top after the offer for HR Tech. And you were in no position to sell any.

"What happened? You sank millions into your big discovery, and after the enthusiastic press and further analysis, you found out you had a dry hole?" He glanced at Boston, who was focused on Henry. "That's what they call it in the energy business. I heard BP lost a billion dollars drilling a dry hole on the North Slope of Alaska years ago. I thought it was a freak one-off until I asked the oil guys."

McBain looked back at Henry as the light bulbs went off.

"So, since you couldn't sell and you knew someone would find out at some point, you did the next best thing. You set up a bunch of secret options contracts to bet against AFR and arranged them so it would just look like those jealous Chinese were the bad guys who were out to get you and sabotaging your project to get you out of Angola—their territory."

"That's how I knew it was you and nobody else," Boston said. "The art. *Mona Lisa.*"

Henry frowned and nodded at her, fingering his watch. "As I've said, you are as intelligent as you are beautiful."

McBain felt his face heating again. He smiled to suppress the anger. "I thought of something my partner said at the beginning—that you wanted HR in the worst way. All this time, I've wondered why. With all the mining rights, it should have been no big deal. I get the whole vertical integration thing, but there were a bunch of options for you on that play. Why pay such a large premium above market for a company you didn't really need to have. But you did have to have it, and fast. AFR had to have something of tangible value in place before the truth came out about the Angola project. What happened? You spent all this money buying up the mining rights, then during your sample testing, you discovered there was almost nothing there?

"So the plan was to claim all these rare earth minerals to boost the value of AFR. When you found out the mine was a dry hole, you decided to keep it to yourself, hide it from investors and almost everyone else, and use the high stock price to buy Rogers's technology. Once you had that, you could offset the fake asset value with the value of the real high tech you had. The stock would plummet temporarily, but you would still have assets to use and sell. You had to make sure it was all kept quiet until you bought HR Tech. Eventually, the mines would turn out not to be quite as productive as people thought. Or else you could just cause an accident or find some excuse to hold off further production or investigation by the governments. As long as the right people got paid off, it could probably go on for years.

"Hardly anyone is willing to take the risk to travel there anyway without your people. You take the reporters or analysts to the mine, give them a dog-and-pony show with the huge operation and faked mineral samples, and presto—new believers to market your cause. Hell, with the US government and Pentagon on board and salivating at the potential, that part was probably easy. So you paid off people along the way to go along, or did you just threaten them with ruin like the analysts on the Street who can't find work anymore?"

Henry finally took his eyes off Boston and looked at McBain. "Something like that. A little of both. With some sleight of hand thrown in. Initially, we really did think it was a major strike. It still may be someday. When a deal has this kind of momentum and high-level support, it isn't difficult to convince people to get onboard. When Meghan discovered the EIA wasn't accounted for, we had to adjust and buy time. So the only option left was sabotage. Machado was going to do as much as he could to undermine the project to have it shut down in the next few months."

At the sound of that name, McBain almost spat on him. "No matter who he had to kill or how savage he had to be, right? How many others did you have him kill along the way, Henry? Or did you reserve some of it for yourself?"

Henry pointed at McBain with cold steel in his eye. "I am not responsible for the action of one out-of-control hire. Our out was the government. At some point, the ministries in Angola and Zambia are going to put our rights into limbo and conduct a review based on suspected irregularities. The environmental impact assessment Meghan identified, for one. After she found out it was missing, everyone else was aware of it, so we had to have one manufactured. It will freeze operations for years. Maybe talk about putting the rights up for bid again. It will look like typical African government corruption and bureaucracy."

McBain smiled. "Meanwhile, the stock gets a pasting," he said. "And now Rogers is CEO, so he's on the hook, especially if any fraud turns up over the next year or two as a result of the new inquiry. Meanwhile, you've generously given up even more of your share of the company and stepped to the side. And, of course, when the shit hits the fan, it looks like you took a bath on your stake in AFR along with every other investor. Then when Rogers gets canned, you come back in as the savior. Nobody has to know that someone had massive short bets against the company. And if they do find out, well, lookee here, they'll say. It must have been those clever Chinese or the boys from Glencore or Trafigura. But hell, the bets are all off market, hush hush, and spread around anyway, so very few people will probably even know about them. And voila, whatever you lost on AFR, you make up on the options side, right? Depending on how far it falls, a couple hundred million dollars, based on my back-of-the-envelope calculation on those OTC contracts."

"Most of it."

"Then on to the next game, right, Henry?"

The steel eyes kept their composure. McBain watched as Henry rubbed his massive hands together and walked over to the bar. He poured himself a whiskey over two ice cubes, sipped it, then turned and leveled his gaze at McBain.

"You must know what will happen if you damage this deal, McBain. This is only one of our projects. You know how important it is that this merger goes forward, and this new company gets created. HR Tech is the last key piece that has to fall into place for the long term. Discovery and processing are vital to the development of these resources. There are mineral strikes all over the world: in Africa, Central Asia, South America, Greenland—yes, even in the US. In a few years, we will even be mining in space.

"You both know how high the stakes are. This is not a game, as you call it. This is a global war for the future, not just for defense or consumer technologies but energy, medical, and environmental breakthroughs. We've seen it before in history, the fights for water, land, gold, and oil. You want to wallow in grief for the murder of one man. We could be talking about millions of deaths. There are already casualties in the pursuit of strategic minerals and rare earths, and they are not all able-bodied men. You saw them yourself. It is vital that we win."

"You mean that *you* win." McBain walked up to within a few feet of Henry. Boston shook her head out of shock and tensed to move.

But McBain just curled his lip and nodded. "I'd almost admire the scale of that kind of rip-off, if I didn't have visions of hundreds of investors losing their money and Africans losing their jobs and hopes."

Henry put the glass down and straightened. "If you put out this story, you know what will happen—the project stops today. As it stands, with my plan, the jobs will still get created for now. The local economy and communities all over will still benefit."

"For how long?"

Henry stepped close to his face. "If you have been there, you already know the answer to that," he said. "Long enough."

As he inhaled the smell of whiskey, McBain could still feel the emptiness in his stomach from days on end without food and water. His few meals since his ordeal could never eradicate the muscle memory of that desperate hunger. The final moments in the darkness of the mine, starving and alone, were now a part of him. As were the last words of Mrs. Neto.

"Until everything goes into limbo," McBain said. "Except Rogers and the rest of the investors won't be so lucky. They'll get blindsided by the announcement, and the stock will be worth a fraction of what they paid for it. Who knows? A guy as smart as you, you're probably already thinking of your next mark."

"You kill this deal, McBain, real people will suffer. We both know it."

For once, McBain kept his cool. He backed away from Henry and walked to the window to think clearly. He remembered what he had seen and learned in South Africa and Angola, from his first conversations at the Elite gala to the meetings with investors and government ministers. His eyes glazed over with visions of the desperate slum dwellers in the *musseques* and the impoverished towns and villages trying to rebuild from decades of civil war across a landscape still littered with land mines and gangs of violent teenagers. He thought of the frenetic energy and lifestyle of the wealthy elite in Luanda, living off oil money while the party lasted. And he thought of Mrs. Neto and her stories of the past, and of her son, and of her final words about justice, wealth, and power.

"What is it going to be, McBain? Bankers, investors, governments, they are all on board and ready to create the company of the future. Are you going to keep quiet and let your client get rich and famous, along with everyone else?"

After another minute, McBain joined Boston by the coffee table. "No," he said. "He's right."

She stretched out her arms. "What?"

McBain glanced at Henry, then down at the files. "This thing could turn into a real mess if we go to the media and the SEC. It will blow up, and everybody loses, including Harold Rogers. But if Henry manages it the way he has planned, on balance it just might work out long term for enough people."

Boston folded her arms and shook her head. "We can't walk away. We can't let our client take responsibility for any of this. He's one of the few decent people in this whole business."

"I know," said McBain. "You're right."

Boston gazed across the room at Henry's hard face in a new way, as if seeing it for the first time. With her anger under control, she turned away from his stare and searched McBain's face. "There has to be a way out. Like Henry just said, everyone is going to get rich. With all the people making money and dying to get in on this deal, we can't let Rogers be the one to get screwed."

And with that, the solution began to coalesce in McBain's imagination. The more he chewed it over, the more it made sense. That, and the fact that to the tainted part of him, it had a certain appeal. It wasn't perfect, and it wasn't ethical, but he had done things in the past five years that were far worse. And the last three weeks had done much to erode the fragments of the moral clarity that remained.

He looked in her eyes. "No, Boston, we won't."

"Well?" said Henry.

McBain walked back to him and folded his arms. "Somebody's going to take the fall, but it won't be our client. Here is our offer: You buy out Rogers's whole stake for cash, not stock. Now, before the acquisition. He gets out whole. You basically show it to the market as a sign of commitment to the deal. It looks like he has changed his mind. So instead of fighting the deal, he sells to you for just below market. Sign him as an adviser or something. He'll leak it that he's got some kind of illness and is heading for retirement. That he's honored, but the CEO role is too big for a man his age. He'll stay on as a consultant for the time being, just to keep everyone calm."

"I don't have that kind of cash available," Henry said. "AFR has funds committed to projects all over the world; we don't—"

"I don't care where you find the money. The bankers love this deal. Get them to finance it, or better yet, underwrite it and buy his shares. Let them take the fall when it comes. Or you take on a bunch of debt and lever up the company. You've got room."

"And if I don't?" Henry asked.

McBain shrugged. "You're probably right. Everyone wants to get this deal done, from Washington to Africa. But if Rogers starts shouting the name Bre-X to the press, it might give people enough pause to start asking questions. Are you willing to take that chance? I am."

"Even at the human cost?"

McBain leaned forward and savored the words. "If it takes you down, fuck 'em."

The ice blue eyes evaluated him for a few seconds. "You're a cold-hearted bastard, McBain."

McBain bared his teeth in the mockery of a smile. "Yeah? Well, we both learned from the best, didn't we?"

But Henry turned, and his eyes focused on Boston when he nodded. "All right. I'll make it happen."

Her eyes were narrow slits as she approached him with her hands unclenched. For the first time in weeks, she was calm, and her emotions were under control. Boston O'Daniel had learned many things in the last few months and even the last few minutes. And she wasn't intimidated anymore.

"I'll agree because it's what's best for my client," she said without a trace of the rage she felt. "And if my partner says it's the only thing to do, then it's the only thing to do. Because I trust him. And because I love my country. But don't delude yourself into thinking what you're doing is OK. I know it's not OK, for those people or for the investors. Not because of anything you said or those government assholes who came to my office, but because of what I've learned on this job. And that's just what it was—a job."

Boston gathered her briefcase from the dining table and walked to the door as the two men watched her. She opened it and took a last look at Henry.

"We all accept the reality of what has to happen, but I'm not going to pretend that it's right."

She left the room and closed the door behind her.

McBain picked up the Bre-X folder and Daniel Neto's report from the table and put them in his backpack. He put on his coat and headed to the door.

"I'll sell it to Rogers and have his lawyers send the draft paperwork over to you. As smooth as you are, figure out a way to sell it to the bankers. We can get the sale done in days. You'll have locked up Harold Rogers's shares before the vote, then you can close. Everybody's happy."

He had his hand on the doorknob before Henry responded. "McBain."

The investigator turned.

"You don't deserve her. She's better than you."

McBain's anger flooded back, and he looked him up and down with resentment at this affront to his relationship. "She's better than either of us, Henry. She actually cares. I understand that. I'm just glad she doesn't."

"I think she's beginning to."

McBain turned his back on Rodney Henry and shut the hotel door, hating the man more than ever and finally understanding why.

THIRTY-FOUR

The elevator ride to the lobby was long, the car filled with the silence of bitter victory. When they reached the ground floor, the hotel was busy with the arrival of families, the red-uniformed staff rushing to bring in stacks of luggage on trolleys while the doorman greeted parents herding their children inside while they played in the spinning revolving door. McBain stopped before they reached the exit and pulled out his phone.

"I'll call Rogers now," he said.

Boston nodded and walked outside to wait, her trench coat and hair flying around her in the lighting of the entrance. She moved down the sidewalk to avoid the arriving guests and stood looking down Boylston Street at the taillights moving toward the Boston Public Library.

After ten minutes, McBain came out of the hotel and joined her. A brisk November wind was gusting across the Charles River and down the long avenue from Fenway Park to the northwest, bringing with it a change of season and the distant siren song of a train. Snow was swirling around them, hinting of a long winter. Boylston was heavy with traffic at this hour of the evening.

"Rogers agreed," McBain said. "I explained the basics to him, assured him that his company was going to survive and prosper but that it would be better for him if he cashed out and took a role as just a consultant so he isn't exposed to anything that happens in the near future. I told him that Henry was going to set him up to take the fall for something bad, but it would be hard to prove, especially in a short amount of time when so many people want the deal to get done. The old guy didn't ask many questions, but you know, he sounded almost relieved. Said something about focusing on research and maybe starting something new. He'll see us tomorrow and explain it to his executives and board members. They won't complain."

McBain watched Boston as she buttoned her trench coat and tied the belt. Snowflakes landed on her eyelashes and cheeks. He wiped the moisture away with his handkerchief.

"I hate him," she said. "I'd respect him more if he was just another shit, if he didn't pretend to care and didn't know what it was like to be poor. It really kills me to let him get away with it. With all our other cases, it was always so black and white. They ripped people off; we made them pay. This was different."

McBain buttoned his own coat and tucked in his scarf. He still had Africa in his bones. "That was superb work up there. How did you know— I mean, the Bre-X angle?"

Boston shuffled her feet and looked down at her black pumps collecting white crystals. "It was a calculated gamble I put together from everything we knew, but especially Daniel Neto's report. It was instinct, but it made sense based on my read of him over the past few weeks. Remember to thank Dee Dee next time we see her."

He nodded and turned his back to the wind, thinking of what not to say.

"I hated giving in, too," McBain said, "but in the end he was in too strong a position. And in at least one respect, he was right. It's hard to explain if you haven't been there. Some people will get some training and have jobs and some money, schools will get built, a couple clinics will go up. Life will get better, at least for a little while until it blows up. And maybe in a few years, it will turn into a successful mine. We had a lot of cards stacked against us. Everybody kept telling us that, even Dee. You did the best you could for Rogers and his company. Maybe we didn't win this one, but we didn't lose. I'm really proud of you."

McBain checked his phone and, shuffling through the messages, he felt a small pain grow in his chest. He glanced at his partner, then down Boylston Street toward the library.

"A couple of our friends sent me some pictures from the gala."

Boston didn't say anything. She stared across the street through the cloud of snow at Abe & Louie's Restaurant.

"You looked . . . ah . . ."

"What?" she said.

"Perfect."

She rolled her shoulders and glanced at her watch, the faint memory of a waltz playing in her head. "It was just part of the job."

McBain swallowed hard and tried to process what he had seen in the photos and upstairs. Somehow, at this moment, his own feelings did not seem to matter. He packed them away.

"I'm sorry," he said. "I guess maybe, in a way, he was everything you wanted."

She drew a heavy breath and looked down at the sidewalk. Then she raised her eyes to his. "Oh, how would you know what I want? You never ask."

McBain was overcome by what he saw in those eyes, a sad hunger he had not seen for four years. He stuck his cold hands in his coat pockets and offered her an arm. "Well, in that case, I'm asking. You want to talk about it? I've got a lot to make up for. And you look like you could use a drink."

A little corner of her mouth went up. "Look who's talking."

"I do have some catching up to do."

Boston put on her gloves and hooked his elbow.

"Abe's is just across the street," McBain said. "Or we could find a quieter place around the corner on Newbury."

"After what you've been through, you probably need a vacation more than a drink."

He shook his head. "Not really. Must be the sobriety. I'm eager to get back to work with my partner. I hear we've got a stack of cases to look through."

They started walking. He reached over and pulled her scarf up around her face. Then noticed her emerald necklace.

"Oh, I almost forgot . . . " McBain dug around in his overcoat pocket and handed her the medallion. "Here."

She stopped and took it in the palm of her hand, then gazed at him, bewildered. "My Seventh Cavalry medallion. I was looking for this. When—?"

"I took it with me for luck. Turns out I needed it more than I knew. So it probably saved my life. Sorry, I know I should have asked."

Boston stared at him for a couple of seconds and bit her lip. With her free hand, she reached over and squeezed his arm. "You're still a jerk."

"I know. Come on, give me a hug."

She put a hand to his cheek and hugged him with her other arm. He pulled her close.

"Maybe I'm the one who got lucky," she whispered. "I don't have the patience to break in a new partner by myself just now. So promise me you won't do anything that stupid ever again. Or at least until we get another partner."

He exhaled. "I promise. Not until we get a partner."

The partners held on to each other as pedestrians raced past them against the driving snow. He looked around and pulled out a pack of Marlboros. "Anyway, it's nice to be back in New England for the change of season."

Boston's sea-green eyes searched his face. "You don't miss sunny Africa?"

McBain tucked her tighter against his side as they started walking again. "Of course not. I prefer Boston any time of the year."

"Very funny." The redhead almost smiled and nodded at the pack in his hand. "Are you going to quit smoking?"

"Anything for you."

"You're a liar."

McBain reached across Boston and tossed the pack of cigarettes through the snow into a garbage can.

"Yes," he said. "But never to you."

ACKNOWLEDGMENTS

THE WRITER WOULD LIKE to thank a number of people who helped in finishing this novel, both knowing and unwitting. Buying gifts for a beautiful woman is a challenge for any man, but trying to dress a character as fashionable and designer savvy as Boston O'Daniel was far too dangerous an enterprise, and called for the expertise of Jenna Smith, *fashionista* par excellence. Any sartorial faux pas in this area are the fault of the writer. Bill Hamlen reviewed the manuscript with the practiced and jaded eye born of years of experience on the commodities trading desk in New York and Singapore. I am grateful for invaluable early feedback from "Professor" Al Smith, Tammy Leslie, Maury Davidson, John Scarperia, Lillian Hayes and Christina Baker, who all provided both insightful comments and encouragement.

Boston O'Daniel and Boozy McBain are works of fiction. Regrettably, their growing business is not. However their unsung counterparts in the real world work constantly to uncover and expose scams, fraud and financial chicanery throughout the investment and corporate worlds. The writer and many others owe a debt of gratitude to the people who are represented by the Association of Certified Fraud Examiners and their global counterparts. The ACFE are a great resource for anyone who thinks they need help or wants to learn more and protect themselves.

On the fascinating subject of rare earths and their importance to our daily life, the writer recommends a number of resources. These include not only the superb Department of Defense/US Geological Survey Reports referenced in the book, but valuable publications on the development and environmental costs of creating the stuff our dreams are made of. I mention only works by Julie Michelle Klinger, Dr. Ned Mamula, Keith Veronese and several reputable newsletters that cover the mining industry such as mining.com.

When it comes to thanking the people who dig up the things that fill our lives with ease or happiness, from professional copper and gold miners to the men on the rigs to the children in the Congo, words are inadequate.

ABOUT THE AUTHOR

Riley Masters is a writer and financial professional. *The Stuff That Dreams Are Made Of* is the second in a series dedicated to those who uncover financial fraud and pursue those who prey on investors or the trusting and naive. Masters previously worked in the intelligence business covertly collecting information, and has degrees in Economics and International Finance. The author was trained in financial analysis, investments and risk management at one of the few private partnerships left on Wall Street that still taught old school techniques of judging companies and character. Masters has worked in the U.S., Europe, Africa and the Middle East as a financial, economic and management consultant, but spends most of his time in Boston and on Haven Beach.

Lightning Source UK Ltd.
Milton Keynes UK
UKHW012026131120
373373UK00010B/711/J